The Trouble with Mr. Darcy

Pride and Prejudice continues…

Sharon Lathan

sourcebooks
landmark

Published by Sourcebooks Landmark, an imprint of Sourcebooks, Inc.
P.O. Box 4410, Naperville, Illinois 60567-4410
(630) 961-3900
FAX: (630) 961-2168
www.sourcebooks.com

Library of Congress Cataloging-in-Publication Data

Lathan, Sharon.
  Trouble with Mr. Darcy / by Sharon Lathan.
      p. cm.
  1. Darcy, Fitzwilliam (Fictitious character)—Fiction. 2. Bennet, Elizabeth
(Fictitious character)—Fiction. 3. Married people—Fiction. 4. Marriage—
Fiction. 5.   England—Social life and customs—19th century—Fiction. 6.
Domestic fiction. I. Title.
  PS3612.A869T76 2011
  813'.6—dc22
                                   2010049265

          Printed and bound in the United States of America
               VP 10 9 8 7 6 5 4 3 2

The Darcy Saga

BY SHARON LATHAN

Mr. and Mrs. Fitzwilliam Darcy: Two Shall Become One
Loving Mr. Darcy: Journeys Beyond Pemberley
My Dearest Mr. Darcy: An Amazing Journey into Love Everlasting
In the Arms of Mr. Darcy
A Darcy Christmas

*This novel is dedicated to my children
who are a constant delight and inspiration.
My daughter, Emily ~
You have grown into a beautiful,
Christian woman whom I am proud
to say is my friend.
My prayer is for your Mr. Darcy
to joyfully enhance your life
as your father has mine.
My son, Kyle ~
You are my baby but now a man
on the cusp of entering the world
away from your parents,
yet I have no fears
because I know God holds you
in the palm of His hand.*

Table of Contents

Cast of Characters

Fitzwilliam Darcy

Elizabeth Darcy

Alexander Darcy: born November 27, 1817

Michael Darcy: born September 14, 1819

Georgiana Darcy

Colonel Richard Fitzwilliam

Lady Simone Fitzwilliam: Colonel Fitzwilliam's wife; sons *Oliver*, the Earl of Fotherby, *Harry*, and *Hugh Pomeroy*

Earl and Countess of Matlock: Darcy's uncle and aunt; residence Rivallain in Matlock, Derbyshire

Dr. George Darcy: Darcy's uncle

Baron and Baroness of Oeggl: Darcy's Aunt Mary and husband

Charles and Jane Bingley: residence Hasberry Hall in Derbyshire; son *Ethan*

Joshua and Mary Daniels: residence London; daughters *Deborah* and *Claudia*

Katherine (Kitty) Bennet

Major General Randall Artois: Kitty Bennet's fiancé

Mr. and Mrs. Bennet: residence Longbourn in Hertfordshire

George and Lydia Wickham: reside in Devon

Dr. Raul and Anne Penaflor: residence Rosings Park in Kent; daughter *Margaret*

Lady Catherine de Bourgh

Marchioness of Warrow: Dr. Darcy's aunt and Darcy's great-aunt

Sebastian Butler: heir to the earldom of Essenton; Lady Warrow's grandson

Earl and Countess of Blaisdale: the former Caroline Bingley and her husband; son *John*

Stephen and Amelia Lathrop: residence Stonecrest Hall in Leicestershire; daughter *Fiona*

Gerald and Harriet Vernor: residence Sanburl Hall in Derbyshire; sons *Stuart* and *Spencer*

Albert and Marilyn Hughes: residence Rymas Park in Derbyshire; son *Christopher*, daughter *Abigail*

George and Alison Fitzherbert: residence Brashinharm in Derbyshire; sons *Andrew* and *Neville*

Rory and Julia Sitwell: residence Reniswahl Hall in Derbyshire; four sons

Clifton and Chloe Drury: residence Locknell Hall in Derbyshire; son *Clive*

William and Charlotte Collins: residence Hunsford in Kent; daughters *Rachel* and *Leah*

Mrs. Reynolds: Pemberley housekeeper

Mr. Taylor: Pemberley butler

Mr. Keith: Mr. Darcy's steward

Samuel Oliver: Mr. Darcy's valet

Marguerite Oliver: Mrs. Darcy's maid

Mrs. Annesley: Miss Darcy's companion

Mrs. Smyth: Darcy House housekeeper

Mr. Travers: Darcy House butler

Mrs. Hanford and *Miss Lisa*: nannies to Darcy children

After a Time

ELIZABETH DARCY WALKED THROUGH the bedchamber doorway and released a heavy sigh as she threw her traveling gloves onto the chair.

"Finally got the baby to sleep. He nursed intermittently, but I do not think hunger was the issue. He definitely does not travel well! I have never seen him so upset, and that is saying something." She plopped onto the edge of the large bed and gazed around the room as she removed her pelisse. "I know I have said it a few times already, but I am amazed that this house has never been sold. You would think the family weary of maintaining a manor so far away for so many years. What is the point?"

This entire speech, including the unanswered question, was directed toward her husband. Darcy lay spanning the whole width of the generous bed, his long, lean body supine with booted legs dangling over the edge by Lizzy's knees and hands loosely clasped in the empty air above his head. By all appearances he looked soundly asleep, but Lizzy was not deceived. The simple facts that his mouth was not parted and breathing not deep were a sure giveaway. Therefore, she continued to ramble.

"Whatever the reasoning, it is fortunate for us. Much more comfortable than an inn or trying to cramp into Longbourn." She sighed again, folded the sable-accented woolen jacket, and absently placed it onto the mattress beside her as her eyes swept over the furnishings and wide windows. "In truth, I will miss this place if they ever sell it. So many memories." Her voice grew silent. A happy smile adorned her lips as one hand caressed Darcy's nearest thigh. "Yes, many memories. Remember the time… Oh!"

"No walks down the lane of Netherfield remembrances as yet, my dear. Put your mouth to better use and kiss me." He had grabbed her elbow and tugged until she lay alongside him, bouncing slightly from the impact.

"William, the door…"

But he turned toward her and engaged her lips before the rejoinder was complete. Nothing improper, they were both fully clothed mind you, but a vigorous kiss ensued for a blissful few minutes.

"Sorry to interrupt the exhibition," declared a voice that sounded anything but remorseful.

Darcy reflexively released his wife and jerked upward, only then registering the voice and tone of latent laughter. "Uncle! Are you unaware of knocking on doors?"

George's brows rose, the feigned expression of surprise not hiding his amusement. "On open doors? What an astounding concept! I must have missed that lesson in my youth." He shrugged. "I only disrupted the romantic interlude to inform you that dinner shall soon be served. Since Mrs. Darcy whined about her hunger for the past hour, feeding two and all that, and I distinctly heard your stomach growl between the infant wails, I thought you both would be interested in the news."

Lizzy's giggle and Darcy's sharp retort were cut off by a sudden piercing scream echoing down the hallway, shut door and stout walls not greatly muffling their son's healthy lungs. Lizzy sighed yet again and closed her eyes for a momentary skyward supplication for strength. Darcy halted her rising, however, leaning for a kiss to her forehead.

"Go and eat, Elizabeth. I will see to it. I doubt it is sustenance he is wishing for, so perhaps I can handle it."

"Thank you! I am famished."

"Just save a bit for me. Uncle, will you escort my wife to the dining room?"

"With honor."

Briskly and bravely entering the nursery chamber, the doting father was greeted by lusty yells, soothing vocalizations, and the faint clunk of wooden blocks being banged together. The former two issued forth respectively from the mouths of his six-month-old son, diminutive face angrily screwed-up and beet red, and the nanny, Mrs. Hanford, who stood near the window swaying and bouncing as she crooned to no avail. The latter noise, barely audible amid the cries, came from the serious, blue-eyed boy sitting on the carpet surrounded by a pile of building blocks in dozens of shapes and sizes.

The toddler lifted his adorable face, azure gaze serenely greeting the tall man, his piping voice calm. "Papa, baby sad."

"Yes, Alexander. I gathered as much. Thank you."

Darcy smiled at his firstborn, stooped to ruffle the wild curls that resisted any form of tamed combing, and turned to the nanny.

"You need not fret, Mr. Darcy. I can attend to him while you dine. Nothing we haven't all seen before!" she concluded, hugging the irate infant and bestowing a loving kiss to his sweaty forehead.

"I do not doubt your competence, Mrs. Hanford, you know that. But Mrs. Darcy will dine easier if I am here with him. Come here, little demon, let your father deal with your tantrum. There, there now. Is it *really* all that bad? Carriage rides not for you? Shall we add that to the list of items that disturb? My poor baby boy! So particular you are, my lamb."

He chuckled as he sat onto the sofa, the baby not even mildly amused, and winked at Alexander who observed the proceedings with quiet interest while still banging blocks. Darcy laid the thrashing, belligerent infant belly down over his knees and proceeded to bounce and pat the diapered bottom. It took awhile, but experience gleaned narrowed this down to the best avenue to hush and pacify.

Alexander rose, tossed the blocks aside, and grabbed one lumpy leg of a tattered, stuffed hound dog. He walked to his father's side, adding soft pats to the firmer ones calming the infant who was now intermittently gasping while sucking on a plump thumb. Leveling his small face with the smaller one, bright azure eyes engaging the teary cobalt ones of his brother, he added phrases in a soothing voice mimicking Darcy. "Go sleep, baby. Hush, hush now. Papa here. No more tears, sweet baby. Be happy."

Darcy smiled, watching Alexander bestow soft kisses to the wet cheeks as angry eyes glazed with serenity and sleepiness. For several minutes after regular breathing was reached, Darcy and Alexander continued to administer pats at a gradually lessening pace. Experience had also taught them not to trust the newest Darcy's complacency too swiftly, a fact they were recently reminded of when his mother's declaration of slumber was proven erroneous.

Michael James Anton Darcy was born on the blustery afternoon of September 14, 1819, after a mere seven hours of labor. His birth, a good month earlier than Dr. Darcy's soonest estimate, caught everyone by surprise, especially his father who galloped frenziedly up the drive and barreled through the bedchamber door an hour and a half before the blessed event, as no one, not even Lizzy, had anticipated the imminent delivery that morning when he blithely rode off to attend to estate business. The uneventful pregnancy and easy birth of the delicate five pound, premature baby was in no way an indication of future complacency.

Darcy teased that their second son was simply fashioned after his mother. Lizzy could not dispute these realities too vigorously, as the stories of her infant years were gleefully related by both parents to an amused spouse. She had searched through the journals, but alas, the writings of Anne and James Darcy conclusively revealed a child Fitzwilliam who was even-tempered and tranquil. George Darcy, who delighted in teasing his serious nephew, could not disagree.

Her counter argument was to blame it on their holiday at Matlock Bath, neither her or Darcy doubting Michael was conceived within that three-day span of crazed lovemaking. After an extended business trip to London, Darcy returned to Pemberley and an ill wife. It was his idea for a recuperative visit to the healing mineral waters. Frenzied intimacy amid the untamed atmospheric conditions was a bonus; the humorous jests of personality traits of the unborn being influenced were not taken seriously until after Michael was born.

Alexander was a happy baby and contented toddler. He rarely cried and tantrums were exceedingly unusual, but spontaneous hilarity and uncontained laughter were infrequent as well. He naturally dwelt in a state of calm neutrality and quiet humor, the stoic twenty-eight-month-old so like his father it was uncanny.

Michael, conversely, was perpetually at opposite ends of the mood spectrum. When not in a rage over some perceived slight, he was bursting with mirth. Thankfully, his sprightliness was infectious and all it took was witnessing one episode of wiggling gaiety to forget any moments of pique.

At six months of age, his devoted parents and loving brother had long since fallen under his spell and learned ways to avoid or remedy the tantrums. Waiting until absolutely certain Michael was asleep, Darcy transferred the snoring babe to his shoulder with steady competence. Alexander climbed onto the settee, settling against the welcoming warmth of his father's side with faithful stuffed companion secure on his lap. Darcy embraced his firstborn, his strong arm hugging tight, and called to Mrs. Hanford.

"Mrs. Hanford, could you please inform the kitchen to bring our dinner here. I will dine with Alexander." Once alone, he looked at his son and asked, "What do you say? Shall we build a tower to the sky once we have dined?"

In true Alexander fashion, he thought it over carefully before replying. "Nanny say it bath time after dinner."

"I believe I can overrule Nanny's orders just this once." He winked at the staid face, Alexander assimilating the words before nodding and smiling happily.

"Aunt Giana here, Papa?"

"Not yet, my sweet. Soon she will be here. I know she misses you and will hurry to Netherfield as soon as it is possible."

"Gramma and Grampa here? Aunt Kitty?"

"We will see all of them tomorrow. Longbourn is only three miles away, but it is late. Michael was in no mood for extended visitations. Tonight it shall just be us, but rest assured your grandparents are anxious to see you."

Alexander nodded at that statement of fact, reaching to pat his sleeping brother's back. Yet the tiny crease between his brows did not disappear.

"Do not worry, my son. Everyone will be coming for your Aunt Kitty's wedding. You will be reacquainted with dozens of relatives and meeting new ones. Far more than your young mind will be able to absorb." He paused, dwelling momentarily on the intelligent gaze of his son and shook his head as he continued, "On second thought, I would be unwise to underestimate your memory. You have not seen Aunt Giana in months and ask about her every day! Come, help me tuck your brother into bed and then we can get started on that tower while waiting for our food."

Netherfield Hall, the finest country manor in all of Hertfordshire, had remained greatly unoccupied over the intervening years since Mr. Bingley first let it over four years prior. The question as to why the owners continued to do so was a mystery that none of the current lessees knew.

On the occasion of Mary's nuptials two years ago, the Darcys had resided in the local inn; a modest establishment that served well if humbly. One other time they had stayed at Longbourn. That was one of the longest weeks in Darcy's life and he stubbornly, and not too kindly, refused to do so ever again! Space for their family was not an issue with only Kitty still at home, but seven days with Mrs. Bennet in close proximity was intolerable. An additional distress was being cramped into a bed not designed for two grown people in a bedchamber surrounded by thin walls that made the necessary joy of loving his wife impossible.

Thankfully, Netherfield was not rented to another party this March of 1820, so they were again able to dwell in comfort. This was a convenience for the Darcys, but also for the other visitors who would be staying there for the wedding. Once again this building belonging to strangers would play host to a gathering of folks intimately involved with the Bennets.

There was never a question of Darcy and Elizabeth occupying the bedchamber that Darcy had inhabited since his first sojourn at Netherfield. The memories surrounding this suite of rooms were special for a host of reasons, but also because of the view of rolling green pastures and a small lake. A nearby chamber served as a nursery, the Darcys insisting on their children staying close. Mrs. Hanford and her daughter, Lisa, who was now employed as an assistant nanny, slept in a bed located behind a privacy screen. This was essential due to the fact that Mr. Darcy nightly crept into the room his boys occupied to check on them.

The need to ensure their contented rest and security was an urge he could not deny, thus it was no surprise when, much later that night, he ignored the post-lovemaking languor that screamed for his body to succumb to satiated sleep. Instead, he kissed his dreaming wife, untangled his limbs from hers, and slipped quietly from their bed.

Soft snores reached Darcy's ears as he padded lightly to the bed where Alexander lay curled around Dog. Four other stuffed animals lay near his body. Darcy moved the gibbon gifted by "Uncle Goj" during Alexander's second Christmas so he could sit beside the toddler. Alexander slept as Darcy did: with lips parted as dreams wove through a submerged consciousness. He knew from experience that he could grant dozens of kisses and caresses without Alexander flinching. In fact, he slept so deeply and lengthily that already, at not quite two-and-a-half, Alexander was eschewing the need for a long daily nap.

As the babyish profile and body matured, he weekly grew to mirror his father. There was a great deal of infantile fat here and there, but he seemed to grow taller by the hour. There was a masculine cast to the youngster that disallowed any doubt as to his sex and promised a future figure as powerful as the man who sired him. The squared jawline had a tendency to clench when considering a puzzling toy or dilemma; the thick eyebrows straight on a mildly ridged brow with the left arching in humor or contemplation. His nose was long and prominent to Darcy's dismay but Lizzy's delight, his forehead wide and high, and he had a full lower lip accenting a firm mouth. It truly was only the coiled curls that prevented him being a duplicate of his father.

Darcy bent and kissed the ruddy cheek, whispered words of devotion, and tousled the magnetic springy tresses before rising with a contented smile. He turned to the cradle sheltering Michael.

The infant's plump fists curled beside his head, chest rising steadily with each breath, and skin almost translucent in the dim moonlight. Both of the boys had inherited Darcy's fair complexion, Alexander even beginning to display a faint scattering of freckles over his nose and shoulders as his father did. Michael, however, aside from the blue eyes that seem to dominate the Darcy clan, resembled neither of them overly. His once delicate, premature body was now stout and strong. His facial features grew daily bolder with a wide nose, almond-shaped eyes framed by thick, arching brows, high cheekbones, and plump lips outlining a generous mouth. His brown hair, a trait both parents possessed, was dark, sparse, and waved gently.

You do have your mother's temperament, the proud father thought, smiling as he leaned to bestow a kiss to the baby's prominent forehead.

He brushed one finger over Michael's breastbone, cautious and light so as not to disturb. His heart swelled as his eyes swept over the precious features of his newest child. He was pierced with fresh waves of gratitude for the bonded relationship and love he possessed for Michael. The early months following Michael's birth were painful to recall. The period when all his dreams of family had seemingly disintegrated beyond salvage was still too real to be forgotten.

The emotions of gratitude and love were followed by a rush of fierce protectiveness. For a second, his eyes were blinded by powerful sensations, his heart skipping a beat and respirations hitching. The years of being a husband and father had changed him profoundly. He felt complete and stronger, yet also vulnerable as never before. Elizabeth and his children were everything to him, his life utterly revolving around them, and living without them was not an option.

He shook his head, relegating the disturbing emotions to a hidden chamber within his soul. He murmured a soft *I love you* and turned sharp eyes to scan the room one last time. He looked for he knew not what, but only when assured that all was well could he return to his wife and the happiness of his dreams. Lizzy sleepily opened her arms, Darcy nestling and kissing the curve of her neck before they settled into the mattress for a satisfied sleep devoid of unpleasant memories or unfounded fears.

CHAPTER ONE

An Excursion Abroad

IN THE WEEKS FOLLOWING Colonel Fitzwilliam's marriage to Lady Simone Fotherby, the reality of Elizabeth Darcy's second pregnancy was affirmed. The spring to fall months of 1819 unfolded in peace, exciting travel, and the anticipation of new life with no problems of magnitude occurring and no warning of the winter troubles to come.

One *may* presuppose that Darcy's giddiness over watching their second child grow within his wife's womb would be less ridiculous having experienced it once already.

They would be wrong.

The unparalleled ecstasy of fatherhood as he daily interacted with Alexander, who he loved with an emotion formidable in its power, augmented his delight in anticipating the appearance of their second-born.

Alexander was young but seemed to grasp in his immature intellect that a special event was taking place. He joined his father in patting and talking to his mother's expanding belly, reverently touched the amassing pile of tiny garments, and gradually assimilated that all of this strange activity meant a baby was soon to join their family.

Lizzy's symptoms of pregnancy never reached beyond the standard vague discomforts of the first trimester and were less severe than with Alexander's gestation, the comparison to how perfect she felt while carrying Michael notable.

Lizzy's vitality meant there was nothing to prevent Darcy from proceeding with his secret plans to travel abroad with his family. Lizzy gleaned a few hints and suspected he was plotting something extravagant for her birthday in May—after all, he had a reputation of overindulgence—but was flabbergasted when he dramatically unveiled the entire itinerary over a romantic dinner one night in March.

From that moment on, Lizzy and Georgiana were dizzy with excitement over the trip. Darcy's arrangements included shopping expeditions and modiste appointments for the trunks of new attire they would need. Neither woman argued over it, instead leaping into action with Lady Matlock alongside, since she and Lord Matlock were joining the journey.

Despite not being able to embark upon a gentleman's Grand Tour of Europe due to his father's precipitous death, Darcy had traveled throughout the countries across the English Sea numerous times so knew of the fundamental requirements and the various hazards. Organizing was second nature for him, and with the proper assistance and references from friends, he enjoyed the process, leaving nothing to chance. Lord and Lady Matlock seemed to have acquaintances in nearly every city in Europe who were agreeable to accommodating the travelers, and when that choice failed the finest hotels were reserved. Elizabeth was dumbstruck at the amount of pre-planning and assembling of equipment necessary for an expedition abroad. Darcy refused to divulge the cost, but she knew enough to conclude it must be staggering.

The company consisted of Darcy and Lizzy, George, Georgiana, Alexander, and Lord and Lady Matlock. Mrs. Hanford, Samuel and Marguerite, Mrs. Annesley, and Lord and Lady Matlock's personal servants accompanied as entourage. Darcy and Lord Matlock insisted on shipping their private carriages with them rather than trusting the ofttimes poorly manufactured rental coaches.

They departed England in April. Having their resident physician as part of the traveling troupe with his assurance that all was well with the expectant mother eased Darcy's lingering worry. The anxious father and husband did fret somewhat, as was natural, yet aside from an ever-increasing abdominal girth, Lizzy was vigorous throughout the whole escapade.

The weather held favorably for the Channel crossing from Dover to Calais. That was a major boon for the non-seafaring Darcy men in one respect as the calm waters did not jostle the ship, but not so fortunate in that the lack of wind extended the time of the crossing. George and Darcy kept to their bunks in various degrees of misery for the entire ten-hour voyage, but Alexander did not suffer as acutely as his father or uncle. Lizzy held him in her arms and stood at the railing. She loved the rolling waves and relished the spray and smell of seawater for every moment of the journey.

The port of Calais was another matter entirely. It was chaotic, dirty, fetid, and plain frightening in how ramshackle the docks, at least to her untrained eye. Darcy assured her it was perfectly stout and safe, but considering his frantic need to disembark and place his feet on solid ground, she was not trusting of his guarantee! There were no mishaps and the hours necessary to unload their equipage gave them time to recuperate within the warmth of a hospitable inn near the docks. Lizzy discovered her fascination and agreeableness returning as she observed the diverse humanity and unfamiliar activities from behind a glass window.

"What are they doing there? What is that contraption? Who are those men, do you think?" And on it went, the others patiently answering her inexhaustible queries while Lizzy jotted notes into the blank journal Darcy had gifted her for the journey. Georgiana's curiosity was as intense, but she maintained a semi-serene demeanor in sharp contrast to Lizzy's blatant enthrallment.

It took nearly four hours to unload, examine everything for damage, take care of the proper legalities, and hire the required help. Brokers lined the harbor with shingles hung above dingy doorways to offices squeezed between pubs. Recommendations gave the men a starting place rather than trusting to luck, and the third businessman approached possessed what the foreign travelers would need: an experienced coachman and former soldiers with impeccable records who knew the roads, and were brave and skilled with firearms.

The women had been prepared for the demand to hire trained escorts prior to leaving England, including the fact that each gentleman would carry loaded weapons with additional pistols secreted inside the carriages.

"Decades of war and terror and then Napoleon's defeat have left far too many people homeless and starving—thousands of ex-soldiers without employment and no skill other than how to kill. Some turn that to lucrative business, such as those we will hire to be our guards. Others turn to thievery and highway robbery." Lizzy shivered at Darcy's words, remembering their lethal encounter with bandits. "We will be cautious," he finished firmly, embracing her tightly.

Traveling in larger groups also tipped the odds in their favor, making it less likely that an attack would occur. As luck had it, two other families were on their ship and thrilled to join them for the journey to Paris, and two other companies were already ashore waiting for the next ship to dock in hopes of adding members to their caravan before departing. It was fortuitous for all involved.

Finally they regrouped, leaving Calais for a leisurely meander toward Paris. The careful plotting by the men succeeded, the days of travel passing pleasantly with halts for rest or interesting sights to explore.

Then Paris! Georgiana's feigned serenity disappeared as the vast city drew near, and upon crossing the first cobbled bridge spanning the Seine her giddiness equaled Lizzy's.

"Are we there, Brother? This is Paris?"

"The outskirts. Paris proper is yet a few miles and then we must cross a quarter of the city to reach Marais."

"How long shall it take? Will we pass the Bastille? Or the Luxembourg Palace? Or Notre Dame? Or…"

"I shall stop you there, Sister! I have no idea whether we shall pass any of those places on our way to Hôtel d'Arlatan."

Both Lizzy and Georgiana stared at him in shock, Lizzy finding her tongue first. "Are you admitting to not knowing the precise route and layout of Paris?"

"Remember that I was last here several years ago when I traveled with Mr. Bingley. I am certain much has changed with Napoleon's restructuring plans and now Louis XVIII continuing the project, not that I tried memorizing routes then. I can tell you that the Place de la Bastille lays within the Marais arrondissement, but where it is in relation to Hôtel d'Arlatan I do not know. In fact, I trust Uncle Malcolm on this aspect of the journey as he knows the owners."

"So you are not fully versed on every detail of the townhouse we are to stay in, not even where is it?"

Darcy smiled at his wife's tease. "I know it is on the Rue Andre Dolet near the Parc du Rolens Croix, that the view is reportedly incredible, and the hôtel beautiful. Beyond that I am at the mercy of guides, thus why I shall not attempt to play navigator. That is why we hired Parisian coachmen in Calais."

"Ah, I did wonder about that," Lizzy nodded. "Quite wise. Well, I do pray they are recent residents if the streets are under construction."

"Paris, and actually all of France, has suffered decades of unrest. The evidence is visible still."

He was correct in the latter statement. Buildings in partial states of repair were common, as were piles of rubble and destroyed gardens. They kept to major thoroughfares so views of poorer neighborhoods were rare, but glimpses revealed areas of filth and decay not yet touched upon. But clearly the coachman leading the way knew his job, diverting frequently from blocked avenues or unsightly obstacles, weaving in a haphazard fashion along roads laid without a pattern remotely organized.

Most of the scenery was pristine and beautiful so the lengthy ride was enjoyed immensely. Darcy pointed to certain architectural oddities or vegetation not indigenous to England, but he was ignorant to a large degree. Paris was much like London in the ancientness to the city, meaning there was little cohesiveness to the styles. Modern Greek neoclassicism stood alongside medieval Gothic, the disparity bizarre but expected. Elaborate gardens were frequent, as were gated lawns and miniature woods. The deeper into the city they went, the grander the passing surroundings until finally they crested a residential avenue lined with palatial private homes and halted before the iron gate of number eighteen, the plush mansion owned by the Marquis Dissandes de la Villatte.

The elderly marquis, an acquaintance of Colonel Fitzwilliam from the war, greeted them with warmth and hospitality. As Darcy had promised, the townhouse was beautiful, with ornate, spacious guest quarters overlooking the courtyard gardens. Every top floor window afforded stunning views of the city streets, a nearby park, and glimpses of the Seine.

Their host and hostess were courteous in every way. The food was delicious, the servants exceptional, and the accommodations superb. Their three weeks in Paris passed in a blur of fêtes, operas, museums, and sightseeing. It was not enough time to adequately view all that Paris had to offer, but eventually they bid adieu to the Marquis and Marquise Dissandes de la Villatte to embark on the second leg of their journey.

"I completely filled my journal with memories of France." Lizzy patted the thick, leather-bound book in her lap, her eyes riveted on the disappearing Paris landscape.

"No worries," Darcy squeezed her hand, "I have another in my trunk. Two, actually, just in case."

"You think of everything, do you, Mr. Darcy?"

"I do try." He grinned smugly, leaning to kiss her nose.

"Well, I am sure I will recall something I missed to add in betwixt the future delights to jot down, so thank you for your foresight and thoughtfulness."

She sighed, gazing again out the window. "I do wish we did not have to leave. Who knows when we shall be able to return, what with babies being born and all," she concluded, rubbing her slightly rounded midsection.

"I am sure William will manage to bring you again, Lizzy, along with your children." Georgiana tugged on Alexander's jacket tail, the seventeen-month-old perched on his Aunt Giana's lap with his face pressed against the window.

"Easy for you to be philosophic! You will return later this year to dwell for months, after trekking through exotic Italian locales. You must visit all the places we missed in Paris with details written and sketches drawn. I insist you do so to allay my raging jealousy."

"Have no fear, dear sister." Georgiana laughed. "William has purchased extra journals for me as well, and I have my paints stowed carefully for colored visual renderings. It will be as if you were there!"

"Now that peace reigns in Europe, travel is easily accomplished. I do promise to bring us back, Elizabeth. And I am sorry the trip must be truncated, but we must be home before our baby is born."

Lizzy leaned against his side, smiling into his serious face. "Silly man! You know I jest. Well, for the most part. Indeed I wish we could tarry longer, but what would that truly accomplish? There is not enough time to see the entire world so there would forever be more. I am blessed to see what I have as it is more than I ever imagined. I thank you for that, love."

"You are most welcome. It is my pleasure."

"And now we are on to another adventure! What do you think of that, Alexander?"

"Go. Bye," was his answer, adding an enthusiastic bounce.

"We shall see very high mountains in a few days, sweetling." Darcy pulled his son onto his lap, nuzzling the soft neck. "When you spy them you will be amazed! Your Great-Aunt Mary has a lovely chateau at the base of the Alps. We shall have enormous fun."

The Swiss estate owned by Baron Oeggl sat on the easternmost bank of Lake Genève in Switzerland near Villeneuve. Darcy had visited his Aunt Mary and her family twice in his adult life, but on both occasions he traveled to their home north of Vienna in Austria, never venturing close to the Alps. Of course, one could see the towering, perpetually snow-clad mountains from many portions of Austria and Switzerland, but the dramatic effect was lost with distance. Thus his eagerness was equally distributed between visiting family and touring the countryside.

George's thoughts on this portion of their trip were vastly different.

Cold weather was not a friend to the man who had dwelt in India for the greater part of his life. He had anticipated his robust Englishman's blood reasserting itself, thickening as it were, to tolerate the cooler climes of England. Certainly he had never been bothered by the chill when a youth and young man, and his transition to the heat and humidity of India had been fairly easy. *Perhaps it is old age*, he mused with chagrin. Naturally he was stubborn about it, continuing to don his preferred warm weather garments while dramatically whining about the freezing air until everyone assumed he was exaggerating. Therefore it was with surprise all around when Dr. Darcy launched into a spending frenzy in the weeks before departing England that was equally as involved as the females. He had numerous appointments with Darcy's tailor—something else to grumble about—with a dozen thick wool suits, three overcoats, hats, sturdy boots, and woolen stockings the result! All were of the finest cut and modern style, but sported something daring or dashing about them. He was still flamboyant George, after all, and thus enjoyed the taunts received.

The temperature in Paris proved to be a bit warmer than London in March. This offered him the chance to wear the elaborate sherwanis brought along for formal events just in case, the exotic effect better than usual among strangers not immune to his charms. However, the idea of Switzerland any time of the year gave him shudders. It was not the main reason he had never visited his eldest sister, but his reluctance to trudge through snow did weigh in there to a degree.

"When did you last see your sister, George?" Lizzy asked one day as they were preparing for their holiday.

"When I was at Cambridge, two years and a bit before I completed my apprenticeship, she and her family traveled to Pemberley. I took a hiatus and spent a month at home before I needed to return."

"And that was the last time?" Georgiana asked, turning from the trunk on the floor to stare at her uncle.

"Do not be so incredulous, Georgie. I am not a horrid brother, not really. You must remember that Mary is eleven years older than me. We were never very close, partly due to the age difference but also because Mary was unlike the rest of us."

"How do you mean?"

"She was serious and prim, more like our father, whereas Estella, James, Alex, and I were like our mother. Carefree and adventurous. Or hellions, depending on the perspective. That was Father's perspective to be sure. I swear the man never cracked a smile in all my growing up days."

"He smiled often with me," Darcy interjected. "Must have been the hellions driving him to a state of utter annoyance."

George agreed with a hearty laugh. "Oh indeed! I am sure that was part of it! Of course, Aunt Beryl will tell you how stoic he was even as a child. I have gleaned that she and a couple of their siblings began the tortures in his youth, long before we arrived. And I do not wish to give the impression that he was harsh or unloving. Quite the contrary! He was a wonderful father, affectionate in his way, and devoted to his family and Pemberley. But he was also strict, reserved, highly disciplined, and frankly humorless. However, James did often write how altered Father was in his later years. Time mellows people, I imagine." He sighed, somber for a moment while remembering his father, with regret that they had seen so little of each other during the final years of his life. "I rather hope this is true of Mary, although it will be delightful to see her again no matter. It has been far too long."

"William speaks fondly of her," Georgiana broke into the silence, "so I think you will be surprised."

"Not to dampen what I am certain will be a wonderful reunion, but as pleasant as I have found Aunt Mary to be, it would be erroneous to intimate that she has evolved into a woman as gregarious and warm as Aunt Estella or you, Uncle. I have seen her smile and laugh, but will admit it is a rarity." Darcy shrugged. "I admire her restraint. She is extremely intelligent and talented in numerous ways. Conversation was never boring."

George nodded. "Yes, that sounds like my sister. Not overly demonstrative but intriguing and admirable in her accomplishments. Ah, it will be great to see her!"

"You must have missed her all these years," Lizzy murmured sympathetically.

"I suppose I did, although it has not registered until recent years. I too have mellowed with age." Darcy grunted at that, but George went on, "We have written to each other, but not with great frequency I am ashamed to say. Numerous reasons for that, not the least of which was the difficulty in finding me. And my busy life did not allow for regular corresponding. Traveling home was arduous, hence my visiting Pemberley so rarely, William. Diverting to Austria was simply not an easy option. Of course, under different circumstances I would have found a way, but as I said, Mary and I were not close."

His smile was soft and slightly melancholy, but the low chuckle was devilish. He continued, "While growing up Mary could not tolerate any of us. This was a well-established fact between her and James and Estella before Alex and I were old enough to appreciate the emotion. By then we were part of the group and one of our greatest joys in life was to torture poor Mary." He laughed, shaking his head in remembrance. "We truly were awful brats about it. No wonder she married a man who would take her thousands of miles away!"

"Do you think so?" Georgiana asked, brows lifting in amazement.

"Well, probably not. I cannot be sure, as I was too young to be aware of such intrigues as love and romance. I saved that mockery for James," he grinned. "No, she met Baron Oeggl through the Vernors. There is some family connection, quite distant, and he was visiting during a tour of England. We go abroad and the Europeans come here. Interesting, is it not? Massive bear of a man, he was."

"He still is," Darcy interrupted, "or was last I saw him. Old and gray, but 'bear' is an apt description."

"Apparently it was love at first sight and all that rot, although Mary was twenty and the Baron over thirty. Father was less than thrilled with the notion, but hearts prevail. Before the year was out they were wed and gone. We were eleven," he reminisced, reverting to the long lost custom of speaking plurally with his twin, "so the party was more exciting to us than all the romantic falderal. Now I am older, a tiny bit wiser, and can regret that Mary and I were not closer. Yes, it will be lovely to see her again and meet my nieces and nephews."

The roads in France, especially those closest to Paris, were well maintained and broad to accommodate heavier traffic. The rural roads they were obligated to take were not always as smooth with holes and residual muddy areas remaining from the winter rains adding to the places left damaged from the wars. Caution was necessary to avoid serious mishaps and twice they were diverted due to construction, the detour avenues inevitably worse, so the pace was slow. Then, of course, there were the higher elevations and steep hills to climb once in Switzerland that slowed the horses to a crawl and required frequent rests.

Their armed guards rode alongside, searching the horizon and passing terrain for odd disturbances or ambush possibilities. Fate smiled upon them and nothing happened in that regard.

Nothing horrid happened but some troubles were bound to occur. One horse lost a shoe, causing a period of anxiety as they were ascending a sharp rise at the time, but a hamlet nestled in the narrow valley beyond, providing shelter and a smith to replace the horseshoe. Upsets to scheduled nightly halts with hosts or at quality hotels were inevitable, and two times they were forced to lodge at dubious inns, all of them thankful to have packed their own bed linens and silver *necessaire* for dining.

For two nights they rested at a luxurious hostelry in Geneva, the recuperation needed by all. Lizzy felt nothing beyond the typical weariness of hours in a carriage and unfamiliar housing. She experienced some nausea from time to time, but they all did with the constant swaying and pitching. Darcy worried, but not overly since it was clear that any discomfort she felt was readily erased with a brisk walk on firm ground and a full night of sleep.

The older members suffered various aches and disturbances in their sleep, the younger members tended to suffer most from boredom, but Alexander took it all in stride. He fell asleep whenever the need struck him—soft bed, warm arms, or padded carriage bench made no difference—ate well of whatever was placed in front of him, rarely complained, stared at the passing landscape with rapt fascination, or played contentedly with his toys. It was truly remarkable, a fact the more experienced parents on the trip pointed out with increasing wonder.

The countryside teemed with life as spring took a solid hold. Farmers were busy, the rich aroma of freshly tilled earth and manure a constant, as were the fragrances from new blooms. Birds chirped a musical background to the rolling thud of wheels, and the laughter of playing children often greeted them as they passed through villages. The weather held, except for one rainstorm requiring they waylay for an unexpected night in Dijon, but that served to lighten the air and please the flora and fauna.

Yet despite the fun of adventure, after two weeks of exhausting travel, they were universally relieved to reach their destination. Their caravan of carriages entered the wide gates leading to the three-story, sprawling wooden farmhouse of Freiherr and Freifrau von Oeggl, to use their Austrian titles. Baron Oeggl stood on the topmost step leading to the open doors of the massive house constructed of thick oak beams and logs, his shape visible from afar and oddly dwarfing the house. He was indeed a "big bear of a man" and if not for the sunny smile creasing his lined face, it might have been frightening to have such an enormous stranger bounding down the steps. For a moment Lizzy thought he was going to bowl them over or enfold them in a welcoming embrace with arms the size of young trees crushing the air from their lungs, and felt a wave of relief when he halted before doing either. But her startlement lasted only a minute, even with the booming voice that sent tremors into her bones, as the greeting was amiable and sincere, if a bit difficult to understand due to thickly accented English. When Lady Matlock responded in German, the Baron's smile grew bigger and the subsequent minutes gave Lizzy a chance to examine their host.

He was tall, of course, but not as tall as George or Darcy. Rather, his bulk was in the broadness of his shoulders and sheer muscle mass. Some of that muscle had evolved into fat over time, the Baron well into his eighties, but he was still a powerfully built man. He sported a bushy white beard to match the silvery-white hair slicked back from his face and worn long, to tie into a tail hanging midway down his back. Alexander's fascination with his flowing hair and coarse beard would be a running joke and memory to highlight the trip. His elderly face was handsome with grayish-green eyes under thick brows, Lizzy easily able to imagine how stunning he must have been when young. No wonder George's sister had fallen instantly in love with him.

That thought caused her to glance around, but no one matching the descriptions of Mary Darcy stood amongst the crowd of a dozen souls, adult and child, who milled about offering greetings. More people flooded out of the house, apparently the entire Oeggl clan spending the spring to summer season in Switzerland. In time she would discover that this was nearly the truth, but for now they were ushered into the house amid great fanfare and a cacophony of German and English voices.

The Baroness was waiting in the parlor, sitting on a large, leather- and fur-lined chair beside the fire, and no one needed to question why. Mary was obviously not a well woman. In contrast to the robust Baron she could have been mistaken for his mother rather than a wife ten years younger. The tragedy of her illness created a minor pall over the visit, although the extensive family prevented too much sadness from prevailing. George brought every ounce of his medical expertise to bear but in the end could not change the inevitable. Instead he settled for quiet fellowship with his sister, spending the majority of his time talking with her about their childhood and catching up on the lost years.

Lizzy never warmed to Darcy's aunt. She was not unkind or rude in any way, but extremely priggish and humorless. Her austere demeanor was intimidating, Lizzy preferring to interact with the children and grandchildren, who seemed to largely possess Baron Oeggl's effervescent personality.

In the end it did not matter. The wealth of activities both outside in the lovely weather and inside the vast house kept all of them busy. The month passed quickly with endless entertainments to be had. Alexander had few opportunities to use his newfound walking skills since some cousin was usually holding him and the abundance of children meant playing from sunrise to sunset. Darcy fulfilled his dream of climbing the Alps, or rather the lowest pinnacle, in a two-day jaunt up the closest summit with several male kinsman. Not George, of course, he refusing to go anywhere near the snow or pretending for a second that the higher temperatures were adequate enough to please him!

The gigantic house included a well-stocked armory so hunting was a frequent occupation, Baron Oeggl tirelessly stalking miles along with the younger men for the plentiful game roaming the foothills, and fresh meat appeared at nearly every meal. The game room included a billiard table, Darcy's smile beatific upon spying it, and every last male relative felt the sting of defeat ere they left. George joined in for some of the manly exploits but preferred to stay with his sister. That also meant he was often the only male present in a house of females and children, a position he gladly accepted. The children thought their new uncle a treasure, the constant clamoring for his undivided attention provoking a jealous streak in Alexander, who made sure everyone knew this was *his* Uncle Goj!

CHAPTER TWO

In the Shadow of the Alps

CROSSING THE ALPS INTO Italy was never an easy endeavor, although it was undertaken with enough regularity to organize properly. Five of the Oeggl grandchildren, young adults all, as well as the eldest son and heir to the barony, Herr Jens Oeggl, and his wife, Anita, had decided to join the caravan as soon as they learned of Lord and Lady Matlock's plan to take Miss Darcy on a grand tour. All the arrangements were made, including connecting with several other friends who wished to travel and, as expected, the locals in Switzerland were stocked with every supply needed. A larger company moving together was the safest plan, Darcy immeasurably relieved and thankful to learn of the family's inclusion.

"Tours across Europe are popular for the Darcy kinsmen this year." It was twilight on May twenty and the main parlor, stretching across the rear of the house with a panoramic view of Lake Genève, was packed with adults lounging about in that hazy place of contentment after a day replete with activity and a sumptuous dinner. Baroness Oeggl's murmured statement was easily audible to all since most were reading, silently playing games, or staring at the scenery.

"Yes," Darcy responded first, laying his book aside and attending to his aunt, "we are a platoon-sized force blazing across the continent. Somewhat ostentatious at times."

The corners of her mouth lifted slightly at his joke. "Oh yes, I recall the feelings of pretension when traveling in the past. Our recent journey from Vienna was a formidable host, more of a battalion with all of us." She swept her eyes over the loungers, most of who were listening to the exchange with smiles on their faces. "However, I was not only referring to those currently residing here. Your cousin Maria and her husband are in Russia, of all the outlandish places to visit."

"I think Russia would be a fascinating place to tour. It is an ancient culture with architecture found nowhere else."

Lizzy's zealous interruption was met with a faint frown, the Baroness continuing as if she had not spoken, "Freiherr Oeggl's youngest brother and family are already in Italy, since last fall, and currently the Marchioness of Warrow is dwelling at our house in Vienna."

"Aunt Beryl is in Vienna?" George blurted.

"Lady Warrow," Mary corrected primly, "is accompanying her grandson, Mr. Butler, while he studies music in Vienna."

Darcy looked toward his wife. "I believe he mentioned his plans to tour abroad when we met him last year, did he not Elizabeth?"

"He did. I was not sure of details in his plans, however. Did he speak of it to you, Georgiana?"

"We conversed for a few minutes only and then about the pieces he wrote. I know nothing of his private matters, but I am not surprised. If the compositions played for us are an indication of his talent, then it is sensible to further his study. He plans to tour Italy, I assume?"

"Not as yet. My understanding is that he hopes to be a student at the Paris Conservatoire de Musique…"

"Oh!" Georgiana blushed at her interruption but could not hide her animation. "How extraordinary! For a foreigner to be admitted is an incredible honor. Mr. Butler surely possesses a talent vastly exceeding my impression if he has such expectations. How extraordinary," she repeated, face dreamy as she lapsed into silence.

"He does play beautifully," Mary resumed, "and with my knowledge of music I can assert he is prodigiously skilled. I am sure in time he will comprehend the importance of visiting Italy to study opera where it originated and reigns supreme."

"If he is as precious to the musical world as it appears then hopefully he will sail to Italy rather than risk his magical fingers or genius brain to the rigors of crossing the mountains!"

Laughter rang out at Herr Oeggl's exaggeration, only his mother pursing her lips and remaining silent.

"Jens teases at Mr. Butler's expense not out of maliciousness, Miss Darcy, but because the two instantly bonded in friendship. Mr. Butler is as humorous as my husband, if one defines sarcasm as humor." Anita Oeggl winked at her spouse, Herr Oeggl bowing in mock salute.

"Only desiring to avoid a tragedy that would wound us all, my love."

"Is the crossing into Italy as formidable as they say?" Georgiana asked. Her voice and expression showed exhilaration at the concept and not a shred of fright, music and Mr. Butler forgotten.

"Oh, indeed it is," her cousin answered in an ominous tone, winking sidelong at Darcy, who frowned. "The pass of Saint Bernard through the Valais Alps to Aosta is roughly fifty miles of narrow winding pathways overlooking plunging gorges and rising to elevations over eight-thousand feet. All around you are towering snow-clad mountains touching the heavens. It is breathtaking to behold! God at His greatest display of artistry. One must be hardy to cross and incredibly brave."

"You have crossed it yourself, Herr Oeggl?"

"I have, twice I am proud to say."

"An adventurous soul is my son," Baron Oeggl declared.

"I am Austrian. And Austrians climb mountains fearlessly, yes, *Mutter, sein*?"

"So I am continually informed," Mary agreed dryly.

Herr Oeggl grinned. "You shall see, *lieblich* cousin, that the Great St. Bernard is a marvelous adventure. We shall tread the road bloody Napoleon crossed with his army of 60,000, descending into an unaware Saint-Rhemy with war chariots and gun carriages. He was branded a fool to attempt crossing in May while the heavy snows blocked the pass, but fool or tactical genius his ploy succeeded. History is plentiful along the pass."

Lizzy shivered. "One hears such tales of woe related to that pass. Are you sure it is wise to take that way?"

"It is the closest and well traversed, Cousin. Thousands of people travel that way each year. One must be diligent and prepared, naturally. That is why we will not depart until well into June, for one thing, and we will move slowly with guides."

"And you will shelter at the hospice for a day or more of rest," Darcy ordered.

"Goodness knows I will need the hiatus." Lord Matlock stretched his legs as if already imagining the ache from an arduous ride.

"The monks who honor Bernard of Menthon by maintaining the hospice will treat you well, my lord. The food is hot and satisfying, the fires raging, and the travelers constant through the pass. The monks and their dogs also patrol the trails for unsavory folk bent on thievery. That is no longer the concern it once was."

"I hear the dogs of St. Bernard are as big as mastiffs. Is this true?"

"It is, Cousin," Jurgen, youngest son of Herr Oeggl replied, leaning forward in his chair and holding his hand shoulder level. "Like small horses they are, but gentle. They gaze at you with their enormous brown eyes and compassion touches your heart. You can see why they love rescuing stranded people, risking their own lives selflessly to aid humans. It is beautiful."

"My son is a lover of animals." Herr Oeggl smiled fondly. "He wishes to join the monastery I believe and devote himself to breeding the St. Bernards. Hence his interest in this journey, unlike my lovely nieces who want to shop in Milano."

"Milano designers and fabrics are unlike anywhere else, except perhaps Florence." Romy sniffed. "It is worth any hardship for fashion."

"Well," countered her sister, Viveka, "Milano excites me as well, but I am also intrigued by the reputed brilliance of spring wildflowers that cover the meadows, the lakes and waterfalls, and any other vistas along the pass. I will be bringing my paints and pad, praying for flat terrain."

"Painting while riding? You are talented to attempt it. You must show me how."

"My pleasure, Miss Darcy, if you teach me how to play the harp as brilliantly as you." She squeezed the blushing Georgiana's hand.

"Not to put a damper on the youthful enthusiasm, but I am happy *not* to be making the trip; enormous dogs and stunning landscape are not enough to tempt me."

"Why, Dr. Darcy"—Lady Matlock laughed—"after your adventures a steep mountain pass gives you pause? I am shocked and disappointed."

"One word, madam: snow. No offense, Baron and Baroness, but I think my blood is now frozen solid and fear removing the three layers of stockings I wear, as I am positive I have frostbite!"

Everyone laughed. Georgiana leaned into her uncle, hugged his arm, and spoke to the crowd, "My dear uncle is delicate it seems. I, on the other hand, am determined to be brave and enjoy every moment!"

"That is the spirit, Cousin." Herr Oeggl slapped his hand onto the chair's arm. "Remember that only half of the journey is uphill. The rest is a descent, and how hard can that be?"

Lizzy filled two journals with notes and etchings of their time in Switzerland. Many of her entries were stories recounted by Darcy's female cousins, those same ladies who taught him to dance the waltz so many years ago. Their remembrances were highly amusing, at least to Lizzy. Darcy flushed and attempted to correct their embellished reminiscences to no avail. He did prove, however, that their lessons in the Viennese waltz were intact, Lizzy reaping the benefits several times at the balls held in their honor.

Yet for all the entertainments and family memories, years later, Darcy would maintain that the best part of their stay in Switzerland was when he felt their baby move for the first time.

A week after arriving, on a night in May, Darcy reclined on a chair in their guest bedchamber with his feet crossed on the ottoman and mind engrossed in a book, while Lizzy sat at the desk writing in her journal. Silence ruled other than the crackle of the fire, muted tick of a clock, and scribble of her pen.

Sudden Lizzy released a sharp gasp and jumped up from her chair. It was so precipitous that Darcy had no chance to react before she plopped onto his lap. He grunted with the unexpected pressure, the book toppling to the floor when she grabbed his wrist with a jerk. Without a word she pressed his palm firmly against the small mound of her belly, smiling at his bewildered expression.

"Wait," she whispered, "he will kick again, I am sure of it."

He stared into her eyes, waiting as she said with his hand tight over the warm flesh encasing their baby. Lizzy held his gaze, lifted her legs until stretched over his, and leaned back onto his chest with her head resting on his inner shoulder.

"He is usually quiet in the evenings. When I feel him you are never around or we are in public. It has been frustrating."

"I agree with the frustration," Darcy breathed softly. "He, or she, is uncooperative. Hopefully not a sign of what is to come. Behave, little one, let your father know you are there."

Lizzy shifted, moving his fingertips to the left side. "I think his legs are over here more. Wait."

But the word barely left her mouth when their unborn child jabbed back at the seeking fingers invading his space, Darcy sucking in his breath at the sensation. He swiveled instantly misty eyes to her abdomen, as if possible to outwardly see the feeble movements.

"See, he is a cooperative boy."

"He is amazing! Ah, how I have missed this miraculous feeling." He buried his face in her hair and closed his eyes. He relaxed his taut muscles, inhaled deeply, and settled in to enjoy the profound emotions sweeping through him as their child lazily stirred under his broad hand.

It was only two or three minutes, the baby yet too small to exert energy for long. Darcy could sense his stretches spacing, and then a palpable rolling motion as he presumably flipped inside his watery home and ended the interlude. Still Darcy cradled the soft bulge, silent and at peace with his wife in his arms and the newfound connection charging through his veins. He could almost hear his heart expanding, each beat sending life-giving blood to the cells created to love this addition to his family, his head dizzy with the glorious feelings flooding over him.

"I love you, Elizabeth. You are a marvelous gift to me, and now you are blessing my life further with our children. I will be content with whatever God allots us, but I must say I selfishly wish for many."

"Be careful what you ask for," Lizzy chuckled. "*Many* is rather vague and as we are constantly being reminded, most children are not as complacent as Alexander!"

"It makes no never mind. I absolutely adore being a father and will gladly accept them all."

"I shall note that remark in my journal in case I need to jog your memory of such a bold promise. The next one may well possess my personality, or worse yet, your father and George's!"

He smiled benignly, cupping her face and rubbing a thumb over her cheek. "I will take my chances." The kiss that followed was lengthy but soothing and soft. His fingertips brushed over her jaw for a momentary caress before returning to cradle the mound where his second child lay. With his other arm he drew her closer to his body, Lizzy instinctively curling and melting into the contours of his form.

A low hum of pleasure purred from the back of her throat when he finally released her lips, the sound wafting as a breath over the curve of his neck when she buried her face there. He held her, contentment a tangible blanket surrounding their bodies, and continued to fondle the pillowy swell for a long while. The baby moved occasionally, faint and fluttery but discernible now that he knew what to expect, but remained quiet for the most part. Eventually Darcy's eyes grew heavy and he carried his sleeping wife to their bed to nestle with his hand tight over her belly and unconscious mind registering every prod.

Toward morning but while the sun yet hid below the surface of their area of the world, Darcy was roused by movement on Lizzy's side of the bed and a brief but cold blast of air across his shoulders. He was on his back and rolled toward the space she typically occupied, only then sleepily assimilating that what roused him was her returning to bed.

"Why were you up?" he grated.

"Nature's duties. I apologize for waking you." He garbled something that sounded like *never mind* and reached for her body, Lizzy keeping a distance and whispering, "My gown is chilled and toes like ice. I will make you cold."

He grabbed her anyway, strong arms slipping her over the sheets as if a feather, the heat radiating off his skin pouring through her. "Do not be ridiculous," he rumbled, sending fresh shivers through her flesh, although not from the cold as Darcy thought. "I will have you warm in seconds."

It was true. She cuddled against his hard chest and leeched the heat generated in droves by his internal furnace. She cinched her icy feet between his naked shins and while they thawed, the remainder of her body flared quickly to hot, especially with his hands drowsily rubbing over her back.

"It may warm up during the day, but at night it is as freezing as December," she murmured, pressing an icicle nose onto his breastbone.

He chuckled, the hoarse sound reverberating under her face. "Trust me, it is much colder here in December. I will stir up the fire." He started to draw away, but Lizzy clutched onto his thigh and held fast.

"No need. I am quite warm now. I have my own personal fire and he rapidly incites my internal flames." And just in case he missed the innuendo she kissed his chest and caressed pointedly up his thigh and around to his rear.

Darcy, of course, was not an imbecile even if half asleep. The lazy caressing continued for several minutes while Lizzy planted kisses across his chest and Darcy smiled into her lavender scented hair. He snaked a hand under the thick nightgown she wore during the winter, pushing the cloth upward as his hand skimmed over her leg. He sighed contentedly, allowing the excitement to build in languid increments, savoring the tactile delight of her skin under his palm without a conscious agenda.

"He is quite active at this moment."

Her whispered words broke into the silence, momentarily halting the fingers trailing over her hipbone. Eagerly they altered their random path, purposefully brushing along her inner thigh until reaching the swell above. As she said, the baby was moving with gentle nudges against his palm.

"Hmm... Wonderful. You continually say 'he' as if sure of the sex. Another vivid dream as with Alexander?"

"No. Not this time. More of a feeling."

"Ah, *a feeling*. So scientific." He accented his tease with a tiny pinch.

"As scientific as my dream, but that proved true."

"Very well then. I suppose that means we do not have to assign a female name, and since Alexander was instantly agreed upon, we have a task on our hands. Any choices? Do you wish to name him after your father?"

"Thomas? Perhaps, although we could reserve it as a secondary name after your father's. James should be chosen before Thomas."

"I do want to pay homage to my father if possible, yes. However, I do want to add Charles as a secondary name as well, if you do not mind? He is a dear friend and instrumental in my meeting you." He gently drew her away from his chest, attempting to see her eyes in the dark, but to no avail so he kissed her instead, his fingertips flittering over her most sensitive zones while maintaining contact with their unborn child.

"How sweet," she said once her mouth was released. "Charles is mutually agreed upon. So, we have numerous secondary name choices but nothing for the Christian name. Do you have a favorite?"

"I have always liked Nathaniel. And Adam. Not common, I know, but nice names."

"Possible. What do you think of Gabriel? Lisle's son is Gabriel and it struck me as pleasant."

Suddenly Darcy chuckled. "Gabriel, Thomas, Nathaniel, Adam. I think we are cornering Biblical names!"

"Indeed," she joined his laughter. "Of course, if we have this *many* babies you alluded to last night, we may work our way through the entire Bible. Just do not ask for Methuselah. I draw the line there."

"Does that mean Shadrach and Meshach are eliminated? And no on Potiphar or Boaz?"

She shook with laughter and a fair dose of arousal now that his fingers had crept to the apex between her legs and were confounding her senses with their antics. "Absolutely not! I have no urge to torture our son with a hideous name. What say we remain in the realm of non-ridiculing names like Matthew or Daniel or Michael…"

"Michael," Darcy interrupted, although Lizzy's voice had paused on the name. Even his fingers had ceased moving, a fact Lizzy did not initially register as she too was dwelling on the name. "That has a nice ring. Michael. Michael Darcy. Michael Charles Darcy. What do you think?" He tried vainly to see her eyes, but the room was still too dark. He felt her gaze upon his face, the gap of inches separating allowing him to feel her exhaled breaths. Somehow he knew she was smiling.

"I love it. Yes, very much. It does not have to be definitively settled as yet, but… It fits for some inexplicable reason. Michael Darcy."

"Michael Darcy. Yes. At least the choice for the present and much better than Methuselah. Shall we seal it with a kiss, Mrs. Darcy?"

"More than a kiss please," spoken huskily and with a demanding press to the immobile hand resting on her pubis.

"As you wish, my love." His fingers resumed their teasing, Lizzy moaning and arching into the magic that was his touch.

Baby names were forgotten in the wake of escalating incitement. Lizzy's amorousness that was dampened while discussing the baby flared into a raging inferno of desire. This was becoming a pattern and Darcy teased that her fervency was due to pregnancy wrecking havoc on her insides. It was true that she typically possessed more restraint in comparison to his voracious sexual appetite, but her craving for him at odd times was not unheard of, pregnant or not. Whatever the truth, his skillful manipulations rapidly achieved the desired results. Then his lips left her mouth to travel down her neck to the breast freed from the gown's bodice with a flick of his little finger and he drew the sensitized, puckered nipple in for a sharp suck instantly turning her pants to gasping shouts as spasms buffeted through every muscle.

Darcy groaned, growled really, but held on and rode the cresting wave of her release, encouraging the pleasure to arc ever higher with practiced strokes. He waited, knowing the precise moment when the sensations began to wane. It was then that he lifted his body, rolled smoothly between her legs, and plunged in as deeply as possible. Raspy moans vibrated against her lips as he parted them with a greedy tongue bent on plundering deeply. Yet instead of initiating a furious rhythm of lovemaking he held still. Buried completely, he absorbed the final tremors, kissing ravenously as the feel of her wildly increased his desire to the point where *not moving* was necessary or their interlude would be over in a second.

And that would never do. What had begun as an unplanned assignation in the darkest, coldest hours of the night need not be swift. Darcy was wide awake now, his body thrumming with urgency and passion. Every sense was alive, except for sight since the darkness prevented even a glimmer of the beloved person pressed so deliciously under his solid frame. But he knew her face intimately, could picture each feature vividly, and the deprivation of light only enhanced every other sensation. This fact was proven true when she squeezed with her lissome legs, lifting her hips in a clear indication that she wanted more. The rivers of flame rushed from his toes to the crown of his head, animalistic lust and rapturous love demanding he respond.

And he did, hard and fast. Heaving breaths accenting the furious strokes and his hands held her hips in place for each fierce push.

"*Yeeeesssss…*" Her sibilant utterance spurred Darcy on, the pace of his thrusts varying as they undulated together in no rush to end the pleasure.

After nearly three years of wedded bliss Darcy could not claim to recall each time they made love in specific detail. Always their unions were amazing and satisfying, but there were those times that created lasting memories. Their wedding night, of course, and not merely because it was their first time together as well as the first time either had shared such intimacy with another person, but also because it was perfect in every way. His soul had truly come alive that night; his heart irrevocably changed when his wife entered inside and took up residence.

There was the time they made love in her bath on Christmas Eve, discovering the unique joy and delight in mixing water, soap, and desire. After her brush with death as a result of Lord Orman's wicked attack, their passion was augmented by their thankfulness to be alive. On her birthday when she undressed for him in an erotic dance. In the seawater of Caister-on-Sea. When she staged a romantic tableau in their bedchamber for their rejoining after Alexander's birth. Her surprise intrusion into his dressing room mere weeks after their marriage. That one night when passion consumed and they made love in the billiard room, on the billiard table. Under the willows in Hertfordshire.

He knew even before this session of lovemaking began that it would join the mental montage. Just as when they loved after he felt Alexander for the first time, profound emotions raced through his being, adding to the transcendent physical bliss of satisfying sex. It was a celebration of new life and the love that created this life.

Gone was the caution in expressing their passion too vocally due to thin walls of the chateau. Did their neighbors sleep through their shouts? They would never know. Nor would they care.

CHAPTER THREE

Summer Draws
to a Close

THE TIME TO SAY good-bye, or *auf Wiedersehen* as it were, to the Oeggl multitude came for four of the English travelers during the second week in June. Lizzy continued to feel incredible, but with her pregnancy advancing they were forced to depart. It was difficult to leave for a host of reasons. Mary's illness, although never spoken of openly, left no doubt that they would never see her again. The impact on George was striking, even as he presented his typical comical front. He embraced her tightly, murmuring into her ear, and the surreptitious swipe at wetness collecting on his cheek was noted by many.

Darcy's parting from his sister was difficult, but not as intensely painful as he had imagined.

"I will miss you every moment of every day, Brother," she whispered while holding him tightly.

Darcy smiled, pulling away an inch to kiss her forehead. "I shall miss you as well, Georgie. I shall think of you constantly and expect letters; however, I do not anticipate that you will be thinking of me every day, let alone every moment. In fact, I would be greatly disappointed if you did! I want you to experience life and art as you have long desired. This is your time to shine and enjoy."

"Thank you, William."

"Just promise to be safe and return with stories to tell."

"I promise."

His brave face remained calm as they said their official farewells. Lizzy was not fooled by the lightness, nor was Georgiana. Lord Matlock was surprised to only receive a handful of warnings regarding Georgiana's safety and was sympathetic to Darcy's emotions, so he did not tease or counter argue. Darcy's melancholia coupled with George's sadness over Mary cast a pall on the initial days of their return journey, but gorgeous scenery and intriguing places overcame.

They set a faster pace as they traveled north from Geneva to Luxembourg and then west to Calais. Lizzy suffered not a twinge of discomfort as her abdomen continued to grow, yet as the baby exerted more influence, Darcy's gut coiled tighter. The urge to be on English soil and in their home became stronger with each passing mile. Nevertheless, they did pause for frequent periods of rest or sightseeing, finally boarding the ship as the first days of July dawned.

The distance from Dover to Rosings in Kent was only some thirty miles, a fact Darcy and George were blissfully happy about, as the seas were rough for the short crossing. Lizzy suggested tarrying in Dover until they recuperated, but the vehement insistence to get as far away from the ocean as possible was heeded. The carriages were unloaded as speedily as possible, the suffering men collapsing into the cushions and not notably improving even when the smell of tar, sea, and fish was finally left behind. The swaying carriage did not help, Lizzy fully expecting one or both of them to succumb to churning stomachs. Fortunately the buckets she brought along just in case were never used, but whether that was due to the Dr. Darcy–brewed tonic they sipped nonstop or sheer willpower she never knew. Alexander was not as fortunate; the Darcy gene for seasickness activated this time. He did recuperate once on dry ground and did not vomit after leaving the docks, a boon Lizzy was eternally grateful for since his retching would certainly have affected the men in a most negative fashion.

Anne Penaflor, née de Bourgh, greeted their carriage alone. She stood calmly on the steps before Rosings's imposing entrance, her fragile figure dressed in a fashionable gown of pale yellow and green that gathered in an attempt to hide the swell of her abdomen. The clever design was unsuccessful mainly due to a breeze shifting the fabric over her body but also because Anne held one hand atop the precious bulge. Lizzy smiled at the gesture, understanding precisely why she wore the voluminous garment—her mother's requirement, without a doubt—but also why Anne would rebel in this small way.

This was Anne's fourth pregnancy and the first to carry past the initial months. The anemia that plagued her adult life was pernicious and unexplainable. Her husband devoted a vast amount of his time in searching, consulting, and experimenting in hopes of finding a cure for her illness. So far the skilled physician had managed palliative measures only and pregnancy had proven a challenging state. Twice she miscarried early in the initial weeks when her condition was not completely certain. The third miscarriage occurred in the fourth month—after quickening had given them greater hope. Emotionally these losses were draining, but the serious affliction was physical. It was as if all the progress made prior due to the medications and treatments by Dr. Penaflor and Dr. Darcy were erased. Anne bled for weeks afterwards and grew frighteningly weak. But each time she healed and regained her newfound vigor and serenity with life.

The image Anne presented as she walked toward them onto the graveled drive was not of a woman suffering ill health. Yes, she was thin as she always had been and it was doubtful Anne would ever possess true ruddiness to her skin, but her cheeks were pink and her entire being glowed. Darcy had verbalized to Lizzy his doubts over the wisdom of Anne marrying and then continuing to conceive. Yet now, as they gazed upon her visage, they both realized how wrong that assessment.

She embraced Elizabeth first, their protruding abdomens bumping together and inciting girlish giggles. "Welcome, Elizabeth! You have no idea how you have been missed! Now we shall have even more to talk about." She rubbed over her belly briefly and then turned to Darcy with a beaming grin. "Oh my, Wills, obviously the Channel crossing took a toll. You look positively dreadful."

"Thank you. Just what every man prefers to hear from a woman." He smiled wanly, kissing her hand. "Thankfully, I cannot claim the same for you, dear cousin. You are radiant. I would embrace you but fear the outcome may be unpleasant."

"You can embrace Lady Catherine instead. That would be amusing."

Anne choked a laugh at Lizzy's remark. Darcy tried to frown but his features were so pinched it came out as more of a sour grimace. George voiced their feelings succinctly when he exited the carriage. "This physician's treatment plan is brandy, or better yet whiskey, in large quantities, and a bed. Not necessarily in that order."

"As you wish, Doctor." She turned, arm in arm with Lizzy, leading into the cavernous foyer and directing servants with ease and confidence. "Unfortunately the greeting to my mother will have to wait. She is visiting an ill friend in Ashford. Sorry to disappoint your amusement, Elizabeth"—she winked sidelong at her companion—"and my husband is at the hospital. We were unsure when you would arrive. I do apologize. Now," she paused before the parlor doors, waving her hand toward the staircase, "off to bed with the three of you." She inclined her head to include Alexander, fast asleep in Mrs. Hanford's arms. "Your indisposition allots us time to chatter and gossip."

And almost like wayward boys being scolded, Darcy and George obeyed.

For two weeks they dwelt at Rosings.

Lizzy inevitably felt odd whenever their paths and duty took them to Kent. The memories associated with the first time she ever came here were not necessarily pleasant. She and her husband had long since buried the past misconceptions with a love so profound that any guilt or sadness was washed clean. Nevertheless, one does not ever forget, especially when boldly confronted with places triggering those memories.

This alone may not have created a great burden. Lizzy and Darcy were able to find ways to erase or supplant bad remembrances with happier ones—just ask the silent walls of Netherfield or immobile willows near Longbourn! Making love on the floor of the Hunsford parlor or Rosings drawing room was clearly not an option, but even if it were, Mr. Collins and Lady Catherine would still be there to annoy Elizabeth when the pleasure abated.

Lady Catherine's acerbic tongue and outward disdain toward Elizabeth were carefully curbed. During their first visit to Rosings, Lady Catherine's subtle slurs led to a second confrontation, minor compared to the one in London shortly after their marriage. Nevertheless, Darcy's barely controlled rage, now seen twice by his aunt, and promise to leave the area never to return effectively quashed her lingering ire toward Elizabeth. Or at least it prevented her openly declaring her scorn. Now the two women tiptoed around each other. Lizzy would never like her and received perverse joy in vexing her, even if the behavior was unbecoming. She just could not help herself and Darcy gave up scolding her for it. Besides, it was rather amusing—not that he would ever admit it—to see his aunt befuddled by his wife's clever wit.

"How can you allow your son, the heir to Pemberley, to wear such outlandish garments?" Lady Catherine indicated Alexander, who was running about the lawn with Rachel and Leah Collins, and the flowing tunic of Indian silk painted with jungle vines and monkeys that he wore.

"We want him to be a free spirit." Lizzy's voice was gay, bordering on vapid. "And besides, it allows the genitalia to grow freely." She tossed George's words out, Lady Catherine's lips puckering so tightly in response that Lizzy was forced to jump up and join the children in their play to avoid bursting into laughter.

Another time: "You intend to walk to the village alone? In your condition? What does Fitzwilliam think of this?"

"Of the walk or my 'condition'?" Lizzy asked innocently.

"Of you walking *in* your condition!"

Lizzy shrugged. "I did not ask specifically about *this* walk, but usually he does not tend to inhibit my walking. And the 'condition' I am in does not seem to influence his attitude on the subject in a negative way, as far as I have been able to ascertain. It is partially his fault, after all, so he cannot very well argue my need for exercise, now can he?"

Lizzy grabbed her bonnet by the strings, curtsied to Lady Catherine, and turned to make for the door.

"Are you not going to put your hat on? The sun is bright and without hat or gloves on you will become tanned." Lady Catherine uttered the word "tanned" as if the worst curse word imaginable. "I cannot imagine Fitzwilliam would be pleased at that."

"He has never complained before. But I promise that if he expresses any distaste, I shall henceforth don my bonnet from the outset." She smiled brilliantly, curtsied again, and left—with the bonnet dangling by her side. Needless to say, Darcy did not mind her bronze skin in the least.

Another time: "Here is your book, Elizabeth."

"Thank you, William."

"May I ask what you are reading, Mrs. Darcy?"

"Of course, Lady Catherine. I am reading *Evelina* by Frances Burney. Have you read it?"

"I most certainly have not," Lady Catherine sniffed. "I prefer to read books of intellectual quality and strong moral lessons rather than the nonsensical romanticism of novels."

"As you have admittedly not read *Evelina*, how can you assert it is nonsensical? Romantic to be sure, but the titular character's virtues and attention to upright morals in the face of difficulties are to be admired. *Evelina* is a lesson in etiquette and propriety."

Lady Catherine was not convinced. "I am surprised you would allow such reading material for your wife, Fitzwilliam."

"I do not dictate my wife's reading material, Aunt Catherine. Her choices are invariably sound ones. Although in this case, I would disagree with Mrs. Darcy's assessment. I found Evelina to be somewhat boring as a character. But perhaps my judgment is colored as I prefer women with spunk and a ready wit."

He smiled at his wife but did note his aunt's incredulous expression. "You read this… novel?" she sputtered.

"Indeed I have."

"He tolerated it," Lizzy put in with a laugh. Then she added, looking directly at Lady Catherine, "He much prefers a novel with a bit more excitement and controversy, like *Tom Jones*."

Lady Catherine was so stunned she could not form a reasonable response. Darcy shot his wife a glare, but she noticed the twitching of his lips. Denying the charge was impossible since it was true, so he said nothing. Thankfully the topic turned away from dubious literature at that point!

But the worse forms of irritation to the priggish woman were unintentionally caused, and that was the blatant affection between her formerly staid nephew and the woman who had driven that good sense and propriety out of him. She was pleased on a certain level that Darcy was happy, as she was for Anne and Raul, finally accepting that her daughter never would have given Darcy what he needed and vice versa. She also accepted that the Darcys truly loved each other, and as ridiculous as she regarded that emotion, she was forced to acknowledge that Lizzy had not pursued him for his wealth and position as Lady Catherine had surmised. That acceptance did not necessarily mean she approved of his choice or saw Lizzy any differently than she did before, however. Witnessing his frivolity, as she interpreted it, and catching them amid loving displays only served to confirm her opinion of Elizabeth's character.

Anne and Raul knew when to show affection, and that was behind a firmly closed door. The two were overwhelmingly in love, but other than polite pecks on the cheek or sappy gazes, they restrained themselves. Lizzy and Darcy had never learned to master that extreme caution, nor had they overly tried. They did not wantonly embrace or kiss in public, Darcy sooner dying than to go that far, but they were definitely more demonstrative than typically customary and, if alone, they could, and often did, lose control to a degree.

"William, come! A whole family of ducks is being herded by Lady Catherine's corgi. It is hysterical!"

He rose from his seat to join his wife by the library window where she stood watching the antics of the corgi, he intent on rounding the uncooperative ducks and ducklings. "I believe my aunt would have a seizure if she knew her prized pet was playing with farm animals," he rumbled, breaking into a laugh when one of the ducks snapped at the yipping dog's tail, missing by less than an inch.

They watched the entire escapade, the corgi finally triumphing when every last duck entered the pond. Darcy unconsciously caressed the small of her back, his hand gliding over her waist when she turned and leaned into the window's edge. "He does well for a little thing. Perhaps we should think of getting one. They are quite cute."

"Dogs are meant to guard and protect, not be useless balls of fur labeled 'cute' that yap constantly and tread through the house."

"You mean like our cat? That worthless ball of fur who ends up curled by your feet and has never once been kicked aside as you threaten to do on a daily basis?"

Darcy smiled, reaching to slowly sweep a loose curl off her cheek and tuck it behind her ear. "He catches mice, therefore earning his keep. Plus he keeps my feet warm."

"Your feet are never cold, Mr. Darcy, so I am not buying that for a second. I think a fluffy corgi would worm his way into your heart until you are spoiling him worse than I. Dare you deny it?"

"I shall maintain my silence on the subject." His fingers brushed over her cheeks and down her neck, his eyes following. "What I shall not deny is how lovely you look with the sun striking your skin and that amused sparkle in your eyes. I am breathless and suddenly thirsty."

"Shall I pour you some water, sir? Will that alleviate your distress?"

"Not in the least, minx." He bent his head, planting a delicate kiss to her collarbone, right where the sun's ray illuminated. He continued to deliver airy kisses and feathery touches of his tongue all along the glowing beam painting her skin, traveling ever closer to her décolletage.

Lizzy was helpless to do anything but to close her eyes, melting into the hard wall and instinctively slipping both hands inside his jacket to hold onto his waist.

"This only serves to make me thirstier," he growled, stopping before kissing the furthest edge of the beam, conveniently located precisely between her breasts. He straighten, only for a moment, before leaning into her body, pressing and pulling at the same time, and engaging her lips this time for a searing kiss. "Alexander is asleep and the house is quiet," he continued some minutes later, "so I say we take our appetite upstairs, yes, Mrs. Darcy?"

Lizzy nodded in agreement but chose to bridge the narrow gap between their mouths and crush his hard body closer rather than take a step toward the door. Darcy chose to deepen the kiss, grind his lower body against her softness, and release a long moan of pleasure rather than taking a step toward the door.

The door which opened at that moment to admit Lady Catherine.

Her gasp was lost in the air, the click of the rapidly closed door not registering to the impassioned lovers who soon composed themselves enough to exit the room still ignorant of the interloper. They took their tryst to their chamber to be completed without any interruptions. Lady Catherine took to her bed also, smelling salts on the stand just in case!

Then there was Mr. Collins to irritate Lizzy. Or rather both of them, as Darcy abhorred him. Luckily he rarely had to encounter the obsequious little man other than at dinner upon occasion. Lizzy was not as fortunate, by her choice, since her friendship with Charlotte remained.

Yet, as time passed, her friendship with Charlotte was subtly altering. Perhaps it was a natural progression due to the distance between their current homes with visits rare and brief. But upon serious reflection Lizzy knew it was not that. While her newfound friendships with ladies such as Chloe Drury, Julia Sitwell, and Amelia Lathrop—all who lived a distance from Pemberley— flourished, her relationship with Charlotte Collins diminished. How much of that had to do with Lizzy's distaste for Mr. Collins and her persistent disbelief that sensible, warm Charlotte could stoop to marry him or the differences in their social status Lizzy could not decide.

She felt embarrassed by the uncomfortable silences that came while they visited. It was odd to realize that they had little in common anymore. She could not share her happiness with Darcy since Charlotte would never possess half that joy in her union. They talked about household management and charity work, but in both cases their experiences and duties were vastly different. Frivolous gossip about people or events was limited, since they knew few of the same people and their perspectives were quite varied now. The safest topic was children, so that is what they shared in largest portion.

The twin Collins girls were plain in appearance, but lively creatures just a few weeks older than Alexander. He thought they were fantastic fun, the three of them running and rolling about the lawn while their mothers sipped tea and talked. At times like this, with the breeze blowing and the women relaxing under a shading tree, the years erased and they were just Lizzy and Charlotte again.

Until Mr. Collins appeared.

"Mrs. Darcy"—he bowed—"I am honored to welcome you to our humble abode. I apologize profusely for not greeting you as is proper for the master of the house, even one as quaint and modest as ours, to do. More so, I daresay, as a great lady such as you condescending to pass through our simple doors is a tremendous courtesy and should not be ignored. Of course, I mean no disrespect to our parsonage, you understand? Lady Catherine, our gracious patroness, has contributed bountifully to enhance our home and we are eternally grateful and in her debt."

"Have no worries over it, Mr. Collins," Lizzy interrupted the tide. "Lady Catherine is abundantly aware of her charitable acts and how appreciative her subjects are."

He bowed again, missing the hidden slur. "That is a relief to hear. Thank you for informing me. And thank you for visiting with my dear Mrs. Collins. She, I know, is as honored as I by your consideration. Most likely her overwhelming gratitude is why she neglected to alert me as to your arrival, an understandable omission, I know, perfectly understandable under the circumstances. Still, if I had been notified I would have hastened from my work, as important as it is to the nourishment of God's children and the furtherance of His church, to welcome you immediately. As it is I am late, but my happiness and sincerity are surely as intense."

"Thank you, Mr. Collins. You are the soul of hospitality. As is Charlotte. Indeed we were caught up in our mutual delight and forgot all other considerations. Please forgive me for preventing her carrying out her duties, as I am sure she would have."

"Indeed! Oh, indeed there is nothing to forgive!" He cast befuddled eyes about the yard, noting the laughing children. "Ah, your son has grown, Mrs. Darcy. What a fine lad he is. Mr. Darcy must be immeasurably proud to have a son who is so handsome and robust."

"We are indeed proud. You must be as well?" He knit his brows, lifting a brow in question. "About your girls, I mean," Lizzy explained. "They are lovely girls and healthy."

"Yes, yes of course. They are wonderful and we are naturally cognizant of God's grace and beholden to Him for His mercy. However, as remarkable and special as girls are, and we dearly love our Leah and Rachel, Mrs. Collins and I, one cannot deny the desire for a son to uphold the family name and potentially, hopefully, walk in a father's steps." He sighed, unconsciously glancing to a flushed Charlotte. "A man naturally wishes for such a gift. Alas, it is not always granted."

Lizzy felt the tension in the air, the heaviness of it pressing into her chest in a most uncomfortable manner, and Charlotte's pained expression distressed her. Mr. Collins was always annoying, but Lizzy typically offset her irritation by oblique insults that he never comprehended but that amused her and made his presence tolerable. Not this time, however.

"Charlotte," Lizzy stood, not giving Mr. Collins another opportunity to pontificate, "how about we take the children for a stroll in the Park? I love the walk through the roses."

Taking their leave of Collins was not as easy as she hoped, but eventually they were alone. They pushed the prams over the rocky walkway, admiring the flowers in inane phrases that only served to heighten the strange tension. Finally, Lizzy could hold her tongue no longer.

"Charlotte, I have to ask. Are you unable to have more children?"

Her companion was silent for a long while. Lizzy feared studying her face, assuming the grief over an inability to conceive must be great. She knew that Charlotte's delivery of the girls was tortuous, although Charlotte had never given details. It was not uncommon for injury to occur of a nature that made pregnancy impossible or unwise.

"No," Charlotte answered in a grave tone. "I am sure I could have more children. I simply do not wish to have more."

"Oh! I see. That is, I can imagine the birth was difficult so, yes, it would make sense…"

"I do not fear birth or being with child, Lizzy."

Her voice was so low and raising from the middle of Charlotte's chest due to her hung head that Lizzy had difficulty hearing the muttered words. But she did hear them and sad comprehension dawned instantly.

"I do not wish to do what is required to conceive. *That* holds no interest to me. I prefer the humiliation of not providing a son over the humiliation of… performing the *act* needed to create one."

Lizzy wanted to cry. They salvaged their afternoon's outing but Lizzy's heart was heavy. She rushed into Darcy's arms the second he walked into their chamber, practically knocking him off his booted feet. He managed to squeak out a few words of concern and question, but not many before she latched on to his lips with a desperate urgency that was thrilling—as his body instantly reacted to it—but rather frightening.

"Elizabeth," he croaked, regaining his equilibrium enough to draw her away and meet her eyes. "I hate to sound as if I am complaining, but what is the meaning of this barrage? What has happened?"

"A conversation with Charlotte that has unsettled me greatly but also rekindled my appreciation for you and what we have together. Have I told you lately how much I love you?"

"Just this morning as a matter of fact. Several times. Of course you also cried my name mixed with that of a deity, but I am certain you meant the part about loving me."

Lizzy shook her head at his attempt to tease, clasping his face firmly within her palms. "That is precisely what I mean."

"I am afraid I do not follow."

"William, we are blessed in so many ways I can no longer count them, but our richest blessing is in how we love each other. How we desire each other and the pleasure it brings into our life and relationship is a true miracle."

"I will not argue that declaration, dearest." He kissed her softly, and then clasped her hand to lead toward the sofa. "Now tell me what this has to do with Mrs. Collins."

"On the bed," she tugged his hand, turning the opposite direction. "I will tell you but I must love you, Fitzwilliam." He did not resist, but felt it obligatory to point out that dinner was served in less than an hour and they still needed to dress. "Some matters supersede dinner hour, even in your aunt's house."

She pushed him backward on the bed, immediately bending to kiss him deeply while stimulating with well-placed strokes. Darcy kissed back, totally forgetting about dinner engagements or the Collins question in seconds. Lizzy did relate the conversation with Charlotte in between kisses and peeling away restricting clothing. Darcy sympathized with her sadness over the plight of Charlotte but was unable to generate much of his own, especially under the present onslaught. All he could think was how grateful he was that she was his wife and not, God forbid, married to Mr. Collins. Imagining any woman engaged in marital relations with that sniveling pathetic excuse for a man was a vision he simply could not conjure. Nor would he ever try.

CHAPTER FOUR

Addition to the Loving Family

THE ROSINGS VISIT WAS brief. Darcy was anxious to return to Pemberley and finalize preparations for their baby, and it was also the time for harvest and settling estate matters for the winter ahead. The latter could be handled by his steward and other staff, but Darcy thrived on being a part of the management.

The two weeks passed pleasantly for the most part. Lizzy divided her time between Anne, who she had grown fond of over the years, and Charlotte. The latter made no further mention of marital issues, a fact Lizzy was thankful for since there was nothing she could offer on the subject under the circumstances. By the final afternoon, sitting with Charlotte while the children played on the lawn, their conversations were light and almost as easy as in the years of their youth. Lizzy was pleased, even though she knew that the months apart would add strain to a relationship that was altering.

Lady Catherine was polite, or as polite as she ever was, but the combined annoyances of Lizzy and George Darcy had clearly worn on her nerves! Lizzy avoided Darcy's aunt as much as possible and her teasing was subtle and checked, out of respect for her husband. George did not possess the same restraints, so his egging of her was more blatant, leading to verbal sparring bordering on arguments. There was no doubt that Lady Catherine was happy to usher them into the waiting carriage, her farewells brief.

Parting from Anne was bittersweet, both Darcy and Lizzy caring for her greatly and knowing it would be many months before they saw her again. Witnessing her pregnancy advance with health and happiness intact eased their minds. Still, even with the current evidence pointing to a positive outcome and the obvious devotion from her husband—Dr. Penaflor's skills as a physician supreme and given an added boost via consultations with Dr. Darcy—they would breathe freer once the birth was over and the babe reported healthy.

They veered northwest to London, tarrying at Darcy House for a little over a week so Darcy could handle the numerous business affairs that had arisen while he was out of the country. Lizzy occupied her time with purchasing both necessary and frivolous items for the baby. Social activities were nonexistent, partly due to the time of year, since few of the ton stayed in London for the summer, but also because of the haste Darcy employed in completing his business so they could get home.

Finally the adventure came to a close. By mid-August, after nearly six months away, the family was comfortably resettled at Pemberley.

The first order of business was to move Alexander from the nursery into the spacious chamber that had been prepared for him while they were gone. Freshly painted and redecorated with varying shades of blue, the chamber was bright and cheery with a large bed that was perfect for parent-son playtime and story reading.

The room faced south with a panoramic view of the River Derwent and pastureland beyond. Sheep roamed freely over the grass, Alexander mesmerized by their sedate activities as observed from the tall windows while he played. It would be a few years before Darcy was told that whenever he and Parsifal went for a run across the meadow Alexander would sit on the window seat, transfixed for as long as he could see them. Mrs. Hanford positioned the rocking horse near the window and Alexander would "ride" the toy horse while watching his father and faithful mount streaking over the tree dotted glade, sheep hastening to move out of the way.

Transitioning from small nursery to larger room was not without problems, however.

He was happy to have wide areas of empty floor to set up his tiny armies and the miniature castle built by Uncle Goj and his papa. The collection of wooden blocks was assigned the northeast corner where they stayed within the allotted area but were never neatly put away. The fanciful replica of Noah's

Ark with ever-increasing pairs of animals was given a table with painted land and water for the appropriate creatures to dwell while waiting for the flood. The chest constructed by his father sat under one window and housed his favorite books, colored drawing chalks and crayons, and stacks of paper. Additional toy chests and shelves lined one wall. For a busy, nearly two-year-old, it was paradise on earth.

Then the nighttime came. Transferring to the big bed, even with his stuffed animal companions to keep him company, proved to be a traumatic event. He refused to fall asleep in the bed, so for two weeks straight he stayed with his parents until asleep, before being moved to his room. Unfortunately he would wake later, something that was extremely unusual for him. Mrs. Hanford tried to sleep with him but the bed, although large for a toddler, was not large enough for a grown woman, some dozen animals, and a child who flipped about constantly. Often he cried out when waking suddenly from a disquieting dream, bringing his nanny quickly to console. Other times he simply woke, grabbed Dog, and padded down the short hall seeking solace from his parents. This came with risks, such as the first time he did so when Darcy and Lizzy were taken utterly by surprise and learned a valuable lesson in privacy and security.

On the night in question, they deposited a deeply sleeping Alexander in his own bed and then retired to their chamber for adult entertainment of a most intimate nature. It was nearing midnight and not five minutes after a mutually dizzying culmination with their bodies yet joined and Darcy crushing his wife into the soft mattress. He lifted his head with a groan to bestow an intense post-loving kiss. Pulling away and bending to kiss her glistening shoulder, Darcy noted movement in his peripheral vision. He turned, freezing instantly and barely halting the reflexive expletive that rose to his lips, eyes locking with the wide-eyed gaze of Alexander.

The toddler stood not a foot away in the gap between the bed curtains, serious face unperturbed as he said, "Papa, I scared. Bad dream."

Lizzy jerked and squelched a scream, turning toward her son, both of them paralyzed where they lay for what seemed like hours. The foremost thought was one of intense embarrassment, although both were sending silent prayers that they had chosen to keep the covers over their bodies as they loved and that the curtains were drawn. However, they had no idea how long he had been standing there, neither noting anything other than their own zeal for the past half hour at least.

Darcy carefully disengaged from his wife, blankets held securely, although there was really nothing either could do about their nakedness. "I am sorry, sweet. Come here, Papa will make it all better." He opened his arms and Alexander climbed onto the bed, nestling snuggly in the warm circle of his father's embrace, clutching Dog tightly.

Lizzy had regained her composure, barely, rising to look over Darcy's body and reaching to comfort her son. "Are you better now, darling?" She smoothed the crazy curls on his brow, his eyes meeting hers in the dimly lit darkness.

"Better," he replied. "You better, Mama? Bad dream gone bye?"

"I am fine, sweetie. What do you mean?"

"You scream. Ogre get you too?"

Darcy howled, Lizzy slapping his back and hiding her instantly scarlet face in his shoulder. "It is well, Alexander," he affirmed with a gasping laugh. "Papa was here to make Mama feel good… very, very good."

"Fitzwilliam!"

Darcy had enormous fun with that one, but from that day forward, he did remember to lock the door securely no matter how caught up in their passion they were. Of course, they also remembered to unlock it later just in case a frightened youngster tiptoed in, as was the case from time to time.

Alexander's transition was aided remarkably by the admission of Mrs. Hanford's daughter Lisa as assistant nanny. Alexander knew the nineteen-year-old well, loved her even, so was delighted to have her close by at all times. Lisa was smaller than her matronly mother and accustomed to sleeping in a bed crammed with nieces and nephews, so slumbering with just Alexander was a luxury! By the time Michael made his appearance, the upheaval was adjusted to and Alexander would dwell in this room until his marriage many, many years hence.

Aside from that drama, the weeks after returning to Pemberley were tranquil. Their excitement was high, of course, but they were also calm and well prepared, having been through it once before.

Shortly after returning to Pemberley, father and son stood gazing at the massive tapestries tracing the Darcy ancestry that hung in the grand foyer. Darcy traced the lines, reciting the names to the raptly listening baby who said nothing until his father read the name Anton Darcy.

His chubby thumb exited his mouth with an audible pop, followed by a moistly declared, "Anton."

"Yes. That is correct, Alexander. Anton Darcy was our ancestor, over two centuries ago. His son was Herbert Darcy, then John…"

"Anton."

Darcy looked at the face so close and resembling his own, the baby's eyes riveted to the fine threads scrolled to form the name Anton. Darcy smiled. "Indeed. Anton. Probably from the Roman influence. A shortened form of Anthony, or perhaps for Mark Antony, the Roman general who ruled for a time as Emperor. Do you like that name?"

"Anton."

And that is how it began. Everything and everyone was "Anton" from there on. Even Dog was dubbed Anton for a time. When they told him that if the baby was a boy he would be named Michael, Alexander nodded calmly then pointed to Lizzy's belly and said, "Anton." They laughed and tried in vain to correct him, but what happened instead is that they grew to love the name and realized it flowed nicely. Thus it was decided that their second child, if a boy, would be christened Michael James Anton Darcy. They did toss around a few girl names, but Lizzy was convinced she was having a boy, so serious deliberation was ignored.

The waning days of summer led into a mild fall. Darcy was busy nearly every day, but always allotted time to play with Alexander. Now that he was older, Lizzy relinquished her hovering concern to a degree and Darcy was able to take his son into the stables or town, to visit with Mr. Vernor or Mr. Hughes, and once to Rowan Lake for naked bathing. Darcy chose a docile mare to ride around the corral with Alexander on his lap, the toddler unrestrained in his joy over the activity, much to Darcy's delight and Lizzy's resignation.

In every way life was picture perfection. Nothing marred the tranquility permeating the atmosphere of Pemberley as they enjoyed the sunlit days and nights of family felicity. Neither Lizzy nor Darcy took it for granted, but it was natural to relax into the contentment and almost assume that it could be thus forever. Very shortly they would discover that life is never perfect and that even the best marriages can suffer.

⎯⎯✦⎯⎯

Considering the probable conception time, when Lizzy began experiencing symptoms and quickening, and how the pregnancy was advancing, Dr. Darcy's professional calculation was for a date of confinement roughly one month before Alexander's second birthday, November 27 of 1819.

Of course, they were wrong. In fact, they would be proven wrong on numerous counts regarding the outcome of their second child's arrival into their happy family.

Aside from the fact that Michael delivered on September 14, nearly one and a half months before anticipated, labor onset took Lizzy utterly by surprise. She hummingly proceeded to sew, decorate, and arrange household matters in the days prior to his birth, sure that she had over a month yet to go. She suffered none of the weariness, backaches, or false contractions that had been rampant toward the latter months of Alexander's gestation, and aside for a mild ungainliness, she was healthier than ever before.

On the day of his birth there was absolutely no warning. She serenely wrote a letter to her mother while Alexander played with his Noah's Ark on a rug by the window of her parlor, ignoring the minor irregular cramps that did not cause her to breathe heavily. In fact, she was more than halfway through the process before she believed it was real, calling for Dr. Darcy a bare four hours before the infant made his appearance.

Nearly every groomsman in Pemberley's employ was sent to scour the estate for its Master and Mr. Keith, who had not thought it essential to share their agenda with anyone. Darcy was found and did arrive before the blessed event, relieved of his considerable self-reproach by a barely sweating Lizzy who assured him with a smile that she was feeling fine!

"Is it not too early, Uncle?" Darcy's voice cracked, his face screwed into a worried frown with sweat beading on his brow worse than Lizzy.

"Babies come on their own timing," George answered with a jovial smile. "Early or not, your son is coming, so let's not worry about that right now. Fortunately you have me, the best physician in all of Derbyshire, if not England, and since it appears my formidable skills will not be called into play for the deliver of this precocious infant, I may prove my worth after he is born."

"No offense, Uncle, but I hope not."

"You worry too much, William." Lizzy patted his cheek, gazing into his face with shining eyes from her perch against his broad chest. He was trembling, partly from the frantic ride back to Pemberley and pell-mell dash up two flights of stairs, but also from excitement mingled with fear. He could not believe it was happening today! Lizzy, conversely, was calm in between contractions. She spend more time trying to comfort him than the other way around, only losing her composure once it came time to push the baby out.

The wild drama was somewhat anticlimactic as Michael slipped into the world with minimal effort on Lizzy's part. That was a miracle it would take her months to fully appreciate due to her and Darcy's all-consuming preoccupation over his survival.

Michael was a fragile infant who required careful handling. The respiratory distress that George most worried about never transpired. Michael's lungs were healthy, as he would display in due course. Rather, his delicacy arose in the vicinity of his gastrointestinal area, Dr. Darcy indeed proving his worth. The initial month was a trial, no other way to state it. Lizzy produced copious amounts of milk, but Michael simply did not have the strength to nurse on more than one side at a time and often was too sleepy to do even that. In the first week he lost precious ounces he could not afford. George encouraged the anxious parents to wake him every two hours for feedings, a schedule that did work in filling his tiny stomach, but was exhausting on Lizzy and irritating to an already finicky newborn.

Additionally, he was extremely sensitive in the amounts he could consume. Vomiting after each feeding became the norm with the fussiness of true colic following. Lizzy monitored every bite that passed her lips, obsessed with discovering what foods were most distressing to his stomach. Lizzy insisted on keeping him close and attending to caretaking since no one else could feed him, and he notably slept and digested better when nuzzled onto her chest. Darcy barely managed to touch his son in those early weeks, Mrs. Hanford even less. Without realizing what was happening, Darcy gravitated toward caring for Alexander since Lizzy seemed to have forgotten the toddler's existence.

George experimented with numerous herbal tonics, not finding the precise combination that allayed the worst of the messy symptoms for nearly three weeks. It was only then that the babe began to gain weight and achieve a healthy, ruddy glow with plumping cheeks, softening skin, and brightening eyes. By his one-month birthday he had reached six pounds, a day of rejoicing for his frantic parents.

It was not until Michael began to improve and life settled into a semblance of order that the exhausted Master of Pemberley gazed beyond the confines of the nursery, Alexander's room, and the bedchamber. The first shocking revelation was the physical appearance of his wife. The weight gained during her pregnancy had gone, leaving her gaunt and pale. Gray circles rested under her troubled eyes. Once rosy, full lips were chapped and dull.

Darcy's aspect was not much better, he too having missed more meals than normally required to keep a man his size functioning, but he was hale compared to Lizzy.

Dr. Darcy watched them closely during those stressful first weeks and did his best to encourage rest and an adequate diet. A couple of thorough examinations determined that Lizzy was recuperating speedily from the birth itself, so other than plying her with strengthening teas and trays of hearty meats and fruits—most of which were left barely touched—he took no overt action, confident that once Michael improved they would as well.

Darcy, however, was profoundly disturbed. He was also disgusted with himself, engulfed with guilt at what he perceived as failing in his obligations. Therefore, in true Darcy form, he took charge of the situation.

"Elizabeth, Michael is past the crisis. His temperamental nature and crankiness is probably here to stay. You, however, are becoming increasingly cranky. I am ordering you to rest more often."

"Ordering?"

"Do not bristle, darling." He smiled at her scowl. "I am not demanding anything untoward. You need to rest and consume healthier meals for Michael's sake as well as your own."

Initially she complied. She left the nursery from time to time, dined in the dining room with Darcy and George, took walks in the hallway, and twice was enticed into the private garden with Darcy. She slept better at night and napped during the day with Michael. She refused to leave the bedchamber close to the nursery—this was extremely annoying to Darcy—and she always hurried back after any absence. But the improvements were pleasing to him, and to George, and for a week or so it seemed as if the tide was changing.

Yet on one point she stood firm and that was her unwillingness to abdicate Michael's care to his nanny. She was compelled by some untamable force to touch him and check on him constantly. The fear of losing him had taken hold of her heart and she could not yield. Furthermore, she guiltily plunged into an urgent desire to care for and be with Alexander, thus consuming more of her time and energy.

Rapidly, her tenuous grip on health faltered as the stress of her set demands took a toll. When Darcy attempted to reassert his authority she refused to listen, no matter how calmly or rationally he spoke. Frustration mounted and petty spats were the result of nearly every conversation. Darcy's natural patience held for a time, but the first in a series of intense arguments transpired over Michael's christening.

"He will be six weeks old tomorrow, my love. He is healthy and strong, the weather is relatively fair, and it must be done before Richard and Simone depart for Europe."

"No. He is still too small."

"Elizabeth, be reasonable! He is nearly eight pounds now. He eats well, rarely regurgitates, and the colic is lessening with Uncle's tonic. You are allowing your fears to rule your judgment."

"If anything happens to him..."

Darcy gently clasped her arms, speaking softly. "Nothing will happen to him, dearest. He needs to be named and blessed. This is important..."

"More important than his life? Would you doom him to an early grave?" She spat, shaking off his comforting hands.

"Elizabeth! That is unfair and ridiculous! I would never do anything to jeopardize his life. How can you intimate such a thing?" Darcy was truly aghast.

"I will not allow him out of the house. That is final, William. It can wait until spring."

"His christening will not wait until spring." He spoke flatly, anger constrained and simmering. "I will grant one more week, that is all."

"But..."

"There are no buts, Elizabeth. *That* is final."

Lizzy stared furiously, trembling in rage, eyes filling with tears. Darcy sighed, moved despite his anger by the emotions he knew controlled her logic. He reached to caress her cheek, but she stepped away. "If he dies it will be entirely on your head, Mr. Darcy." And she pivoted, exiting the room without a backward glance.

CHAPTER FIVE

A Marriage in Crisis

THE TENSION WAS THICK on the air for the following days, but Darcy stubbornly proceeded with the christening plans. Lizzy's emotions grew wildly unstable and dozens of trivial disagreements and major rows broke out between them, when she talked to him at all.

Darcy was in a constant state of turmoil. Vexation battled with disquiet. That Lizzy was irrational in most matters was obvious, but he seemed unable to calm her or appeal to the analytic intellect he knew she possessed.

When Lizzy was not riled over some perceived slight she was crying. More than once Darcy walked into the room to discover her curled in a ball weeping. These moments, fleeting as they lasted, were the few times she permitted him to embrace her.

And therein lay another point of contention.

As the weeks turned into months, they had yet to resume their intimate relations. Far more important than the purely physical annoyance of sexual deprivation, Darcy was deeply concerned by Lizzy's total disinterest in any form of contact. They shared the bed in his mother's old chambers—Lizzy still refusing to return to their bedchamber and the contention over that subject ongoing—but she spurned all affection. Naturally, he had expected nothing more than cuddling for the first weeks, truthfully too fatigued and anxious even to think about the matter, but as time marched on and the danger passed, he began to dwell on the topic quite a bit!

Yet, as his desire escalated, hers waned into nothingness.

She drew away from his kisses, no matter how gentle or light. Any caress was met with stiffening or evasion. She slept curled on her side of the bed, clothed in the concealing nightgowns of a maiden, and extended no overtures. More than once he was awoken from a sleeping state by a sharp jab from an elbow or forceful shove as a result of dreamily straying toward her body.

Darcy's confusion grew, as did his anger. He tried to understand her reluctance, but it was impossible to comprehend, especially since she refused to talk about it. When he cautiously advanced the subject, she flared, accusing him of only thinking of his needs and ignoring what she and the children wanted. Obviously this was ludicrous, but Darcy was wounded and guilt-ridden nonetheless.

The combination of her vacillating moodiness and bodily detachment caused an ever-widening breach to separate them. Darcy watched it happening but was powerless to halt it. Lizzy did not seem to care.

Michael's christening took place on the Sunday before Darcy's thirty-second birthday. The ceremony was a minor affair compared to Alexander's. Most of their family was not present, so it was mainly a few friends from Derbyshire and those relatives who lived close by. Michael cried through the entire procedure, but Reverend Bertram managed with aplomb, even while hastening the obligatory rituals. There were some private comments regarding Mrs. Darcy's unusual somberness, but the couple presented a united front that no one suspected was false.

George's perceptions pierced through the façade, noting the tension underneath. Medical matters had kept him away from Pemberley a large portion of the time, the christening bringing him back to the Manor for a handful of days. Yet casual inquires to his nephew yielded nothing, Darcy rigidly uncomfortable discussing his marriage with anyone. It disturbed George, but even his discerning eye could not penetrate the mask or deduce the troubles as severe.

The days following the christening were oddly calm around Pemberley. The persnickety infant settled into a standard routine, his health robust and growth steady. George was again consumed with medical needs in the surrounding communities and was rarely home. The cold of winter settled in, further isolating the traumatized couple.

Darcy's birthday came and went with minimal fanfare, the birthday dinner and "party" arranged by Mrs. Reynolds. Well aware of his wife's distraction and disinterest, he was thus shocked that she spared him enough thought to provide a gift of several books he desired and a stunning pair of abalone and silver cuff links.

"Elizabeth," he breathed, truly moved, "these are wonderful. I love them! Thank you."

He kissed her cheek, Lizzy leaning into his lips and blushing prettily. His heartfelt thanks seemed to penetrate the icy cloud surrounding her heart, eliciting a tender smile and brief caress to his hand that nearly caused him to burst into tears.

The combination of christening and birthday celebrations helped ease the tension between them, bringing a measure of peace. Only Darcy was fully aware of how strained their relationship remained and his pride would not allow him to seek help. Rather, he determined to deal with their troubles with his typical forthrightness, and her hesitant touch on his birthday gave flight to his hope. She remained distant but smiled at him several times over the ensuing week as they planned for Alexander's second birthday. She met his pained eyes with a glimmer of her old brilliance, spoke without the sharp edge that had become so familiar, and laughed at a dry comment he made about one of their notoriously irritating tenants.

One night he decided to take the initiative, much as she had done after Alexander's birth. He reasoned that whatever residual worries were clouding her mind, their love was ultimately too profound to be extinguished and their passion for each other too powerful to be harnessed indefinitely. *Elizabeth merely needs to be reminded of this*, he deduced.

As always, he found her rocking in the chair located next to the cradle. One hand rested on the wooden rail causing the cradle to sway with each rock of the chair, her face a study in serene happiness. Darcy observed her unawares for a moment, his breath catching at the transcendent beauty of the scene.

Oh God, how I love her!

The ache was tangible, felt all through his body, and his heart swelled to agonizing levels with the hunger to hold her. Several deep breaths were necessary to calm the raging seas within.

He approached unhurriedly, desperately needing this night to go well, and afraid, as he had not been since long before their wedding, that one misstep could cause it all to dash into a million pieces. She turned her face to his, smiling sweetly and lifting a hand. He swallowed to muffle the moan as he knelt before her knees, hands resting on her thighs. For long minutes they simply stared. Darcy held perfectly still while Lizzy lightly played with the tips of his ruffled hair.

It was unbearable. The yearning pounded through him. His skin was electrified, each inhale a gasp of longing. How long since he had felt her lips? It was impossible to delay, but he refused to frighten her. Rising slowly, eyes locked with hers and noting the flickers of ardor seen therein, he leaned closer but did not touch.

"Come, my heart, let me take you to bed."

Lizzy nodded dazedly, lost in his darkened orbs, feeling the feeble tendrils of desire rising. It was all so befuddling. Her love for him infinite, the attraction acute, but the typical surge of passionate flame a dim memory. The tingles were there, buried deeply in every cell of her body and crying to burst forth, but like the prisoner begging for freedom, the escape was denied by some internal force beyond her control. She hardly knew what was happening as he lifted her into his strong arms. His heart beat vigorously against her chest with his heat emanating in droves into her chilled skin. He brushed her lips once, a soft moan escaping his mouth, but she did not experience the jolt of pleasure that she recognized he did and knew she should.

It was wrong, she knew this, and panic rose inside her breast. *I love him so! Why can I not feel?*

He sat her onto the edge of their vast bed, Lizzy only then realizing they were not in her bedchamber. The panic flared anew. "William, I do not want to be so far…"

"Shhh…" He caressed a thumb over her lips, placating and holding her gaze. "Mrs. Hanford knows where we are and will ring. All will be well, beloved. This is where we belong. In our room. You will be more comfortable here, and God knows I will, as that bed is about three inches too short for me." He chuckled softly, smiling. "Let me pour some wine."

Lizzy watched him walk to the small table by the fire. It was easy to appraise his figure in the clinging material of his belted robe, especially as he bent over to pour the wine, and Lizzy was not so unnerved not to appreciate the view. Time had not diminished the superb manliness of his physique, Darcy as trim, muscular, and potent as on the day they married. Again the faint flutters erupted inside, but without their previous capacity to turn her entire body into a quivering pool of desire.

Tears of frustration and irritation welled in her eyes. She blinked and glanced away from the disarming sight of her handsome spouse to the chamber she had not set foot in for months. Darcy had muted the lights, candles strategically located about the room to lend a comforting blush of romantic ambience. The fire burned sedately, the crackles and pops adding beautifully to the intimate tone. The drapes were drawn except for the balcony curtains which allowed the moon's glow diffusing over the rippling surface of the trout lake to radiate through the glass. The warm burgundy and rich mahogany of the furnishings had an inviting burnish. The relaxing creams and autumn colors that she so adored soothed the tumult in her soul. All the homey touches that were so uniquely hers and his were evident upon every wall and corner. She loved this room, truly loved it, and the wealth of joys experienced here buffeted through her mind and brought a sincere smile to her face.

It was this smile Darcy beheld as he returned to her side, his relief and happiness manifest in mien and voice. "Here, beloved. Your favorite French merlot."

"Thank you."

They sipped in silence. Lizzy was nervous but content to gaze around the room, while Darcy's eyes were engrossed by her face. He waited, the craving to touch her searing, until she turned to look at him. He was bewildered by the traces of fear he saw there, but encouraged by the cheeriness and soft smile.

He reached to cup her cheek, voice husky as he whispered, "I love you so profoundly, Elizabeth. I have missed you more than I can articulate. I need you. I want you, my precious lover, fiercely and eternally. Lord, please tell me you feel the same! I cannot live if you do not love me as deeply!"

Lizzy's throat constricted, the conflicting emotions swirling and terrifying. His face was awash with passion and the agony of doubt, and it pierced her heart. *Why, oh God, why do I feel so disoriented and numb?*

"I do love you, Fitzwilliam. Please have no doubt of that."

He groaned loudly, capturing her lips in a heated kiss. Wine glasses were set aside, by some miracle not spilling. Robes were discarded. Darcy was gentle but determined. Hunger and thirst tore through every fiber of his body. The need to love her, to reestablish their sacred bond, to reawaken the immutable passion they shared, and to join with her body and soul was driving him onward feverishly.

Lizzy responded intermittently; the fervor swelling and dampening in a chaotic jumble that left her panting with desire one second and freezing in terror the next. Nothing made sense, her nerves assaulted by the blissful sensations resulting from his masterful touch and the internal icy paralysis that blotted out the pleasure.

Darcy, ever attuned to his wife's cues, detected the sporadic retreats. But the frequent moans, writhes, clutching hands, arches, and gasps spurred him on. His desire spiraled higher as he employed every trick in his vast erotic arsenal to please, titillate, arouse, and satisfy. The ache built beyond the point of rational thought or lucid control. If he noticed her intimate zones not as welcoming, those soft places touched only and forever by him not as warm and moist as typical in response to his attentions, it registered dimly. Only as he joined with her, as her cry of pain and stiffened limbs jerked through his inflamed mind, only then did he recognize his mistake.

But it was too late. A line had been crossed and his passion was too great to be denied. He tried, God knows he tried, but her pain was inevitable as he took his pleasure.

He collapsed onto her. His physical satisfaction momentarily overruling the screaming awareness that he had hurt her. Lifting finally, the self-recrimination threatened to buckle him yet again as he noted the tears leaking from her tightly closed eyes.

"Oh my God, Elizabeth! I… Please, look at me! I am so sorry! Beloved, I love you! I did not mean to…"

"Please stop, William! It is not your fault. Believe me! It is me, all me. I just… cannot feel… nothing is normal anymore!" And her sobs burst forth as a damn. She clutched him, shaking violently as she wept.

Darcy rolled to his back, embracing her tightly as she cried, baffled and deeply disturbed. She slept finally, clinging to him, and no other words were exchanged. He lay awake for long hours afterwards, his own tears silently shed, thinking furiously and questioning without any answers forthcoming.

❧

The two weeks that followed were terrible beyond the initial weeks fretting over Michael. The baby flourished under the diligent ministrations of devoted parents, loving nannies, and spellbound brother. He was temperamental, as they were coming to expect was his natural disposition, but also jolly and extremely healthy. Any cause for sincere anxiety as to his wellbeing was nonexistent.

Yet Lizzy refused to concede.

Darcy watched his wife immerse herself in the children and the Manor to a greater degree than prior. From sunrise to well after sunset she was constantly on the move. Suddenly, Alexander's birthday and Christmas became vitally important to prepare for, although she never mentioned their anniversary. Darcy was wounded and the gulf widened as her preoccupation prevented her from sparing him any time.

The fragile claim on her health wavered further as she gradually lost the weight she had regained. She was clearly exhausted: pale and tremulous. Her emotions continued to fluctuate crazily, outbursts of tears and ire randomly occurring with no apparent cause, but primarily she seemed to sink into a daze of gloom.

Nothing Darcy said or did reached through to her, although he persisted in trying. Any overtures for affection were spurned, vigorously. Attempts to discuss their anniversary were ignored. It was as if he were invisible.

Alexander's second birthday was celebrated with an elaborate party. Dozens of Derbyshire friends partook of the fun, their children the honored guests as playmates to Alexander. Lizzy was a buzzing bee in her desire to provide for her guests and her son. At times, her behavior crossed into frenetic with shrill laughter and addled sentences. Every last person noted her altered appearance and fragility with concern.

Yet somehow she managed to hold herself together until it was over. Visibly shaking, she bid her last good-bye to Harriet Vernor, sagging against the door as soon as it was closed. Darcy reached for her, but she snapped at him and pushed him away. He watched helplessly as she climbed the stairs.

"Dearest, you need to come to bed." Darcy pleaded that night, entering the nursery where Lizzy sat beside the cradle.

"I want to make sure he is asleep," she countered, eyes centered on the slumbering Michael.

"He is asleep. As is Alexander. I read with him until he fell asleep. I barely managed to read one sentence without him interrupting to talk about his party. His enthusiasm is as intense as yesterday and he will likely be up at the crack of dawn to play with all his new toys. Poor Miss Lisa." He chuckled, vainly attempting to lighten the mood. "Maybe it is just as well I have no business plans tomorrow so I can devote some time to manning the castle with the new set of tin Spartans and Mongols. He would not rest until he testing the catapults for himself." He laughed again, sincerely this time as the thrill of this birthday with his son displaced the melancholy. "I confess I am as anxious as Alexander. Sharing the joys of presents with a child is superior to anything I can imagine. Goodness knows he has enough gifts to keep us occupied for hours!"

He paused, realizing that Lizzy was not listening. She stared at Michael, no expression on her face, eyes dulled and drooping. Darcy's insides clenched painful, as they always did when he encountered her obvious affliction and decline, but lately he had noticed other emotions rising: anger, frustration, impatience, and, most frightening of all, a horrid sense of detachment and grief, as if something precious had died.

He sighed, closing his eyes briefly and offering a silent prayer. "Come, Elizabeth, take my hand."

She did, listlessly rising and walking to his side. She stood by the bed complacently as he removed her robe, strong hands stroking over the silky skin of her arms. He cupped her face, lifting it to meet his eyes. "Please, beloved, tell me what is troubling you? I am so worried for you." His soft voice, brimming with concerned agony, brought tears to her eyes.

"I do not know," she whispered. "I am so tired... all the time tired."

"I keep encouraging you to rest, do I not? You must not push yourself so, my heart. Relinquish the chores to Mrs. Hanford and others. Let us help you! Please, Elizabeth, heed my advice."

In an instant her eyes were angry. "Oh yes! Mr. Darcy who knows what is best for everyone! Must you control the entire world, William? Tell everyone what to do?"

Darcy paled, stepping back a pace in utter shock. But Lizzy followed, her face enraged, finger stabbing him in the breastbone. "I do not need you to tell me how to be a mother! I am a *good* mother, an excellent mother! My babies need me, not a servant! Stop... just stop... ordering me..."

Her voice was shrill and body shaking as her eyes welled with angry tears. It was her wildest outburst yet and Darcy had never felt so cold.

"Elizabeth Darcy, listen to me." He spoke in his authoritative voice, normally more than adequate to quell any adversary. "You are irrational and raving. Calm yourself and let me help you. Try to be reasonable!"

But his words were cut short by a stunning slap to his left cheek. He gasped, recoiling as his hand rose to cover the sting. It was not so much the pain, although his wife did have a strong arm, but the mind-numbing astonishment of what she had done.

Lizzy instantaneously crumbled in remorse. Hands covered her mouth as an anguished moan escaped. "Oh God! William, please forgive…"

"I shall be in my study if the children have need of me," he icily intoned, eyes dead as he pivoted and left the room, slamming the door behind.

Lizzy stood paralyzed for a long time, eventually releasing a wail of sheer animal intensity, her heart breaking asunder as the world spun and swirled. She whirled about, frantic for anything to relieve the twisted emotions ripping through her mind. Lunging toward the balcony, she only thought of escape and punishment for the sufferings caused by her words and deeds.

She halted abruptly at the railing, wheezing and crying. She grabbed onto the freezing stone in a white knuckled grip, staring at the cobbled stones of the walkway far below. Oblivion from the pain called, but some small kernel of sanity beckoned. Perhaps it was the frigid cold restoring a hint of clarity. Perhaps it was a guardian angel stopping her steps. Whatever the case, she fell to her knees, sobbing until there were no tears remaining, only then finding the strength to stumble to the lonely, cold bed.

CHAPTER SIX

Healing a Great Love

ALEXANDER, IN THE INNOCENCE and unawareness of a two-year-old, was oblivious to the tension and chasm between his parents. George was more observant and he was shaken to the core by what he witnessed.

For the month of November, and much of October, he had been busy attending to his duties at the Matlock hospital and throughout the surrounding communities. It was the time of year for influenza and injuries sustained from the cold weather or wet conditions. Several days in a row would pass before he returned to the Manor, often for no longer than it took to bathe and sleep a day before leaving again.

His intermittent interactions when able to relax at home had hinted to a strain between the two, but he had thought it no more than what would be expected with two young children, one who was quite demanding. Darcy's natural reticence and intense urge for privacy did not always foster blunt communication, even as close as they now were. There were many topics Darcy did not hesitate to discuss with his uncle, but his marriage, which he perceived as sacred and solely his responsibility to deal with, was not one of them. George respected this, and aside from the gentle teasing that brought him such pleasure as Darcy persisted in flushing and stammering when the playful topics were tendered, he avoided broaching anything too intimate. Of course, until now there had been no need, since his niece and nephew appeared to possess a relationship uncommon in its intensity and felicity.

Thus, due to his busy schedule and faith in their relationship, George had remained ignorant as to the seriousness of Lizzy's status. A catastrophe in Chesterfield calling for emergency assistance had kept him away for Alexander's birthday and the week following. Upon his return to Pemberley, the exhausted physician was flabbergasted by what he discovered.

Without hesitation, Dr. Darcy decided to take action, even at the risk of offending his proud nephew. However, he first dealt with Lizzy. Her predicament was at a critical level and needed direct, immediate intervention.

As a physician, he diagnosed Lizzy's illness instantly, recognizing it as a rare infirmity seen from time to time after the birth of a child. No one knew the cause, although speculation was rife. Most judged it a failing in the mother, if they acknowledged it at all, but George did not ascribe to that philosophy. He had observed dozens of decent, loving women succumb to bizarre, uncontrollable emotional breakdowns after birth and did not believe it an inherent flaw in their character.

He was circumspect in his approach with Elizabeth, partly because it was necessary to ascertain the scope of her condition but also because he understood how fragile her emotions. One wrong move and the essential trust would be gone. Fortunately, he was immensely skilled and within a couple of casual conversations over tea, she broke down. The seeming irreparable rift between she and her husband, who now rarely entered any room she was in and spent nearly every hour in the library or his study, acted as a strange catalyst toward candor. While on the one hand she sunk deeper into her misery, she also admitted to a serious problem.

As guilty as George felt for not noting the sickness consuming his beloved niece, it was fortuitous. A month or even a week previous, Lizzy would probably not have listened to anything he said, despite his mastery in persuasion. The dire situation she now found herself in—with a beloved spouse who was disengaged—and her weariness remained all that propelled her to embrace anything the good doctor recommended.

George enlisted the services of the relieved Mrs. Hanford, Mrs. Reynolds, and Marguerite, all of whom had observed the drama with heavy hearts. Thankful to be proactive in the matter, they gleefully took orders from Dr. Darcy. Finally they could be firm-handed, bossy actually, as they had not felt the liberty to do under Mr. Darcy's confusing requests and Lizzy's stubborn commands. There were several tonics and strong teas concocted by

Dr. Darcy as a beginning treatment. Her diet was tightly stipulated, specific foods requested of the kitchen staff and demanded to be consumed whether Lizzy wished for them or not. Rest was requisite; long daily naps to be followed by walks in the brisk air as often as feasible. Personal hygiene was stressed. Last, but not least, was the forced abdication of her self-imposed obligations.

This latter was the hardest to enforce. A careful balance of assuming tasks while watching closely for negative effects was imperative; one step too fast could lead to an emotional backslide, but the determined group of caretakers were diligent.

The final and equally important aspect of her recovery to the old Lizzy they all adored was the presence of a certain man vital to her ultimate happiness.

Darcy, however, had isolated himself. He practically lived in the lower rooms, most nights falling asleep on his study's sofa after working to a state of collapse. Occasionally he slept in their bed, waiting until long after she was asleep, but usually he mounted the stairs only to head directly into his dressing room or to visit Alexander. His only joy was in those hours he spent playing with his eldest son. Michael he rarely laid eyes on, tiptoeing in at the deepest hours of the night to gaze upon the child he felt such a mixture of emotions for. His heart swelled with love when gazing upon his child's perfection, but weeks of detachment rendered it nearly impossible to bond with the baby as he had Alexander. To his profound shame, he perceived a growing hostility toward the innocent babe, illogically blaming him for the cause of his marriage falling apart.

For a week he held hope that she would apologize for her actions or simply express her love and that she missed him. Every knock on the door or tread heard in the hallway caused his heart to leap painfully, but it was never Elizabeth. When they did encounter each other she refused to meet his eyes and exited the room as soon as possible. Twice he saw her duck into a chamber clearly not where she intended to go for the express purpose of eluding him. Each incident was as a nail in the coffin of their union and his grief was overwhelming.

In addition to the sadness and shame was an increasing self-loathing. Darcy was a man capable and brave who did not shrink from the troubles of life. Rarely had he encountered problems that were unfixable or at least unable to be controlled. Courage and straightforwardness were character traits innate to his being, yet in this instance he was utterly at a loss as to what to do, as all his efforts thus far had been futile. Dimly he recognized that his damnable pride prevented asking for advice. Yet, until Elizabeth, he had never revealed his soul to another, admitted his frailties, or confided personal matters. This reality compounded his hopelessness and indecisiveness.

Worse yet was the fear lodged deep within his bones. Fear of what she might say if he spoke to her again, fear of the future, fear of his lost control, fear that there was no remedy, fear that he was weak, fear that he was a failure. It was a terror so engulfing that he withdrew, denying the facts and cowardly hiding away as he had never done in his entire life while the negative emotions ate him alive.

Thus it was a paler, thinner Darcy that George found staring into the white landscape outside his study window one afternoon about a week before Christmas. His face was ravaged with whiskers of at least three days growth, cravat loosened, and hair mussed by nervous hands. Dull eyes turned to the sympathetic smile of his uncle as George took the chair across.

Darcy cleared his throat, attempting to reinstate the guise of a man in control, and smiled faintly. "Forgive me, Uncle. I did not hear you enter. What have you been up to these days? Is the hospital lessening its demands on you?"

"I have not been to the hospital for nearly three weeks now."

"Oh, I was not aware. You come and go so frequently that I lose track of your schedule. Since you are home perhaps we can play a game or two of billiards tonight. It has been a while since I thrashed you."

"I am delighted to hear you jesting, my boy. Tells me not all is lost, although you look as if you have been dragged behind an unfriendly horse. Has Samuel forgotten how to shave you?"

Darcy reached to his chin, honestly startled. "Well, work has kept me busy." He waved vaguely toward the nearly empty desk and then shrugged. "I was attempting to write a letter to Georgiana, but the snow distracted." He sighed and turned again to the view outside the window. "I do miss her."

"Yes, it is a shame. She would be a stabilizing, comforting presence to be sure. She will be home in the spring. I am positive she is hardly missing you, caught up in the whirl of fêtes and Italian social life." Darcy nodded absently, George watching his face as he continued. "I encountered Mr. Gerald Vernor the other day while visiting the apothecary shop in Lambton. He asked about you, Elizabeth, and the baby. Of course I told him you were all well, but we know that is not the truth of it, agreed?"

Darcy glanced up sharply. "What do you mean? Is something amiss with Michael?" The stab of fear was acute, his eyes penetrating George's face.

"Do not be purposefully obtuse, William. Have you learned nothing of me yet? I am a notorious busybody, to be sure, but I also adore my family. Additionally, I am a rather remarkable diagnostician, although in this case I regretfully made assumptions I should not have. Elizabeth is ill. Surely you have gleaned this yourself?"

Darcy's alarm escalated, choking off his air supply. His face paled and eyes widened. "Ill? What do you mean ill? She works too hard, as I have given up chastising for, and does not eat as she should, but she is not ill. You are exaggerating." He stated the last firmly, denial decisive.

"It is not necessarily an illness of the body, or at least not in the way you presume. She is suffering from a melancholia we see in women after birth. It is mysterious, and affects the mind primarily, which in turn has an effect on the body, but has been recognized by physicians since Hippocrates. Some speculate it is entirely spiritual, a weakness of the psyche, but I do not agree. I am not a researcher, but I found the lectures by physiologic chemists such as Saunders and Babington fascinating…"

"Uncle, what are you babbling about?"

"I am trying to explain Elizabeth's condition, William. You need to understand this, and I am certain your intellect capable of grasping the science."

"My wife is not ill." He declared stubbornly, rising with a burst of anger to begin pacing about the room, fingers flickering. "She is… unhappy. I will admit to that, as much as it pains me to do so. Two children so soon is obviously too much for her. I should have been more… responsible. Not so demanding. It is my fault she feels as she does. Her… hatred toward me"—he swallowed, hands rifling through his hair—"is understandable. In time the pressures will ease… in time. Then, perhaps, she will not… she may learn to love… me again as she did. I can wait. But she cannot be ill! No, she… no, I will not allow it…"

"You would prefer to believe your wife does not love you than to admit she is sick and therefore needs you?" George's quiet voice broke through, Darcy pausing with his back to the older man. "Be sensible and listen to me. Come, sit, and hear me out."

Darcy sat, wooden and tight-lipped, his face closed.

George resumed. "Our bodies are complex organisms, William, you know this. Think of how traumatic it is for a woman to carry another individual in her body and to give birth. It goes beyond the physical. There is strong evidence pointing to chemicals that control many of our functions and may affect our minds. We do not understand it and probably never will, but I have seen unexplainable things in my years."

"What does this have to do with Elizabeth?"

"Some believe, myself included, that there are those women who suffer negative effects on an emotional level after childbirth. Is it the trauma itself? Something caused by a reaction to the individual infant, his or her body inadvertently upsetting a careful balance? We do not know, but I have seen it several times and Elizabeth's symptoms are classic."

"What symptoms precisely?"

"Moodiness, irrationality, and dispiritedness primarily. I know you have been the brunt of these and probably more. Ofttimes there are physical manifestations such as tremulousness, pallor, fatigue, although most of that is probably an effect of not caring for themselves. Also sexual apathy and the inability to rouse."

Darcy stiffened noticeably at the latter, his face tightening further as he looked away. George nodded grimly, another piece of the tragic puzzle falling into place.

"Is it permanent? Can you help her?" Darcy finally choked out.

George nodded. "I have been on the job for a few weeks now and have seen improvement. She is more balanced, sleeping better, and not as overwrought. She is still gloomy, but I am beginning to believe the cause is not her illness as much as it is sadness over the situation with you."

Darcy barked harshly, unable to control the skepticism in that statement. "I rather doubt that. She avoids me completely and has made it abundantly clear how she feels about me." His fingers rose to press on his left cheek, the memory of her slap searing as the day it happened.

"You are a fool," George snapped.

"I will not listen to you insulting me, Uncle. I appreciate your concern for our well-being and am willing to accept some of what you have said, but you are not privy to our intimate relationship. You do not know what you are talking about!" He launched from his chair, eyes blazing. "You march in here after weeks away, declaring that my wife is unbalanced"—he shuddered at the conjured image of an insane Elizabeth locked in some sanatorium or distant chamber—"talking about chemicals and psychology and other rot. Furthermore you claim to have our relationship all figured out! You have no idea what has gone between us, how hard I have tried to reach her."

"That is precisely my point, Fitzwilliam," George interrupted calmly. "Reasoning with a woman in her state is fruitless."

"I see," Darcy interjected with heavy sarcasm. "You know all. Well, let me tell you what I know. My wife shudders at my touch. She hides from me. Does not speak to me unless it is in anger. She…" He stopped with a sob, twirling away and swaying slightly before heading firmly to the liquor cabinet.

Silence fell. George waited as Darcy drank not one but two shots of whiskey in rapid succession. "That will not help, you know." Darcy did not answer, pouring a third glass instead. George sighed, rising, and speaking quietly. "I understand that you are hurting, William. So is Elizabeth. Trust me in this. I will give you both time to heal, overcome your fears and pride. But, you see, I know something that I think you two have forgotten in your pain and misery. Great love does not die so easily. Years apart do not sever the bond, nor does death. Elizabeth needs you, and you need her. It really is that simple."

And he left. Darcy sat the filled glass down, bowing his head and standing immobile for a long while before climbing the stairs for a much-needed bath and shave.

Feeling improved once clean and properly attired, Darcy passed the afternoon in deep contemplation of his uncle's words. He began by scouring the medical texts—not due to doubt in the knowledge possessed by Dr. Darcy, but out of a need to clarify. Unfortunately, the books were silent on the subject other than vague references to melancholia or lethargy in the immediate post-partum periods. Not helpful in the least.

He considered every word spoken and forced himself to look at the situation from a different perspective other than the one clouded by pain and misery. The concept of Elizabeth being ill with an organic, curable ailment had never occurred to him. Although his insides chilled at the idea of his wife ravaged by sickness of any type, it did offer a plausible explanation for the bizarre evolution from loving to estranged wife that he had often questioned, as it seemed unfitting when explained as simple exhaustion and worry over Michael. Her total withdrawal from him and the relationship they had fought so hard to forge was unfathomable, even if that is how it appeared to be.

Weeks of turmoil could not be rationalized or erased in one afternoon of analysis, but a glimmer of hope touched Darcy's heart. Now he needed to decide the next step and put aside his fears.

George presented a possibility by insisting they dine together that night as a family. Darcy quailed at admitting it, but he was relieved that someone else took the initiative in bringing them together. Bolstering his flagging courage, he entered the dining room first, determined to assess his wife's demeanor and overcome this obstacle as they had prior ones.

He was stiff with nervousness, feeling twice the fool for being so uncomfortable and flustered in his own home and with his own wife. The constant mental chastisement to relax only served to tighten his nerves. Rehearsing casual conversation and solicitous remarks when they should come naturally only annoyed him, which caused him to forget them anyway!

Then George breezed in, as sprightly as always and carrying Alexander, who was wearing an Indian style tunic of so many colors Darcy lost count at twelve. He chatted effervescently, tickled a giggling Alexander as the toddler was placed into his seat at the table, and took the seat beside him without a mention of the unusual circumstances. Darcy supposed his uncle's blithe attitude and Alexander's outlandish dress were designed to calm him, and was surprised to find that it did! Plus it helped to have Alexander there to attend to, the art of proper table manners one he was still learning and not very proficient in. The edginess remained, but Darcy felt a few coiled nerves unwind as he assisted his son and they waited for Elizabeth to arrive.

She was late, sprinting in through the open door with head down and making a beeline for her usual place setting on the other side of Alexander. She jerked to a stop when she realized George was seated there, thus leaving the chair immediately to Darcy's right empty. Her eyes darted to his face, a flush spreading over her cheeks as she bit her lip and resumed her hasty steps to the table. She murmured her greetings, plopping into the chair and unfolding her napkin with spastic motions.

Darcy's breath caught the second she entered the room. So riveted was he to her presence and stunning beauty that specifics were unnoticed initially. Her hair was dressed elaborately, the curled tresses lush and vibrantly shining as they had not been at their last close encounter that fateful day she slapped him. Her cheeks were full and flushed, and her skin bronzed rather than sallow. She wore one of his favorite gowns, his heart lurching at the sight and the memories evoked. Her appearance rattled him, his body responding violently so that he pressed his thighs tightly together and clamped his hands onto the chair arms before embarrassing himself totally. Every muscle hardened, literally, and his blood pounded so loudly all extraneous sound disappeared.

He hungered to see her eyes, but when she glanced his direction it was swift and indecipherable. Darcy frowned, finally registering that she had paused, flushed after looking at him, and was clearly disturbed to be seated next to him. Did she not know he was to dine with her?

His scrutiny began with his observing the details missed initially. She was beautiful and definitely healthier, but there were dark circles under her eyes not able to be hidden with cosmetics. The dress clung to her full breasts—Darcy quite distracted by that fact—but was loose at the waist and shoulders. Beyond the physical signs indicative of residual weariness and illness were the flustered movements and reticence so alien to her usual deportment.

Taken altogether, they confused Darcy more than ever. Over time, his skill in reading his wife's thoughts had grown, but now he felt lost. She was entirely shut down and so unlike her usual self that he simply had no idea what to say or do. All his carefully rehearsed phrases vanished and he was left to stare open mouthed, not even standing when she entered as he should have.

George continued to talk, Lizzy answering with nods and monosyllables for the most part. Darcy realized he was staring and pulled his eyes away, reaching for the wine glass and proceeding to swallow half the liquid in one gulp in hopes of calming his frayed nerves and relieving his parched throat.

"Papa, spoon for soup this way?"

Darcy started, not aware that the soup course had been served, and turned toward Alexander. "Yes," he croaked, pausing to clear his throat with another sip of wine before leaning to help, "but not too much in the spoon or you will drip. And never slurp, as fun as that is to do."

"You can slurp all you want when eating with nanny," George said, "but for some reason it is not allowed in public."

"Manners, Uncle. It is called proper manners."

George shrugged. "In some places they just pick up the bowl and drink right out of it. Did you know that, Alexander? Indeed they do. Gets the food in much quicker and the meal ends sooner than the interminable affairs we have here."

"Look on the bright side, you get to eat more if the meal lasts a long while."

"True. That is a benefit. Forget what I said, my boy. Take your time and we shall see who eats the most."

"A connest?"

"That's right, a contest. I bet you win."

"Highly unlikely that even I could win that contest"—Darcy laughed—"but give it your best attempt, Alexander." The boy set to his bowl with serious intent, Darcy laughing again. As he straightened in his seat he glanced to the right and caught Lizzy gazing at him. Her eyes were round and glistening, lips parted slightly, an expression of pain crossing her features.

A frown of concern knitted his brows and instinctively he extended his hand toward her. Unfortunately, his body was crooked in the chair and his fingers knocked against the edge of the soup bowl just hard enough to clang it against the wine glass. To make matters worse, Rothchilde bent at that precise moment to pour more wine, not only missing the glass as it moved, but also obstructing Darcy's view of Elizabeth and interrupting his words. So what intended to be a sincere inquiry as to what was distressing her came out as, "What is wrong… Oh damn!" as the wine spilt onto the white linen tablecloth.

The minor mishap was exacerbated by the curse word, Darcy embarrassed by his uncharacteristic outburst and Rothchilde surprised to hear it. The footman erupted into apologies as he wiped up the crimson fluid with Darcy hastily blotting with his napkin while assuring it was nothing to be concerned over. In seconds it was done and Darcy's glass was refilled, but the moment to reach out was past. Lizzy was again eating her soup with studied intensity, her face composed and hands steady. She had, he noticed, scooted her chair further away but whether to give Rothchilde room to sop the mess or to place space between them he did not know.

Dinner proceeded with the strange tension thickening as the minutes ticked with agonizing slowness. The courses were served and consumed, not that Darcy would remember how they tasted or what was served. Lizzy did add to the conversation from time to time with voice subdued and comments minimal. She ate well, Darcy was pleased to see, and smiled frequently at Alexander, but she rarely glanced Darcy's direction and maintained an erect pose throughout. Was she angry? Nervous? He could not ascertain and the dinner table was not the place to boldly confront, so he reverted to the familiarity of his taciturn nature. It restored his composure to a degree, or at least kept the pain at bay.

Luckily, Darcy was distracted with Alexander and the constant chatter from George, who cleverly steered the dialogue to drag them in. Nevertheless, the strain mounted and Darcy genuinely felt a breaking point arising beyond his control. Before matters spiraled wildly, for better or worse, Alexander inadvertently intervened. He reached the end of his forbearance when his tiny stomach was filled and the need to sit still became impossible.

At the first protest, Lizzy jumped up and dashed around the table, grabbing Alexander out of his chair and exiting the dining room with haste and few words. Darcy watched her go, longing and sadness etched upon his face.

George sighed. He stood, shaking his head as he addressed the air in general. "You two are so perfectly suited for each other. Both of you are stubborn, blinded, and ridiculous. If I were a voyeur I would wish to be there when you finally overcome your foolishness. It will be a remarkable reunion, I am sure."

❧

"But he was so stern and stiff! He barely glanced at me, frowning when he did, and barely spoke a word to me. When he did his voice was angry and he swore!"

"You see what your aching, fearful heart chooses to see, Elizabeth. Between that and a fair amount of bullheadedness, I may need to lock you two in a room together before this is over. But I would rather the resolution come naturally. Now, drink your tea, all of it, and get some rest." George sat the tray on the small table beside the fire and turned to clasp Lizzy's shoulders. "Do not dwell on your clouded perceptions of dinner but clear your mind instead. I think you will then see a different interpretation."

"I just want him to laugh with me as he did Alexander," she whispered as the tears welled, "but how can he ever forgive me?"

"Forgiveness has nothing to do with anything since there is nothing to forgive."

"That is rather cryptic, Aristotle," Lizzy grumbled.

George chuckled, pushing her gently but firmly into the chair. "You will figure it out. Now, drink and eat all the fruit. No arguments! Then sleep. Tomorrow will be brighter, I am sure of it."

Lizzy grunted but took a large bite of apple even as she glared at the doctor's retreating back. She stared into the flames as she absently chewed and sipped, rehashing dinner over and over. Had she misinterpreted? It certainly is true that she had barely looked at her husband, shame and nervousness sapping every ounce of fortitude.

"What a blasted coward I am!" she muttered, throwing the core into the flames and sending sparks flying.

When George had informed her they were all to dine together that night, couching it as an order, she had grown weak with anxiety and relief. Her improving spirits did not like acknowledging that she needed someone else to push her, but that was the fact of it. Armed with determination to take a positive step toward reuniting with her husband, even if it meant groveling, she chose her attire carefully, dressing to entice as well as bolster her confidence. If all else failed, simple seduction may do the trick!

What she had not anticipated was his effect on her. Hearing his resonant voice, smooth as melted chocolate, forcibly pierced her heart before she entered the room. Waves of the purest lust jolted through her, quite unexpected considering the apathy of the past months, with heat rendering her muscles weak. Her cheeks flamed and her musings were so libidinous that she was afraid to look at him. Then when she did, it only multiplied the emotions a thousand fold. Yet he was frowning and so rigid in his chair that her heart sank, sadness warring with the desire until she could not speak for fear of falling to pieces.

Dinner was torture, but she could now admit that the chaotic sensations were not conducive to clear analyzing. Lizzy sighed, the prune pits following the apple core into the fire. George swore he did not brew her evening tea with any sedative herbs, but inevitably she grew sleepy after drinking it. *Just as well*, she thought, *perhaps my dreams will be better than the dismal reality.*

A few hours later Elizabeth was dreaming.

She and William were on a beach. It was not Caister-on-Sea, but rather an empty expanse of sandy shore with no hint of habitation. The waves lapped gently against the sparkling sand, the roar of the tides was muted, the call of birds rang in the azure sky, and the sun shone warmly on their naked bodies. They lay on a spread blanket, entwined and caressing. His hard body covered hers, the heat rising far beyond what the blazing sun administered as his hands moved expertly over her skin.

It was delicious! Delirium mounted with each kiss and caress.

Her sleeping body writhed and tingled as her dream-self responded to her lover. No words were uttered. None were necessary as their hearts beat in unison and passion overwhelmed. Joy and pleasure were exalting as they moved together in tune with rapture certain and cataclysmic when it occurred.

Slumbering-Lizzy cried out, waves of delight sweeping through her flesh as dream-Lizzy clutched onto her husband's inflamed figure, neither Lizzy wanting the sensations to ebb.

Then, as dreams have a way of doing, she was suddenly standing on the water's edge. William was swimming away, far beyond the safety of the gentle waves. She called to him, panic spiraling, but he did not look back. She rushed into the now surging tide, realizing with a start that she was clothed in the gown worn at dinner. The heaving surf dragged at the thick cloth, tangling it about her legs as she screamed for her lover to return. But he grew smaller and smaller until only a dot of dark hair. Then he was gone.

Lizzy cried in anguish, vaulting up in her bed as wakefulness crashed over her. Her heart beat wildly, the lingering sensations of sexual excitement and dreadful loss rushing through her cells. The blankets were a knotted mess, her legs trapped, and she flailed crazily to freedom. William's side of the bed was empty, the covers disrupted from her thrashing, but the pillow was plump and mattress smooth.

She released a choked sob, lunging from the bed and grabbing the carefully folded robe from the chest at the end of the bed. It was his old robe, freshly splashed with his cologne. She had taken to wearing it again the past few days, the fabric comforting, but also a vivid reminder of the emptiness in her soul. She thought of that now as she dashed from the room, inhibitions completely gone. Flying on bare feet down the hall to the stairs, she prayed he was in the study or library. What if he had had enough, especially after the disastrous dinner, and left entirely? Gone to London or anywhere to escape her. The thought caused all air to vacate her lungs and she ran faster.

The library was dark and vacant. He was found in his study, and Lizzy nearly collapsed from the relief. She paused on the threshold, clutching the solid wood, and gazed at him where he slept on the sofa with soft snores reaching her ears. The fire burned low, one lit lamp on the nearby desk casting a liquid golden glow over his handsome face. He lay with his head resting on a small cushion, lips parted and thick lashes lying on shaven cheeks. He wore long trousers, boots discarded, and his shirt. A thin quilt covered partially, one leg bent and resting against the sofa back. It was clear that he intended to sleep here all through the night, purposefully choosing the hard, narrow sofa over the comfort of their spacious bed.

She hesitated, sadness causing her to tremble. *Perhaps he does not want me?* Then she remembered George's assurances of William's confusion and grief.

She entered, kneeling by his side and taking the cold hand that dangled over the sofa's edge. She kissed it and pressed it to her cheek, tears welling, as the fingers of her other hand lightly traced over his face. Reverently touching each precious feature, holding his hand tightly as it warmed, she murmured, "I love you so, William. Please forgive me. Tell me you love me as well."

He mumbled indecipherably, turning his head toward her gently stroking fingertips. The hand lying on his chest rose slightly, golden band glinting in the firelight with fingers seeking before falling sleepily. "Elizabeth…"

"Yes! It is I! Wake up, William. Please! I love you and need to feel your eyes upon me."

He groaned, stretching and lightly clasping her hand as he bestowed a tiny kiss to the palm. "My Lizzy," he mumbled, beginning to turn toward the hand touching his face, his dreams incorporating the fleshly reality and holding fast.

"No, dearest, wake up! I am here and I love you!"

Suddenly his eyes flew open, dazed and uncomprehending. He saw her, but rather than gathering her into his arms as she so desperately needed, he released her hand and sank further into the sofa. "Elizabeth? Is something wrong? The babies?"

"No, no. They are fine. Soundly asleep." He dropped his gaze to the hand she held cinched next to her cheek, returning to her eyes with confusion evident. As she gathered her thoughts, observing him in the dim illumination, she could detect the faint hope deep in his eyes.

"Beloved"—his brows rose at the endearment—"I… I dreamt of you tonight. We… we made love on the beach in broad daylight as you always wished we could." She smiled, feathering hungry fingers over his befuddled face. "It was so beautiful. You were beautiful. I felt you… truly felt you, even beyond my dream. I… desired you as I have not in weeks and it was wonderful. Only it was not real. And then you swam away and refused to answer me and I woke terrified to find you gone, again, and I needed to see you, touch you, and tell you that…"—she sobbed—"I love you and that if you do not, I understand, but I will die and…"

"Please, Elizabeth, do not cry! I cannot bear to see your tears anymore!"

She shook her head, pierced by the pain in his gaze. "I do not want to cry anymore, my love. I just want to hold you." And she leaned forward, capturing his mouth in an encompassing kiss.

He moaned, encircling her back and lacing sturdy fingers through the hair on her head, drawing her tightly to his body, and returned the kiss with all the pent up agony released in their yearning to reconnect.

It may only be a dream, he thought, *but it is a dream I want and need.*

Lizzy broke the kiss first, but not to draw farther than his neck. Hundreds of warm kisses and nibbles were bestowed, hands traversing the quivering plains of his chest as buttons were undone and fine linen pushed aside.

"Sweet Lord! I love you, Elizabeth!" Darcy gasped, his emotions surging blissfully. Dimly he heard his uncle's voice: *You are a fool*. It seemed impossible that he had ever doubted their love as her luscious lips and arousing hands declared a passionate need. Yet the residuals of fear remained. He stroked her back and shoulders, vocalized his pleasure, but allowed her to lead.

Kissing down the middle of his torso to the rigid muscles of his flat abdomen, she lifted the shirt upward and attacked the area with gusto.

"Oh God…" he moaned, arching his hips as his head fell back, giving in to the sensations.

The shirt was rolled away as she kissed back up to his neck, catching the fabric around his outstretched arms as he lifted to assist. She paused then, holding his hands captive over his head, and gazed into his dark orbs.

"We shall talk later, my soul. There is so much to say, for me to apologize for…" She kissed him to halt the negation, stilling his shaking head with a gentle grip to his chin before leisurely rubbing downward toward his groin. "Right now I only want to show you how much I love you," she whispered against his lips, "show that I am sorry, show that you are everything to me." She suckled along his jaw to earlobe, voice husky amid his rising moans. "I want to renew our bond, bring you pleasure as you have me, give and give until you cry with joy. Please, Fitzwilliam! Let me love you!"

Darcy absorbed every word through the mists of heightened ardor, his body rocking and trembling in response to her tactile stimulation. Crashing sensations burned stupendously and clouded his senses. The trials of the past months faded into nothingness. She was here, beside him, electrifying every nerve, filling his heart with healing phrases far more beautiful than the fervor of their mutual lust.

She released his hands, the shirt falling forgotten to the floor, and he instantly grasped her tightly. Ravenous hands explored the contours of her shape, kneading and stroking, reacquainting themselves with the beloved flesh as familiar to him as his own.

Lizzy drew away, standing as Darcy wheezed *No!* But she only spared a moment, the robe falling in a puddle at her feet, before straddling his thighs and merging in one smooth motion. They simultaneously expelled loud sighs of pleasure and then laughed. Darcy sat up partway, clutching her to his chest and cupping her face as she began to sway with a rhythm as old as time, yet forever satisfying.

He kept her close, lips and noses touching, eyes locked with heated passion blazing. The furious, maniacal urgency of a few moments ago waned somewhat in the gratification of feeling the other's body surrounding. They absorbed the flowing energy and mutual love with no desire to rush the experience.

"I love you, my wife."

"I love you, my husband."

The endearments and affirmations fell interspersed with nuzzles and fondles. The pace quickened after long minutes of temperate loving, finally culminating with blinding rapture. They fell to the sofa, harsh gasps echoing through the room and sweat glistening flesh heaving as they clung together.

Lizzy buried her face in his neck, sobs of joy caught in her throat. *I will not cry! I am done with tears!* She breathed deeply of his masculine scent, that magnificent mixture of woodsy cologne, musky perspiration, and some unidentifiable aroma only present when they made love. It soothed her.

In time their hearts returned to fairly normal paces. Darcy moved then, shifting until her face was near his, fingers stroking lightly over her cheek. He smiled, eyes radiant and shining, his voice rich with throbbing emotion. "There is nothing to talk about, Elizabeth, if you say again that you love me."

She laughed breathily, the last vestiges of anxiety releasing in a gush. "With all my heart I love you, Fitzwilliam Darcy, now and for all eternity."

His grin was enormous, dazzling her senses seconds before he kissed her, rolling toward the back of the sofa as he embraced her so securely she could barely breathe. Yet before the need for oxygen invaded the fantastic delight of his lips, he released her, rolling and rising to his feet in one graceful motion. She propped on an elbow, admiring unabashedly as he fastened his trousers and bent for the discarded quilt. A second later she was enveloped in the material and swooped into his arms heading for the door.

"Where are you taking me?" she teased, tenderly biting along his neck and utterly indifferent to her naked dangling feet and bare shoulders—not that it was likely they would encounter anyone in the middle of the night.

"To our bed where I intend to kiss every inch of your skin and make love to you again and again until you fall asleep exhausted and satiated in my arms. Then I intend to keep you there for at least one or two whole days and do the entire procedure over again. Numerous times. Does this meet with your approval?"

"Indeed it does."

He was serious, adhering to his promise with gleeful dominance, not that Lizzy argued the matter. It was a welcome respite, in fact. In an uncharacteristic display of laziness, Lizzy barely left the bed for a week. Darcy was there every minute, frequently expressing his happiness in a physical way, but also joyously assuming care of Michael. Father and son's relationship flourished during those days, Darcy falling deeply in love with the three-month-old whose unique personality was swiftly emerging. Alexander joined them, the family of four playing together on the large bed for long hours at a time.

On Christmas Eve the foursome gathered in the upper story bedchamber after dining with their guests. Darcy read the nativity poems of Henry Vaughan and the first Christmas story from the Bible until both boys were soundly asleep. He sat the Bible aside and glanced to Lizzy, who was barely awake and propped half reclining with Michael curled against her chest. No words were spoken but communication was clear. He smiled, brushing lightly over her cheek before leaning to extinguish the bedside lamp, and then drew Alexander into his embrace. They slept as a family, unknowingly beginning a tradition that would carry down through the years.

Christmas came, Lizzy's crazed planning paying off in a lavish celebration with local friends that could now fully be enjoyed. Everyone noted the restoration to the Lizzy they had grown to love, although no one commented of course.

Nevertheless, Lizzy's full recovery from the strange illness that had beset her was gradual. There were moments after their heavenly reunion when emotions and melancholy assaulted her. Thankfully, they rapidly receded both in frequency and intensity. Darcy was never far from her side, his attentiveness more acute than typical and welcomed by Lizzy. George insisted on administering the special herbals and dietary requirements to reestablish the balance to her body, but as he had suspected, reuniting with her husband was the best medicine.

By the time they packed up their belongings and two children for the trip to Netherfield for the event of Kitty Bennet's wedding, Lizzy's symptoms were eradicated and she was her old self in every way. The mutual love the young family innately possessed was more than adequate to overcome the months of hardship.

As with many such trials one faces in life, this was one they would never forget or wish to repeat; yet they could not deny that further lessons were learned and their bond was stronger as a result.

CHAPTER SEVEN

Again at Netherfield

WHERE ARE YOU TWO boys off to?"

Darcy turned toward his wife. "Nowhere in particular…"

"The stables!" interrupted the ringing voice above his head.

Lizzy laughed, glancing at her sheepish husband before gazing into the shining eyes of Alexander, perched on Darcy's shoulders. "Well, it is nice to know you have learned the lesson of honesty, Alexander."

"We plan to start in the stables, but one never knows where one may end up. That is all I meant," Darcy intoned with a straight face, reaching to tickle Michael, who was waving every limb in wild mirth from his comfortable roost in Lizzy's arms.

"Of course. Alexander, you understand that Xerxes is not here but home at Pemberley with the other ponies?"

"Yes, Mama. Papa say we ride Moon."

"Oh, did he now?" She looked sharply at her spouse, who was now making faces at a giggling Michael. "Do you really think this wise, Fitzwilliam?"

"Moon is as docile as old Sheba. We will only be walking around the yard. Nothing more, I promise, and he will be on my lap. I will hold on very tight, dearest. You need not worry." He bent to kiss her on the cheek, securely clasping Alexander's legs to his chest, and then blew into Michael's neck, sending the baby into fresh gales of laughter.

Lizzy looked from her sincere husband to the enthusiastic face of her firstborn and sighed. When it came to horses her authority was nonexistent. Darcy's infatuation with all things equestrian had been passed to Alexander.

"Very well. Just be careful."

"You know I will." Darcy caressed her chin. "I love you, Mrs. Darcy. Have fun with your mother and sister planning wedding minutiae."

"I am sure I will, although Mama will be heartbroken not to greet her favorite son-in-law."

"She can share her delight in my presence tonight," he responded to her tease. "Perhaps by then the bulk of her raptures will be exhausted."

"I would not count on that! So you will not be taking tea with us?"

He winced. "Ah, well, I was thinking I would take Alexander into Meryton later and…"

Lizzy shook her head as she rose to bestow a tender kiss. "I understand. Be prepared for some scolding, however, as my mother is anxious to see Alexander and will be vexed that you have spirited him away."

"I daresay she will be easily comforted in spoiling Michael all afternoon. Feel free to expose my selfishness in keeping Alexander with me before he is diverted by dozens of cousins come tomorrow. Undoubtedly I will barely glimpse any of you once Netherfield is descended upon."

"Poor Mr. Darcy!" Lizzy laughed up at him. "Now go and enjoy yourselves."

"We will." He bent for a last kiss for himself and Alexander.

"Bye, Mama! Love!"

Lizzy waved as they exited the manor, Darcy bouncing and weaving side to side with Alexander laughing and holding on tightly to his father's collar.

Both parties passed pleasant afternoons their first full day in Hertfordshire—Darcy alone with his son, exploring the stables and countryside, and Lizzy with her mother and Kitty. Evening would bring them together again as they hosted the first of several planned dinners.

Lizzy and Darcy stood in the parlor, the warm, spring-like evening air of mid-March flowing through the open windows.

"There," she said with a tug to her husband's impeccably tied cravat, "you are perfect."

"Thank you, madam. I am sure Samuel will once again rest easier knowing my wife has given her approval." He kissed her cheek and then turned to Alexander with a solemn nod toward Lizzy. "What have I taught you, Alexander?"

"Mama, you beautiful. Pretty dress."

Lizzy curtsied, brown taffeta crunching. "Why thank you, kind sir." Then she laughed gaily, kneeling for a tight embrace. "You are as handsome as your father, sweetheart. How do you like your suit?" She fingered the frilly, chambray collar framing his round face, brushing invisible lint from the blue flannel jacket tailored to mimic a gentleman's coat only far looser and lighter. The roomy breeches were adorned with simple gold buttons, white-stockinged feet encased in basic house slippers of kid leather. It was the first time the toddler had ever worn anything other than the typical free flowing children's dresses, or the airy Indian garments his godfather managed to provide no matter how Darcy frowned. He was a bit young for his garments, but he did look absolutely adorable.

Nonetheless, it was clear by the expression on his face, coupled with the constant tugging on clinging fabric, that he was far from enthusiastic about the change in attire.

"Itchy, Mama."

"It is flannel, love. It cannot be scratchy. You will grow used to these clothes in time, but I promise you can change into your nightgown soon. Try not to squirm. Look at your papa. He is not fidgeting, is he? And his jacket is wool, which is scratchy."

"Your mother is correct, Alexander. Try to be strong."

"Ah! The corruption begins already!" George strode through the door at that moment, breezy and regal in an Indian silk of navy blue and silver, his three years in England not affecting his clothing preferences appreciably. Alexander took one look at his unencumbered godfather and assumed a childish pout astonishingly similar to his father's frown.

"We were beginning to presume you had decided not to join us, Uncle. The Bennets should be here at any moment."

"I was assuring that the chess set was ready. Elizabeth's father has now surmounted me by three games at last count. I must prove my superiority!" He dramatically lifted his chin, fist high in the air, and winked at Alexander, who erupted in giggles, itchy clothing forgotten.

A footman entered, announcing the arrival of the Bennets. George scooped a still giggling Alexander into his arms as they moved into the foyer to greet their guests.

Mr. and Mrs. Bennet had changed little in the past years. Mrs. Bennet continued to bemoan her husband's imminent demise, but the older gentleman showed nary a sign of going anywhere. If anything he held himself with an unusual spunkiness. Apparently the joys of observing his eldest daughters find happiness while providing him with an ever-increasing clutch of grandchildren had restored a semblance of youth. Mrs. Bennet was as breathless and flighty as ever; the consolation of fulfilling her appointed task in marrying her daughters adequately not yet penetrating her consciousness.

"Why, Mr. Darcy! How delightful it is to see you! How can we ever repay you for leasing Netherfield for the wedding? Your generosity is a testament to your excellent character!"

"Thank you, madam, but once again I must assert your error. All praise must be extended to Mrs. Darcy."

"Nonsense! We know it is your doing, sir! Blessed we were the day you entered our lives, is it not so, Lizzy?"

"Absolutely, Mama. However, in this instance I fear my husband is telling the truth. You see, he preferred the joy of dwelling at Longbourn until I prevailed upon him the need for additional guest quarters. Quite distressed he was at the sacrifice, but I insisted."

"Oh! What a dear, dear man you are!" She daubed at her teary eyes, missing Lizzy's smirk and Darcy's barely concealed frown of disgust.

Greetings erupted in earnest. Alexander was engulfed with hugs and kisses while the men greeted each other with more restraint. Lizzy promised that Michael would be brought down later, only then able to steer her sister to the back of the small crowd for a private chat.

"Have you heard from your fiancé?"

"Not as yet. I know he is busy in his own way to prepare for our wedding, but I do wish he would hurry along."

"Have no fears, sister dear. I am sure he is as frantic to be with you as you are to be with him." Lizzy smiled at Kitty's pretty blush. "Surely you do not believe otherwise?"

Kitty shook her head. "No. I no longer doubt his devotion and honesty. I merely persist in a ridiculous fear that an unnameable force will separate us for yet a few more months!"

"I doubt that shall happen. When do you expect him to arrive?"

"Tomorrow or the following day. He was unsure, but he is insistent on passing a few days with the entire family prior to our wedding. How about Georgiana? Have you heard from her?"

"Not since they departed from Paris. William is fretful, not that there is anything remarkable in that." She glanced fondly toward her spouse. "I assure him that all is well. She is in competent hands and would not miss your wedding."

Kitty halted her just outside the parlor doorway, lowering her voice seriously. "Lizzy, I must inform you. We received word today that Lydia and Mr. Wickham will be coming to the wedding. I did not expect them; after all, they did not stand at your and Jane's wedding, or at Mary's. I am very sorry!"

"Do not be anxious. It was inevitable and we have been fortunate not to encounter Mr. Wickham in all these years. I appreciate you warning me so I can prepare William and Georgiana." She looked at Darcy, who was currently in amused conversation with his father-in-law while Alexander tugged on his grandfather's bushy muttonchops from his perch in the older man's arms. "They do not anticipate residing at Netherfield, I pray."

"Oh no! Papa disabused Mama of that notion immediately! There is more than enough room at Longbourn." She too glanced toward Darcy with warmth. "I would never allow such disregard for Mr. Darcy's feelings, nor Georgiana's. I am truly sorry, Lizzy!"

Lizzy smiled warmly, kissing Kitty's forehead. "Think on it no further, my dear. This is your time to celebrate. Nothing shall be allowed to mar that. Come, let us start the rejoicing now."

❦

The evening's festivities were over, the Bennets safely returned to Longbourn after a delicious meal. Mrs. Hanford hummed while she knitted and kept an eye on Alexander, who was finally rid of the encumbering garments and nestled in sleep wearing a loose, cotton nightgown and hugging Dog against his chest. Miss Lisa read a book by the fire, all comfortably ensconced in the chamber selected to serve as nursery for the duration of their stay. The remaining Darcys relaxed in the tiny sitting room attached to their favorite Netherfield sleeping chamber.

Darcy sat at the small writing desk attending to a stack of papers that Mr. Andrew Daniels, his London solicitor, had sent to Netherfield. Mostly they were lists of various business matters to be handled upon his arrival in London, nothing urgent thankfully, as Darcy was distracted by the vision of his wife nursing their son.

As always, Lizzy respected his preference for silence as he worked. Her gentle murmurs and crooning to Michael were dulcet. She rocked slowly, eyes intent on the calm face of the babe, by all appearances ignoring her husband. If there was a bit more breast showing than was strictly necessary for the task it *seemed* to be guileless.

Darcy smiled, turning his gaze toward the parchment before him. He was not really fooled by her ploy, reasonably familiar with his wife's tactics. Nor was he in the slightest bit dismayed, except that he really did want to peruse these lists and pen a brief note for Georgiana to be posted on the morrow.

He frowned. As Lizzy had intimated to Kitty, he was concerned that there was no letter from his sister. She may have been twenty years of age and well cared for, but some habits never die and one was the need to protect her. And, of course, he simply missed her horribly and was anxious to be reunited.

Movement from the chair again diverted him, pleasantly so as Lizzy transferred Michael to the right breast and apparently forgot to cover the left. She glanced up at her husband, the expression of contented innocence belied by a twinkle in her eyes. Darcy smiled in return, certain that his eyes were glowing even though he avoided directly gazing at the abundant display.

He pulled a blank parchment from the pile, dipped the pen as a prelude to writing while his thoughts veered not to wayward sister, but to his beautifully sensuous wife. A fresh wave of joy and relief washed over him, borne not from what he was certain would evolve into a delightful night of pleasure, but from the peace that now ruled after what had been several months of difficulty.

He shook his head, willed the unpleasant memory aside, and concentrated on his letter, unaware when Lizzy exited to the next-door nursery to place Michael into his cradle.

Lizzy brushed over the wispy hair on Michael's head and tucked the blanket tightly around his plump body. She knew she would tell Darcy about Wickham, just not tonight. It was not cowardice—well, not completely—but rather because she wanted and needed this time to focus solely on her husband.

Lizzy was indeed fully conscious of her actions while nursing Michael. Last night's lovemaking was wonderful as always, but somewhat perfunctory after days of forced abstinence due to preparations for their departure from Pemberley and residing at an inn while traveling. Tonight's seduction was designed to evoke a response!

The memories surrounding Netherfield were numerous, as she had said upon their arrival earlier yesterday. They dated to the beginning of their relationship and involved dozens of strange and incredible moments. She paused in her caress over Michael's skin, smiling as she recalled one particularly erotic encounter that sparked her plans for tonight. She crossed to their chambers, halting only for a last minute pinch to her cheeks, to fluff her flowing waist-length hair, and to loosen the ties to her gossamer robe.

"Are you almost finished with your letter?"

Darcy jumped, not hearing her sneak behind him, and grasped the hand running inside the opening in his shirt. "Nearly. Give me a few minutes, please."

"Hmmm… In a few minutes I may be asleep. Then what would you do, Mr. Darcy?"

"Wake you."

"How ungentlemanly! I am appalled." She escaped his grasp, resuming her exploration of his chest, and poked the tip of her tongue into his ear.

Darcy groaned, grabbed the searching hand tighter, and bent his head away from her lips. "Patently unfair! Seriously, love, please give me a few minutes. I really want to send this at first light."

"You do worry too much, dearest. Georgie will be here. She has probably decided to surprise you." She stood, running her fingers through his hair and massaging his temples. "Richard will play the wounded soldier for you having so little faith in his capacity as protector, and the rest of us will have to endure his dramatics. Have you no mercy?"

He laughed, clasping one hand and kissing her palm. "I am certain Richard will have far too many delightful stories to tell for overt dramatics. Now, leave me be for a bit and I promise I shall make it up to you."

"Very well." She kissed the top of his head. "I shall be in there, alone, trying to stay awake." She glided toward the bedchamber doorway, diaphanous robe billowing, and paused halfway to glance seductively over her shoulder. Darcy watched her, pen poised over the parchment. She held his gaze and proceeded to peel the robe off her shoulders, revealing one of Madame du Loire's skimpy concoctions.

"Ah, Lizzy! You vixen!"

She laughed and sauntered into the bedroom with a toss of her hair.

Less than fifteen minutes later he was there, warm hands stroking over her arms and moist lips nuzzling the bend of her neck. She stood by the window, gazing at the familiar landscape bathed in faint moonlight.

"You are still awake."

"Waiting for my obsessive husband."

He chuckled, arms clasping hers around her slender waist and drawing fast onto the solid surface of his body. "Yes, indeed I am obsessive. Obsessively in love with and desirous of you. I abhor traveling if for no other reason than it is difficult to relax with you in an inn with our sons upset."

"Oh, you seemed comfortable enough with Michael asleep on your chest and Alexander curled between us."

"As much as I adore our babies I concede I would rather you be on my chest." He ran two fingers under her strap, knuckles grazing over a fragile collarbone and then down to a swelling breast.

Lizzy melted further onto his body. "I do believe, husband mine, that it was on my agenda to seduce *you* tonight."

"Hmmm… Is that so?" His mouth was now at the nape of her neck, the other hand stroking over a thigh. "How did you intend to go about your seduction? It really does not take all that much, you know."

"This is true, but I have discovered that driving you a wee bit insane does heighten the experience."

"I cannot argue that fact. Merely picturing you in this slip of satin"—his fingertips smoothed over the fabric covering her belly—"has kept me pleasantly distracted while attempting to compose a brotherly correspondence."

She sighed, loudly and theatrically. "Unfortunately, I have had to wait for so long that I think I am no longer in the mood." She twisted from his embrace and strolled with a sway of her hips to the middle of the room.

Darcy grinned, leaning against the wall with arms and feet crossed in a picture of blasé attitude. "What a pity. Is there anything I can do to restore your interest?"

She tapped a finger against her lower lip as she studied him contempla-tively. Then she shrugged, arms waving as if bored by the question although she managed to sweep through her hair and push her chest out. "Oh bother! I suppose you could remove your shirt. That may spark my enthusiasm. If you do it properly."

He lifted a brow. "Are there varying methods to removing a shirt?"

"Oh, indeed, yes! I daresay if one performs adequately it can be quite stimulating. Have you not discovered this to be true, lover?"

She leered—there was no other way to put it—and Darcy flushed.

The truth is that even after three years of marriage and numerous seductive stripping dances on her part, always observed with tremendous enthusiasm, he still did not grasp that she experienced the same titillation from observing him disrobing. He had lost track of the number of times she joined him in his dressing room with that singular expression indicating passionate arousal. Samuel still blanched and scurried from the room. And how often she had lingered over each button and tie, unveiling him as she kissed and caressed until she was wild with need.

That she esteemed his figure was obvious, and highly appreciated, but his humble nature shied from taking it to the next level. As she grew bolder in her attire and the flirtatious exposing of her flesh to his eyes, he quailed at the idea of such exhibitionism. However, the brightness in her eyes and lascivious smirk were encouraging, so he decided to do his best to please her.

He started with the buttons, the top two already undone, feeling utterly ridiculous as she avidly watched.

"Now, slowly pull the ends from your waistband."

His eyes widened in surprise at her command, realizing that she intended to talk him through it! He blushed deeper, but also felt a scorching surge of lust, especially as her gaze was no longer on his face, but clearly inventorying his person with rising ardor.

"Take it off, Fitzwilliam, unhastily, while turning in a circle."

His face was scarlet but only partially from embarrassment. Heat was flowing through him, her vibrant voice and covetous stare enlivening.

"Hmmm… I love the way your muscles flex as you move," she whispered with a reflexive moan.

She kept up the train of admiration and instruction, the removal of breeches never taking so long in his life. It was awkward, and he felt a bit the fool, but it was obvious by her deepened voice, panting breaths, and visible shivers that she was profusely pleased by his performance. By the time every bit of clothing was removed, he too was intensely aroused, much to his surprise.

Then she floated toward him, hands lifting to airily brush over the hairs on his chest, and he thought he would burst into flames. She touched him everywhere, murmuring appreciatively over each feature, finally leaning into his back. With lips pressed between his shoulder blades, the level most comfortable for her to reach, and hands stroking intimately, she asked, "Are you adequately seduced, my love?"

He growled in response and stilled her stimulating hands. "Are you adequately in the mood, sweet love?"

"Come to bed and we shall see."

Quite some time later, the bed tousled and their bodies entangled and lying diagonally, Lizzy rose on one elbow to gaze at her gasping spouse. She kissed his chin, fingertips dipping into his navel. "You performed stupendously, my love."

"Yes," he agreed with a smug leer, "I sense you are pleased."

Lizzy rubbed over the fingertip-sized pressure marks across his posterior shoulder blades. "Indeed I am satisfied, but I was not primarily referring to your prowess and ability to send me to the moon. I was talking about your impressive disrobing. I was not sure if you were up to the task. But considering the last time we were here and my excellent lesson in the art of seductive undressing, I trusted you had learned capably."

"Ah! Indeed I remember quite vividly. So that was your impetus, was it?"

"I was praying for an adequate, perhaps somewhat neophytic, performance, but you wildly exceeded my expectations."

Darcy grinned, snatching her teasing hand and bringing it to his mouth for a kiss. He drew her body closer, encircling her with both arms and delivering a long, lazy kiss.

"Mmmm… I forgot to ask if you remembered to lock the door."

He nodded as he swept the snarled hair from her face. "That lesson has been indelibly etched into my brain! Yes, the door is locked. But now that you have touched upon the subject, I am going to ease my mind of their welfare ere I fall asleep in your arms. I shall return momentarily." And after another kiss, he left.

Lizzy stretched and sighed happily, belatedly recalling the foul news of Wickham. *Tomorrow is soon enough*, she thought, nestling deeper into the linens warmed by their love and yielding to drowsiness.

❧

The tentative knock that roused the Darcys on their second morning in Hertfordshire brought instant wakefulness to Lizzy but only a rumbled groan from Darcy. She leapt from the bed and grabbed her robe, while Darcy turned onto his stomach and burrowed deeper into the mattress. No bell was installed to alert of a hungry infant, but the morning routine was ingrained.

A half hour later Lizzy returned. Darcy had not budged and was breathing regularly, but instead of snuggling gratefully into his welcoming warmth, Lizzy stirred the fire and curled up in the chair. She gazed into the flames as her racing mind drifted to matters both pleasant and distressing.

It was always a joy to visit with family and friends after the long winter sequestered in Derbyshire. This year was extra thrilling due to the wedding and new lives born in the intervening months. Letters passed over the miles at a regular pace, but there was only so much information that could be inscribed onto parchment. Long hours of fellowship were required to catch up on all the news.

Lizzy sighed and drew her legs against her chest. She knew it was imperative that she inform her husband of Wickham's appearance before he heard of it from a less understanding source, like her mother.

Oddly, she did not know how Darcy would respond to meeting George Wickham after all these years. He certainly would not be thrilled by the idea, but she was unsure how deeply his animosity yet ran.

It was nearly two years since the information reached them of Wickham's discharge from the army and his subsequent relocation to Devon. Letters to Lizzy from her flighty sister were nonexistent, but Mrs. Bennet received sporadic updates. They were always vague, no one sure what the full details of their living conditions or Wickham's employment were. Knowing how irresponsible her sister was, it never crossed Lizzy's mind to consider the mystery a sinister one.

Darcy relinquished his guilt over Lydia's situation, recognizing that they were a married couple who were responsible for their own lives. The dearth of explicit information with only Lydia's giddy ramblings to discern from together with the great distance to Devon meant that it was not a topic often broached. Darcy, like Lizzy, simply did not think of the Wickhams.

Now they were to be here for Kitty's wedding. Why? It was baffling and she feared Darcy would interpret it as an ominous sign. She hated to see her husband or Georgiana discomfited and she fretted over Kitty's wedding being disturbed, her own thoughts dark as she stared into the flames.

Darcy roused, groggily noted the emptiness of his arms, and groped for where his wife's luscious body should lay. While his sleepy mind decided she was probably nursing Michael, his eyes slit open and noted with surprise that she sat by the fire. After a few seconds of sluggish mental assimilation, his gravely morning voice broke the calm, "Beloved? Are you well?"

"I am fine, love. Just thinking."

"Come back to bed. I need you."

Lizzy joined him under the quilted counterpane, their arms embracing naturally and hands caressing. Darcy nestled his head onto her right chest, cheek pillowed by her bosom with warm breath wafting over her sensitive skin, humming in cat-like satisfaction.

"I love you, Mrs. Darcy," he mumbled in a thick sleepy voice.

"I love you more, Mr. Darcy," she retorted with the standard playful response, feeling Darcy's amused smile against the soft flesh of her breast.

"How long do I have you all to myself before your mother and sister descend upon Netherfield?"

"They will be here mid-morning, before noon. Charles and Jane should arrive shortly thereafter."

"Yes, and that reminds me. Do you mind terribly if Bingley and I desert you all this evening and spend some time at the Meryton billiard hall? Mr. Bennet has informed the men of our visit and although I am sure they are more delighted at the prospect of Bingley's presence than mine, a dinner and games have been arranged."

"They undoubtedly fear being humiliated once again at the billiard table." She responded, rubbing her face against his silky hair. Darcy snickered evilly, offering no rebuttal to the plausible truth. "Do not fret about us womenfolk, my love. We can entertain ourselves without the dashing men about to liven the atmosphere."

"I have no doubt of that. I was most concerned for Jane. Do you think she will be distressed to have Bingley gone?"

Lizzy shook her head after thinking on his query for a moment. "I do not believe so. We can dine at Longbourn as planned and I judge that the familiarity of family with the children playing at our feet will soothe her. She needed to distance herself from Hasberry for a while and this is a perfect place to start." She continued to play with his hair, fingers running through the brown locks absently. "Physically she has recovered and is overcoming her grief. Also, Ethan's walking has evolved to running so she is keeping busy!"

Again she felt Darcy's smiling lips graze her skin. "Indeed! Life is never the same again once they begin to walk. Alexander was easy to control, but I have a feeling I will need to install stout locks or barricades over the stairways to prevent escape and severe tumbles when Michael begins to toddle, which, considering his precociousness, will likely be well before Alexander did."

They both laughed and nodded. Darcy's hand traveled from its warm roost on her hip to the flat expanse of her abdomen, pressing gently into the soft flesh, his voice low when he spoke. "I do not like to think on the sadness of losing a child. Bingley has recovered from the loss for the most part, but it must be extremely difficult for a woman."

Lizzy squeezed tightly and said nothing. The trauma Jane suffered in miscarrying her second child during the middle of her pregnancy was profound, as they both knew, thus words on the subject were unpleasant. The midwife assured them that Jane was healthy and should conceive and carry easily in the future, as the stillborn, a girl baby that Charles would not allow Jane to see, was malformed, hence the cause of the miscarriage. It was a tragedy nonetheless, the past three months a difficult period for both Bingleys. The sturdiness of their now nearly two-year-old son was a balm to aching hearts.

Silence fell for a spell. Darcy closed his eyes, stroking his wife's velvet skin, utterly at peace. Lizzy, conversely, was tense. Breaking the news about Wickham's imminent return into their lives was not a topic she relished relaying, yet she knew it needed to be spoken, before events intruded and he discovered the information in a more startling manner.

How to broach the subject? For the past hour she had played through scenarios, practiced the best words to ease his distress, but nothing would make the blow any easier. *Just say it!* She chastised her cowardice and opened her mouth to speak…

"How long ago did Michael nurse?" He interrupted in a sultry drawl, fingers initiating the subtle frolicking over her skin that drove her mad. "Experience has taught how diverted we become with family and activities intruding, so I think it essential we make love while we have the opportunity to do so. Agreed?"

"Lydia and Wickham are coming to the wedding."

Darcy froze, the hand that encompassed her left breast clenching.

Lizzy bit her lip, the blurted statement shrilly spoken in her haste to forestall his amorous attentions that would surely have driven thoughts of offensive family members out of her mind. She groaned and cringed at her lack of tact. "William, I…"

"Yes, I know they are coming."

"You... What?"

He rose up, serious eyes engaging hers. "Mr. Bennet told me last night. He thought I should know and be prepared." He smiled, smoothing the hair by her startled eyes. "Your father does not know all the details of my past interactions with Wickham, but he knows there is a certain... animosity, shall we say? I gathered that he is none too thrilled either, although I am sure he is anxious about Lydia and will be pleased to see her." He paused, frowning and cocking his head. "Is this why you were sitting by the fire in thought rather than nestling with your husband?"

She nodded. "I was trying to think how to tell you. You... you do not seem too upset. I thought you would be furious."

"I am not sure how I feel. I have known our meeting was inevitable, but over these past months I have given up dwelling on it. Time does heal some wounds, I suppose. That is not to say I trust him." His face grew sterner, mouth pressed into the thin line Lizzy recognized as stubbornness and a precursor to a domineering demand. "I command you to avoid him as much as feasible, Elizabeth. And I forbid him to have any interaction with our sons. My opinion has not changed and my decree that the Wickhams have no place in our lives persists."

"Do you think him dangerous?"

"I put nothing past him. I know for cert that he has no love for a Darcy and do not want you or our children subjected to his tongue or possible exploitation. Primarily I merely wish to avoid any unpleasantness. Perhaps we will all be shocked and discover him to have matured or tamed or found God. Who knows? But I will not take any chances with my family. Do you understand?" She nodded, Darcy intently examining her eyes for the tiniest hint of disobedience, but in this situation she was in total agreement. "As we have discussed in the past, he is not a man to be taken lightly. I will be watching him closely, so you do not need to fret. I want you to enjoy this time with Kitty. Leave the vigilance to me."

"You are worrying me, William."

He smiled, bending to kiss her forehead. "Forgive me, dearest. You really have nothing to be concerned about. I doubt if Wickham will attempt to cross me, and remember that Richard will be here as well. Wickham was always far more terrified of him than me, for some reason. Even now that he no longer wears the uniform, Wickham will be quelled by the presence of Colonel Fitzwilliam."

He brushed a thumb over her lips, leaning closer while pushing his taut muscled body onto hers. "Now, what say we return to the previous topic? The far more pleasant one involving me loving you." He lingered, lips a scant hairbreadth away from hers. "I am positive I can drive all other thoughts from your mind, Mrs. Darcy."

"I would accuse you of arrogance, but in this matter you speak the truth, Mr. Darcy."

He laughed, rolling to his back with her encased amid strong arms and long legs. Every muscle rippled, Lizzy shivering at the feel of his solid thighs tenaciously clutching her hips and the radiant heat oozing from the steely plains of his torso. He lifted his head to close the small gap for a kiss, but Lizzy withdrew.

"William, I worry for you." His brow rose questioningly and eyes widened. "Promise me you will avoid Wickham as well. Do not let him bait you into acting foolishly."

"Elizabeth, I have greater forbearance than you give me credit for!"

"Do you? I seem to recall a rash urge to strangle him with your bare hands not too many months ago! You are a man of great passion, my love, despite your uncommon self-control and wisdom. Your emotions do, upon occasion, overrule your temperance and reserve. Thankfully your shortswords and dueling pistols are secured at Pemberley! Please be careful, that is all I ask. Remember your family in the present and not the conflicts of the past. Promise me."

"I promise. I will happily pretend the man is invisible as much as is possible. Even if that means being a poor host."

"It will give you a ready excuse to stand in the corner and glower, since that is what you prefer in large gatherings anyway."

Darcy grunted at her tease, pulling her firmly to his mouth and tightening every muscle enclosing her body. "Can we stop talking now? My need for you has taken on an urgency that I fear may be interrupted at any moment by a demanding baby. Thwarted sexual satisfaction will put me in a fouler mood, and we would not want that, now would we?"

Lizzy's laugh and retort were stayed by a fervidly seeking tongue, communication essentially nonverbal from there on. No interruptions occurred, both exiting the bedchamber sometime later tremendously satisfied and in buoyant spirits.

CHAPTER EIGHT

Anticipating a Marriage

CONTRARY TO DARCY'S TEASE about the women spending hours dedicated to wedding plans, there really were few left to finalize. Kitty had arranged everything with a straightforward simplicity that drove Mrs. Bennet into nervous fits. Mrs. Bennet had apparently decided that as the final Bennet daughter to be wed, it needed to be an affair of pomp and renown. The morning and early afternoon visitation as the three waited for their assorted guests to arrive would follow a typical pattern.

"I am certain Mr. Hennings could provide a few more flower arrangements in short order," Mrs. Bennet declared, Lizzy rolling her eyes for the umpteenth time while Kitty calmly waited for her mother to finish the thought before rebutting it. "This is a meager amount! Only four around the altar and the one you will be carrying? Not nearly sufficient!"

"Mr. Hennings has provided what I asked for, Mama. There is no need to burden him further." Kitty did not look up from her embroidery hoop.

A few minutes later: "I spoke with Mr. Janssen yesterday, Kitty. He said he would be delighted to bake the cake for you."

"I plan to cook it myself, Mama, as you know since you helped me purchase the ingredients three days ago. The fruit is drying already and the marzipan is prepared. I pray you did not impose upon Mr. Janssen for an item we do not require?"

"No, no! It was merely a suggestion."

Then again, following a heavy sigh: "I do wish you had prevailed for a special license. His family connections are illustrious enough to afford it and you certainly had the time."

"That is not the point. We had no need to apply for such a thing."

"Of course, it should have been you, Lizzy, who had done so," Mrs. Bennet interrupted, having not listened to Kitty's response, her eyes dreamy as she continued. "It would have been marvelous to see Lady Lucas's face when one of my daughters was married after noon with leave by the Archbishop of Canterbury himself!" Her eyes grew mournful as she turned to her younger daughter. "Really, Kitty, if you could only think of your poor mama you would have granted me this one wish."

"Mama, please!" Lizzy scolded. "The wedding will be perfect as it is. It is Kitty's happiness that counts the most."

"Of course! Yes, yes, you are correct, Lizzy. I only want what is best for my dear girl! Are you sure the kitchen staff here is adequately prepared for the occasion? Perhaps we should scrutinize the menu again, add something more. It is such short notice, but it must be stupendous!"

"It is only breakfast. They will handle it superbly."

"But what about the dinner that evening? Two meals in one day of such magnitude?"

"The bride and groom will be gone and it will just be family, Mama. No need for ostentation. The Netherfield staff can manage it, I assure you."

And on it went until mid-afternoon and the relieving disruption by the footman announcing the arrival of the Bingleys. Darcy was sent for from his solitude in the library, entering the foyer as the group massed for hugs and greetings.

"Bingley!"

"Darcy old man. How are you?"

"Well, quite well indeed. Mrs. Bingley." He bowed toward Jane, who smiled and curtseyed.

"William, I expected to see Alexander trailing behind. Ethan has spoken of nothing else nearly the entire journey."

"I forced him to nap, much to his chagrin, so it is fortunate that Ethan is clearly in the same state." He inclined his head toward the Bingleys' nanny, whose arms were laden by the sleeping form of the Bingleys' young son.

"Mrs. Geer, a room has been prepared for you and Master Bingley. Arguston will escort you there, if you approve, Jane?"

"Please. He was a terror, I am embarrassed to admit, refusing to sleep or sit still until we began pulling into the drive whereupon he suddenly collapsed in exhaustion."

George laughed. "I am convinced your dear son holds not a candle to the youngest Darcy in terms of a wicked temper."

"I wish I could argue the point, but I am afraid it is the truth." Darcy grinned, clasping his wife's hand in the crook of his arm as they filed into the parlor.

It was a bedlam of voices and bodies as they refreshed the new arrivals with tea and spirits, exchanging pleasantries with Kitty gladly answering the identical questions asked of her by Lizzy over the past two days. Jane was paler than typical, but otherwise outwardly recovered from the horrendous ordeal of miscarrying her second baby. Her countenance was cheery as Kitty gushed about the wedding to come.

Lizzy leapt for joy to see Kitty reverting to her giddy self. The past year and a half had been filled with trials and heartache, her present happiness often seemingly not in the fates with her newfound strange reserve a remnant of too many disappointments. Additionally, Lizzy prayed the presence of family and a blissful event would wash the residuals of grief from Jane's heart—at least as much as was possible after a tragedy of that magnitude.

The cacophony had dimmed only slightly when a fresh outpouring erupted upon the surprise arrival of Mr. Bennet with Joshua and Mary Daniels in his wake. They had halted at Longbourn first, Mary physically evicting her father from his study to accompany them to Netherfield. Hugs, kisses, formal bows from the menfolk, and two more slumbering children were relocated to waiting chambers while fresh tea and edibles were brought in.

Kitty once again embarked on a question and answer session, not tiring in the endeavor. Sitting as the guest of honor on the sofa amid a gaggle of Bennet females, she waxed on as only a bride-to-be can do.

Mr. Daniels greeted his brother-in-law with staid formality, never considering Mr. Darcy more than a client. A tied packet of documents was delivered with appropriate rectitude, Darcy not even cracking a smile although his eyes glittered humorously. George casually leaned against the liquor cabinet, whiskey decanter in one hand and brandy in the other as he served drinks to the gentlemen gathered around.

"May as well get started on the celebrating," he said jauntily. "Bingley, Daniels, drink up. Get a jump on the other gents at the pub!"

"The pub?" Mr. Daniels asked, taking the whiskey tumbler automatically as it was thrust into his hand.

Mr. Bennet answered, "The men of Meryton are gathering for an impromptu dinner and games. News of our guests has spread. Mr. Bingley especially has many friends in the neighborhood."

Mr. Daniels paled. "I am not certain… that is I should stay with Mrs. Daniels and the girls."

"Nonsense!" George airily waved the brandy toward the clutch of jabbering females. "All these women talking weddings and mothering? Lord, be merciful! We need to be surrounded by manly sweat, drunken cursing, and discourses on hunting and politics to remind us we are of the stronger sex for at least one night. Pity Colonel Fitzwilliam is not here to test my skill at darts."

"Perhaps it is for the best, Dr. Darcy," Mr. Bennet offered with a smile. "Humiliation at games of skill twice in a row may not be healthy for your ego."

"My ego is towering enough to handle it, I assure you. Besides, the chess-board shall not sit idle for long, Mr. Bennet. Be wary. 'Pride cometh before the fall,' as the Good Book says."

"Indeed," Darcy said. "But does it not also ask, 'Why beholdest thou the mote that is in thy brother's eye, but perceivest not the beam that is in thine own eye?'"

George laughed heartily, pouring more whiskey into Darcy's untouched glass by way of answer.

"Speaking of Colonel Fitzwilliam, have you heard from him, Darcy?" Bingley asked.

"Not for a couple of weeks," Darcy answered, frowning into his glass.

"I still am in a state of shock that Colonel Fitzwilliam is now a married man," Bingley said. "I do not know him as well as you, Darcy, but I have to say I thought bachelorhood had a firm grip upon him. The abruptness, his choice of wife, the whole matter took me so by surprise."

"And many others, myself included!" George declared, features falling into a pitiable expression of mourning. "I am the lone bachelor in the crowd now. It is a tragedy."

They all laughed, Mr. Bennet speaking with false placation, "Rest easy, Doctor. I am sure we can find you a nice lady somewhere."

George gasped dramatically, hand clutching the vivid green silk swathing his bony chest. "Perish the thought! You wound me, sir!"

"I have an aunt, sir, who may be perfect for you."

They collectively gaped at Mr. Daniels, not due to his statement, but due to the obvious teasing tone it was uttered in. Stunned silence fell for a heartbeat, Mr. Daniels's face beginning to color, but the lull was broken by Dr. Darcy's loud bray and a reverberating clap to the young man's shoulder.

"Well done, Daniels! Well done! Here, have some more whiskey."

"Married he may be, but it will be pleasant to see him again. It has been months. I hope he arrives soon."

Darcy nodded at Bingley's words, the frown intact. "I am a little concerned, but trust that they will arrive in time. Georgiana will not fail to attend Miss Kitty's nuptials, so my wife assures me."

"Elizabeth is correct, William," George agreed. "The wedding is several days away. We have yet to see the groom even! In fact, I am betting they will all arrive together. At least then we will have more men to counteract the feminine twittering. This brings me to back to tonight. How are you at darts, Mr. Daniels?"

Meanwhile the women sat in a semicircle with Kitty in the middle. Lizzy poured tea and distributed tiny plates of cakes and fruit while the bride-to-be described her dress in minute detail. "A rosy pink with green ribbons and sash. Green is Randall's favorite color," she finished in a soft voice, her rosy cheeks dimpling.

Jane and Lizzy shared a glance. Even the serious, unromantic Mary found herself smiling tenderly as memories of her own nuptials and those heady days of blooming love were recalled. Each young woman glanced unconsciously toward the knot of laughing men by the liquor cabinet, eyes seeking out their spouses.

"Well, I was of the opinion that a regal silver or gold would be more fashionable," Mrs. Bennet interrupted the sentimental fancies. "Green is so… ordinary. Who picks green as a favorite color?" She shook her head, reaching for a scone.

"I think it sounds lovely," Mary said, patting Kitty's hand. "In the end it does not matter what color the dress as long as the choice of husband is a wise one." She nodded sagely. "Kitty has made an excellent match."

"Indeed she has. Do not be distressed, Mama. Consider how wonderful it will be to have Kitty married! Then all your daughters will be safe and securely

SHARON LATHAN

established elsewhere, and you can turn your attentions to other matters, having accomplished your primary task in life. Think what a joy that shall be!"

Mrs. Bennet's face fell at Lizzy's innocently uttered words. Jane nudged Lizzy's knee, shaking her head ever so slightly with a stern look, but Lizzy merely shrugged.

Mary changed the subject. "Lizzy, I do hope Michael wakens soon. I cannot wait to see him. Does he still look more like you than Mr. Darcy?"

"His appearance is a melding of us both but mostly unique, I think. In temperament I fear he is me."

"Strange how that happens," Jane mused. "Alexander so incredibly resembles his father while Michael resembles neither. Ethan too is a melding of Charles and I, with some features that come from only God knows where."

"Well, we know where he gets his red hair, to be sure!" Mrs. Bennet offered. "I never could figure such things as there seems to be no logic. Jane's fair coloring has always been a mystery. Mr. Bennet was as dark haired as Mary before turning white, if you girls remember. I do not think there are any blondes in the family."

"Deborah's locks are sandy, although not as light as yours, Jane, but that could well be from my husband's side of the family. Joshua's mother is blonde."

"And Claudia?" Jane asked. "Is her hair light? I could not tell with her bonnet on and did not wish to disturb her sleep."

"Never disturb a sleeping baby!" Lizzy declared firmly.

"I daresay you would know *that* truth!" Jane teased.

"I am anxious to meet this tempestuous nephew of mine. You have me burning with curiosity. How does Mr. Darcy handle his personality?"

"William has enough experience dealing with me that it has been an easy transition," Lizzy answered Mary with a tiny chuckle. "In fact he has far more patience than I, not that there is any shocking imparted truth in that statement. Patience is not a virtue I overwhelmingly possess whereas William is a walking example of the attribute. I have decided that God plans these matters carefully and with tremendous forethought, thankfully."

"Yes, He does. To answer your question, Jane, Claudia is completely bald, I am afraid. She was born with a few wisps of light hair, but they fell out within a couple of weeks. Mrs. Daniels assures me that the same thing happened with all of her children and they now have lovely hair."

"Ethan developed bald patches that were moderately unsightly. Caroline said he was piebald, which irritated Charles no end. Luckily his hair evened out and is now thick like his father's. How are you feeling, Mary? Have you recovered completely?"

Jane spoke softly, treading too close to an area that elicited painful emotions, as her own recovery from the birth process was not balanced by the joy of holding an infant in her arms. Mary sympathized and squeezed her sister's hand. "I am well, Jane, thank you. Claudia's birth was easy. Now if I could lose some of this extra weight, I would be right as rain."

"A bit of flesh on the bones after becoming a mother is proper," Mrs. Bennet asserted. "A maternal appearance is expected! Men prefer their women rounded, I daresay. Why, Lizzy and Jane stay so thin it is a wonder Mr. Darcy and Mr. Bingley remain romantically interested at all."

"Mama!" Jane blushed scarlet, eyes inadvertently darting to her husband.

Lizzy, however, after a furtive gaze toward her handsome spouse, retorted, "I thought learning ways to divert our husband's romantic interests was one of your chief lessons, Mama. I seem to recall a wealth of wise education on the subject during our engagement, remember Jane? Not that any of it seems to be working, sadly." She sighed dramatically. "You know how men can be, yes, Mama?"

Mrs. Bennet fluttered her handkerchief wildly, one hand grasping at the lace at her throat, "Oh, Lizzy! How you do try my nerves! Speaking of such things!" She stood abruptly, muttering as she retreated to the window.

"God may well strike you down, Elizabeth Darcy," Jane whispered in a quavering voice. Mary too looked near to bursting into giggles. Lizzy just shrugged.

"Oh!" Mrs. Bennet exclaimed loudly, the whole room glancing toward her. "A fine carriage approaches! And two men on horseback!"

Kitty gasped, rising and dashing to join her mother. One squeal erupted before she pivoted and flew from the room.

"See, I told you they would all arrive together," George declared calmly. "Should have taken wagers on the matter."

"Any profit gained would have been lost tonight as I see one of the mounted men is Colonel Fitzwilliam," Darcy grinned at his uncle. "Sure you still want to try your hand at darts?"

"Perhaps marital felicity has softened him as it has others whom shall remain unnamed."

"Are you insinuating to have defeated Mr. Darcy in billiards?" Mr. Bennet asked in true surprise.

"Ha! He wishes!"

"Not as yet," George spoke optimistically despite Darcy's declaration, "but I have gotten close. And I hear that Major General Artois is prodigiously skilled at billiards, so Darcy may be in for a humbling experience this evening."

"I daresay anything is possible, but we shall see who is humbled. For now, the speculations must rest as my present concern is greeting my sister properly. Excuse me."

Any additional comments on the subject were left unsaid by the entrance of the Continental travelers and Kitty's fiancé. The latter was somewhat inhibited in extending suitable greetings due to a glowing Katherine Bennet apparently soldered to his left arm and side! The Major General was clearly not disturbed by his clinging fiancée, everyone managing to bid him welcome and offer congratulations without deficiency.

With so many people clamoring to hug, extend cordial greetings, and report the past months events in one fell swoop, it was over an hour before Kitty and her betrothed were politely able to absent themselves for a stroll alone. The stroll, not surprisingly, quickly led to a secluded copse not too far from the house, whereupon Artois instantly drew Kitty in for an embrace and thorough kiss.

"I have missed you terribly," she whispered, once able to use her mouth for speaking. "Two weeks apart is far too long. Every time you leave I fear never seeing you again!"

"And yet each time we part I always return. Do I not, my lovely Kitty? You must learn to have faith."

"I have complete faith in you, truly I do, Randall. But…"

He halted her with another kiss, a soft one that soon left her lips to travel tenderly across her face while he murmured. "No doubts, kitten. I have waited patiently all my life for you. Fate wills us to be together, so what is there to fear?" He expected no answer, not that Kitty could formulate a negative emotion while her betrothed was kissing her.

The romantic part of Major General Artois's nature would forever wish he could tell their children that he fell madly in love with their mother when they met in the darkened library during Colonel Fitzwilliam's marriage to Lady Simone Fotherby. Alas, this would be an untruth.

The fact is that they spoke for a few more minutes, laughed over their circumstances, and then recognized that the risk of being caught alone was too great. So they discreetly exited the library and rejoined the assembled guests with renewed spirits. Kitty was introduced to Major General Artois's father and two brothers, military men all, conversing politely until individual duties to family separated them. Aside from warm glances across the crowded room, Kitty and Randall would share no additional words that day. Before either could digest their impressions or the impact of the encounter, the day was over and they had gone their separate ways.

In the three weeks that followed, Major General Artois would think about Miss Bennet from time to time. He admitted that she had struck a chord within him, her wittiness and beauty intensely intriguing, and was honest when he told her that she was one of life's glories. Meeting her had been a pleasure and he contemplated seeking her out, but decided that boldly appearing upon the doorstep of Darcy House was inappropriate. He felt no fervency over the encounter, not out of a negative response to her, but rather because of his natural inclination.

General Artois had almost given up on his son. The father of seven, widowed since the youngest was only five years, was in many respects like Mrs. Bennet in that he keenly felt the tremendous responsibility to ensure his offspring were safely married. Aside from the purely selfish desire to be surrounded by grandchildren, he wanted his sons and daughters to find the joy of steady companionship that he had experienced with the departed Mrs. Artois. To this end, he had succeeded with all but his third child, Randall.

Like all the five Artois boys, Randall had joined the military, displaying a subtle mind, sharp intellect, and reckless bravery. He rose fast in his chosen career and already outranked his two older brothers. General Artois was immeasurably proud but remained baffled by his son's personality and outlook on life. Randall had endeavored to explain his feelings on the subject of life and marriage to his father on numerous occasions, but it was futile.

It was difficult for Randall to articulate because he did not comprehend his odd peace either. All he knew is that from a young age he had looked at life as something that largely passed by with minimal control on his part. Some would call him a fool, and maybe they were partially correct, but Randall preferred to see it as a peaceful reliance on something greater than him. He did not necessarily attribute it to God, although he was willing to accept that probability, but rather to a serene trust in destiny unfolding as it was meant to be.

Melancholy never afflicted him nor did great passion. Nothing riled him. This steady temperament contributed to his success as a soldier and officer. As for women, the same complacency ruled. He enjoyed women, in every way one can, but strong emotions did not exist. The perfect gentleman he was, treating them with kindness and respect, but easily able to walk away.

This detachment might have bothered him except that from his earliest forays into the world of women, he had known, simply known, that there was a woman out there just perfect for him. Thus he proceeded to amble through life, advancing in his career, amusing himself with friends and family and the occasional lover, all while confidently believing that *she* would fall into his lap when the proper time came.

Therefore, he was not remotely surprised when he rounded a corner onto Bond Street and nearly physically bumped into Miss Kitty Bennet. Again. She blushed becomingly but demonstrated the charm that he recalled from their wedding introduction. The conversation was brief, both remarking on the humor in both encounters involving nearly plowing into each other, and he seized the opportunity to ask if he could call upon her.

Within a month of frequent social interactions Randall was in love and had not the slightest doubt that Katherine Bennet was the woman fate or God or whatever had been preparing for him. His entire family adored her, his father so relieved to see his reluctant son clearly in the throes of love that he would have blessed the union no matter what her background!

Kitty, however, struggled with her emotions. The joy she felt with Randall Artois was intense, but the wounds from her previous romantic misfortune intruded upon her complete happiness. Her heart was thawing, but fear of further pain and disappointment made it difficult for her to trust fully.

Randall sensed her reserve and patiently persevered with no demands placed upon her fragile shoulders. He never pushed for an explanation, and when she finally revealed her previous heartbreak, Randall interpreted her disclosure as a positive development and his heart soared. Of course, he also wanted to dash off and beat Mr. Falke to a pulp for hurting his Kitty and then extend profuse thanks to the idiot for allowing such a treasure to slip through his fingers!

He did neither, naturally. Instead he trusted in the familiar serenity that ruled his life, knowing without the tiniest doubt that Miss Bennet would someday be his wife. He offered friendship only, kept the depths of his senti-ments controlled within his heart, and allowed their relationship to advance in small increments toward the goal he knew was inevitable. When the summons came to leave for an extended deployment, he was not disturbed. He was granted permission by Mr. Bennet to write to Miss Bennet via her father while he was away, confident that fate was playing a part in their unusual courtship.

The restrained tears in Kitty's eyes when they said their good-byes were pleasing. As he hoped, the separation with frequent letters filled with details of his daily life and humorous ramblings allowed her love to blossom. Her trust in his steadfastness grew as his correspondence never wavered, his voiced affections never diminished, his devotion to her never waned, and his respect never faltered.

When he returned to London after months away and trials within their separation, his reception was more than he could have dreamed of. The self-possession employed to prevent launching into his arms the second he walked through the door did not inhibit radiant joy from infusing her face. Major General Randall Artois had never been so happy. Less than a week later he proposed; his happiness lifted to rapture when she accepted. With the date set, Major General Artois anticipated the future with the same calm assurance that had been a comfort all his life.

Until, that is, he kissed her for the first time.

He had never doubted the passion lurking inside Kitty, even during the early months of their friendship when she was emotionally guarded. She was too alive, too bubbly not to have the potential for wantonness. That natural aspect of marriage was important to him and he considered Kitty's animation as another positive sign.

Then, the day of their engagement, after the congratulations were exhausted, he finally found a moment to be alone with his betrothed. They were only in the small garden at Longbourn and his only intention was to steal a chaste kiss. And in the end that is all it was. A slow, regulated, closed mouth kiss with their hands clasped together between their bodies.

Randall was utterly shaken by the sensations provoked! He was far from an innocent, knowing the joy of a woman's touch from a relatively young age, but *never* had it felt like this. And that was merely a kiss! In the six weeks since, she had grown bolder, while he grew increasingly rattled. His innate patience had deserted him to be replaced by vivid images of them together, teetering restraint, and an aching yearning to possess her. Every ounce of energy went into dampening his need and the physical arousal experienced nearly all the time—this from a Major General well into his thirties!

Staying away for two weeks had been a choice made to curb his passion and regain clarity. Yet before a handful of hours passed he realized the danger was worse than ever.

He leaned against the wide tree trunk with Kitty weakly sagging onto his chest, her breasts agreeably squeezed to the point of nearly spilling out of her décolletage. Discipline learned over years of military service was harshly brought to bear to avoid plundering her body right there and then.

Suddenly the wisdom of whisking her away seemed poor indeed. She engaged his lips forcefully in a kiss more intense than he intended and grazed her fingernails over his scalp while running through his hair. He groaned and his knees weakened in response. Then, God help him, she pressed her entire body onto his with a wiggle he assumed was unconscious, although maybe not, targeting a certain part of his anatomy that definitely did not need to be encouraged at this point.

Fire radiated in a piercing arc from groin to every other part of his body, a fierce growl emitted as he deepened the kiss far beyond what her innocence deserved. He grasped onto her bottom, every sense of decency gone in blinding surges of desire, holding fast with the dim hope that pressure would alleviate the painful need.

He was wrong, of course. But before he could assimilate that fact, and before morality and gentlemanly behavior restored a modicum of lucidity, she started rocking her hips and releasing soft gasps into his mouth. Randall stiffened, hands stilling where they held her derriere, surprise startling him into coherency. In all his struggles it never occurred to him to consider that she might be feeling the same uncontrollable passions.

Bursting with delight, he shoved the final vestiges of gentlemanly concern away and decided if giving her this gift eased her ache for him, he would happily comply. He readjusted his hips, one hand still cupping her bottom to aid her unsure movements with subtle guidance while the other lifted one leg over his waist, and met her writhing with counter-pressure. So lost was he in observing the beauty of her impassioned face, listening to her pants and moans, and absorbing her shudders of release that his throbbing need was momentarily forgotten.

She sagged into his arms and he held her tight, hands caressing over her back as her trembling ebbed and breathing normalized. He whispered into her hair, "I love you, kitten. Always. You astound me with your innocent needs and trust. I am honored by your faith, my respect and love stronger each day."

"That was… amazing," she interrupted his assurances, lifting to stare boldly into his eyes. "Better than I imagined or have felt in my dreams of you. And I know this only scratches the surface of how it will be when we are completely together."

Randall's eyes widened with astonishment. "You… imagine us? Dream of us… together?"

"Does this shock you, Major General?"

Her satisfied smile and husky timbre sent fresh jolts of desire through his body, making speech difficult for several moments. Then he grinned lasciviously and pressed her into his swollen groin. "I am surprised I suppose, but pleasantly so. I want you badly, but did not anticipate the same in return. I am not sure what to say, Kitty, other than that I love you so much it hurts."

"Your misery can end soon if you wish, Major General. I will be staying at Netherfield for a few nights at the behest of Georgiana. We have so much to catch up on. But once that is completed, I could, well"—her eyes lowered, a blush spreading over her cheeks—"it would be easy to slip into your room."

"No," he wheezed, swallowing the lump in his throat and willing his brain to lead rather than his overactive libido. "No, Kitty. God help me, I have never wanted anyone more than I want you right now, right this very second. The thought of you being in the same house with me, abed, in nightclothes…" He paused, looking away from her lustrous eyes and face still radiating with sexual heat. "Quite frankly I think it may well be more than I can bear. Have pity! Do not tempt me further. As it is I will need to drink myself into a stupor at the pub tonight to prevent banging your door down."

"I like that vision. So manly and romantic."

"Are you enjoying my suffering, Miss Bennet?"

"I am offering you relief from your suffering, Major General, as well as mine. This"—she pressed against his straining groin, Randall groaning and buckling slightly—"was not enough for me and it was no help to you at all." Then she grew serious, the teasing lilt gone from her voice as she clasped his face in her hands. "I am tired of waiting. I want to be your wife now, Randall, not a week from now."

"We have waited this long. What are a few more days?"

"An eternity."

They stared at each other. Kitty's eyes were firm and resolute. Randall's were a bit wild. His will was wavering, badly, and her next words did not help his stability.

"You believe in fate. Fate brought us together. Fate kept us faithful to each other while separated. Fate has now brought me into your bedroom, so to speak. How can we ignore fate after she has been right all along?"

"I will lock my door," he offered feebly.

But Kitty just smiled, lifting on tiptoes to kiss him slowly, after whispering, "No you won't."

And he knew she was correct.

CHAPTER NINE

Mysteries of Love

GEORGIANA'S SOFT KNOCK UPON the door was answered with a rushing swing before her knuckles finished rapping. In less than a heartbeat she was gathered into Kitty's arms.

"I tarried, but you are dressed for bed and have completed your toilette, I see." Georgiana laughed, pulling away although still affectionately clasping Kitty's shoulders.

"Faster than you, Miss Darcy. If I was not so anxious to gossip and be a silly girl for one night I may have snuck out to see my handsome fiancé!"

"In your bedclothes? How utterly shocking and improper, Miss Bennet. Fortunate that he is out with the men presently so you could not act upon your scandalous inclinations."

If only you knew, Kitty thought, laughing gaily at Georgiana's tease. The two linked arms and walked to the sofa before the fire. "It was only a momentary thought. I am not so shameless as to risk Mr. Darcy's censure or my fiancé's displeasure," she said nonchalantly.

"I rather doubt your fiancé would be displeased to see his beloved in her bedclothes. Quite the opposite sentiment is more likely the case."

"My! Listen to who speaks of intimate sentiments!"

"It is the natural way of such things. Although hopefully your trousseau consists of nightwear a bit more stylish than that," she indicated Kitty's robe of thickly quilted velvet with a high collared and plain cotton gown worn underneath.

"Oh my, yes! Mama nearly fainted when seeing the pretty, lacy slips Lizzy gifted me. I daresay I never would have braved purchasing such garments. Yes indeed, even I blushed and demurred!" Kitty asserted at the unbelieving expression on Georgiana's face.

"It might, therefore, be wise to don the nightgowns for a few nights before your honeymoon so you will not be too uncomfortable with your new husband."

"I have taken your wise advice ere you rendered it, dear Georgiana. I too pray that prior application will benefit. And as to being uncomfortable in regards to new husbands, my experienced sister has been preparing me. Her advice is far better than Mama has given, I am relieved to say."

"Well, this is profitable information. I will know who to ask when time to acquire my wedding trousseau and prepare for a wedding night."

"Oh really? So tell me, Georgie, who is he?"

"Who is who?" Georgiana calmly bent to pour tea into two cups, only the faintest smile and rosy cheeks belying her aloofness.

"Some gorgeous Italian, I imagine," Kitty went on dreamily. "Or perhaps a Frenchman with dark eyes and a poetic accent. I shall divine the truth in time!"

"You are ridiculous, but I have missed you terribly despite your penchant for over dramatics. I can assure there is not a single Italian or Frenchman to tell you of." She handed the cup to Kitty with a sincere smile. "Two spoons of sugar and a spot of cream as you like it."

"Oh, Georgiana! It has been far too long! We have so much to catch up on and so little time before I shall be parted from you."

"And so happily parted that you will undoubtedly not think upon me for weeks. Or at least I would hope your mind consumed with pleasanter thoughts." Again that impish lilt that had Kitty searching her friend's face in wonder, but Georgiana continued before Kitty could inquire. "That is why I invited you to stay with me here at Netherfield. Not for clandestine engagements with fiancés, no matter how handsome. I shall be watching you, Miss Bennet, so control your impulses!" She sternly shook her finger at Kitty, who pretended to bite the digit, bringing on a fresh case of giggles. "You must share all that I missed. Letters, even those as diligent and comprehensive as yours, do not tell all."

"My letters must have been painfully dull compared to your adventures, more than half of which I am sure you never enlightened me of."

"Absolutely not! Letters from home staved off my homesickness, which did threaten to overwhelm at times no matter what adventures I was having."

"Ah, to see such exotic places as Paris and Rome." Kitty sighed.

"You will travel far and wide in due time, Kitty. Major General Artois is a man of the world and financially prosperous. He will delight in squiring his beautiful bride to military galas at every capitol of the world."

"When he is not engaged in armed battle or getting himself wounded, you mean."

Georgiana clasped her friend's hand, squeezing to comfort. "Was it so horrible? When he was injured and beyond your reach and knowledge? I knew you kept it light for my sake, which you should not have, but I could discern your distress within the lines and words."

Kitty shook her head, smiling slightly to offset the threatening tears. "*He* made light of it so I endeavored to do the same. And of course he is now as hale as can be." Then she released a short laugh, meeting Georgiana's gaze and speaking with her typical humor. "Is it not the height of irony that after years of swooning and dreaming of soldiers in their smart red coats, imagining the life as an officer's wife one of honor and dazzle, that I never thought about what a military man actually *does* for a living? And now I have secured an officer, much to my mother's endless verbal delight, and I am terrified amid the exalting happiness!"

"Life definitely has a way of surprising us, I will concur."

"There it is again! That inflection of something more behind your careful words. Georgiana Darcy, you must spill all!"

"Well, if *all* is on the agenda for tonight perhaps we should call for more tea and cakes and get started posthaste!" Georgiana laughed giddily, every trace of reserve erased. "Very well, you have gleaned my hidden secret thoroughly for one who has not seen me in months. I had no idea I was so transparent! Although Lizzy was peering at me strangely, so I must conclude that love is indeed visible upon the skin as the poets declare."

"Aha! I knew it! Who is he? Where is he now? And does he have a most marvelous accent and speak phrases of love in mellifluous French?"

"Stop! One question at a time! Our discussions must have order or we will merely be talking one upon the other. My story of romance needs to wait until Lizzy arrives. No sense repeating it all twice. You tell me more of your courtship with the dashing Major General."

"But that is unfair! You know of my romance and yet I am to die of curiosity waiting for Lizzy?"

"Patience is a virtue," Georgiana piously intoned. "However, I would not wish for my dear friend to *die*. That would be most discourteous of me. So here, I shall give you a name and you must content yourself with that." She paused, dramatic flair always a subtle Darcy trait, then spoke with the rich tones of one violently in love, "Mr. Sebastian Butler."

Kitty gasped. "The composer! Truly? But I thought he was merely a friend? You were so specific. Oh my! This is a tale indeed! How did you…?"

"A hint only, I promised, to prevent your perishing!" She laughed, clasping onto Kitty's hand, her smile radiant. "It is a fabulous tale, Kitty, and I shall do it justice. But first, you. We must somehow manage to cover the past months apart before dawn. Major General Artois would be most vexed with me if his bride approached the altar with purple circles under her eyes from lack of sufficient sleep!"

"If I must sit in suspense I shall, Miss Darcy. But so you know, it is torturing me!"

"Your pain will diminish as you wax eloquent about your true love. Go on. When I left for Europe you were deeply in love, we all knew it, except for you, foolish girl. Tell me of his letters. I wish for details!"

And with a great deal of giggling and exclamations, Kitty told of her strange reluctance to trust a man who, by all outward appearances, was wonderful. She read a few of his letters aloud, having brought them to Netherfield for just this purpose. She told of how her heart gradually opened while he was away, finally admitting to the fullness of her love when the message arrived saying he had been wounded. The agony of waiting, of not knowing, was terrible, but it had served to strengthen her resolve and secure her heart.

"What a difference just a year makes," she said introspectively. "When Mr. Falke abandoned me I thought the pain more than possible for a heart to bear. My affections for Mr. Falke were real, I know that. I may be fickle to a degree, but not so nonsensical as to fabricate emotions where none exist. Certainly I never experienced an attachment to a man before him. Yet I can now comprehend the variance in my emotions between the two. The heartache and vision of Mr. Falke's face are detached, whereas my Randall is firmly entrenched."

"My dearest Kitty, dare I say how altered you are from the girl I met three years ago without offending?" Georgiana spoke with tones of warmth and pride, Kitty blushing at the recollection of how frivolously she once approached life. Lydia's influence greatly attributed to her shallow attitude, as the stabilizing influence of Georgiana Darcy had positively aided her comportment. Nevertheless, traumas of life and passage of time were the main contributions to forming the woman who was days away from being a wife.

"No offense, Georgiana. It is simply the truth. Dare I say that we have both altered over these years of our friendship? Tribulations of the heart proficiently temper one, do they not?"

"Indeed. Oh yes, Kitty, I know precisely what you mean."

"Oh! Of course you do! And how thoughtless of me to forget! Foolish, scattered Kitty yet rears her vapid head! Please accept my apologies, my friend. I speak of past affairs that are sure to revive thoughts of Mr. Wickham, even though I know you have asserted no lingering affliction, and compound the insult by brainlessly forgetting to inform you of a matter that personally affects you!"

"Kitty, you must calm yourself. I assure you once again that Mr. Wickham's name and memory afflict me not in the least. Surely you must know this? After all, if you can so readily distance your emotions after a year, how much easier must it be for me after five?" Georgiana laughed, shaking her head at her distraught friend. "Besides, I was not referring to Mr. Wickham. In fact, that man did not enter my mind! You are silly at times, my dear. Yes, still quite ridiculous!"

"If not Mr. Wickham then I am doubly curious to hear of your romantic entanglements. I shall accede your label of silly and ridiculous gladly in hopes that it will not distress you too greatly when I report that my sister Lydia and her husband will be arriving any day now. The family was informed not two days ago that they planned to attend my wedding. Frankly, most of us wish it were not to be, although it will be nice to see Lydia after so long a separation. Are you distressed overly, my dear?"

Kitty's inquiry was met with slightly raised brows but no other sign of agitation. "No, I am not distressed. I am sure it will be moderately uncomfortable, but then again I rather doubt it requisite for me to interact with either of them, is it?"

"I see no reason, other than simple politeness if encountered in the crowd. They will be dwelling at Longbourn and the plan is to keep mingling to a minimum."

"Then you see? All is well. I refuse to allot Mr. Wickham the power to unbalance me. I, like you, have grown stronger and now have a relationship worthy of prideful boasting and happiness. Agreed?"

"Oh, yes, Georgiana! The depths are so different! With Randall everything is different and vastly superior. His touch and kiss, even his eyes upon me are intense as never dreamed or experienced. Dare I say he is perfect without having you laugh at me?"

"No, because I understand that you do not mean he is 'perfect' in that his character possesses no faults, as we all have faults. Rather you mean that he is perfect for you. Your match, I suppose. Once again, I know precisely what you mean."

"Again an allusion to your romance. I am bursting with intrigue!"

"Do not burst as yet, please! Finish your tale, or rather bring it to the present as the story has no end."

"Being with Randall is a joy unlike anything ever felt, to be sure. That alone convinces me of my love. But the true test was his constancy. I gave so little in the way of a promise, and yet he persevered. Always patient and not demanding. He told me later, after our engagement, that he was certain of his affections and our future after a month!" She shook her head. "I still have difficulty believing that. I was downright rude at times! I was so sure that he would disappoint and wound that I... well, I suppose I was testing him. Or attempting to guard my heart by pushing him away before he burrowed in too deep, only then to have him reject me."

They were silent for a spell, each dwelling upon their romances with the bizarre twists and chaotic emotions that accompany falling in love.

"Love is a wonderful emotion and state of being," Georgiana said, breaking the silence, "but hazards are found within."

"Indeed. I would not wish for anyone other than my Randall, and to have discovered the secret of loving someone and knowing they love you is indescribable. It is well worth the risks from vulnerability!"

At Georgiana's urging, Kitty completed her romantic tale, replete with detailed information. Laughter was constant, questions frequent, and teasing interspersed. Kitty reached the point of repeating herself and lapsing into saccharine reiterations of Major General Artois's attributes when another knock on the door announced the arrival of Lizzy.

"My youngest son would choose this night to resist slumber and suffer a bellyache. Have I missed all the romantic disclosures?" Lizzy also wore comfortable sleeping attire, plopping onto a plush chair and pouring a cup of tea before curling her legs and settling in for a lengthy session of girl talk.

"Not all," Kitty answered her sister. "I related my story in the fullest, all of which you know, Lizzy. I fear I was on the brink of lapsing into maudlin verse and embarrassing namby-pambyisms since Miss Darcy refused to reveal her romance until you arrived."

"As I suspected!" Lizzy leaned forward, gazing intently at Georgiana, who was blushing profusely. "Indeed, we must hear all. Yet before we embark into what will undoubtedly be a delightful topic with abundant joy and laughter, I regret I must insert an element of disturbance. It is best to have it over and done with, unless, of course, Kitty has already spoken of Mr. Wickham?"

"She did," Georgiana answered with a nod, "and I assured her, as I shall assure you, that I am not unduly disturbed. Rather I am pleased for the Bennets, who surely have missed Mrs. Wickham all these years. It shall be strange to see Mr. Wickham, uncomfortable, I am certain, and I am glad of the warning, but I refuse to allow that man to discompose me."

"Well spoken," Lizzy declared. "We are united in our resolve to bear it bravely and delight in Kitty's happiness."

"How did Mr. Darcy accept the news?"

"He was told by Papa, already assimilating the fact prior to my speaking of it. He was calm as typical of his character, but expressed distrust of Wickham's motives." Lizzy shrugged. "I fear William cannot ever be indifferent where Wickham is concerned. He will be watchful and prudent. I intend to avoid him utterly, even if William had not ordered me to do so."

Georgiana laughed at that; the expression on Lizzy's face at being "ordered" to do anything, even something she agreed to be perfectly logical, was priceless. Still, Georgiana knew that her brother's animosity toward his once childhood playmate was intense and a result of more than her foolish near-elopement with Wickham, so she did not flippantly disregard his response to the news.

She never had solved the puzzle of their strained relationship, having no idea there was an unpleasant history until after the events at Ramsgate. Her childhood memories of Wickham were pleasant; hence she was so easily duped by the scoundrel. Darcy's protection of his sister included not shattering her happy thoughts of a charming young man who treated her with wit and humor and kindness. In retrospect that decision was unwise, but chosen with her serenity in mind, Darcy never suspecting that Wickham would have an opportunity to hurt Georgiana. The ugly confrontation between Darcy and Wickham at Ramsgate left no doubt of their past involving serious incidents, but her brother refused to enlighten her.

"If William feels that strongly after the passing of several years, I can only bow to his wise counsel." Georgiana smiled at a frowning Kitty, squeezing her friend's hand. "Besides, I am sure he will behave with William and Richard glowering at him! Surely he is merely acquiescing to Mrs. Wickham's desire to visit her family. And it is a wedding, after all! Love and rejoicing to high degrees shall erase ill will."

"Indeed you are correct, Georgiana," Lizzy firmly declared, her voice cheery and light. "And, speaking of love, it is time for you to enlighten us as to when you fell in love with the eminently worthy and supremely handsome Mr. Butler!"

Georgiana gaped at her sister. "How did you figure *that* out?"

"When Madeline mentioned Lady Warrow and Mr. Butler traveling across the Channel and into London as part of your group, you nearly jumped out of your skin. Then you reddened and glanced at William. So, Mr. Butler it is? He is the fortunate man to steal your heart?"

Lizzy and Kitty were grinning, Georgiana flushing further at their attention. Or perhaps it was the mention of Mr. Butler that caused her heart to flutter and heat to rise. Whatever the direct inducement, she was concerned about one point. "Lizzy, do you think William suspects anything?"

Lizzy blinked in surprise then harrumphed. "William? Are you serious? Your brother is unskilled in the subtle indicators of romantic sentiment, bless his adorable heart. He may catch on in a few weeks if you persist in growing dreamy-eyed whenever Mr. Butler's name is mentioned. Or perhaps if Mr. Butler were here bestowing hand caresses and adoring gazes he might draw a conclusion!"

"Oh, Lizzy! You are too harsh!" Kitty exclaimed amid the laughter.

"Of course I am teasing and exaggerating. But Georgie knows the truth of it. But why the secrecy?"

Georgiana shook her head emphatically. "No secrecy, I assure you. Aunt and Uncle, Richard and Simone as well, know of our affections and wishes. Uncle and Richard, as temporary guardians, have given blessings and consent for Mr. Butler to court. It was Sebastian—Mr. Butler, I should say—who requested he properly speak with my brother and formalize our desires."

"Why did he not accompany you here and speak to Mr. Darcy now?"

"It is your wedding, Kitty. He did not feel it was appropriate. And as much as I miss him and wish for our future to be secured, I have to admit I craved time devoted to my family. I have missed all of you so very much, especially my brother and you, Lizzy."

"William has missed you as well, dear. I agree it is judicious to focus on one romance at a time! However, surely you do not fear your brother's displeasure at your choice?"

"No! Oh, how could he? Mr. Butler is a wonderful choice, even if I did not love him fiercely. Nevertheless, I can foresee William being a tiny bit dismayed to have his 'baby' sister return after months away with a fiancé in tow!"

They all three laughed at that truth, Lizzy breathlessly responding, "He will merely be surprised. Not dismayed in the least. He was impressed with Mr. Butler's manner and talent when we met at the ball last year. What I am curious of is when your heart was captured. You never hinted of an attraction beyond friendship in any of your letters, deceptive girl! Nor do I recall a particular interest when he played for us, other than enthusiasm for his music. So my curiosity is piqued most high."

"Yes indeed, it is time! Your story now, Georgiana!"

Georgiana's dramatic tale of convoluted misconceptions, blossoming love, a classic lover's triangle, and triumphant mutual accord entertained for a long while. Fresh tea was requested, the sugared cakes devoured, and the fire stirred twice as they laughed and conversed. The night passed the chiming of midnight ere they exhausted the subjects of love and future affinity enough for one sitting.

❧

Major General Randall Artois was determined to get rip-roaring drunk. So drunk that he would need to be carried into the house and poured onto his bed. Inebriated to the point of complete unconsciousness so that even if the house caught on fire he would be unaware. Since reaching such a state of utter intoxication was a task accomplished numerous times in the past, there was every reason to think it could happen again.

So why was it he barely sipped his way through two brandies?

When that plan failed, he thought maybe he could pick a fight with someone. A rousing brawl would either, one, get him knocked unconscious, or two, land him in jail for the night. No better place to cool simmering lust than in jail. He knew that from past experience as well.

But damned if every last man in the pub was so bloody *nice* that insulting one of them or hauling off and punching for no reason was not an option. And if a small voice inside his head reminded him that those issues had never bothered him before when he felt the urge for a friendly tussle, he told it to bugger off!

Then he prayed that their return to Netherfield would be a quiet one. Everyone would be asleep at one in the morning—everyone, right? They could tiptoe up the stairs to their designated rooms with no one the wiser. Of course, none of the other men had any problem with getting rip-roaring drunk. Not even Mr. Daniels! No amount of shushing stopped the off-key singing and heavy steps, no amount of leading kept them from bumping into every last hall obstacle. It was bedlam and several of the ladies emerged to assist in pouring the drunken menfolk into their beds. He apologized profusely, stating over and over that he had tried to keep them quiet, but the fact that his heart fell when Miss Bennet was not one of the ladies exiting her bedchamber, in her nightwear, revealed his hypocrisy.

An hour later he paced in his room. He had tried to sleep, for about five minutes. He downed another brandy, not that three would have any effect on his level of consciousness. His feet veered toward the door more times than he could count, but whether that was with the intent to lock it—which he had not done—or exit it to skulk down the hall he was not sure.

Oh, who are you fooling, Artois? The only reason you have not gone to her is because you do not know where her room is!

Maybe she does not know where your room is.

And that thought brought him to an abrupt halt. He stared into space, admitting in that moment that he *wanted* her to come. Had counted on it. And now he felt bereft. Another week did seem an eternity of yearning for her while in her presence and going mad with desire.

"God you are pathetic," he muttered, "and you are not a gentleman."

"Yes, you are. A gentleman that is."

He whirled around, his heart skipping several beats but only partially from fright. It was relief, a dizzying relief that overwhelmed until he thought he would collapse right there on the floor at her feet.

She stood near the door, it shut and locked behind her, wearing a long robe of blue that covered her from neck to toes, yet she was so beautiful he could not breathe. He had never seen her hair down and that alone was enough to fan the flames of his ardor to levels never attained before. For a brief second he wondered if he could survive this night. Sex was one thing, something he had done countless times. Making love was a new experience and he prayed—seriously this time—that he was capable of pleasing her while attending to keeping his heart beating during the ecstasy he was now beginning to suspect would supplant anything previously known.

And just as it dawned on him that not once had he honestly contemplated not being with her tonight, before they were legally wed, and the guilt flickered into existence, she stepped closer to him.

She was smiling. She was calm. She was beautiful beyond words to describe. And before she spoke he knew she was his, just as he was already hers, and that today or a week hence their hearts would feel no different.

"You did not lock the door."

"My door will never be locked to my wife."

Kitty smiled wider, dazing him with the glory of her, and started to loosen the thick belt holding the robe together.

"Wait!" She glanced up, and he could tell she was prepared to argue, but he crossed the distance, taking her hands into his and bringing them to his lips. He held her eyes, slowly lowering her hands to dangle at her sides and reached to the belt. "Let me."

A moment later, the robe heaped forgotten at her feet, Randall was again assailed with doubts as to how he would ever make it through this night. His heart beat erratically, although how that was possible when surely every ounce of blood in his body was pooled below his waist he did not know.

She wore a gown of sheer white satin edged with lace and ribbons gathered at all the correct places to accent her lush figure, her golden-brown hair a cloud of curls falling as a veil over her shoulders and back. She smelled of peaches, the scent rising from her creamy skin enticingly so that despite his paralysis and longing to simply examine her figure, the hunger to discover if she tasted like peaches overruled.

And she did. His lips and tongue skimmed over her neck, dining on the succulence that was her bare skin. She was the sweetest ambrosia imaginable. He ran his hands over her arms, pulling her closer as he nibbled across her delicate collarbone.

She inhaled sharply, trembling with the sensations educed and sagging into his arms. "Do not worry, I have you. Hold on to me," he whispered, and she obeyed, snaking her arms over his shoulders to lock behind his neck. Pleasure shot like a bolt of electricity through his body, but he could not discern if it was the feel her arms and hands caressing his bare neck or the softness of her bosom under his mouth. Probably both.

Savage desire gripped him. With a hoarse groan he crushed her to his body, initiating an uncontrollable kiss that bordered on feral. Amazingly, she did not flinch, returning the embrace and kiss with the same ferociousness, a muted growl communicating she reciprocated. His shirt was yanked out of his waistband, her hands plunging underneath to stroke up his back, Randall gasping at the flames streaking across his skin and into the marrow of his bones. Each touch of her hands was exquisite to a degree that defied logic. Pleasure, desire, bliss, lust, and more were felt to a level unprecedented, and they had barely done more than kiss!

With herculean effort he tore away from her lips, respirations ragged and hands rough on her elbows to still the caressing that was about to shatter his remaining wits. He fought for control, or a semblance thereof, eyes closed and forehead resting on hers.

"I need a moment," he croaked, "or I will toss you onto that bed and ravage you like a beast. God, Kitty! What you do to me!"

"I am sorry."

"No, no! Please do not be sorry." He opened his eyes. "It is my problem to deal with, not yours. I should be the one in control, leading you gently and not rushing in like a bull in his first rut! Yet this is new to me, how I want you and how much I love you. I have never done this before."

"Oh! I did not… That is, I thought you had, well, experience." She blushed to her toes—he knew because he was looking at them and thinking that even her toes excited him—and tried to step away.

He stayed her retreat, clasping his hands around her face, smiling and chuckling. "*This* is new to me," he repeated, brushing a kiss to her lips. "Being with *the* woman I love. Being with my wife. Kitty, I know now that I have never made love before this, before you, and it terrifies me and fills me with awe and joy at the same time. I confess to feeling a bit lost and overwhelmed by my emotions."

"Then we are on equal footing, except that I have no fear of you or our emotions and passion." And before he realized what she was doing, the satin gown slithered down her body to join the robe, rendering him speechless and transfixed.

"You are beautiful," he finally managed, his fingertips lightly sliding from her shoulder blades down to the outer swell of her breasts, circling. "Perfect, absolutely perfect." He cupped each breast, their fullness heavenly, filling his large hands and spilling over. He brushed his thumbs over her nipples, her gasp and instant hardening deeply satisfying. "Yes, perfect. I bet they taste like peaches." And he bent his head, taking one into his mouth while continuing to rub the other.

She was wondrously receptive, her ardor affected by every touch and kiss. To his amazement he suddenly did not feel so rushed. He craved exploring her body, inch by glorious inch. He reveled in witnessing her awakening to passion.

For the first time he experienced rapture from nuzzling a woman's breast, ecstasy from stroking the velvet skin over a curved hip, and jubilation from lithe legs squeezing his waist. Her hands on his chest was unparalleled euphoria, her mouth on his nipple delirious, her nails grazing his buttocks unimaginable bliss, and his name panted into his ear an angelic chorus.

And when he finally entered her, making her his wife, the words to describe how he felt did not exist. It was new. Everything about making love with his Kitty was unique. She was paradise on earth, holding him tightly and riding the wave with him at every point.

Kitty stayed with him until well after the sun rose. It was risky, they knew, but the pain of separating was not something they looked forward to. They did not sleep. They cuddled and talked, explored each other's bodies, and made love again.

"I hope I have not hurt you too much?" he asked, eyes scanning the figure now illuminated by the rising sun and revealed as more glorious than in soft candlelight.

"I may be a bit stiff, but nothing a hot bath will not cure. You were very gentle," she assured, kissing the frown away, "not that you always have to be."

"Keep talking like that and I will never let you leave my bed."

"Oh please, not that!"

He laughed, nuzzling her neck. "Once we are married and I do not have to let you go I won't."

"Part of your devious plan, is it?"

"It is. And now that I know how incredible it is to love you, I look forward to it even more. This night only whets my appetite, Kitty. I shall never, ever get enough of you!"

"I can tell." She slid her hand between their bodies, encircling the evidence of just how strong his appetite, Randall groaning loudly.

"Lord, woman! Have mercy! You need to leave before the house rouses, and I do not want to cause you pain with my uncontrollable lust."

"My only pain is in saying good-bye. Do not ask me to do that yet, please?"

How could a man passionately in love resist that? He did not, responding to her tug and rolling onto her body with a contented sigh that rapidly turned to muffled moans followed by stifled shouts sometime later.

Before he opened the door to check the hallway, he carefully inspected her for any overt signs of their tryst just in case she was caught outside her room. "Do not worry," she whispered, "I am not stamped with a sign that says, 'She has been making love all night long.'"

"I am not so sure. You do look properly ravished." He pinned her against the door with an arm on either side of her body, leaning close but not touching. "I would doubt my abilities if you *did not* look properly ravished. But you should be safe enough, at least I hope." He caressed over her cheek. "No regrets, Kitty? Even if caught?"

"No regrets. And if I am caught then we can get married today, which would suit me just fine since then I would not have to leave you again tomorrow morning."

She lifted to kiss him, but he pulled away. "Are you sure that is wise? God knows I want you to come. Lord, I do not want you to leave now! By tonight I will be in a frenzy to hold you. But I can wait rather than risk…"

She interrupted with a kiss and then slipped under his arm, opening the door a crack to peer outside. "All clear. See you soon. I love you, Randall."

"I love you, my Kitty." But she was gone.

CHAPTER TEN
Brash Intrusion

AFTER KITTY LEFT HIS room Randall agonized for hours. Had she been seen? When Mr. Darcy did not come pounding on his door with pistol in hand he assumed she had safely reached her chambers. Then, despite her assurances, he worried that she would regret what they had shared, that once alone the guilt might overwhelm. He chastised himself for weakness, for being a rogue and taking advantage of a fragile female who trusted him to be a gentleman and leader. He started to doubt how passionate and receptive and willing she had been, twisting specific actions or words to emphasize his loutishness. When he finally walked into the breakfast room his nerves were seriously on edge.

She was there and turned instantly as if sensing his presence before he crossed the threshold. She smiled radiantly. In fact, her whole countenance was radiant, glowing, and breathtakingly beautiful. All of his doubts evaporated, leaving behind a rush of pure love and excruciating desire. So much for the idea that tasting of her delights would curb his hunger since it was tenfold what he had ever felt in her presence. He staggered from the assault, literally, Mr. Darcy instinctively grabbing his arm to steady.

"Hold up there, Major General. I did not think you drank all that much last night. The rest of us should be the unsteady ones. Personally, I wish someone would take pity and darken the sun."

Randall noted Darcy's pained grimace, collecting himself with a shake that Darcy again concluded was the by-product of excessive carousing.

The day passed in sedate activities. Most of the men were recuperating from varying degrees of indisposition as a result of their public house revelry so did not leave the drapery drawn rooms. The ladies embarked upon one long walk with the children scampering alongside, but also spent a fair portion of the afternoon chatting as they lounged in the spacious parlor. Disappearances in the latter hours of the afternoon were mostly for rejuvenating naps, Kitty especially needing to regain her strength for what she hoped was a second long night of passion.

She and Randall finagled a few minutes of alone time, both of them suffering acutely with the need to touch and kiss. By that evening, when the wedding party gathered in the Netherfield parlor awaiting the announcement for dinner, he could barely stand straight due to the churning sea of ardor wrecking havoc on his insides. But having his fiancée clutching his left arm and agreeably plastered against his side was wonderful in its own way. Plus, he was momentarily content to be surrounded by her family.

He was familiar with enormous family gatherings and delighted in the pleasing atmosphere of community and love prevailing even in this mixed group. This assembly, although reminiscent of the boisterous Artois collectives with all seventeen of his nieces and nephews loudly playing and dashing underfoot while the adults engaged in vibrant conversation, was far more refined.

There were children, but only five of them. Ethan Bingley, Alexander Darcy, and Hugh Pomeroy sat in the corner rolling a ball back and forth. They were under the watchful eye of Mrs. Geer, who held fourteen-month-old Deborah Daniels on her lap while the toddler avidly observed the boys at play. Harry Pomeroy, the eldest son of Lady Simone Fitzwilliam, was content as retriever for the frequent wayward ball, smiling and only slightly bossy in his instructions for proper ball aiming. The babies, Michael Darcy and Claudia Daniels, remained in the nursery with Mrs. Hanford.

The adults were scattered about the room, standing and sitting, but in a rough circle that focused on the centrally located sofas and chairs. Talk was animated and filled with laughter, but with an air of restraint and formality that was lacking with the Artois crowd. The event which brought them all to this place at this time may be the upcoming wedding of Major General Randall Artois and Miss Kitty Bennet, but for the present, the prime topic of conversation was the adventures of the Continental travelers.

"I know I could not definitively appoint a particular event or place as number one on a list of favorites," Georgiana spoke in her cultured tones. "The list of museums, fabulous gardens, beautiful castles and chateaus, picturesque rivers and lakes would be unending, I am certain, with a dozen fighting to inhabit the top five and none prevailing!"

"It becomes rather muddled after a time, does it not, Georgiana?" Lady Simone asked with a laugh.

"Indeed it does," Lady Matlock agreed, "and I have toured the various towns of Europe several times in my life. Perhaps that is why I now delight in visiting relatives and friends while on holiday abroad, as another garden or opera house is likely to overwhelm the cluttered section of my brain that stores such information."

"Personally I was content to stay in France, especially Paris," Colonel Fitzwilliam interjected. "It was wondrous to walk the streets so radically altered since I last walked them in the immediate aftermath of the war. There is yet a great deal of unrest and disquiet, but Louis XVIII and his Bourbon restorationists are establishing order and a functional constitution. Decazes is managing capably with a moderate approach that appears to please the populace, for the most part."

"Frankly I grew tired of the discussions. French politics are messy and boring since none can agree, and most revel in the argument with no true desire to conclude," Lord Matlock rumbled from his chair. "But then, that is the definition of all politics, post-Revolution France or England."

Laughter and nodding met that statement, Lady Matlock patting her spouse's hand as she spoke. "Precisely why we should let the topic drop for the present. I can debate politics when in the mood as ably as you, my lord husband, but would rather not do so now."

"As you wisely wish, Mother." Richard inclined his head in respect to his parents before turning a mischievous eye back toward Georgiana. "So, fair cousin, claiming a favorite may be impossible, but surely Paris itself stole your heart more than the other great cities?"

"Indeed it did," she replied levelly, only a hint of rosiness touching her cheeks. "The Conservatoire alone was adequate to cement love of Paris within my heart. However, Rome, Milan, and Florence equally intrigued. And not only for their beauty in landscape and music, as I discovered a surprising interest in the history." She smiled toward her brother, teasing as she continued. "You may be shocked, dear brother, that your lengthy discourses on ruins did penetrate my stubborn skull. Imagine my own amazement when the commentaries of the tour guides resonated and piqued my attention! There I was climbing over crumbled medieval remains searching for clues to the past."

Darcy laughed, bowing in mock approbation. Bingley visibly shuddered and groaned, speaking with exaggerated relief. "Thank goodness for miracles! Now you can haul your wife and sister on your excursions over dusty, moldy ruins and never pester me."

"It is a promise, Bingley. You are safe from here on."

"Well, I cannot claim that to be my favorite part, but it was not as painful as imagined, unless you count poor Uncle's sore feet."

"Not to worry, Georgiana dear. It was nothing days of languishing by the fire with a brandy in hand did not cure," Lord Matlock assured. "Personally, I would rather traverse over cultured lawns and well-tended pathways, such as the Borghese gardens. Hours in the serene atmosphere of the vivarium healed every ache."

"William, the Galleria Borghese was everything you declared it to be. I spent countless hours wandering the rooms, gazing in awe. We visited often, and it is not that large a museum compared to the Louvre especially, yet I failed in assimilating the full wealth of art and beauty. It touched me so." Georgiana shook her head, clasping Lizzy's hand. "Oh, Lizzy! You would have loved it! I thought of you so often. The gardens would have overwhelmed you."

"Indeed," Darcy offered, "the gardens are astounding and I daresay put Mr. Clark to shame. However, it is the marbles that I would most adore sharing with my wife. Bernini's works alone are worth the trip. My grandfather acquired one of his pieces, but I was not so fortunate when I traveled to Rome."

"I refuse to lament what I was unable to view," Lizzy said with a laugh. "I struggled with absorbing all the wonders I was gifted to canvass, much of the journey yet dreamlike, so am relieved to stage it gradually over my life."

"If you two can manage to space out the task of creating inhabitants for every empty bedchamber in Pemberley, you may be able to arrange another trip before the sculptures erode into dust, or whatever happens to marble."

"I believe, my dearest, that marble is nearly indestructible," Simone chastised her husband, Colonel Fitzwilliam winking at a blushing Lizzy before smirking at his expressionless cousin.

Lady Matlock smoothly intervened. "I delighted most in the gardens, I must confess. It was a popular locale for artists. The landscape and architecture offered an endless opportunity for sketching."

"Quite true. An additional trunk was required to haul the creations home."

"As if you were not delighted by Aunt's drawings, Uncle. Raved on and on, rightfully so."

"You do have an astounding talent, Lady Matlock, and I have not forgotten that you promised the Rotunda to me."

"Nor have I, Simone. As soon as it is framed, it is yours."

"The little ponds, rivers, and impressive lakes were arguably everywhere. I always thought of you, dear sister." Georgiana again squeezed Lizzy's hand. "I know how you adore the water."

"Adore?" Mrs. Bennet interjected with a nervous flutter. "One would think you half fish the way you immersed yourself in the pond every chance you got. Clumsy, Mr. Bennet would insist to help you avoid the thrashing you deserved, but I never believed that!"

"Indeed I was awkward and clumsy, Mama, as Papa declared. Never as graceful as other Bennet sisters I could name." Lizzy glanced to Jane, who blushed. "However, when it came to the pond it was simple rationality. It was hot and the water cools. Plus, it is fun to float and swim."

"We have a large pond near our family home in Berkshire," Major General Artois offered. "Two of my sisters were 'fish' same as you, Mrs. Darcy. They are both married with children now, but I am certain if possible would yet be daily swimming."

"And why should they not?" George Darcy asked. "Ridiculous notion. Sea bathing is acceptable, why not jumping naked into a lake as men do?"

"Gracious!" Mrs. Bennet murmured with a vigorous wave of her fan.

But Lizzy laughed aloud. "Oh, do not fear, Uncle! Not all ladies are as prim as you imagine. Let us merely say that Rowan Lake has been utilized from time to time, although I shall not elaborate on the bathing attire." Laughter rang out all around, even Darcy smiling at his wife's jest.

"Aunt Giana?" Alexander appeared at Georgiana's knees, arms extended. She gathered him into her embrace, nestling him onto her lap with a soft kiss on his crown.

Darcy's smile widened, voice tender as he spoke. "Did you practice your painting as well, Georgiana?"

"Sporadically. You know I am not so proficient or enamored with painting. Aunt taught me some and I did improve, but music was what drew me most." Her eyes grew dreamy. "The wealth of styles and compositions, arrays of instruments and grand orchestras, all unlike anything I have ever heard." She sighed, "It was wonderful."

"Georgiana paints beautifully," Lady Simone said. "But I believe her greatest advancement was in playing and in composing. You will be impressed, Mr. Darcy, at the music she has written."

"Indeed I know I shall. You must share your new compositions with us, Georgiana."

Georgiana hid her rosy cheeks in Alexander's curls. "I wrote nothing spectacular. Where some are inspired by nature to draw or paint, I was inspired to compose. But my skill is infantile compared to most."

"Georgiana is modest. Mr. Butler found your compositions impressive, and that is high praise indeed," Lady Matlock noted, turning the conversation smoothly away at that point, no one but Lizzy noting the increased color to her new sister's cheeks at the mention of the young grandson of Lady Warrow.

The effect of Georgiana's eight months abroad with culture and Society at its finest surrounding her at every turn was evident, even to Major General Artois who previously had limited exposure to Miss Darcy. He glanced about the room, studying the occupants with a keen eye. He found the differing characters and stations intriguing, familiar, and amusing.

His immediate family was much like the Bennets. Comprised of gentleman stock with a long history of prestige through military achievements with a historical host of field marshals and generals heading the ancestral corps of lesser ranks, they possessed modest familial estates scattered throughout the southern regions of England and were all blessed with incomes and inheritances above sufficient if not grand. The casual upbringing, middling finances, and gritty occupation made for a family that was broad-minded and somewhat boisterous.

Nevertheless, he also belonged to an extended family of extreme wealth and high social class. A number of titled gentry graced the secondary and tertiary branches of the Artois tree, capping it all with a great-uncle who was a duke. This, coupled with the strict discipline of the Royal British Army, meant that even the humble members could blend into any social situation capably.

Mr. and Mrs. Bennet were precisely akin to a couple of his retired military uncles and their wives. Now dwelling at and managing the family estates, they were simple folk who loved the land they had given so much to protect. Mr. and Mrs. Daniels were like a few cousins, and also his youngest brother, Reginald, who were content to be clerks or serve in other noncommissioned capacities.

Mr. Darcy, although far younger, reminded him greatly of his father. General Artois was tall, brawny, and unbending. Unlike all but one of his sons, Randall's eldest brother, Roderick, General Artois seemed physically unable to relax his ingrained military demeanor. Yet he was wry and witty, his humor and empathy emerging through the regulated discipline so that even his numerous grandchildren knew he was lovable.

The other six Artois offspring were universally ebullient with emotions worn on their sleeves. This fact was primarily why his brother Roland had gravitated toward Richard Fitzwilliam during Academy, the two developing a tight friendship that more often than not lead to rabble-rousing and activities best left omitted from polite conversation! It was also why Randall meshed with the natural gaiety that ruled his fiancée's relatives. Lord and Lady Matlock, and the widowed wife of the famous Lord Fotherby, were warm in their formality, teasing and laughing frequently. It was an altogether pleasing assembly, and he accepted the situation with his inborn peaceful assurance that it was meant to be. He looked down at Kitty, meeting her eyes and squeezing the hands resting so lovingly on his arm, contentment wrapping his soul.

Later, he would wonder if it was a divine warning of events to come, but at the time Randall merely thought it odd that in the midst of his happiness he reacted so strongly to the interruption. Yet, the instant he heard the raised voice in the outer corridor, before the words consciously registered, his instincts prevailed.

"I tell you we are expected! We are family and do not need to be announced!"

The indignant exclamation rang through the open door, the Major General stiffening before the first words were released. Impulsively, he nudged Kitty away from his side, turning his body toward the door and in front of her while his left arm shot out as a barrier before her to shield. Simultaneously, his right hand swung about in a flash to grasp the hilt of the sword that normally would be hanging on his hip. He squelched the curse that threatened to pass his lips at the realization that, in this setting of familial felicity, he was not armed. He had no time to experience embarrassment at his reflexive response due to the palpable tension that invaded the room when the visitors revealed themselves.

The owner of the brash voice was a young woman dressed in a revealing gown of a fashionable style. She wore a feathered hat cocked to one side, with her brown hair curled becomingly and framing a pretty face. Rouged cheeks and painted lips lent an air of maturity to what was obviously a young face devoid of intelligence or wisdom. All of this the trained military man concluded in less than a second—observing, categorizing, deducing, and dismissing her as not the cause of his hackles being raised.

Rather, that came from the man who trailed behind her. He traveled in her wake but strode into the room as if he owned it. Of medium height, slender-framed with a small paunch, dark blonde hair stylishly cut and curled, and dressed in a fine suit of beige wool, he swaggered in and swept the room with dark blue eyes inundated with condescension. His face was handsome but arrogant, and with a lewd sensuality inherent in the set of his full lips and half-lidded eyes. His gaze rested on Randall, noting the mass of medals and ribbons on the officer's chest and the rank insignia on his collar before lifting to meet the older man's return inspection. Steely black eyes pierced the blue ones that momentarily lost their haughtiness to flickers of fear. Randall noted the unease and foolishness behind the bluster in the younger man's gaze before the haughty survey moved on to inventory each occupant of the room.

"Mama! Papa! Oh! You are all here!" The woman clapped her hands, rushing toward Mrs. Bennet, who had already rose.

"My Lydia! My baby!!" Mrs. Bennet sobbed, embracing her youngest daughter. "We did not know when to expect you! Oh, Mr. Bennet! Is it not marvelous?"

"I could wait no longer, Mama. I told my Wickham we needed to make haste. We only tarried at Longbourn, briefly, so I could freshen up. I wanted you to see me looking my best! Is not this dress divine? And my hat? I told this servant here that we were expected and welcome. Such impertinence treating us so! Oh, Kitty! Look at you all grown up and getting married! An officer too. Well done, Sister, ranked higher than my dear Wickham, but I shall not be jealous! Papa! Have you missed me? I have missed you so. Devon is such a dreadfully long way away. Such a horrid journey it was, and you would not believe what we had to pay to have the coach take us out to Longbourn! As if it is so far away from the Meryton Station! Nonsense! And then we had to wait until Mr. Hill hitched the phaeton, I hope you do not mind, Papa, but I could not walk all this way! We were afraid we would miss dinner. But we clearly did not!"

Lydia Wickham's voice pierced the abrupt quiet that had fallen. She appeared utterly unaware of the taut atmosphere as she chattered in an endless stream. Mr. Bennet joined his wife and daughter, embracing and attempting to insert normalcy into the situation. Richard's sunny expression settled into the rarely seen commanding mien of a colonel. Darcy's neutral face held except for a fleeting clench of his jaw and frigid iciness infusing his eyes. Dr. Darcy's countenance assumed an identical pose as his nephew's, Randall momentarily interrupting his appraisal of the overall scene to register how strange it was to see anything other than gay animation on the physician's face.

Kitty patted Randall's arm, drawing his engrossed attention back to her. "It is well, Randall. I have told you of my sister and her husband. I apologize again for their attendance at our wedding. Are you so distressed?"

He smiled, face softening as his body relaxed slightly. "No dear, I was merely startled. Anything that pleases you pleases me."

"How gallant! You need not pretend completely, however. Nor express any great enthusiasm toward Mr. Wickham. I daresay he will receive little welcome, but you know some of that matter." Her face shone with pride as she leaned closer. "You far outrank him, as Lydia said, and are physically superior in every way. So my guess is he will be frightened of you."

"Excellent! A secret, Miss Bennet, for your ears only..." He leaned to whisper into her ear. "I delight in frightening my underlings. They all think me terrifying. It is a reputation I feed as often as possible."

"I shall keep your secret, Major General. None but I shall know what a lamb you truly are."

"Come, you two lovebirds!" Mrs. Bennet interrupted. "Do not be so rude. Welcome your sister, Kitty, and introduce your fiancé."

Everyone but the oblivious Mrs. Bennet felt the undercurrents, but few knew the entire tale of Wickham. In fact, only Darcy, Richard, George, and Lizzy knew all of the history from childhood on to the present. Georgiana knew of her own travails with the scoundrel, but only hints of his past interactions with her brother. Lord and Lady Matlock knew of Georgiana's narrow escape, of Wickham's wild ways during University, his squandering James Darcy's honest inheritance, and the attempt to swindle Darcy later, but nothing of his youthful mischief or the seduction and subsequent forced-marriage to Lydia Bennet.

Mr. Bennet knew the entire tale of Wickham's seduction of Lydia and Darcy's rescuing of her in London, but only vague fragments of Darcy's past connection to him. Darcy had never shared his information regarding Lydia's marriage and life in Newcastle with his father-in-law, seeing no profit in worrying him further. Kitty knew some of it, but from Georgiana's point of view and via whispered conversations between her parents, the bulk of which she had passed on to Randall.

The remainder, no matter what tidbits they may have gleaned over the years, instantly sensed the tension as well as cringing at the abrasive manner of Lydia. Where Mrs. Bennet was tolerated by the more refined members of Darcy's family, as long as contact was minimal, Lydia's crass words chafed. Darcy had anticipated this, even if he was not prepared for the contact to occur when the entire wedding party was amassed in his temporary home with him as host. Nonetheless, his impeccable breeding and need to establish firm ground with Wickham overcame his chagrin. "Mrs. Wickham." He bowed, stepping into the fray urbanely. "Welcome to Netherfield. Indeed you are in time for dinner. Setting for two additional diners is not in any way troublesome. Please, make yourself comfortable as you surely must be wearied from your journey."

He gestured to the sofa, briefly meeting Lizzy's eyes in silent communication. His wife nodded, grasping Lydia's elbow and steering toward the middle of the room, the Bennet clan following.

Richard and Dr. Darcy sidled over as Darcy turned to face George Wickham. Randall remained behind, curiously observing the changing expressions while his own internal alarms yet rang.

"Wickham," Darcy stated flatly, eyes flinty and piercing his old playmate. "You are welcome to Netherfield as well. Miss Bennet's happiness is of the utmost concern. For her sake you are accepted, but you will be watched, have no fear of that."

Wickham inclined his head, cocky smile fixed in place. "No need for threats, Darcy. I come in peace, and only at my wife's urging, I assure you. Hertfordshire holds no happy memories for me, nor do you frankly. Colonel Fitzwilliam, I understand congratulations are in order?"

Richard nodded curtly, not replying.

Wickham nodded as well, feigned sadness touching his eyes. "I see. And you must be Major General Artois? I will assume you know of my unfortunate history with His Majesty's Army, so I will not pretend that being surrounded by officers is all that appealing to me."

"I suppose in that regard we are on equal footing, Mr. Wickham, as I do not find being in the company of insubordinates all that appealing either. But for the sake of my fiancée I will manage to overcome my repulsion."

Wickham inclined his head politely, smile in place. "Understood. Congratulations to you as well, Major General. Miss Bennet has matured nicely, I daresay, from the girl I last saw. But it is oddly comforting to know not all has changed, such as her preference for military men. I am certain Mrs. Bennet is delighted at her daughter's… resourcefulness and has welcomed you into the fold with lavish praise."

His eyes turned from the stiffened Randall to Darcy. "More congratulations are in order, I see. Mrs. Darcy appears every inch a Mistress of Pemberley, to the point of speedily presenting you with not one, but two male children! Amazing development and how *proud* you must be. Your heir is a handsome lad, without any doubt your son. *This* must be a comfort to you."

"Is this your idea of coming in peace, Wickham?" Darcy growled.

Wickham shrugged, spreading his hands. "Just getting the insults out of the way, Darcy. Then we can have it done with and move on to the happy event. Should I complete your expectations by remarking on how lovely a woman Georgiana has become?"

Richard took a step closer, his face ruddy with anger. "Be careful, Wickham. You are not among friends here."

"Oh, how well I know, Colonel. But I do not think either of you want to start a brawl here in the parlor. Mustn't upset the delicate females. That would be highly improper. Frankly, I am outnumbered, so am counting on the famous Darcy restraint to persevere. If Darcy truly wanted to harm me he has had plenty of opportunities to do so before this one."

"Fitzwilliam." Lizzy fortuitously interrupted the escalating scene, touching his sleeve. "Dinner has been announced."

She sternly held his gaze, finally hearing a deep inhale as his face resumed its typical controlled seriousness. "Of course. Thank you, Elizabeth." He offered his arm, Lizzy taking it with relief, both turning their backs on Wickham as Darcy's elegant voice rang out in formal announcement. Richard and Randall left to claim their partners, none noting the smug expression that crossed Wickham's face before it settled into its usual arrogant lift as he escorted a babbling Lydia into the dining room.

When Lizzy entered their bedchamber that evening, after nursing Michael and putting him to sleep, it was to a familiar sight. Her husband stood before the fireplace staring into the flames with one elbow resting on the mantel and the hand fisted against his mouth. The other arm hung at his side with fingers twitching. Jacket and cravat were discarded, negligently tossed over a chair, and shoes and stockings were piled on the floor. His hair was ruffled, sticking up in places, and his thick brows were furrowed with creases deep in between. She could not see his lips under the fisted hand, but she knew without a doubt that they were harshly pressed together. Even without additional evidence, such as the steady tic in his rigid jawline, she would have known the state of his emotions, as his entire posture was common when he was extremely agitated or angry.

Tonight she was not sure which it was. Agitation? Anger? Both? She entered quietly and curled up into the chair opposite his stiff body. She watched him for a few moments but could not bear it, so assumed her own contemplation of the fire.

Time passed. The only sounds were the crackles of the flames and Darcy's heavy breathing. The only movements were the occasional shifting logs and his hand that continued to fidget and rifle through his hair.

"I am sorry, William," she finally murmured into the silence. "Your anger is understandable and I wish I could alleviate it. Having to deal with Wickham… having him as… family is…"

"I refuse to listen to you apologizing for this again, Elizabeth," he snapped, not moving or looking away from the fire. "This has nothing to do with you, or at least not in the way you persist in seeing it. You are my wife and he is my brother-in-law. That is the fact of it and I would not choose otherwise, so please desist in the self-recriminations! I cannot deal with your misplaced guilt at this juncture." He inhaled vigorously to calm the anger and jerked away from the mantel, pivoting toward Lizzy. "I would prefer if you put aside your foolish guilt and use your intellect to help me figure out what his motives are!"

"And I would prefer, Mr. Darcy, if you lowered your voice, got control of your emotions, and quit glaring at me. You want me to tell you what I think Wickham's motives are? It is this! He wants you raging and distressed, and flaring angrily at your wife. He desires discord among the family. You are allowing him to win, William, and you cannot do that!"

He stared at her for a few seconds and then began pacing, the other typical attitude when he was agitated or angry. She was angry as well, but his rudely spat words had done the trick of finally dissolving the residuals of her guilt. She would never again doubt his love for her—never—and knew beyond the tiniest shred that he counted any difficulty worth being her husband. Goodness, he tolerated her mother! What more proof could she possibly require?

Besides, she well knew that this was not a result of wishing, however remotely or unconsciously, that he did not have to deal with Wickham. The sad truth was that Darcy believed that Wickham would always have been a thorn in his flesh, Elizabeth or no Elizabeth. When would he have to again encounter his lifelong adversary and how would the threat arise? His bravery or mastery was not the question, but the stakes were increased due to his love for her and their children. His anger and agitation arose at the unknown possible harm to those he was sworn to protect.

Lizzy had been married to this complex man long enough to know it was best to allow him to expend his passionate irritation. It never lasted too long. Darcy was not a man, in general, who wallowed in his emotions. He was zealous in apportioned allotments and in appropriate situations, such as their bed, but was predominantly a man of superior restraint and vast intelligence. To him it was illogical and foolish to waste time and energy on fits of temper, thus he always rapidly gained control over his baser drives.

While she waited, her own vexation cooled and she found herself wanting to smile, although she held the impulse in check. As painful as it was to observe his distress and as potentially serious as this situation was, she never failed to obtain a physical rush in watching her handsome, virile, passionate spouse display his power and masculinity. He paced with feline grace and determination, tall body erect, long strides measured, and attractive face set as he worked through the problem. Then, just as she expected, after a dozen rushed passes before her, his rhythm slowed and the words came.

"Certainly, no matter what else he may have up his sleeve, sowing discord is one goal. That and annoying me. Damn! How could I allow him to witness my discomposure? Idiotic fool that I am! Very well then. You are correct, Elizabeth. He wants to vex me and he succeeded tonight. As humiliating as it is to admit, he won this round. I should not have allowed it, I who knows more than any other how capable at manipulation he is. I recognize that my anger is primarily at my own gullibility." He waved his hand in the air before again reaching to vigorously comb through his hair.

"Stop that or you will yank every last hair out and I would rather not have a bald husband as of yet."

He paused both his pacing and nervous gesture, looking to her smiling face. Releasing a sighing laugh, he closed his eyes and shook his head, dropping his arms with hands coming to rest on his hips. It was only a few seconds of silence before he straightened, inhaled deeply, and looked at her with his customary controlled expression in place.

"Very well then," he repeated, "I concede that time clearly has not healed the past wounds as much as I thought, and that my vaunted forbearance is not as well established as I bragged, at least where Wickham is concerned."

"Even you, my darling, are allowed to possess a few faults." She smiled winsomely, Darcy again shaking his head and chuckling breathily. "The truth is, William, you boys cornered Wickham the second he walked in the door. Although I do not know what was said and certainly do not trust him any more than you, I can well imagine that having four men with heightened tempers surrounding would not bring out one's best manners."

"Perhaps, but he did not attempt the slightest civility or show a modicum of remorse for past deeds." He proceeded to tell Lizzy about the parlor encounter, leaving nothing out.

"May I safely propose, dearest, that none of *you* attempted the slightest civility or extended a hint of grace for those past deeds?"

He did not reply, instead pressing his lips together and holding her gaze without any apparent shame.

Lizzy continued, "Dinner was no more uncomfortable than it ever is with such a mixed group of people. The tension level was a bit higher than normal with all the glowering menfolk. But Wickham was fairly polite and aside from a few borderline slurs was amiable."

Darcy grunted, finally sitting on the sofa opposite Lizzy. "Yes, indeed. He is quite charming."

"That is not what I meant. I merely want to cautiously advance the possibility that he intends no harm or has some nefarious plans. We only need to get through these few days and then we will be in London and have no reason to see him or Lydia again. As long as he is pleasant and causes no trouble, I think we can survive."

He was staring at her, eyes dark and penetrating. "I noted that he brought a smile to your face once or twice, and a laugh at one point. His amiability and magnetism overcame your skepticism, I deduced."

"Oh my God, William! Are you jealous of George Wickham?"

Lizzy laughed aloud while Darcy's frown deepened into a surly pout. "I see nothing humorous in the situation, Elizabeth. By your own confession you once succumbed to his charm, however briefly, as well as his lies."

Lizzy rose, still chuckling, and sat onto his lap entwining her arms over his shoulders. "Fitzwilliam Darcy, you are ridiculous and pathetic. And somewhat insulting. But, I shall forgive your offense against my character and momentary questioning of my love and devotion to you as I understand your fragile sensibilities and vulnerability."

"Do not tease me, Elizabeth. I am not in the mood for lightheartedness."

"I shall tease you nonetheless. And make you suffer for accusing me of any unfaithfulness, no matter how slight. Furthermore, you should be punished most severely for not recognizing when your loyal, adoring wife is fulfilling her role as Mistress of Pemberley and Mrs. Darcy, paramount hostess of Hertfordshire. However, since it is Mr. Wickham, and I know how distressed you are, I shall be merciful."

She leaned to kiss him, but he halted her with firm hands grasping her face and fingers embedded into the curls pinned at the nape of her neck. His eyes bore into hers, no amusement evident within the dark blue depths despite her teasing, his voice a rough growl. "Elizabeth, sharing your smiles with other men is forever a torture for me. It is occasionally a struggle to avoid strangling my cousin or uncles. I am possessive, selfish, and covetous when it comes to you. George Wickham flashing his dazzling smile and dimples toward my wife brings all those unattractive characteristics to the forefront."

He pulled her in then, kissing voraciously while his fingers searched for the pins holding her hair up. Lizzy melted into his body, a low moan escaping, but he abruptly drew her head away. "Add to my jealousy the fact that I do not trust Wickham as far as I could toss him, and I judge my temper forgivable."

"I always forgive your tempers even when you do not deserve it." She kissed him softly and released the top buttons on his shirt. "Just as you do mine. As for any jealousy, if I thought for one second you truly imagined that Mr. Wickham could spark the tiniest iota of interest within me, I would begin to doubt your ability to reason rationally. I would likely be forced to call Bethlam to take you away for insanity."

"You do delight in teasing me, Mrs. Darcy."

"Indeed I do, Mr. Darcy. It is your own fault, of course, as you make it entirely too easy an employment. Anyway, you should know by now that charm and amiability are not what intrigue me. As absurd as it seems, I apparently prefer serious and reserved. Dimples still pique my interest, but only those found on strong chins or faintly appearing in cheeks with brilliant, devoted smiles directed only at me in the privacy of my chambers."

"Is this an exhaustive list of what enthralls you?"

"I like big men, tall and masculine, with firm muscles over every inch. Dark hair is beneficial. A rugged, clean-shaven jaw… well, perhaps a mustache. I am not sure, but definitely not a beard."

"No?"

"No. I am certain of that. I am partial to soft, plump lips easy to kiss without interference."

"Anything else of major importance to induce affection?"

She laughed breathily, maintaining her perch on his lap and relaxing into the armrest as he peeled her gown's sleeve off her shoulder, initiating a methodical and sensual disrobing. "A resonant, authoritative voice is essential. Nothing weak or wavering. I love eyes as blue as the sky with intelligence and passionate fervor readily evident. Broad shoulders and a sculptured chest blanketed with downy black hairs. Hmm… Yes, indeed. Hands that are proficient, strong yet tender with elegant, gifted fingers…"

Her whispered words trailed away into a soft moan resulting from the blissful sensation of her husband's lips upon the exposed flesh of her neck. Eyes closing at the added exhilaration of his roving fingertips that now brushed over her collarbone and downward over her breast, she mutely enjoyed the tactile stimulation.

"Continue, Mrs. Darcy. I must know what attributes intrigue you so I can be on alert for any potential competition," he huskily demanded just before his warm tongue teased her bared bosom.

She gasped, resuming with a stuttering inflection. "A strong, prominent nose…"

"Forget the nose," came a muffled voice.

"Indeed I shall not as the nose is highly important. Must be defined and forceful, making a statement of boldness and distinction. Plus, a perfect nose draws attention to the kissable lips beneath."

Her words were cut off by abrupt movement. Darcy grasped her by the waist, lifting and pivoting in one powerful, smooth motion until a now naked Lizzy, except for stockings and slippers, was seated on the sofa with him kneeling between her thighs. He swiftly removed his clothing, drew her legs around his waist, and leaned his muscled frame over her smaller one.

"Any other necessary features to complete the package and drive your ardor to unnameable heights?"

She pointedly looked down to where their bodies met. One hand leisurely played over his exposed flesh, while the other entwined into his hair and drew his head closer. She pressed her lips against his earlobe, hot breath tickling deliciously as she whispered words for his hearing only.

Lizzy was correct in that Darcy was not seriously all that jealous of Wickham. His faith in their mutual accord was too tremendous. Nonetheless, he *was* a possessive man and the sudden entry of his enemy, a one-time rival for his wife's affections, had upset him in a way he had not anticipated in his fretfulness over other concerns. Lizzy understood this and no matter how ludicrous she found it, and despite her gentle teasing, she wanted to assure him in the most elemental but glorious way that she was his. Only his.

There were no further words uttered. The only sounds were harsh grunts, rasping respirations, and sighing moans as they enjoyed the pleasure derived from each other. Love surged in an electric arc between their flesh and blinding bliss was attained simultaneously.

Later, after heartbeats slowed and lungs refilled with oxygen, the words flowed. But they were only declarations of eternal love and devotion. The topic of Wickham was left alone, neither giving it another second's contemplation.

CHAPTER ELEVEN

Glimpsing the Past

LORD AND LADY MATLOCK departed the following day with plans to visit Lady Catherine and the Penaflors at Rosings. Their vacancy was barely felt due to the arrival of Major General Artois's father and siblings. A different carriage rattled up Netherfield's drive at sporadic intervals over the ensuing days depositing exuberant guests for the Darcys to greet and interact with.

Every day the women gathered to talk and prepare for Kitty and Randall's wedding. The atmosphere was one of constant fluttering and laughter. There was not a great deal in the way of wedding arranging left to do, but with six Artois females added to the six Bennet ladies, Georgiana, and Simone, the gaiety was feverish.

The menfolk tended to vacate the manor as often and as early as feasible. The impetus was partly the desire for masculine pursuits and companionship since the weather remained fair with sunshine and blue skies perfect for hunting and long horseback rides. However, undeniably the drive was also to place distance from the females before roped into arranging flowers or, God forbid, weaving ribbons!

Darcy joined the gentlemen on their various jaunts but found the ladies' giddiness charming. It brought back happy memories of those exhilarating days prior to his marriage. Now, as then, he had no clue what really went on and why it was such a cause of frivolity, but it was part of the female condition and thus oddly comforting to witness. In the evening Lizzy would rattle on about ribbons and flowers and lace and confectionary while he sat with one or both of the boys on his lap, indulgent as he attempted to comprehend it all.

One night he sat by the fire with Alexander and Dog curled against his chest. They watched Lizzy as she rocked the baby and listened to another discourse on the table decorations. Or maybe it was the food itself; Darcy was not sure which. At one point Alexander looked up at his father with a baffled expression that clearly questioned the purpose to the speech. Darcy just shrugged, smiling and winking before nestling his son closer and kissing his forehead. He returned his attention to Lizzy, now saying something about one of the main entrees, a dish with Cornish hens and rosemary gravy, and he perked up, as food was something he could understand to a degree. He did not have too much interest in the actual creation of the food, but did not attain his six-foot-three-inch height and broad bulk without appreciating tasty cuisine!

Kitty contrived extending her stay at Netherfield for three additional nights before the room occupied by her was needed for Randall's family. Each of those nights she crept along the shadows to the far side of the manor where her lover waited, the door opening when her knuckles barely touched it. He would pull her into the room, pivot with her in his arms and, already kissing her lips, lock the door with one fumbling hand.

Clothing fell in a trail as they frantically groped and kissed their way blindly to the bed, tumbling in a heap of limbs, and joining together in a heated rush. The first time was always furious and fast, the long day of wanting each other producing constant states of arousal that increased drastically as the hours slowly ticked by until a blissful release attained in minutes was necessary. Then they could relax, enjoying the hours with conversation, short periods of sleep, and leisurely loving until dawn.

"I know you must return to Longbourn tomorrow, and it is for the best I suppose, but I do believe these next three days will be the longest of my life." He smoothed the tangled hair from her face, studying her beauty in the half-light, committing it to memory in hopes it would sustain him in the lonely nights to follow. "How will I ever sleep without you here with me?"

"You have slept little with me here," she teased.

"Do not be surprised if you are yanked into a linen closet or pulled behind a large bush, kitten. It will just be me showing you how insanely I love and need you."

"Hmmm, that is not a bad plan. Any particular bushes you had in mind? Just so I can casually stroll by it?"

"Do not tempt me, love," he grated, burying his face between her breasts and squeezing so tightly the air whooshed out of her lungs. "It was only a jest, although now the image will haunt me. I think I have shed twenty years since meeting you. I am as randy as when a youth." He laid his head tenderly on one breast, Kitty stroking through his curls. "It may prove my undoing, but I will harshly exert the discipline I know lurks within me somewhere, God knows where it went, and save my energy for when I am truly your husband and have you alone in the cabin. Be prepared, as I intend to keep you completely naked for several days."

"You already are my husband, Randall, and that is a fine plan as long as you are naked too."

He rose, grinning lecherously and rolling a nipple between his thumb and finger. "Naked and inside you as often as humanly possible, which lately, to my happy shock, seems to be frequently possible."

She squirmed, pressing his hand hard into her breast. "Tell me more of this cabin so I can dream of us there."

"It is in east Hampshire, so will not take us long to get there, thank God. It is owned by a buddy of mine; it is a hunting lodge actually. Small and quaint, but comfortable. I have been there many times. We will have two weeks totally alone, not even any servants. It has been prepared with everything we will need and no one, especially none of my brothers, knows about it. Paradise, it is. Or will be with you there."

"It does sound heavenly. How about we stay there for the entire month and forget about Bath?"

He laughed, rolling onto his back with her atop. With a simple shift of position and smooth thrust they were already in heaven.

At noon the next day Randall drove the phaeton to Longbourn, needing this time alone with her. As soon as they were out of the sight of Netherfield Kitty leaned against his side, her intention just to be soothed by his closeness, but the sensation of flexing arm and leg muscles as he controlled the horses had the opposite effect.

"Up ahead there is an entire copse of bushes, Major General. Care to inspect them?"

"They look to be lovely bushes, Miss Bennet, but any inspection shall have to wait." He glanced at her dimpled face, smiling and giving a quick peck to her nose. "I have decided to salvage what remnants of control and decorum I possess and behave in a manner befitting an officer and a gentleman. Then again, maybe I am simply imagining how incredible our wedding night will be after three days without you."

"It will be incredible in any case, because then I will be yours completely, in every way, and you will be mine." She stretched to kiss across his jaw while one hand tickled up the inside of his thigh. Randall groaned and gripped the reins so tightly his knuckles turned white. Just as he began to think the copse would be inspected after all, *resolutions be damned*, she withdrew, sliding over the seat as far as possible. "But you are correct, on all counts. I will remember that I am a proper young lady with a measure of restraint in there somewhere. I shall be good, I promise," she finished, her smirk contradicting that claim.

"After we are married you can forget that promise."

Her answer was laughter.

~❦~

The days passed pleasantly with none of the drama Darcy had feared. The local gentlemen of Meryton welcomed the visitors with open arms, offering a wealth of diversions both day and night. Sir Lucas organized an impromptu tournament of games at the pub with Darcy again proving his superiority at billiards while Richard soundly trounced everyone at darts. Area families of distinction held dinner parties every night, Netherfield included one other time. Through all of this activity Wickham conducted himself with the utmost civility. He frequently was not present, his time spent in amusements unknown. Yet when he was present he was polite, charming, and strangely unobtrusive, fading into the background and doing nothing to draw attention.

Darcy managed to douse his rage over Wickham. His natural levelheadedness and self-discipline were too immense to falter for long. The few times Wickham was in his presence Darcy ignored him, by all appearances indifferent. But he noticed everything, observed his enemy's tiniest gesture or expression, and listened to each nuance in his words. It was subtle, but in those times when the family interacted, Darcy's hulking proximity to Lizzy and their children was a strong deterrent to Wickham attempting any contact, if he was thinking along those lines, which he gave no indication of.

Daily Lizzy was reminded to be cautious and nightly she was quizzed regarding any accidental confrontations. She strived to halt the instinctive eye rolling, especially when Wickham seemed to be politeness itself and paid neither her nor Georgiana particular mind besides the normal deference. Lizzy did not agree with Darcy's apprehension, but she knew it was real to him. The constant fretting over his loved ones while pretending serenity was deeply fatiguing and disturbed his sleep, this paining Lizzy greatly and causing her to wish the wedding was sooner so they could depart for London and leave the Wickhams behind.

The day before the wedding she drove Netherfield's curricle back to their temporary home after a morning at Longbourn. Michael, mesmerized by his brother's delighted grin and wind-tossed curls, was nestled in the sturdy basket secured on the wide seat between Lizzy and Alexander. The two-and-a-half-year-old was thrilled by the experience, even if they were crawling along at a turtle's pace.

"Hold on tightly, Alexander. Keep your hands on the rails."

The admonition was redundant, of course, as Alexander was one of those rare children who followed rules to the letter. Keeping her focus between the well-maintained avenue and her sunnily grinning son, she did not note the approach of a rider until the horse pulled alongside the passenger seat. Alexander turned his bright face to the mounted man, who smiled in return and tipped his hat.

"Master Darcy," he greeted, looking then to Lizzy. "Mrs. Darcy."

"Mr. Wickham," she returned in a level tone.

"I was returning to Longbourn when I saw you leaving, so I followed. We have had no opportunities to converse privately."

"I have no desire to converse privately with you, Mr. Wickham. Nor would my husband appreciate you accosting me on the road."

"Ah yes, Darcy. He always did have an overdeveloped sense of control. Of course, I suppose one could argue that that desire to dominate is essential to the Master of Pemberley."

"Mr. Wickham, I will not allow you to insult Mr. Darcy in front of me and his children."

He inclined his head. "Forgive me, Elizabeth. I meant no disrespect, truly." He looked at Alexander, whose smile was beginning to fade from the sensed hostility between the two adults. "I remember a time when Darcy smiled more, laughing and playing as a boy. Your son looks so like him. Rather uncanny." He looked again to Lizzy. "I think you, Elizabeth, would have preferred that Darcy. The one who was jovial and free spirited, before he grew so serious and dictatorial. That is all I meant."

"Mr. Wickham, let me be clear. I appreciate my husband precisely as he is and would not prefer him any other way."

He shrugged, sunny smile in place. "If you say so, Elizabeth. It still baffles me, I confess. The Darcy I know is completely unsuited to you and I admit I have puzzled over the subject since I heard of your marriage. Was it obligation, Elizabeth? You felt you had to marry him after he 'saved' your sister from the bad man who compromised her? I know he regarded you at one time but never would have imagined him stooping to marry…"

"Mr. Wickham," she interrupted, glancing to Alexander. "You do not know me in the slightest or Mr. Darcy. I will not listen to your poison, now or ever. Furthermore, I would appreciate it if you would not address me so informally."

"Just curious, forgive me. And are we not brother and sister? You can call me George."

"I think not, Mr. Wickham." She stressed his name, turning a glare his way. "And as for being your sister, that is a fact I would rather not be reminded of!"

"What a pity. Indeed, I had hoped that your gaiety and plucky wit would have rubbed off on the old man, brought some lightness to his personality. Quite the shame to see it has worked the other way around."

"Mr. Wickham…"

"Very well then," he interrupted her angry rebuttal, his own voice and expression abruptly gay with dimples flashing. "We shall change the subject. I must confess it is lovely here in Hertfordshire. I am delighted to be back. Devon tends to be cloudy. And the wind!" He shivered dramatically, winking at Alexander. "At times I fear it may blow me out to sea! Have you felt such winds as that, lad?"

Alexander shook his head. "No, sir."

"No, I suppose not. Derbyshire is not known for her winds. Beautiful springs and summers are more the standard. I recall, Mrs. Darcy"—he emphasized with a grin—"that you were always one to walk. Miles upon miles. Is this still true?"

"Yes, it is still true."

"How you must adore the grounds about Pemberley. The endless trails amongst the trees and the pathways through the beautiful gardens surely delight. Mr. Clark is yet head groundskeeper?" Lizzy nodded. "He is a marvel to be sure. One of the finest gardeners in all of England, I daresay. Do you not agree?"

Again Lizzy nodded and kept her eyes straight ahead while her mind furiously wondered how to rid them of his unwanted presence without disturbing Alexander.

Wickham continued as if nothing was amiss, turning his attention to a baffled Alexander. "Do you enjoy watching the plants grow, son? Pulling nasty weeds and playing in the dirt until your fingernails are caked with muck?"

The toddler was further confused, as the epithet "son" was associated with his parents and odd coming from a stranger's mouth. He glanced to his silent, clearly annoyed mother before meeting Wickham's beaming face. But politeness was an inherited trait as well as a virtue enforced by his parents, so he responded accordingly. "Yes, sir. Mama show me how to dig and pack seeds and pick flowers. Papa teaches bot... botumy."

Wickham laughed. "Botany. Yes, Darcy would teach science to a two-year-old. And do you like to walk like your mother, Alexander?"

"Yes, sir."

"Be sure your mother or nanny takes you to Hyde Park to feed the ducks, Alexander. They live in the smaller lake near the Grosvenor Square entrance."

"Ducks and frogs at home in our pond. Cook gives us crumbs to feed. Michael 'fraid of ducks, but not me!"

"No. I am sure you are very brave."

"Papa says I brave boy."

"I am sure he is right. At Hyde Park, near the pond, are hedges to hide in. And bulrushes along the lake edge. It is great fun and since you are so brave you could hide very well. Play hide and seek, and your nanny would never find you!"

"Mr. Wickham, please do not encourage my son to misbehave!"

"Not to misbehave, but to have normal boyhood fun. Your father and I, when we were boys together, Alexander, had some crazy adventures. Hiding and exploration is what a boy is supposed to do! Yes, son?"

Alexander frowned, thinking carefully, and then shook his head slowly. "No, sir. May scare Nanny if gone long."

"Oh no, my boy! Nannies expect brave boys to be a little wild! It makes their job fun!"

Alexander held Wickham's gaze, assessing as typical, with the tiny creases between his brows deepening. Wickham winked as if sharing a great secret. "Just imagine the fun, Alexander. The ducks often lay their eggs in the hedges too, so you may find a treasure while on your quest!"

Alexander thought in silence, finally giving a short, solemn nod.

"Now I see the grave Darcy peeking through. He has a serious bent as his father; however, I hope his humor remains intact. And your youngest, Mrs. Darcy? Is he molded after you with a ready laugh and sparkling eyes?"

Lizzy did not answer, her angry eyes fixed on the road.

"I shall pray that he does. Too much stuffiness is unhealthy, I think. Do not be afraid to test the limits once in a while, Alexander. That is what brave boys do."

"Mr. Wickham, we are nearly to Netherfield and it would not do for Mr. Darcy to see you with us. I am sure you agree?"

He grinned, again inclining his head. "Yes, I am sure you are correct, Mrs. Darcy. I shall bid you good day then. It has been a pleasure. Master Darcy. Mrs. Darcy. Until tomorrow."

The encounter seemed innocuous enough, but Lizzy was disturbed. She dreaded having to broach the topic with her husband when they were so near the wedding and then being able to put the unpleasantness behind them altogether. That it would enrage him was a given, and she wanted to weep at causing him any further anxiety or grief.

But, they had vowed long ago to have no secrets between them. They were aware that the other frequently glazed over during the maundering discourses that were a necessary part of their lives, ears listening to the words that recounted their day, but the details not always penetrating into the deeper memory banks. They did pay heed for the most part, however, with only the occasional slice of information forgotten and thus leading to humorous teasing or a minor argument later.

The drawback to all this communication, if one looked at it from a certain perspective, is that after all this time it was ingrained. Lizzy could no more withhold the interaction with Wickham than halt her breathing. But that did not mean she ceased fretting about it or wishing, just this once, she could remain mum.

A stroll along the twisting pathways through the grass and wildflowers was decided upon as a necessary exercise to soothe her frayed emotions, so she bundled the sleeping Michael into his perambulator, grabbed Alexander, and set off. Joining her extemporaneous excursion was Jane carrying Deborah, Mary pushing Claudia in her carriage, Georgiana, Mrs. Hanford and Mrs. Geer, and Simone. Ethan, Hugh, and Harry skipped alongside Alexander, staying in the open fields and miraculously managing to discover every remaining mud puddle from the winter rains. Laughter was prominent, birds were chirping in nearby trees, and the slight breeze was invigorating. Nevertheless, Lizzy's pensiveness continued.

She unconsciously sighed, drawing the attention of Jane. "Are you well, Lizzy? You seem distracted."

"Oh, it is nothing really." She glanced around, but the children were picking dandelions and blowing the seeds, and the other adults were spread along the trail. She lowered her voice. "Mr. Wickham accosted me on the way back to Netherfield today."

Jane gasped, Lizzy squeezing her hand as she continued. "It was nothing horrible, so rest easy. He made a few remarks against William, but generally was friendly and harmless. He spoke with Alexander about gardening and the ducks in Hyde Park." She shook her head. "It was odd really. There seemed no point in it at all."

"You will tell William?"

"Of course. We keep no secrets. But I will confess, Jane, that I hate to do so. He will be furious and so troubled. He has been certain from the beginning that Wickham meant harm of some kind. I have not been so sure of that and am still not convinced by this encounter, but William will assuredly perceive it as such."

"Poor Mr. Darcy! To be so plagued by this one man. Oh, how could Lydia have been so stupid as to align herself with such a terrible individual?"

"Lydia is a fool, Jane, and I doubt she sees beyond that he provides for her needs."

"And he seems to do that well enough."

"Yes, it is strange, is it not?" Lizzy paused, staring into the air sightlessly. "She dresses fine, as does Mr. Wickham, yet she cannot say what he does for a living. Where does he get his money? William has mentioned that several times with suspicion. He is positive it a nefarious undertaking of some kind." She laughed but with little humor.

"All Lydia says is that he keeps late hours and disappears for days or weeks at a time. She complains of that, but then boasts of all the parties they attend in the next breath. I overheard her tell Mama that he works for a rich man in the area, but when Mama questioned further Lydia grew vague. I gathered she does not know the details and was embarrassed by the fact. It was merely a feeling, but her face was flustered for a moment." She shrugged. "It could be innocent. Mr. Wickham is an educated man, well-spoken and cultured…"

"Thanks to the late Mr. Darcy!" Lizzy interrupted with some heat.

"Indeed. But the point is he could be serving as a steward or some such capacity, could he not?"

"It is possible, and William has thought of that. But why be so secretive about it? If it were a position of esteem he would probably be bragging loudly, even if it was a huge exaggeration, just to annoy William." She shook her head. "No, it is odd however you look at it but not conclusively criminal. William will be irritated and I cringe at the thought of enlightening him. Perhaps I shall wait until later tonight before we retire and he is especially mellow."

"Lizzy!"

She looked at her sister's shocked, red face and laughed aloud. "Oh Jane! You are a treasure!"

"Mama, wellow 'lion for you."

Lizzy turned to Alexander, who stood before her with a handful of yellow dandelions held up. She knelt and took the offered bundle with a flourish, inhaling the acrid odor as if the sweetest perfume. "Thank you, my lamb. They are beautiful! Now, repeat after me, 'yellow dandelion.'"

"Yellow dannilion."

"Close enough!" She squeezed him until he squealed, chubby arms gripping her neck as she rose with him in her arms.

It was then that she saw the carriage.

Their group strolled along a trail that ran beside a narrow creek. The wide expanse of meadow on the other side of the creek was laden with wildflowers in bloom amid the tall, waving grasses, but was barren of trees or larger bushes, thus the view of the road was unobstructed so she could easily see the parked carriage and, presumably, whoever occupied the carriage could easily see them. It was a simple coach, well constructed, but without any embellishments or identifying markings. The driver wore nondescript clothing, not livery, and sat erect upon his seat with eyes staring straight ahead and paying them no mind.

There were probably a dozen reasons why a carriage may be halted on the side of a road with no houses or buildings in sight, so Lizzy's gaze barely noted the vehicle's presence before beginning to slide away. But a sudden movement from within the interior caught her attention.

It was a mere flash. An arm reaching, the golden head of an ornate cane held in a pale hand rapping onto the ceiling as a signal. Then the barest glimpse of a face appearing in the window, eyes looking her direction. For a heartbeat only their eyes met, recognition knifing through her brain with an accompanying physical pain before the image was gone. As rapidly as it started the sensation began to fade, her stunned consciousness already doubting what she had seen since it just could not be possible. It was unfathomable that it was *him*.

"Mrs. Darcy? Are you well?"

She turned dull eyes to Mrs. Hanford, the nanny's kindly face wrinkled with concern.

"Mama? Dannilion?" Alexander pushed the fisted flowers under her nose, sensing his mother's fright and naively trying to comfort despite his innocence.

Lizzy looked to the carriage, but the windows were dark and empty. It was slowly rolling away, picking up speed with dust swirling until obscured further.

"I am fine. Just fine. I guess the sun has affected me after all." She smiled at her son, kissing his nose. Another glance showed the carriage rounding a bend and then disappearing altogether. "Now, let's see if we can find some tadpoles, shall we, sweetie? Or, better yet, a big, ugly toad! Your papa would love to see that!"

A man entered the darkened, smoky pub, pausing on the threshold for a moment to adjust to the sudden gloom, and searched the shadowed corners for the person he was scheduled to meet. He spied him finally, readjusted the crutch under his arm, and shuffled awkwardly to the table set into the alcove. With a groan of pain he sat onto the bench across, rubbing his shriveled left leg.

"You are late," the waiting man said flatly, offering no assistance to the older, crippled man other than to scoot a mug of ale closer. "What were you doing? Watching the house again?"

"What I do with my time is none of your concern, Wickham. You are paid to do my bidding and not ask questions. Remember that."

Wickham inclined his head. "Have no fear, my lord. I know where my livelihood comes from and am grateful. You have my loyalty."

"Good."

"However, I am the one putting myself on the line as I traipse back and forth to London with the risk of being recognized. If you want this to succeed you have to stay hidden and trust what information I glean. What if one of them was to see you?" His tablemate looked into the foam in his mug, avoiding Wickham's eyes. "No! Who saw you?"

"It was for less than a second and from a long distance. I am sure there was no recognition."

"Do you truly imagine, all considered, that she would forget your face?"

"Why do you assume it was her?"

"Because if it was him you would likely be dead. Listen, my lord, you cannot allow your impatience to ruin all our planning."

"Quit chastising me, Wickham. Must I remind you again who I am and where you were when we joined forces? You had connived your way into managing that inn and were doing a fair job of it, keeping your wife in the gowns she desires, but we both know it was an impasse. A man like you would never had been content doing that forever. With me you have a future. And, best of all, the means to punish Darcy."

"We both need to be smart then. You have not learned to control your rage and need for vengeance."

"It is too personal," he hissed.

"I understand, my lord. It is personal for Darcy as well, but despite that he knows how to contain his anger. He was always proficient at that." Wickham finished with grudging respect.

"How well I know," the maimed man muttered, brushing a thumb over the long scar across his left cheek before taking a swallow of his ale. He emptied the mug and signaled the barmaid for another. "Now tell me what you have accomplished, if anything. I tire of my rustic accommodations. Have you learned of his activities? Divined any pattern?"

They paused as the barmaid brought fresh mugs of ale. She was a pretty thing, young and buxom, her smile inviting as she leaned near Wickham offering a generous view of her bosom.

"Anything else you needin', sir? We gots a nice lamb stew cookin' to warm your belly and other treats to satisfy if you wants." The coquettish expression and sweep of one finger across her cleavage aided the innuendo, not that Wickham was confused. He winked, dimples flashing as his eyes raked over the breasts less than a foot from his face.

"Any stew cooked here is more likely rat than lamb and the 'treats' are probably the pox."

The girl turned toward the grating voice with a biting rebuttal on her tongue but flinched and recoiled, the words undelivered. The Marquis of Orman glared at her, his dark eyes menacing. His sallow skin stretched over the harsh bones of his thin face, the only color blotches of pink flesh amid the puckered scar on his cheek. The odor of ale and cheap wine mixed with an alien sweetness permeated his clothing and was strong enough to supplant the smell of rot and vomit naturally drifting on the pub's air.

She instinctively took a step backward but was halted by Wickham's hand clasping her wrist. He followed with a sensuous caress up her inner arm, his smile mollifying while still being lewd.

"We are good here, love. I will seek you out when I am ready to take you up on your generous offer."

The simper instantly returned, her lashes lowering in what she reckoned was demure flirting, and without a glance toward Orman, she moved away with a seductive sway of her hips that Wickham avidly observed.

"Later!" the marquis spat. "You can have your fun when we are done talking. Answer my question."

"They have not been in the area long enough to establish habitual routines, especially with wedding plans and local activities. He rides every morning, usually alone, but not always. He forever has done that. The man is obsessed with horses."

"Yes, yes! Go on!"

"But that is no help to us anyway. I am a fair rider but could never overpower him while he is mounted."

"Just shoot him and be done with it."

Wickham shook his head. "Have you ever seen him ride? I am not that accurate a marksman, especially as fast as he runs. I would probably wound him at best, and that is not what we want."

"I thought you were a soldier. Does His Majesty's army teach nothing?"

"I was a poor soldier, remember? And do not be treasonous."

"Interesting morals there, Wickham. You chafe at treason but rejoice in plotting a murder. Intriguing."

Wickham grimaced at the word "murder," particularly as spoken in tones of jubilation. The Marquis of Orman glowed, his strange eyes sparkling even in the gloom and his wheezing pants faintly sexual. Wickham doubted the unbalanced man knew that he caressed over the wounds inflicted by the Darcys when he spoke of how he desired punishing them. It was eerie, especially added to the lopsided grin that displayed his rotting teeth and the crooked, bulbous nose. The once handsome Lord Orman was handsome no longer.

Hiding a shudder, Wickham looked away to examine the room. The place was filthy and dingy, perfect for this type of conversation, and they were the only patrons this time of day. Reluctantly he pulled his gaze away from the enticing view of the barmaid's round derriere swaying as she cleaned a far table.

"The truth is, I have been giving this more thought and think we should change our plan. I have been telling you for months that together we can make the revenge sweeter than merely a quick death."

"How so?"

"Would it not be more satisfying to make him suffer before he dies?"

"I want him dead! Do you understand me, Wickham? Only death is payment for what he has done to me!"

"And what about her? Sure, she will be grieved to lose the man she loves"—he choked on the word, uttering it with loathing—"but will have the consolation of his riches and…"

"You know we cannot touch his wealth," Orman interrupted. "Believe me, I have inquired, but the man is too powerful and too smart. I finally accepted that reality."

"Ah! I think I have a means to hurt him in more ways than either of us has ever imagined. I have your use of inhaled ether to thank for planting the seed of possibility. The effect on you when used cautiously to dull your pain…"

"Pain that is all his fault!" Orman snarled, rubbing over his upper thigh near his groin.

"Precisely why it is justice to use the ether that sustains you, my lord, as a means of exacting our vengeance."

Wickham proceeded to outline his plot with words specific to feed the marquis's ego and madness. The insane eyes across the table grew wilder and more maniacal, his countenance nearly orgasmic in his pleasure at the vision laid before him. His lust for what he envisioned befalling his worst enemy warmed his gut more than any woman ever had, even when he could still physically achieve satisfaction from that quarter.

"Yes!" Orman whispered, closing his eyes in bliss.

"Well, it seems as if you have attained rapture in the way that best pleases you, my friend. I, on the other hand, as much as I shall derive gratification at Darcy's downfall, need release in a more fundamental way." He glanced to the barmaid, who met his gaze with frank provocation.

"Does your wife not satisfy you adequately?" There was no judgment in the question, but a strong undertone of loathing and jealousy.

Wickham laughed gaily, draining his mug in one large gulp. "Let us just say I do not keep Lydia around for her cooking skills. But that fact in no way prevents a real man from tasting elsewhere. Diversity is true living, my friend. Now, go back to your lodge and stay out of sight. I found a chemist with no scruples and have a delivery coming tomorrow. Between that and a well-stocked wine cellar you are comfortably provided for, my lord Marquis. I will contact you in London." He stood and bent close to Orman, smothering his repugnance behind a cheery façade. "I am off to slake my other thirst. Be at peace. We will win this time and be vindicated, I promise you that."

Then he pivoted away and sauntered toward the maid, who deftly caught the coin Wickham tossed her direction.

CHAPTER TWELVE

The Plot Thickens

A BEAMING ALEXANDER PROUDLY gifted his father with the slimy amphibian clutched in his tiny hands, rushing forward as Darcy knelt and showed the appropriate enthusiasm in his son's acquisition. He listened attentively to the tale of how the boy had chased the toad into the reeds and toppled into the river during the hunt. The fact that he was wet with muddy smeared cheeks and grass clinging to his damp curls mattered not. Darcy hugged him, praised his bravery, declared the toad by far the most amazing toad in all of England, and immediately set to the task of providing a temporary home for the pet, after Lizzy replaced the wet gown for a dry one.

A wooden barrel was found in a shed by a baffled groundsman. The Netherfield cook grudgingly gave an old pie pan for a pool after stating firmly that she did not want it returned. Together father and son searched for the best rocks, grasses, and leaves.

"Toss the grass over there, Son. That's it. Now he has a nice bed to lie on if he wishes." Darcy arranged three large stones to form a type of shelter for the impressive sized toad who squatted on a large, flat rock. Darcy crouched next to the barrel with Alexander standing beside as he taught about toads.

"He will probably stay on the rock, or burrow into the grass or under the rocks, but he might go into the water too. However, toads, unlike frogs, prefer to be dry. He probably was not all that pleased when you fell into the water."

He laughed, kissing Alexander's cheek. "They are nocturnal animals which mean they are most active at night."

"Like bats, Papa?"

"Very good! Yes, just like the bats we have near Pemberley. So smart you are, my sweet." He ruffled the dried curls, face flooded with paternal pride. "Remember how we watched them that one night? Flying through the trees?"

Alexander nodded. "Mama so mad."

"Yes, a little bit only. It was past your bedtime and she worries. That is what mothers do. But it was fun, was it not?"

Alexander nodded again, glancing upward with a smile for his father before turning his attention back to the placid toad. "He sick, Papa?"

"No. He is fine. Toads do not really do much, Son. They sit around most of the time and eat bugs." Alexander grimaced. "Spiders and worms too. Give him one of those fat earthworms Mr. Hale brought us."

Alexander dutifully took a wiggling worm from the jar given them by Mr. Hale, one of the stablemen who was also an avid fisherman. He plopped the juicy specimen right before the toad's nose, but the bulbous eyes never blinked. "He not hungry now," the toddler declared authoritatively.

"Perhaps he will eat it later. Fear not, Son, he looks to be fat and healthy." He reached one finger to smooth over the bumpy skin. "Feel how soft he is, Alexander? The warts over his skin will not hurt you, although some types of toads can be mildly poisonous. See these ridges here behind his eyes?" Alexander nodded, one tiny finger rubbing over the mentioned spot. "They are glands that secrete a poison so that predators will leave the toad alone and not try to eat him."

"Poor froggy. No one eat you now."

"No, he is safe enough here. And he is not a frog, my sweet, but a toad. Someday you will know the difference."

"I keep him forever, Papa? Please?"

"I am sorry, Son, but no. He must be returned to his home tomorrow." Alexander's eyes welled with tears, lower lip pouting and quivering. Darcy hugged him to his side, and then pulled him onto his knee and kissed the crown of his head. "Do not be sad. He needs to be where he is happy. He probably has a family who needs him, maybe parents of his own. You would not want to be away from your home, away from your mother and me, would you?" Alexander shook his head emphatically. "Well, neither does he. Tomorrow, after Aunt Kitty's wedding, we will take him back to the riverbank where you found him.

You will have time to play with him before we have to say good-bye. All right?" The toddler sniffed but nodded.

"Let's say good night to your little pet. I better get you up to nanny and your bath before we both get into trouble. Before bed I will read you the Grimm Brothers' tale of a frog prince and the story of the frog plague from the Bible. How is that?"

He nodded again and said good night to the toad, wishing him sweet dreams. Darcy smiled and chose not to remind him what "nocturnal" meant. Alexander gave one last gentle pet to the amphibian, which chose that moment to extend his sticky tongue and snatch the worm before it slithered out of reach, yanking it into his mouth in one neat movement.

Alexander squealed in delight, eyes shining up at Darcy. "See that, Papa?"

"Yes, I did. Now you will not have to worry if he is hungry. Give him a few more worms for the night, Son. Very good. Now, to your bath! You smell like a fishy, muddy boy! If I were a big fish I would think you dinner! Yum!" He slung the giggling, squirming two-year-old over his shoulder, playfully placing nibbles along his chubby arms and waist while making yummy sounds all the way into the house.

Most of the Netherfield residents had gone to Lucas Lodge for a dinner party that evening, leaving only the Darcys and Daniels to dine in solitude since both young mothers needed to remain close to their babies. Darcy sensed Lizzy's distraction even when rhapsodizing over Alexander's toad and when she requested retiring early, pleading a headache, he knew all was not well. He was disturbed but refused to leap to false conclusions and trusted that once the children were asleep she would share whatever was troubling her.

Lizzy reclined on the chaise with Michael at her breast. She wore her usual dreamy expression as she gazed into her baby's face, fingertips caressing over the velvety skin and minute knuckles of his clenched hand. Comfortable in his privacy attire of only trousers and loosened shirt, Darcy sat cross-legged on the floor with Alexander. The youngster was scrubbed clean, smelling of sweet castile soap and fire warmed towels, dressed in a crisp white sleeping gown and stockings. Several errant curls fell over his forehead and into the intent blue eyes that were focused on the assortment of brightly colored marbles arranged before their knees.

In one of his many forays into the dusty attic storage spaces at Pemberley, Darcy had discovered his old collection of marbles. Most of his childhood marbles were of clay or stone, but he and Alexander had since added a number of colorful glass specimens to the mix. Whenever they ventured near a shopping district they searched for marbles. It was a quest, with Darcy seeking used spheres with a history or made of rare materials while Alexander was instantly drawn to the bins of multihued, shiny glass marbles.

Darcy did not yet teach any rules of actual marble play, instead keeping it a simple matter of knocking one marble into another for the fun of making them roll about the large wooden board he had constructed expressly for the game. However, Darcy was learning that his son had inherited his competitive and exacting nature. Alexander would clap with joy when he managed to hit another ball hard enough to cause it to tumble over the flat surface's edge, but most of the time his face was screwed up in deep concentration, the tip of his tongue in the corner of his mouth and brows furrowed as his tiny fingers attempted to aim and launch the marble with the proper technique as learned from his father. Darcy loved that his son studied his actions and mimicked his facial expressions and gestures, but it also made him aware of the reflexive mannerisms Lizzy had been teasing him about for years now!

"Excellent shot, Alexander! Right off the board. Well done! I think you are beating me tonight." He ruffled his son's hair, Alexander beaming with pride. He reached his small body across the board to retrieve the stray marble, one knee nudging the corner and setting the marbles to rolling crazily.

"Oh! Sorry, Papa."

But Darcy was laughing as his large hands spread to prevent the marbles escaping too far while stabilizing the board. "No problem, sweetling. They needed to be rearranged anyway. In fact, here is a new game, let's jiggle the board and see how many we can keep from falling off." His broad grin was met by a smaller identical one and with laughter they set to their new game. Alexander's enthusiasm for the new game brought him to his feet, marbles flying everywhere, and he launched bodily into his father's arms.

Darcy was prepared and caught the soft projectile but feigned surprise and weakness by falling onto his back with a loud, "Oof! You are so strong, my son! Knocked me right over!"

It was a familiar type of play, Darcy instantly continuing the game by lifting the boy high into the air with sturdy broad hands spanning the tiny chest. Alexander stiffened, extended his arms perpendicular, and locked his knees.

"Flap your wings! That's it. What bird do you wish to be today? Hawk? A fearless eagle?"

"Falcon, Papa. A pergin like Mr. Holmes has."

"Excellent choice. Then hold your arms still, soar and glide." He swung his arms, side to side and up and down, Alexander smiling and laughing. "No laughing! Be fierce! Raptors frighten their prey and terrify with a piercing gaze. Show me your peregrine scream, Son. Outstanding! If I were a mouse I would be petrified."

Alexander set his face, attempting to be scary, but it was difficult especially as Darcy kept tilting him downward and bestowing glancing kisses to his face.

"Papa, no! I am hunting. Must be brave. Am I a brave boy?"

"The bravest boy who ever lived. Indeed you are. You killed the ugly spider that scared nanny last week. Remember? So very brave."

"I told the man I was a brave boy. Not ascared of ducks like Michael."

"What man?"

"The man on the horse. Mama not like him." He frowned but then the smile returned. "He say ducks lay eggs in the bushes! I can hunt like brave fox too."

"Yes, of course you can," Darcy murmured. He glanced to his wife where she sat curled on the sofa with eyes closed and cheek resting on Michael's head. The baby was asleep, cuddled against her upper chest. Her face was calm, but without the usual expression of blissful serenity that she typically wore in these moments of maternal relaxation. Darcy's earlier intuition that something was not quite right with his wife came back in a rush as Alexander's innocent remark sent cold shivers up his spine. "The man on the horse" could be anyone considering they were in Lizzy's childhood home, but Darcy knew who it was.

He pulled Alexander to his chest, the toddler protesting for a second before nestling into the warm security of his father's wide torso and embracing arms. His thumb instinctively entered his mouth.

"You are a brave lad indeed, but also sweet and loving and so precious. *My son!*" Darcy whispered fiercely, hands caressing firmly over the tender flesh that comprised his firstborn and heir. "I love you with all my heart, Alexander."

"I lub you too, Papa," he mumbled around his thumb.

Darcy closed his eyes so that other senses would dominate. He felt Alexander's fast beating heart, the heat from the tiny body, the muscles tough but pliantly melting onto his torso, and the steady and deep respirations that tickled his neck. He relished the sensation of Alexander's jaw movements against his left shoulder with each rhythmic suck on the thumb and the plump fingers that stroked the hair by his ear and the linen of his shirt. The springy curls tickled Darcy's nose pleasantly with each breath, the incredible silkiness comforting as he placed gentle kisses onto the youngster's head. The hardy two-year-old was so vibrant and alive, his energy nearly inexhaustible and health superb. His presence in their lives was a constant fount of joy and Darcy loved him with a love that was different than what he felt for Elizabeth, but no less powerful.

He squeezed him tightly, Alexander wiggling and giggling. "Papa! Squeezing my air out!"

Darcy gave another noisy kiss before loosening his grip. Alexander lifted, bright blue eyes meeting his father's worshipful gaze just inches away. "Time for sleep, Son. Tomorrow is an important day for Aunt Kitty and you must again wear your suit." Darcy smiled at the frown that fact elicited. "It shan't be too horrible. And remember, you and your cousin Deborah get to spread flowers. Will that not be fun?" Alexander nodded, although his expression was one of dubiousness. "Now, kiss?" Alexander brightened, inclining to the pursed lips and giving a firm kiss accompanied by a loud, playful *mwah*.

Darcy launched upward abruptly. Alexander shrieked in delight, the noise and movement alerting Lizzy that her two favorite men approached.

"Bedtime for sleepy boys," Darcy said with a smile, placing Alexander on the ground. "Is Michael satiated?"

"Utterly stuffed to the brim. He has already burped and regurgitated the standard amount, so your shirt should be safe."

He leaned over to take the baby and paused to cup Lizzy's cheek with his palm, concern in his voice and expression. "Are you well, beloved?"

Lizzy pressed his hand against her face and then turned to kiss his wrist. "I am fine, dearest. Just tired mostly, but we need to talk when you return."

"Very well. I shall be swift. Come to papa, sweetheart boy. There's my littlest lamb. No, no, stay asleep."

"Story first, yes, Papa?"

"I promised and have the book right over there, Alexander." He pointed. "Grab it on the way out. We will use your Bible for the story of Moses." He turned to his wife, smiling crookedly. "Tales of the Frog Prince and frog plagues."

"Ah! Of course."

Lizzy sat on the edge of the bed brushing her waist-length hair when Darcy returned. Wordlessly he sat behind her while she relinquished the beautiful walnut-handled boar bristle brush gifted to her the past Christmas by him. The mother-of-pearl inlay brush given to her on their wedding night by her new husband had lost too many bristles to be functional, but was tucked into her traveling trunk to be repaired once they reached London. Darcy had provided his wife with several fine brushes since then with no intention of halting the ritual of brushing her lustrous hair. His love for her hair was birthed on that long ago day at Netherfield when she arrived after a three-mile walk to nurse an ill Jane. Her hair had tumbled freely down her back, vivacious and wild, framing her rosy face in a way that was altogether unique. It captured his soul then and the effect brushing her hair had upon him, both arousing and soothing, had not diminished over time.

He clasped the wavy tresses in one hand and passed the stiff bristles through with the other, the sensations flowing through him. Her hair crackled with life, a few individual strands rising as if prepared to fly away while the bulk fell heavily onto his palms, all of them glistening like liquid chocolate with multiple hues of brown. The subtle fragrance of lavender reached his nostrils and he bent to inhale deeply from the mass located at the nape of her neck and bestowed a lingering kiss to the sensitive skin before resuming the task.

"Is your headache entirely gone?"

"Just a twinge in the temples. Nothing significant. It has been warm here compared to home. I think it took my body by surprise." Her right hand caressed over the muscled thigh pressed into hers, eyes closed while he brushed and massaged her left temple with firm fingertips.

Silence descended for some minutes with neither wishing to disturb the intimate experience. Finally Darcy broke the quiet, his voice a resonant whisper. "I doubt it the sun that caused your headache. Tell me what distressed you, love. Who was the man on the horse? Wickham?"

She gasped, stiffening in surprise. "How did you...?"

"Alexander. He mentioned a man you did not like who told him he was brave. And something about ducks and eggs. Not sure about that part." He smiled, trying desperately to internalize his anger and fear. "What did he say to trouble you so?"

Lizzy turned, took the brush from his hand, and dropped it forgotten onto the floor before grasping his warm hands within her own. "Fitzwilliam, please, I beg of you, can we talk about it later? I promise I shall tell all and I assure you it was nothing of any great significance. But right now I ache for you to just hold me and make love to me. I need to feel your protective strength and devotion surrounding me."

She leaned in to initiate feathering kisses over the exposed surfaces of his neck and breastbone, hands seeking more flesh as she gradually peeled the linen away from his chest.

There was something indefinable in her eyes and the tone of her plea that disturbed him tremendously. He knew her thoroughly and her dismay went beyond what seemed likely from an encounter with Wickham, no matter how rude he may have been. Vulnerability or weakness was rarely seen in his strong wife, so he briefly contemplated staying her sensual assault to question her distress. However, her skilled touch was already causing his ardor to rise, and furthermore, he intuitively understood that she needed the special consoling and security that came from their bonding as one.

Gently he clasped her face, lifting away from his chest so he could gaze into her eyes, pouring his love and trust in a look. Then he bent to her mouth, kissing with the lightest of pressures over each lip surface. Tiny suckles, airy grazes with the tip of his tongue, dainty nibbles with his teeth, and minor exhales brushing over her sensitive skin designed to arouse and tranquilize.

Rapidly his alarm diminished. Allaying her anxieties was all that mattered now and he would happily assume the dominant role needed to confer the fortitude she currently lacked. He moved to her neck, applying the same tender nibbles and suckling kisses, while his competent hands roamed with firm pressure over her shoulders and arms. Her dressing gown ties were released, the supple fabrics yielding easily and falling to pool at her waist.

He withdrew to gaze upon her. She was flushed, breathing with the heaviness of beginning passion, breasts firm and rising with each inhalation, expressive brown eyes half lidded. He adored this moment in their lovemaking, when the eddy of burgeoning desire transformed her into his transcendent lover. Elizabeth Darcy, his wife, was a beautiful woman and he never tired of observing her, but the current of happiness and masculine fervor that surged through him in response to her igniting sexual excitement was beyond measure.

He pulled her gauzily draped legs over his, simultaneously reclining her onto the waiting pillows. Gracefully he shifted their bodies toward the middle of the generous Netherfield bed, burrowing deeper into the crisp cotton sheets covering the soft mattress. Propped on one elbow with fingers idly playing with the cascading tresses of her hair, he removed the pretty gown and robe and tossed them onto the floor, his hands caressing and stimulating. His burning scrutiny leisurely scanned the figure spread alongside him. Hunger shone from his eyes and he licked his lips much as a predator anticipates his hunted meal although love and protection drove his appetite. "Fitzwilliam," she murmured, arching into his arousing touch in expectation and desire.

That was his signal, so he bent and kissed her hard.

Their lovemaking took many forms and often she was the leader while he blissfully remained passive to her pointed assault. Typically, she welcomed and yearned for his masculine virility to be at full peak and in command. He had long since relented any fears of crushing her svelte body with his athletic build, knowing she was more than capable of handling his weight pressing into her and his forceful maneuvers as they loved. His prowess so vigorously expressed drove her to heights of insane arousal, and her wanton response was a potent impetus for him.

Tonight she asked for his strength and devotion, both easy for him to give. So he held on to her lips with the penetrating kiss and rolled onto her body until his clothed form swathed her utterly. Lizzy flung her arms over his shoulders, snaking the right under his shirt with hand pressed firmly onto the ridges of his spine below the dip between his shoulder blades. The left clutched his head, fingers twined through his thick hair and holding downward pressure as she returned the feverish kiss with equal intensity.

Never ceasing the delicious attention to her mouth, he grasped her legs and drew them over his waist before traveling his hands with a steady pressure over her silky skin from hips to waist to rib cage and the soft swell of flattened breasts. Long minutes were devoted to titillating play as their passions raged and hunger for more overwhelmed, until Darcy released a guttural groan and gasped her name hotly against the tender space below her earlobe.

"Fitzwilliam, you have far too many clothes on."

"Indeed you are correct," he responded to her whispered words, chuckling breathily. Inhaling deeply to calm his pounding heart, he rose to kneel amid her bent knees. With a sensuous smile he released the remaining clasped button on his shirt, unfastened the cuffs, pulled the tails from his pants, and drew the garment over his head. He then flourished it over his head and pitched it into the darkness beyond the faint lamplight before removing his trousers in the same languid, seductive way.

Darcy arched one brow. "An improvement?"

Lizzy merely nodded while her eyes raked approvingly over his manly torso with lust and yearning unmistakable. Suddenly no longer in the mood to be a passive spectator, she threw her legs about him and tugged. She lifted to meet his advance and shouted his name as waves of pleasure thrummed through her body at their joining. Gleefully she submitted to the furious pace her husband set.

Stamina was one of many marvelous attributes Darcy possessed, along with a divinely gifted ability to cater to their fluctuating passions as they made love. He discerned every sigh and moan, infallibly reacting with a blend of power and tenderness to best please her. With a masterful touch he provided all that she needed.

Every sense was acutely alive in a manner that differed from any other situation. In a beautiful paradox they could vividly feel the sensations in each nerve of their own bodies and differentiate the multiple points where their skin met, while also melding into a single entity ablaze with pleasure until attaining a summit of exquisite glory and tumbling over together.

Lying in a heap of pliant flesh, Darcy made no move to leave the warmth of his wife's trembling body, and Lizzy had no wish for him to roll away. Instead, they absorbed the residual tremors and bursts of energy as they exhaled soft sounds of love between gentle kisses. The final shivers passed and he then lifted to smooth the hair from her face and look into her eyes.

"You are amazing, Fitzwilliam. As my lover and as my husband. You are the only man who comforts me and offers unassailable protection." She impishly added a tight squeeze to his rear for emphasis. "But mostly as my lover. I still fear I shall perish someday from how you set my heart to bursting."

Darcy felt a glow of egotistical satisfaction. All his accomplishments as the Master of Pemberley, or in any area of his life, paled in comparison to being able to ceaselessly gratify his wife. He knew that in some respects that was typical male arrogance and accepted that his manliness and virility were essential to his being. Yet knowing without the tiniest doubt that she attained pleasure of the highest order through him was the true test, and he thanked God daily for the competence to do so.

He nuzzled his lips and nose over her soft skin, and huskily murmured, "I desperately desire to fall asleep with you in my arms, best beloved, which is all the greater reason why we should rise. Let us sit on the sofa, sipping brandies while you share what happened today."

Minutes later he had stoked the fire, poured two half-glasses of fine cognac, and settled their naked bodies onto the plush sofa nearest the blaze. A quilted coverlet draped over the legs lying across his lap and her back resting against the couch's arm.

She sipped the sweet liquid, caressed the strong fingers laced between her thinner ones, and smiled into his alert eyes. "It is as I said before. He said nothing of any significance or that was particularly disturbing. My distress was in the incident happening at all because I abhorred telling you of it." She halted the retort with her fingertips to his lips. "Do not say it, Fitzwilliam, as you should know I would never entertain the thought of withholding information from you." She ran one fingertip over the creases furrowing his brow. "What I abhor is being the bearer of any news that will unsettle you. Even something as benign as delivering a newspaper that announces one of your horses losing the St. Leger."

"That was hardly benign," he grumbled irritatingly, still steamed over an episode some months old. "If Lord Hessing had employed a modicum of sense or listened to any one of us at the Jockey Club he never would have allowed Schreiber to jockey Lady Beth. She could have won and should have if the fool…" He stopped, frown erasing at the amused expression on her face. He shook his head, eyes closing briefly. "Very well, point taken. I shall attempt to contain my temper and listen calmly."

"Thank you." She leaned for a kiss to his cheek, launching into a complete narration of the Wickham encounter, as best she could recall it.

Darcy was unmoved by Wickham's slurs against his personality, grudgingly acknowledging a certain truth to some of them. Nor was he disturbed by the false allegations as to the motive for their marriage. The truth of their mutual love was far too ingrained to be vexed by such ignorance and evil, although hearing Elizabeth's firm reaffirmations was pleasing. He was angered that his sons, mostly Alexander, had been subjected to such lies, but Elizabeth assured him that Alexander was too young and too devoted to his parents to be influenced by vague words from a total stranger.

What incensed him the most was the insolence in presuming an intimacy with his wife and son! He could easily strangle Wickham for that alone. Yet he knew it was precisely this reaction that motivated his childhood playmate to choose the words he did. Try as he might, Darcy could find nothing overtly threatening in talks of gardening and ducks and eggs at Hyde Park or inherited personality traits. The encouragement to Alexander to break the rules or cause mischief was annoying, but Darcy knew his son well enough to know that was unlikely. He interpreted those remarks as nothing more than Wickham wishing to aggravate his nemesis and bring turmoil into their family felicity.

In the end he was forced to agree that there appeared to be no nefarious scheme attached to the encounter. He would remain cautious to be sure, but refused to permit his ire to erupt into full-blown fury. As Lizzy had wisely observed several days ago, his rage led to discord between them, which led to a victory for Wickham. The idea made his blood run cold, and he reflexively pulled Lizzy into his body for a tight embrace.

"So in the end he was Wickham in top form," he spoke into her hair, "spouting lies for the pure enjoyment of it." He released a harsh laugh, tipping her backward to once again rest against the pillowed sofa arm. He stroked over her cheek, gazing intently into her eyes. "I suppose we both expected it. At least I knew he would not be able to resist cornering you for a few barbs in hopes that our love was not as strong as it is."

"Mr. Wickham, I am saddened to admit, likely has no concept of love. Despite my assertions to the contrary, he is probably congratulating himself on reminding me of how impossible our relationship. If it pleases him to do so it matters naught to me. We know the truth and neither of us would convince him otherwise even if we wished to try. But it is sad for Lydia to be bound to such an unfeeling man."

"Is that what yet troubles you?"

"Partially, of course. I would wish more for my sister despite knowing how foolish she is." She sighed. "But, no, there is more. Although now, here in the safety of your arms and after the marvelous expression of our love and this discourse, my vision seems all the more fanciful and ridiculous."

"Elizabeth, I do not understand."

"After we returned to Netherfield I was upset. We went for a walk, all of us, and I told Jane about Mr. Wickham. It helped to talk to her, unburden myself to a degree, but I was so dreading causing you any pain. I will confess, William, that for a few moments at least, I wished we were not always so honest with each other. But it was only a fleeting, cowardly thought as I longed to share the burden with you, knowing that you would ease my heart."

"Just one of the jobs I gladly discharge, beloved."

"I know and I love you for it." She paused and inhaled deeply, her voice muted as she resumed. "It is like a dream that seems so real when you first awake with heart pounding and the sensations vivid. But then the more you try to bring the images into precise focus they become hazier still and slither away until all that is left is an impression that lacks clarity or power. This is like that. After I told Jane, as I was yet wrestling with my emotions, I looked across the meadow to a parked carriage. It was just sitting there, alone, not ominous in the least. Then, for a breath of time only, I imagined I saw a face."

She was staring into the distance, brows wrinkled with concentration. Darcy examined her closely, but she did not appear to be anxious. Rather she looked confused and mildly irritated.

"I cannot think for the life of me why I would imagine him at that moment. There is no connection whatsoever, except that they are both men who have caused us pain in profound ways."

"Who? Who did you imagine?"

She turned back to him, peering unblinkingly into his baffled eyes. "The Marquis of Orman."

Darcy drew in a sharp breath, lips pressing together until nearly invisible, and the spasm that jerked through his jaw was marked. "Are you sure?" He choked out in a low growl.

"No! William that is the point! I am the exact opposite of sure. I could not describe what I think I saw if my life depended on it! That is what gave me a headache and has distracted me all night. Not Mr. Wickham, but the struggle to bring coherency to what is now only a vague impression of a person we shall never forget. I knew I had to tell you, but it does seem rather stupid since I cannot recall the tiniest detail that lends credence to speaking his name."

"Yet his is the name that surfaced in your mind when you saw… whatever it is you saw. Why?"

"I do not know! Except that, if you examine it from a certain perspective, they are, as I said, men who have caused us pain. Perhaps on some unconscious level dealing with Mr. Wickham has unearthed frightening memories of Lord Orman."

"Tell me what you saw, as much as you can recall."

"A carriage, plain and nondescript, sitting on the road some distance away. No movement from the coachman. I did not think much of it initially. Then I detected movement from within. A hand, I think, holding a walking stick and tapping on the ceiling to alert the coachman. William, it truly was the barest glimpse. Perhaps not even that. Did I see a face? I want to say I did, but all

I remember is pale flesh holding a cane, a flash of gold, and dark eyes. Orman's name seared through my brain and I doubled over in pain. That part was real. The pain. But Alexander was there with dandelions, and Mrs. Hanford and Jane expressing concern, and as quickly as it was there it was gone. The carriage too. Lost in the dust and I saw nothing else."

Darcy had risen from the sofa and was standing stiffly before the fire, his face etched with perturbation and fingers fidgeting. "You may judge it nothing of import, Elizabeth, but I do not. It has been years since your last nightmare of Orman. There is no logical reason for you to conjure his name or image unless something you saw in those fleeting seconds reminded you of him. Granted, that is not proof it *was* him, but I will not assume it of no consequence either. You are not typically a fanciful woman."

"What did you last hear of the Marquis's activities?"

Darcy shook his head curtly, voice hollow in his abstraction. "Rumors mostly and I do not attend to gossip. I know he was ill and weak for a long time. Talk of the extensiveness of his injuries varied, many wildly incorrect, as I know since I was the one who inflicted them. No one has seen or heard from him since he left Derbyshire. He retreated to his estate on the southeastern border of Dartmoor and apparently never leaves. He has not been to London at all. I heard once... Wait!" He pivoted sharply, face gray and drawn. "Wickham lives in Devon! What part again?"

"Exeter, I believe, but that is north. It is too coincidental, William." But the faintness of her tone belied the assertion. She suddenly recalled the vague comments by Lydia, as she and Jane had discussed just that afternoon.

"I do not believe there is anything coincidental about it. Rather, it is rational." His voice rose, words rushing over each other. "News travels eventually over the breadth of England. Wickham hears of the incident with Orman, learns he resides miles away, and plots a course of revenge with the one man in the entire country who can not only fund it but has more hatred toward me than he does."

Darcy was pale and rigid with rage. Wrath caused his heart to pound painfully and every muscle to ache from clenching. His voice was flat and icy cold. Lizzy jumped up, crossing to where he stood immobile, and grasped his face between her hands, forcing his darkened eyes to meet hers.

"William! Get control of yourself! You are leaping pell-mell into unfounded conclusions. No!" She interrupted his response before it was uttered. "You listen to me. All you say could, and I stress *could*, be a possibility. But my frayed vision is not proof of anything. Nor is Wickham accosting me for ludicrous maligns against you." She wrapped her arms around his neck, hugging fiercely and pressing her warm body into his chilled skin.

"Elizabeth," he mumbled from the depths of her neck, "I cannot ignore this."

"I know. And you should not. But nothing has really changed. Tomorrow Kitty will be married and the day after we will leave for London. Once there you can exert all your considerable influence to discover what, if anything, is really going on with Mr. Wickham and Lord Orman."

"We need to know for certain. You do understand this, dearest, do you not?" His eyes pleaded with hers, hands steely where they rested on her waist.

She nodded. "Of course…"

But he was already looking over her shoulder, eyes haunted as he drew inward, seemingly forgetting her presence. "I should have killed him when he was under my blade. Swift and conclusive. I was a fool to leave him alive, more dangerous than before." He paused, inhaling expansively. His brow creases deepened, his timbre low and questioning as he asked, "What could they be planning? Orman has few friends and none who are idiotic enough to collaborate with him. Especially against me. A scheme to damage the estate? Pemberley? Wickham would love that!"

He paused again but quickly shook his head. "No, that is unfeasible. Wickham knows nothing of Pemberley finances or management and the Manor is too well protected. Orman does not have the wealth or influence to damage the estate. They cannot harm me in that way."

Lizzy gasped, fingertips digging into his shoulders. "He would… he would not try to… injure you? William! I…"

Darcy was abruptly alert and focused, fully aware of her trembling and panicked eyes. He shook his head decisively, cupping her face within his cool but sturdy hands. "Do not fear for me, love. I can take care of myself and am extremely cautious and vigilant. Besides, that is not Wickham's way or Orman's for that matter."

He wiped the tears off her cheeks with tender thumbs, studying her eyes in an attempt to convey confidence and assurance. But as he gazed into her frightened eyes his essence grew colder and an agonizing tightness banded across his chest. Neither Wickham nor Orman may comprehend love and family devotion from a personal perspective, but as a result of their individual dealings with Darcy, each was wise to the depths of his emotions for his loved ones. Memories of how Wickham plotted and attempted to destroy Georgiana in an effort to wound him flashed through his brain.

"The boys!" He pivoted so precipitously that he almost tripped over his own feet. Recovering instantly, he grabbed the carefully folded robe that Samuel always placed on the chest at the end of the bed and had one arm within the sleeve and was turning back toward Lizzy before she had taken a breath. "They are staying here, with us, tonight and tomorrow night. And you three will not be allowed out of my sight for a second. Do you understand?" The robe was on, if not yet belted, and his hands were gripping her upper arms painfully. She had rarely seen him so intense and would not have been able to disagree in the face of his exigent command if she had wanted to.

He did not wait for a reply or a nod of assent. Her consent was not necessary. He was telling her how it would be, not asking for her opinion. He strode to the door, throwing it open, and was halfway down the hall before properly concealing his nakedness. He did not care. Nor did he acknowledge or apologize for the near heart seizure he gave Mrs. Hanford when he aggressively hurtled through the nursery door. He glanced to both sleeping bodies assuring their reality and safety, crossing toward Alexander's bed. He spared a rapid visual exchange with Lizzy, who he knew was following, and gestured curtly toward Michael.

Alexander was tight in his embrace, vibrant flesh and strongly beating heart pressed into the bare skin of his chest, before he permitted a slight easing in his coiled terror. In a coarse rumble he informed Mrs. Hanford that the boys would be sleeping in the Master's chamber, offering no other explanation. He turned to Lizzy where she stood with Michael clutched in her arms, brushed over the baby's plump ruddy cheek with his knuckles, and then grasped his wife's hand, leading back to their bedchamber in as much of a whirl as the entry.

Not until the four of them were nestled snug and warm under the goose down duvet did Darcy breathe freely. Alexander had barely twitched during the relocation, now curled in a tight ball beside his father and sharing the wide pillow. Darcy closed his eyes and kissed the soft forehead, fingertips smoothing over the disorderly curls while he inhaled deeply of the fresh scent emanating from the toddler's skin. He drew back a few inches, fingers caressing to the open mouth where a slack hand with moist thumb poised on the plump lower lip. Darcy smiled. "I love you, my son," he murmured, bringing the chubby fist to his mouth for another kiss. "You are safe with your father."

He rolled carefully onto his back, looking over his shoulder first to make sure there was plenty of space between his body and Michael. Lizzy's delicate hand ran over his arm, tugging, letting him know it was safe. Naturally, Michael *had* stirred during the displacement but was easy to calm at his mother's breast. Lizzy gently patted his back to assist the release of trapped air, but her gaze rested on her husband's face while she continued to stroke over his arm.

Darcy captured her hand, fingers lacing with hers, and pulled it in for a lingering kiss to her knuckles and light sucks to each tip.

"Relieved, my heart?"

"Marginally," he responded. "Tomorrow I will construct a pallet with blankets and pillows near the fire so we can place the boys there and give us more space. Darcy House is unassailable unless one mounts a siege, and I am in command and know it is secure. I doubt I shall sleep well until then. If then."

Lizzy did not admonish him for overreacting. The incident that afternoon remained hazy at best, and her mind shrank from contemplating the potentials if Darcy's conclusions were correct. She simply could not deal with it and shamelessly relegated the task to her vastly competent spouse. Knowing he was in absolute control, feeling the potency that radiated from every pore, hearing the sobriety in his voice, observing the steadfast reliability in his blue eyes, and having been witness time and again to his supreme dependability and keen intellect was enough to allay her fears.

"I apologize for alarming you with my melodrama, dearest. In the light of day I may feel a bit foolish for reacting so. But I confess I breathe easier knowing you are safe within my reach. I could not bear anything happening to you or our children."

Lizzy nodded, smiling her assurance in his capabilities and understanding of his fears.

"Sleep now. Your eyes are weary." He brushed over her cheek, fingers yet entwined with hers, and touched her eyelids until they closed. "Sleep. I will watch over our sons. I love you." His voice dropped to a whisper, murmuring loving devotions until her respirations were regular.

He watched her sleep, eyes frequently drifting to the tiny body of Michael cradled against her breast and the long-limbed form of his firstborn sprawled to his left. Every muscle ached with fatigue, but he would not fall into a troubled sleep for a long while.

CHAPTER THIRTEEN

A Wedding in Meryton

DARCY WAS JOLTED TO semi-wakefulness late the next morning by a pair of soft but surprisingly heavy elbows landing square on his chest.

"Papa, wake up! We need to see my toad!"

Darcy opened bleary eyes, befuddled brain registering the anxious expression of Alexander, whose face was close enough to see two of him. Darcy blinked and groaned as remembrance seeped into fogged wits.

"Papa!" Alexander gripped his father's chin between pudgy fingers, shaking for attention. "Hurry! What if he is hungry?"

Darcy nodded, reaching to encircle his son's body for a squeeze while rubbing gritty eyes with the other hand. He looked to the right, but the bed was empty. "Where are your mother and Michael?"

"Gone," the boy answered unhelpfully, unconcerned over absent mother and brother or apparently confounded by waking in a bed other than his own. The issue of toad safety was far more pressing a worry!

"Your toad is fine, I promise you. Come, let's find your mother and attend to our own hunger. I am in need of coffee."

"But..."

"Trust me, Son. He is just fine. Now give me a kiss."

Lizzy and Michael were in the sitting room, both consuming a morning meal, when the elder Darcy men joined them. Thus the morning began. Darcy had lain awake theorizing until the darkest hours of the night, finally falling into a deep but nightmare-filled sleep that was far from sufficient for his needs. Being continually prodded by a flipping toddler all night long did not help either. Nonetheless, his superior perspicacity prevailed and he wasted little time before executing the necessary requirements.

He was dead serious when stating that he would not permit his three loved ones out of his sight, but of course in the light of day the realities of such a blanket statement were not as easy to arrange. Lizzy departed to bathe and prepare for her sister's wedding, but only after being sternly reminded to keep Marguerite within shouting distance and to send for him before leaving her chambers. The nursery door was kept bolted, Mrs. Hanford instructed to open for no one other than Mr. or Mrs. Darcy. It was an odd request that baffled the nanny but was executed without question.

Darcy performed his own toilette hastily, returning to the freshly scrubbed faces of his sons with relief. He did not think that Wickham or Orman would boldly storm Netherfield to abduct or harm his family, but he was not going to slacken his defense.

With the boys clean and dressed, and Mrs. Hanford finally apprised of cursory details regarding her Master's strange behavior, the four of them set out to check on the toad, who was fine as promised. With a contented Michael clasped to Darcy's chest, they knelt beside the barrel and supplied the indifferent amphibian with three more fat worms. The baby was mildly intrigued by the animal, but was equally fascinated by the buttons on his father's jacket. Darcy would not relinquish Michael from his arms to the nanny until they were safely sequestered in the library. And then it was only so he could speak to Colonel Fitzwilliam and Dr. Darcy in private, and the three were mere feet away within easy reach, if out of earshot.

"Why the long face, Cousin? Wedding days are ones of rejoicing."

"For some perhaps." George countered as he took the chair across from his somber nephew and smiling friend, addressing the latter with an exaggerated grimace, "I am yet mourning every bachelor I know dropping like flies in winter. Thank the Maker marriage is not a contagion."

"Hogwash! You smiled and danced at my wedding. If you found a lady as perfect as my Simone you would embrace the infection, I assure you."

"I would continue this argument and eloquently prove your misconceptions, however I sense that William is about to throttle us for misplaced jocularity. I deduce you have not summoned us here for a casual chat?"

"Indeed you do appear more serious than usual. Did Wickham finally cross a line? I sure hope so. With all the military men floating about it would be a spectacular brawl!"

"I fear it is worse than that." Darcy recounted the whole tale sans any embellishments. Richard and George listened, faces growing graver by the moment.

"It does seem rather coincidental," George said when Darcy finished. "But as you said yourself, coincidence alone is inconclusive. Devon is a large county. I have been there several times visiting Estella and have heard nothing of this Lord Orman. The odds seem slim that Wickham would stumble across him."

"True, but he may have sought him out. That would not surprise me in the least as Wickham has ever conspired and schemed."

"Exactly my point, Richard."

"But, Darcy, remember that Lizzy was unsure. We must consider that."

"Yes," George interjected, "but Elizabeth is not a woman prone to flights of fancy. She saw something that triggered the Marquis's name, even if her subconscious has submerged the stimulus to that impression. I trust her instinct enough to claim caution, no matter how extreme the likelihood of these two men collaborating."

"That is all I am asking at this point." Darcy nodded, his face relaxing ever so slightly.

"We shall assist in watching over them, Son. Georgiana as well, so have no fear in that quarter. As the colonel pointed out, a veritable sea of soldiers roam the premises. It would be sheer insanity to attempt even the slightest mischief."

"I can offer more than that. I have connections despite my retirement. Certain men I know who are highly qualified to undertake a spy mission and would leap at the opportunity for adventure and intrigue. I will send a message immediately and with luck you will have profitable information within a fortnight."

"Thank you, Cousin."

Richard inclined his head. "Pleased to be of service. Fortunate for you I have not completely lost my edge or forgotten my expertise. My ego is boosted to be indispensable again. You owe me," he concluded with a smug grin.

Darcy grunted. "I am sure the tally is in my favor, Colonel. But I will concede one point as you have given me an idea. I will write to Mr. Daniels.

He can quietly investigate Orman and Wickham, through legitimate channels, unlike how your 'spies' will undoubtedly go about it."

George laughed. Richard merely shrugged noncommittally.

Those tasks accomplished, there was nothing further for the three to do but maintain a cautious vigilance. No alarms were raised and no hints of unrest were allowed to disturb the joyous celebration. Not for the world would any of them wish to distress Miss Kitty's special event.

Shortly before noon, the crowd of witnesses converged upon the Meryton church where the eldest Bennet daughters had been married. The nondescript church was beautified with early spring blooms exuding a pleasant scent into the cool air, green vines and ribbons twined together were hung for additional color, and tall spermaceti wax candles lent a soft glow. The groom stood tall and majestic in formal military attire, the mass of ribbons and medals adorning his chest unable to vie with the proud expression on his face. The bride wore a gown of palest rose with accents all in shades of grassy green, softly woven muslin and lawn drapes that emphasized her curvy figure while maintaining proper modesty. She was a vision, and Randall nearly fainted from lack of oxygen before remembering to breathe!

Alexander walked in front of his aunt scattering rose petals with a studied precision humorous to observe. Laughter rippled, finally eliciting a shy smile from the serious boy, who dashed to the comfort of his father's lap the instant the last petal hit the carpeted floor.

The sacred vows were exchanged, ring placed on the bride's finger, and chaste kiss bestowed in a short, traditional ceremony that was nonetheless lovely and moving. The matrimonial binding of a beaming and lovely Katherine Bennet to a smiling and handsome Major General Randall Artois concluded without incident

The undisputed happiness and love surging forth from the bride and groom was adequate to allay most of Darcy's fears. As when sitting in the audience during Mary's wedding, Darcy held on to his wife's hand, absently fondling the diamond and sapphire ring on her third finger while he mentally replayed their wedding, one of the happiest days of his life. Alexander sat protectively on his lap, and Michael was secure at Netherfield with the other children too young to attend the ceremony. Georgiana sat sandwiched between Lizzy and Richard. Taken altogether, Darcy relaxed tremendously.

Plus, it was amusing to note George Wickham's discomfort.

The number of soldiers of varying ranks perpetually rose higher as the morning progressed until there was practically a whole military company inhabiting Netherfield! Lydia brazenly flirted with the red-coated men, her coquettish nature and penchant for military gentlemen obviously not diminished despite her marriage. Or perhaps she missed Wickham wearing a uniform. Whatever the case, it was appalling to witness but also amusing to observe the increasing glower upon Wickham's face.

Darcy's expression never changed from his usual serious politeness, but his muscles eased in the satisfaction of Wickham's irritation. Eventually the latter collected himself, his native charm and ease overcoming his vexation. He remained unobtrusive for the most part and did not approach Darcy or his immediate family, but did a fair amount of his own flirting.

The wedding breakfast exceeded all expectations. Netherfield's kitchen staff performed brilliantly with an array of delicious dishes leaving none wanting. As expected for such an occasion, happiness and laughter abounded. None, of course, felt as joyous as Randall and Kitty.

"Where did you say you were spending your wedding night?"

"I never said and would not divulge that information even if you applied a hot poker to my skin!" Randall answered his brother Roland's seemingly innocent query with a laugh. "I shudder to imagine what you jokers would spring on me as a special wedding gift."

All five of the Artois men wore wounded expressions, Reginald speaking for all of them. "We are deeply grieved that you would accuse us so, Brother. We are universal in our delight at your happiness and only wish to bestow our blessings upon your union in the most overwhelming terms. Any special gifts delivered shall be designed to enhance your wedded bliss and augment your first night as a married couple."

Randall snorted and rolled his eyes. "How Major Henderson tolerates your long-winded pontificating is beyond my comprehension. Your secretarial skills must be consummate."

"I am the best," Reginald affirmed without a hint of equivocation, "but that is beside the point."

"I was guessing you planned to lodge at Uncle's house in Oxfordshire as that is on the way to Bath," Royce speculated, eyeing Randall and Kitty closely for a telltale response.

He was disappointed. Kitty knew the brothers fairly well between her own interactions with the Artois family and Randall's conversations so merely smiled benignly. Randall's face was blank and he said nothing.

"Quit fishing, Royce." The eldest, Roderick, spoke finally. He gazed at his brothers with feigned reproach. "Randall never said they were going to Bath. Could just as easily be Brighton or the Lake District or…"

"Or maybe we are sailing to France or taking the ferry to Ireland," Randall interrupted with a laugh. "We may spend our wedding night at the inn down in Meryton, Aunt Phillip's townhouse in London, or my house near the barracks. And, since I have mentioned all those places you can therefore conclude it will be none of them!"

"Unless it *is* one of them and you mentioned it to throw us off the scent," Royce inserted with a grin.

Randall shrugged. "Maybe. Maybe not. Face it, I have outwitted you so leave it be. My bride and I will have a perfect honeymoon without any interference, or 'blessings upon our union' from any of you."

"Very well then. We admit defeat to your superior intellect and skills at stealth. Clever you are, Brother, but remember that no matter where you honeymoon, after a month you will be returning to your house in London and we all know where that is!"

Roland's smug mien was mirrored by the others, until Randall replied, "Indeed. Bear in mind, however, that I know where all of *you* dwell. Retaliation would only add to the joy of my homecoming."

And at this point Kitty burst into gales of laughter.

Expressing their thanks and accepting the numerous well wishes was time consuming, but the newlyweds managed to depart Netherfield by mid-afternoon. Georgiana embraced Kitty the longest, whispering her assurance that her wedding would definitely not take place until Kitty returned.

As predicted, the newlywed Artoises were relieved not to be traveling far, although the handful of miles proved enough to wildly escalate their fervency. Randall did not unhitch the horses, instead opting to carry his wife into the house and straight to the bed. The lovely surroundings and exceeding joy in officially being husband and wife added a dimension to their lovemaking that neither had expected. Despite Randall's assertion that he would keep his wife in bed for the whole week, they took a few long walks in the wood and enjoyed the rustic scenery before moving on to Bath. In every way imaginable it was the perfect honeymoon and an auspicious beginning to their life together. But that is for another story.

In the meantime, the festivities at Netherfield continued until late afternoon with the guests occasionally turning their thoughts to the newlyweds but primarily enjoying the food and entertainment. Darcy and Elizabeth performed their duties as host and hostess, but did breathe a sigh of relief when the final guest departed that evening. Darcy was able to slip away with Alexander to return the toad to his riverbank home before darkness made that chore impossible. Just as dusk began to creep over the horizon, Darcy closed the wide front door, threw the latch, and fell against the thick wood to momentarily close his eyes in exhaustion.

George laughed, encircled the weary younger man's shoulders, and steered wordlessly to the game room where Richard, Charles, and Joshua Daniels were already chalking their cues. Several rounds of billiards and a couple of glasses of brandy were just what Darcy needed to unwind. No one brought up the subject of Wickham or Orman, instead chatting amiably about the wedding, politics, horse racing, medicine, or anything else that arose naturally. By the time Darcy rejoined his wife and sons in their chambers he was nearly restored to his old self. He kept the boys close, constructing a pallet of thick quilts by the fire that ended up being a place for extended play and story time.

"Papa, do you think my toad happy?"

Darcy looked into the anxious face of his firstborn, smiling and not admonishing him for interrupting the story he was reading aloud. "I am sure he is content, Son. He is with his family, just as you are, maybe reading a story to his children."

Alexander frowned, meditating on that information for a minute before shaking his head. "No, Papa, frogs not really read. Only in pretend."

Darcy laughed, pulling him closer to his side and kissing the top of his head. "Indeed you are correct. I was only teasing."

"Fuss no more over the toad, Alexander. Let your father finish the story. I want to hear what happens to Gulliver on Lilliput, do you?"

Alexander nodded. Michael squealed and babbled, his hand tapping on the open page of the book Darcy held as if he concurred with his mother's question. He was perched on his father's left thigh, fat body bouncing and wiggling, and the silver rattle gripped in his hand waving about dangerously. He looked upward into Darcy's face and released a stream of bilabial monosyllables that apparently translated into his wish for Darcy to recommence the reading.

After a kiss to his second son's head, he did, resonant voice rising and falling in a storyteller's cadence. Michael calmed, the rattle brought to his mouth for serious gnawing as he listened to the adventures of Gulliver.

The final restoration to Darcy's equilibrium came once the children were asleep and Lizzy was lying snugly against his side with head resting on his shoulder. They wore nightwear and had no plans to be intimate with the children in the same room, but that did not prevent tender caressing under the concealing covers. In light of the exhausting day and extreme emotion, it was soothing to hold each other.

"Miss Kitty, or Mrs. Artois I should say, was a vision of loveliness. Pale colors become her." He drew the long lock of his wife's hair that he had been negligently toying with to his nose. "Of course, she was no match for how stunning you were on the day we married."

"Naturally not! It is requisite for you to make such a declaration. As I must say that your abundant handsomeness on our wedding day was no match for a man in military garb."

"Is it not the truth, Mrs. Darcy?"

She pursed her lips, eyes twinkling, and answered with feigned uncertainty. "Well, the leather, jeweled baldric and gold saber did add a certain panache and éclat missing at our nuptials. Makes a definitive judgment difficult to render."

"I *knew* I should have worn my grandfather's Italian rapier that day!" he declared dramatically. "I feared being ostentatious."

"Never any fear of you being ostentatious, my love. You so easily blend into the background." She laughed, closing the gap for a kiss.

"You must stop that, Elizabeth," he murmured huskily against her mouth, "or I shall not be able to restrain myself and will wildly make love to you unconcerned with giving Alexander an education he does not yet need."

Lizzy halted the activity of her fingers, not aware that she had reached to feather light caresses over her husband's left ear and the hair that curled there. Early in their marriage Lizzy learned how erotically sensitive Darcy was in the region of his ears. The lightest touch elicited faint moans and shivers, and a kiss or subtle breath drove him insane. She found it humorous since her own ears were only ticklish. She also found it useful. A last moment brushing kiss or stroke to his aural area was a gift she delighted in bestowing from time to time as he departed the house. The muted pule caught in his throat and flicker of fire in his sapphire eyes was satisfying. When they made love it was one of a handful of tactics she knew to employ that plummeted his ardor over the edge of control into blissful, wanton abandon.

Now, however, she obeyed the plea, moving her hand to his linen-covered chest and docilely laying it over his accelerated heartbeat. Squelching the instantaneous surge of gratification in knowing how easily her touch provoked his desire, she changed the subject.

"The newlyweds are enjoying the clear air of an exotic locale and tomorrow we will be breathing the clogged air of London, yet I hold no jealousy. Even the busyness of Town will be a welcome respite from recent drama."

"You and Georgiana can shop to your heart's content. Actually, we will all need to acquire new clothes to a greater degree than normal. The endless stream of fêtes to honor our new King will require the latest fashions."

"Interesting that you would mention fashion. Georgiana brought several magazines from France. Styles are changing with Paris designers setting what is vogue, as always. Did you notice the subtle differences in Georgie's gown?"

"I noticed that she was beautiful and wearing a pink dress."

Lizzy laughed. "It was mauve, my darling. Thank goodness your tailor is cognizant of advancing men's fashion or you would be a laughingstock."

"That is precisely why I chose him and gladly pay his exorbitant prices. Like any excellent modiste, he keeps abreast of the whimsies of style trends. Take note of all the magazines you can obtain on the subject as you will need to be brilliantly garmented for the coronation next year."

"Plenty of time to worry about that momentous event," she said, attempting to be casual, but the tremor in her voice divulged her excitement. Darcy smiled in understanding.

It was not every day, or once in a person's lifetime, that a new monarch was crowned. George III had ruled for some sixty years, few remembering his traditional coronation. All of England breathlessly anticipated the procession and ceremonies scheduled to take place next year when King George IV publicly received his crown and scepter from the Archbishop of Canterbury in Westminster Abbey. The rumors of how grand the planned coronation was to be were rife. The latest news circulating was that the King had purchased the famous forty-five carat French Blue diamond once owned by Louis XIV and later given to Queen Marie Antoinette, only to be stolen from the Garde-Meuble and then lost during the Revolution. Speculation as to how the King would use the renowned, two-hundred-year-old gem was only one of numerous coronation-related topics open for discussion. The King vocally determined to have a coronation that outshone Napoleon Bonaparte's in 1804, Parliament voting to provide a staggering fortune to make it so. Thus, though over a year away, the enthusiasm mounted. The benefit of having eighteen months from the time when the Prince Regent became King in January of 1820 until the official coronation was latched on to by Society with the slated parties lavish and frequent.

"I shall need to buy an additional carriage to haul the new gowns and jewels back to Pemberley by the time this Season ends," Darcy said, only partly jesting. "I know you, my dear wife, and am certain we shall exhaust ourselves in revelry."

"Only moderately," she said with a laugh. "I still have a baby at home to care for, so cannot drag you all over London until the darkest hours of the night." She leaned to bestow a slow kiss. "I always prefer to stay home with you and our children over dancing and socializing. Have no fear, love."

He grunted. "We shall see how well that plan holds. I think I will be ready for our restful holiday hiatus in Kent after Easter."

"It will be wonderful to see Anne and Raul again. And the baby." Lizzy spoke softly, laying her head onto his chest and squeezing tightly.

"Indeed," he answered. "I have worried over her so these past years. She has suffered too many health issues and traumas. Perhaps marriage was not the best choice for her, but then I know how she loves Dr. Penaflor and how devoted he is to her."

"It is an unfortunate consequence, I suppose. But you know that even with the losses, Anne would not wish it otherwise. Now they have Margaret."

"Lady Catherine says the infant is strong and that Anne is yet fragile, but largely healed from the ordeal. Still, I will not rest easy until I see for myself."

Lizzy smiled and hugged him again, thoughts momentarily shifting to Kent and the inhabitants of Rosings as they snuggled together and drifted into sleep.

The former Anne de Bourgh, now Mrs. Raul Penaflor Aleman de Vigo, would unequivocally affirm that marrying Dr. Raul Penaflor was the happiest moment of her life. Not a one of the subsequent heartaches in the previous two years could supplant the overwhelming bliss they found in each other. In every way it was precisely as her cousin and lifelong friend had confided to her on the shores of Rowan Lake: "All I can assert with absolute confidence is the astounding joy to be found in a union with one whom you love and who loves you in return."

Anne had found that joy with Raul and felt no regrets. The losses had taken their toll, and privately Anne had doubted a baby was ever to be, but strangely her fourth pregnancy proceeded with hardly a glitch. For the entire nine months Anne was chronically tired and pale, but otherwise proved to be one of those fortunate women who barely notice they are pregnant. She suffered not a single negative symptom, glowed with an inner happiness that superseded the pallor, and had a labor that lasted for four hours start to finish.

Margaret Catherine Victoria Penaflor Aleman de Vigo was tiny but perfectly healthy. Anne remained frail and wan for weeks and was unable to nurse her daughter as she had wished, but gradually the persistent care from her private physician, who loved her obsessively, prevailed.

The next day was their scheduled departure from Hertfordshire. Mrs. Bennet insisted on hosting her family for a last tea at Longbourn before they quit the area. Darcy grit his teeth and did not argue, but he prepared for a last-minute confrontation with Wickham.

The carriages with their luggage and servants were sent on to Darcy House while their coach diverted onto the narrow avenue leading to Longbourn. As soon as they crossed the threshold they heard Mrs. Bennet's voice raised in lamentation. Mary greeted them at the door with an explanation.

"Mama is distressed over Lydia departing today. It has taken all of us by surprise as they planned to visit through Easter. Barely did we sit down for breakfast when Mr. Wickham announced they would be leaving."

"Did he explain why?" Lizzy asked.

"Not with complete clarity, no. He smiled regretfully and pleaded, 'pressing business affairs that pull us away from the delightful company of our family.' He has been effusive in his apologies but firm. They are packing as we speak."

"How odd and how sudden. Was a missive delivered today as the cause of his urgency?"

"Not that we are aware. Who can say, Lizzy? The entire affair is so strange. Why come so far for a week's visit?" She shook her head, steering into the parlor and missing Darcy's muttered *Why indeed* as she continued to speak. "I do apologize for the histrionics, Mr. Darcy. I fear the day may be unpleasant."

The latter was an understatement. Mrs. Bennet refused to be consoled. Lydia cried and expressed deep remorse at leaving one moment only to then rhapsodize over "her darling Wickham's" promise to holiday at Brighton once his business in Portsmouth concluded. What he had to do in Portsmouth remained a mystery. No one directly asked the question and Wickham was strangely quiet.

The minuscule amount of delight Mr. Bennet experienced at seeing his youngest daughter after so many years had rapidly dissipated upon noting she was as foolish and noisy as ever. Wickham, despite being respectful and pleasant, had never been forgiven by Mr. Bennet for his despicable conduct and the scandalous affair with Lydia that had nearly brought ruin upon the entire family.

Mr. Bennet silently endured his wife's ranting for a time before speaking. "Mrs. Bennet, we are all greatly grieved at the imminent emptiness to our family, but surely you would not wish a man as important and influential as our daughter's fine husband to shirk his responsibilities? Imagine the negative cast this would place upon our dearest Mrs. Wickham if her husband were to gain a reputation as feckless and unprincipled."

Mr. Bennet directed his gaze toward Wickham, who startled at the softly spoken double entendre and then flushed with anger before composing himself.

To Darcy, Wickham said nothing, not even a farewell beyond a slight incline of his head and an indecipherable smirk. Darcy was unconvinced it was that simple, but nevertheless, watching the Wickhams' carriage wheeling away on the southwestern road skirting London was encouraging. His greatest relief was when they arrived at the palatial townhouse on Grosvenor Square that evening.

At Darcy House he was in charge and the familiarity of the townhouse pacified his soul. Of course, he did march about much as a general before the deciding battle, reiterating his usual requirements for security and privacy, and extending fresh demands for limiting unknown visitors and increasing protection to his wife and children when he was away. Darcy never lifted his voice above its normal sonorant baritone, nor did he punctuate his orders with gestures or repetition, yet there was never a doubt to any of the staff as to the seriousness of his instructions or the implied consequence if they failed. They responded to his orders with brisk, almost military efficiency.

It was late when he entered their first floor bedchamber. He opened the door from his dressing room slowly, sure that Elizabeth would be fast asleep. But, to his immediate delight and swelling desire, she was not abed but out in the garden somewhere as the patio doors were widely gaping. He found her sitting on the smoothed stones topping the short wall that surrounded the private courtyard outside their bedchamber. She was gazing at the stars visible through the waving branches of the elm that shaded the terrace but turned at his silent entry. She smiled, nestling happily into the ready embrace he offered as he sat onto the ledge beside her.

"I never can sneak up on you," he spoke into her hair, voice vibrant with love and humor, "no matter how stealthy I try to be."

Lizzy laughed, squeezing his arms and lacing fingers between his where they rested on her abdomen. She rotated the gold band that resided on his left hand, the unblemished metal a constant reminder of his unwavering commitment and love. "It is not a negative commentary to your stalking skills, my love. Rather, a testament to our bonding as I am always aware when you are near. My heart feels your every heartbeat and my soul hears your every breath," she said in a lilting cadence with latent laughter.

"Now who is the poet? Abounding in romantic emotion tonight, my lover? Anything I can do to assist you in your sentimental attitude?" He accented his whispered question with several well-placed kisses to her neck.

"It was a poor attempt, albeit the truth, and meant as a hint for you to recite poetry of your own."

He chuckled that singular rich tone of pleasure released against the skin at the bend of her shoulder that sent shivers of excitement cascading down her spine, settling into a private zone deep within her belly that only he could reach. He held her firmly against his chest, heart powerfully beating a soothing rhythm, heat infusing her skin through the thin layers of fabric that separated their flesh, arms sturdy but muscles relaxed as they surrounded her lithe form. His hands were motionless where they clasped hers and lips gentle as they wandered leisurely.

Largely it was indefinable, but Lizzy sensed in every touch and breath from her beloved that he was restored to the man of power and confidence that she had married.

Fitzwilliam Darcy was a curious dichotomy. At once a man of superior intellect and sharp decisiveness who met and resolved the challenges that came his way with barely a blink, while also being a man who required constancy and formula in his life, abhorring any upset to the careful balance he craved. When the two collided, his internal poise was shaken even as he dealt with the crisis head-on. Only one extremely close to him, and that primarily was his wife, ever perceived the struggle waging inside. When the waters calmed and that yearned for composure was once again attained, she knew it.

Her voice was dulcet, barely audible when she spoke. "You have satisfied your worries? Do you feel peace in the situation?"

"I would likely be happier at Pemberley, but, yes, I am at peace. You know how I despise being out of my routine, Elizabeth. It has forever been a fault of my character. Father laughed at me constantly, wondering how I could so enjoy traveling when it annoyed me to be in unfamiliar environs with strangers." He laughed, shaking his head at the ridiculousness of it. "I cannot explain it and am aware of the absurdity, but no matter how I delighted in journeys to foreign lands or learning new customs and ancient history, my muscles did not unwind until breathing the air of Derbyshire and laying eyes on Pemberley's pinnacles."

He turned her body gently, hands smoothing over the softness of her cheeks, and eyes soft in the moonlight as he gazed upon her face. "There are many questions to be answered and we will remain cautious. But right now I am in my second favorite abode on this earth, my children and sister are asleep in the rooms above us, and I am holding the woman I love more than my own life in my arms. The stars are sparkling, the moon is glowing, the pure fragrance of lilac and cut grass is deliciously invading my nostrils, and the lulling music of bubbling water falling over rocks fills the air. Furthermore, after kissing you, my lovely, precious Elizabeth, until you are pliant and breathless with desire I know I shall make love with you until we are utterly satiated. How could I not feel peace in such an atmosphere?"

"Now who is the poet, Fitzwilliam?"

"I shall recite the masters for you, darling, if that is your wish, but I prefer to express the poetry of love with my mouth and hands upon your skin."

"My goodness, both a poet and a wit! How marvelously blessed I am."

"Indeed," he growled, pulling her onto his lap, hands searching relentlessly under her raised skirt. "As much as I would like to love you here in the moonlight, alas this place does not afford us the privacy of our balcony at home. Come, Mrs. Darcy, we can discuss poetry on our bed."

And amid her tinkling laughter he rose with her clutched in his arms, striding purposefully into the candlelit chamber attached and proceeding to fulfill his vow until they were undeniably and utterly satiated.

CHAPTER FOURTEEN

Mrs. Smyth Has a Secret

H AVE YOU NOTICED HOW prolific and colorful the narcissus this year?"
Lizzy glanced over at her sister-in-law where she stood next to
the window facing the broad, cobbled avenue of Grosvenor Square.
"In truth I had not peered out the front windows this morning. I did note the
buttercups on our bedchamber's terrace. I adore spring blooms." She paused,
laying her embroidery aside to gaze contemplatively at Georgiana. "Tell me
truthfully, dear sister. Are you deeply enthralled with the beauty of the Square
or searching the corners for the mail carrier?"

Georgiana turned from the window and returned to her seat across from
Lizzy. "Can both be true?" she asked, the hint of a blush touching her cheeks. She
settled her secretaire onto her lap, dipping her quill into the embedded inkpot but
then pausing above the parchment music sheet spread upon the surface. "Only a
week has passed, yet it feels an eternity. This is the negative to love, I suppose?"

"The poets declare the absence shall foster fondness within the heart, as
in Mr. Bayly's *Isle of Beauty*. True to a degree, as a separation does cause one
to dwell upon their lover with longing leading to an increasingly emotional
reunion. Nevertheless, I abhor William being away from me for any length and
firmly believe our relationship grows stronger with constant communion."

"How marvelous that will be," Georgiana said, her eyes dreamy. "I greatly
desire to begin our life together."

"Very soon you will. Did he promise to write you?"

"Yes. Uncle granted permission. Of course, it has not been long since we parted so my expectations are unfair."

"He knew when Kitty's wedding was to be and thus your return to London. A man in love marks these dates upon his heart. My guess is a letter at the least, and very soon."

Georgiana sighed, and then chuckled as she shook her head. Her eyes were sparkling with humor when she met Lizzy's gaze. "I am rather pathetic, am I not? I was fine while diverted in Hertfordshire, yet here it is a day later and I am moping as a lost puppy. I cannot focus enough to complete this sonata I started on the voyage across the Channel!"

"Missing your collaborator?" Lizzy asked with a lift to her brow.

"I believe it is more that I miss my friend, who also happens to be the man I love and an excellent musical collaborator."

"Your own personal muse?"

"A male muse?" Georgiana laughed. "Yes, I suppose he is to a degree. Oh, Lizzy! I cannot wait for you and William to know Mr. Butler completely. He is warm and delightfully humorous. A valued friend and companion. I do miss him."

"I am sure Mr. Butler is of a like mind and will hasten his return to you."

Georgiana nodded, frowning slightly as she peered at the notes. "Yes, I have faith that this is true. I must be patient. Staffordshire is a distance not easily traversed for a seven-day visit or a letter. Besides, he did propose celebrating Easter with his family before returning, so surely it will be a fortnight at the least. I know how he missed home and his friends. He is undoubtedly immersed in entertainments and familial concourse."

Lizzy cocked her head, brows knitted. "What are you not telling me, Georgie?"

Georgiana looked up in surprise and then flushed. "Oh, nothing really! I fear I am a silly, imaginative girl at times, Lizzy. Pay me no heed."

"Nonsense! And I shall pay heed to your moods. You have a concern, clearly, and I am here to commiserate. Do you doubt Mr. Butler in some manner?"

"No, oh no, not in the slightest!" Georgiana put the secretaire aside and scooted to the sofa's edge to reach Lizzy's hand. "It is just"—she waved her other hand in the air, biting her lip before continuing in a halting voice—"vague feelings regarding Lord Essenton."

"Mr. Butler's father? In what way?"

Georgiana shrugged. "He is a stern man, Lizzy. I sensed this before

Sebastian told me of their relationship. He is rather frightening, if you must know, with a disapproving air. You know how Lord Essenton feels about Sebastian's musical studies and his, in Lord Essenton's opinion, pointless rambles across Europe. I fear he will see our engagement as another whimsy."

"Surely not. Taking a bride is a serious commitment. Certainly Lord Essenton will interpret Mr. Butler's decision as a positive sign for his future settling at Whistlenell Hall?"

"I do hope so. Yet"—she paused, picking absently at her dress—"I do not think Lord Essenton fond of me. He may reject Mr. Butler's choice."

Lizzy was truly shocked. "You must be mistaken, my dear! How…" She shook her head, squeezing Georgiana's hand tightly. "There is no possible way Lord Essenton could deny your excellence, Georgiana. In all ways imaginable you are a perfect choice, even if Mr. Butler was not madly in love with you. Rest your mind, my love. You are allowing your fancies to run amok. I guess your personal sensations of disapproval were merely shadows of Lord Essenton's annoyance at Mr. Butler's situation. Besides, Mr. Butler, if he is the caliber of man I judged him to be and you claim, would not be cowed in this matter any more than he was in pursuing his studies abroad. You have nothing to fear, I am sure of it."

Georgiana rose to kiss Lizzy's cheek. "Thank you, Lizzy. You always speak wisely and ease my fluttering heart."

"Pardon the intrusion, Mrs. Darcy. Miss Darcy, this was delivered for you."

They both started, not hearing the silent entry of the butler. Georgiana recovered and took the sealed envelope from Mr. Travers's hand, absently thanking him as a vibrant smile spread over her face upon noting the sender. She tore the wax, moving toward the window as she read.

Lizzy grinned happily, turning her attention to Mr. Travers, who waited patiently. "Mrs. Darcy"—he bowed—"a servant from the Matlock townhouse delivered this."

"Thank you, Mr. Travers. One moment, please." She rapidly scanned the paper, smiling as she resumed, "Lord and Lady Matlock will be dining here tonight, as well as Colonel Fitzwilliam and Lady Simone. Could you please send word to Mrs. Smyth that I wish to speak with her and adjust the menu? At her convenience."

He bowed and left the room, Lizzy returning her attention to Georgiana, who was rereading Mr. Butler's letter for the third time now.

"From the silly expression on your face I presume your qualms have been allayed? Mr. Butler is in Town, probably has been waiting for days while you tarried and partied in Hertfordshire, and is aware of our arrival some twenty hours ago? The besotted man must be clairvoyant or have spies! Or have you been redirecting me when in truth you evaded William's security forces and snuck out for a clandestine engagement last midnight?"

"You know the latter is not true," Georgiana answered Lizzy's tease with a giddy laugh, her eyes scanning the words. "Sadly the former is not true as yet. He wrote this two days past from Whistlenell Hall in Staffordshire. He anticipates arriving in the week after Easter. He writes cheerily and expresses nothing remiss."

"As indeed I asserted! Are his declarations of unending love properly rendered with a wealth of poetic verse? He is a composer so I expect nothing less."

Georgiana sighed, her cheeks rosy as she reread her beloved's letter, lingering over every word especially the greeting to "My loveliest fiancée, Georgiana."

"He manages sufficiently to appease my heart. And, no, I shall not share his affections, so do not ask!"

"Understood," Lizzy agreed, laughing along with Georgiana. "I am delighted to hear he is to arrive soon. Not only because it will be lovely to meet Mr. Butler again, and under these blessed circumstances, but because I confess it is difficult to secret the news from William."

"Oh, Lizzy! I apologize for placing you in an awkward situation! Perhaps I should speak to William myself and not wait for Mr. Butler."

"No, dearest. I should not have spoken of it. And I do not necessarily mean that it is awkward as in feeling I am deceiving as much as I am bursting with happiness for you. I know William will be overjoyed and thus cannot wait to share with him; that is all I meant. I only pray he arrives prior to our departure to Kent."

A worried frown creased Georgiana's brow. "I had not thought of that. I shall inform him of your plans when I write tonight. Hopefully he can adjust his schedule to coincide as I would hate to postpone matters until later in April when you and William return."

"I am positive all shall be well, even if we must delay our departure and enlighten William as to your engagement."

"And not arrive on the precise day Lady Catherine expects you?" Georgiana asked with feigned horror. "Perish the thought!"

The echo of childish laughter interrupted any further discussion. Laughter was followed by a high-pitched shriek and a deep voice declaring in exaggerated ominous tones, "Run fast, tasty boy, or you shall be my breakfast!"

"Can no catch me, Uncle Goj!"

A loud roar mimicking a lion followed that bold declaration with the pounding of small and large feet growing louder by the second. Suddenly a triumphant roar and shrill yell burst forth simultaneously, two bodies barreling through the open parlor door. George rose to his full height, a red-faced and giggling Alexander dangling upside down across his shoulder.

"Greetings, ladies! I rescued this imp from the boredom of tracing the alphabet"—he shivered dramatically—"and now we are here to enliven the stuffiness of sewing. I believe a walk to the Park is the prescribed remedy. Michael is asleep, Mrs. Darcy, so I am here to rescue you."

"I was not aware I needed rescuing, but a walk does sound lovely. I want to inspect the narcissus I hear are especially colorful this spring."

George lowered Alexander to the floor head first, tickling as he rolled him onto his back. The toddler giggled breathlessly, squirming and wiggling until free from his uncle's clutches whereupon he dashed to his mother.

"Nanny Lisa says I go with Uncle Goj and do letters later. We go see ducks, Mama, please?"

"I think feeding the poor starving ducks of Hyde Park a marvelous idea, sweetling."

"Mrs. Darcy, you wished to see me?"

George turned, grinning broadly at Mrs. Smyth, who avoided his eyes and visibly winced when he boomed, "Good day, Mrs. Smyth! How are you this fine morning?"

"Quite well, Dr. Darcy. Thank you. Mrs. Dar…"

"Have you done something different to your hair, Mrs. Smyth?"

"Not at all, sir," she answered primly.

"Hmm… I do not recall curls escaping your cap. Most lovely, I daresay. It becomes you. Ah! Look at how she blushes so delightfully! Do I detect the look of a woman in love? Is my heart to be devastated at your affection turned toward a secret amour?"

"George, do not tease Mrs. Smyth so shamelessly," Lizzy said with a laugh, George bowing contritely with a hand over his heart.

"I do apologize, Mrs. Smyth. I fear my wits and good manners have escaped me in the overwhelming awe of so much beauty in one room."

"Indeed," the housekeeper coldly intoned, her face neutral except for a glimmer of supreme dislike directed toward George's back when he turned away.

"What causes the rosiness to your cheeks, Georgie? Are all the women surrounding me falling in love?"

"Do not be ridiculous, Uncle. I may be forced to conclude that it is not beauty that scatters your wits but rather senility weakening your diagnostic skills! What a pity if we are required to hire a nurse to keep the drool away from your brilliant green and gold tunic."

"If she is exceptionally comely I welcome the idea." He wiggled his brows, a crooked grin flashing. "And is this suit not astounding? A package from India was awaiting me. Nimesh and Sasi, Jharna's sons, keep me properly garbed, thank the Maker, as I would never wish to draw undue attention from outdated attire." He winked, grabbed an apple off the tea tray, and tossed it into the air. It was caught deftly with one hand followed by a huge bite.

Mrs. Smyth stood ramrod straight, her pinched lips the only outward indication of her disgust as she listened to Mrs. Darcy's dinner requests. Her responses were clipped but correctly rendered, her curtsy a bit stiff but adequate, and she left the parlor with her disdain well concealed. She did not look back and walked at a stately pace down the long corridor toward the kitchen. Each step took her further and further away from the voices and laughter pervading the parlor. Then, just as she reached the door to the housekeeper's pantry located near the kitchen and the nervous twitch behind her left eye began to slacken as the noises fell to a dim murmur, another shrill, childish laugh pierced the relative hush followed by a loud, braying whoop. Her teeth clenched and the tic restarted at full force. Her hands trembled as she fumbled with her chatelaine to find the correct key and she barely managed to retain her dignity as she ducked into the insulated closet.

She fell onto the stool, head dropping against a pile of precision folded table napkins as her eyes closed in relief. Silence. Blessed silence. She inhaled vigorously, willing her heart to slow. The darkness in the closet with familiar scents of silver polish and laundered linens was calming. Her fingers played over the hard metal of her chatelaine and the grooves of the keys attached. It was a ready reminder of who she was.

Only two weeks, she said to herself, *then they shall leave for Kent. After that hiatus, several more weeks of misery before the long, glorious months when the house is all mine.*

It was a litany she repeated frequently and had done so ever since that horrid day over three years ago when Mr. Darcy brought his new bride to Darcy House. Mrs. Smyth shuddered at the memory. Her comfortable, regulated, proper life had been radically changed from that day forward. How could it have happened? It was a question she repeatedly asked herself, but no answer was forthcoming.

Up until that day, Prudence Garrett Smyth considered her life charmed. At the age of fifteen she had joined the staff of Lord and Lady Cheltham in their luxurious London Townhouse. As the daughter of a tradesman father and milliner mother, Prudence Garrett was modestly educated, reasonably accomplished, accustomed to hard work, and considered herself a class above the average maid. It was an attitude that appealed to Lady Cheltham. By the time she was twenty, Prudence was ladies' maid to the teenage daughter of Lord and Lady Cheltham, and by twenty-three was the highest ranking upstairs maid and setting her sights on the housekeeper position.

Soon after, her stellar performance and indispensability to Lady Cheltham allowed her to marry the head groomsman, Mr. Smyth.

It was not a love match, the far older Mr. Smyth more interested in Miss Garrett's physical attributes than her sentiments. But then she was in no particular way interested in his thoughts either. It was a union logical and business-like and they rarely conversed beyond what was essential between man and wife. Never once to dwell on the physical activities between males and females, the new Mrs. Smyth was rather startled to discover they were compatible in that realm. It was a marriage that suited them both adequately, fulfilling the only need they had from the other on those nights when they chose to come together, and making no demands for anything greater. Thankfully they had no children, a shrewd brothel madam providing Mr. Smyth with the herbs and strange devices viable to prevent an accident of that nature, and all was perfect for five years.

Then her foolish husband did the unthinkable and died. One minute he was shoveling soiled hay from a stall and the next he was lying in that very pile of straw, slain instantly from some internal seizure. At nine and twenty she was a widow whose only concern was who would warm her bed and service her body when the desires rose. Far angrier than grieved, Mrs. Smyth attended the funeral with stoic calm and then immediately returned to her duties. Lady Cheltham observed the odd behavior of her maid and falsely interpreted it as profound grief. Deciding that the best medicine for a wounded heart was change, Lady Cheltham arranged a meeting with Mr. Fitzwilliam Darcy.

The young Master of Pemberley was seeking a housekeeper for Darcy House as his current housekeeper, Miss Hughes, was ill with a wasting sickness and none of the current household maids were up to the task. He was extremely dubious due to Mrs. Smyth's young age, but the assurances and high recommendations of Lord and Lady Cheltham, friends he trusted and valued, swayed him enough to agree to an interview. Mrs. Smyth was furious and highly insulted, but then better sense prevailed. The housekeeper of Cheltham House was only in her forties and in prime health, meaning that Mrs. Smyth was years if not decades away from gaining the prestige she craved. Furthermore, the Darcy reputation for honesty, excellent pay, virtue, propriety, discretion, isolation, and stability was too well known to ignore. Mr. Darcy, although young, was the epitome of the rigid, controlled English gentility that she admired. Finely dressed, cultured, sober, taciturn, and excessively prim, he was the classic gentleman. Moreover, it was only him and his sister, a shy creature who barely spoke, so the gossip ran.

For five years all was well, until her tranquil existence and position of respect was abruptly destroyed with the horrible inclusion of Elizabeth Bennet, now Darcy, over three years ago.

Mrs. Smyth shuddered anew, shifting restlessly on the hard stool, hand gripping the keys so hard that red ridges formed on her palm. The memory of her first introduction to the uncultured Miss Bennet, and her later humiliation in front of her entire staff at the hands of the inferior parvenu, were fresh and painful. She had not forgiven and never would. At times she considered searching for another position elsewhere, but then they would depart for Pemberley and serenity would fall, giving her the strength she needed to persevere. The urge had overwhelmed her the previous Seasons with the inclusion of an unruly child who was not cloistered in a distant chamber as he should have been. A child dining with the family, included when visitors called, and who dashed through the halls frequently being chased by a laughing Mr. Darcy! It was unbelievable and cemented her judgment that declining propriety and vulgarity had entered Darcy House along with Mrs. Darcy. How she would survive the addition of a second child to the household was nearly more than she could take. Add to that the brash Dr. Darcy with his outrageous mannerisms and attire, and her nervous condition nearly overwhelmed her reason.

Geoffrey will soon return to comfort me, she thought with a sensuous sigh, closing her eyes and melting further into the stacks of fine linen as her body began to relax.

Vividly she remembered the day they met eight months ago while she was at the market.

The Darcys were expected any day, their journey to Europe and Kent completed, and the fact that they planned to tarry for merely a week or two before returning to Derbyshire before the birth of the second Darcy brat was the only optimistic detail she could cling to. Envisioning the noise created by an undisciplined toddler was enough to exaggerate her eye tic and cause her hands to quaver. So much so that she clumsily dropped the squash she was examining, the hard shell cracking on the stones by her feet and bursting the warm, pulpy meat into a squishy mess over her shoe and soiling two other ladies standing nearby. The ensuing clamor, with merchant demanding she pay for the ruined vegetable and the ladies loudly bemoaning their state while casting angry glares toward Mrs. Smyth, caused her ire to rise. The trembling and tic ceased, her frustration suddenly finding an immediate outlet in the bellicose retailer.

As she puffed up for a full-blown confrontation, a smooth, cultured voice intervened. "Here, my good man, accept these coins for your trouble. This should more than pay for your loss and the time to clean the mess. Ladies, I am to understand that bicarbonate of soda removes such stains leaving not a hint of the damage. Perhaps this information shall benefit when *you* next accidentally spill."

Mrs. Smyth's deliverer, after tossing enough coins to pay for three squashes and gifting the stunned women with engaging smiles, turned to her. "Madam," he began, bowing and speaking in a lush undertone, "allow me." And he knelt, producing his handkerchief with a flourish, lifted her foot, and proceeded to wipe the sticky seeds and pulp off her shoe. His fingers rested on her ankle, searing through her stocking, and he stared upwards into her captivated eyes.

"There, all better now." He rose, holding her gaze. "Madam, if I may be so bold, you appear to be shaken. This dratted London heat." He smiled, deep dimples appearing, and winked as if sharing an intimate jest. "My name is Geoffrey Wiseman and it would be an honor to provide a cool refreshment, if you will allow? Rumor has it that Westin's Café serves the finest lemonade in Covent Gardens, but as a new resident I have yet to sample the beverage to discern if this is fact or fancy. Will you accompany me in discovering the truth?" His bluish-green eyes bore into Mrs. Smyth, rendering her breathless and entranced, hardly aware that she took his offered arm.

From that moment forward she was lost. In times of clarity, usually when Mr. Wiseman was away from Town for a period of time, her native skepticism would rise, wondering how Mr. Wiseman could genuinely be so perfect. Vague mistrust would rear up as she almost grasped a cunning manipulation in his precise phrases, thoughts, and actions that complimented hers and compelled her to speak frankly of matters she did to no other.

Then one glance into his mesmerizing eyes, one word uttered in his sweet voice, one brush of his full lips over her fingers, and one dimpled grin was all it took to catapult her from mature woman to swooning maiden. She could not sincerely say it was love; Mrs. Smyth was far too pragmatic to believe in such a capricious emotion. But it was unquestionably lust. After nine years without male companionship she had buried her urges deep inside, yet all it had taken was one incredibly sensual, captivating man to bring them rushing to the surface.

As a broker for a porcelain manufacturer in Manchester, Mr. Geoffrey Wiseman was required to travel, thus often away for weeks at a time. For the first three months after their meeting in Covent Gardens they saw each other sporadically; not precisely courting as neither expressed such a wish, but merely becoming acquainted. He was absent more than present initially, but as the months passed he stayed for longer periods of time in London, always sending a message to Mrs. Smyth when he arrived.

After another two months they became lovers.

Again, there were no declarations. Mrs. Smyth simply wanted the pleasure of a physical relationship without losing any of her status. The idea of giving up her post to be the wife of a tradesman, living in far away Manchester or even in London was unappealing. What could she possibly do while her husband was gone for extended periods? Live in some waterfront apartment and raise a pack of weeping, snotty children? The notion brought shivers of disgust. No, the arrangement of clandestine assignations at the modest set of rooms he rented on the fringes of Bloomsbury was adequate.

At least at first.

Despite her practical, icy disposition, she was a woman. Geoffrey's sweetly whispered admissions of affection and subtle pleadings for her company touched a hidden region of her heart. His skill in the bedroom far surpassed the unlamented Mr. Smyth and the sensations experienced burned through her body to an addictive degree. Equally enthralling was his interest in her views, Geoffrey caring for her opinions and welcoming her conversation as no one ever had. Gradually she began to imagine more from their relationship, even if her dreams were nebulous and not pondered in the light of day.

Geoffrey pushed to visit her at Darcy House so they would have the entire night together rather than brief minutes of rapid lovemaking. Emotion overruled discretion and she allowed him in to her private apartments, aware that the act was an unforgivable breach of Mr. Darcy's rules. In the aftermath of inexhaustible passion, he asked personal questions about the family, and she enlightened him. As winter waned into spring with the looming onslaught of the family on the horizon, Mrs. Smyth lost all scruples in her craving for the special brand of comfort that Geoffrey Wiseman so capably gave her.

It had been three weeks since she last saw him and she anticipated his return any day, as he had promised. Every prudent bone in her body screamed against permitting him entry with Mr. Darcy in residence, but she knew that she would the moment he sent word of his arrival. A mere day of excessive racket was already wearing on her and she shamelessly needed consoling from her lover. A shiver of anticipatory pleasure raced through her core, settling in her belly. *Yes, indeed I shall let him in,* she thought, *and no one will be the wiser.*

CHAPTER FIFTEEN

Easter at Darcy House

THE SUBSEQUENT DAYS PASSED in the usual manner for this time of year as the official London Season was soon to commence and Easter approached.

Traffic—foot, horse, and carriage—noticeably amplified as the elite members of Society relocated from their pastoral country abodes to their plush townhouses. Vendors of every type hopped into action as purchasing drastically increased with the steady influx of orders for everything from flowers and fabrics to fresh produce and meats. Covent Garden, Piccadilly, Cheapside, Adelphi, and even the smaller shopping districts met the demand with ease after decades of practice. Church ceremonies to honor Christ's death and resurrection were held daily during Lent and Holy Week. Costers took advantage with booths selling hot cross buns, dyed hard boiled eggs, simnel cakes, flower-adorned crosses, white lilies, and palm branches lining the walkways nearby.

Couriers added to the press of bodies, busily delivering the invitations to afternoon teas, salons, and soirees. Musicians, actors, singers, and a dozen other entertainers exhausted themselves in perfecting their art while theatre owners and crewman frenetically primed for constant performances. Museums, art galleries, clubs, gardens, public rooms—every business catering to the entertainments of the ton gleefully threw open their doors, knowing a vast amount of money was to be made and prestige gained. Modistes, tailors, milliners, cobblers, and anyone else associated with providing fine garments and accoutrements worked long hours and employed additional helpers to meet the demand.

The residents of Darcy House passed the days in the usual pursuits as well.

Despite his claim to applaud all forms of laziness, George wasted only two days before reconnecting with his medical colleagues. He scheduled a series of lectures for new students, his reputation as an excellent teacher and expert practitioner well known, and volunteered at the local hospitals where he was welcomed gladly. His never-waning hunger to learn improved or unique methods of diagnosing and treatments prompted him to enroll in several lectures of interest. Of course, his serious, scholarly side did not totally rule with a fair number of frivolous entertainments embraced in between.

Georgiana submerged her impatience to see Mr. Butler. It was not easy, but the delight of shopping and gossiping with the plethora of friends she had not seen in months did soothe and distract. Her prior enthusiasm for balls at Almack's and flirtatious strolls through Hyde Park was greatly diminished, an oddity Darcy noticed but did not comment upon.

Lizzy discovered the same degree of happiness in distraction. The strange vision of Lord Orman and any residual disquiet over Mr. Wickham disappeared with a full schedule of socializing and preparing for the holiday. After three previous Seasons in Town, Mrs. Darcy was acquainted with everyone, close friends with some, and esteemed as worthy company by all, her ability to easily socialize one Darcy remained in awe of.

Darcy spent the first days with his solicitors in their maple-paneled offices. Mr. Andrew Daniels and his sons brilliantly handled Darcy's numerous business ventures while Mr. Darcy dwelt at Pemberley during the winter months with frequent messages passing over the miles. Nevertheless, the pile of documents requiring signatures or careful perusal grew and would take some time to deal with. He relished the work, even as he strived to consolidate and streamline his affairs so as to require less personal attention in the future. Mr. Daniels's service to the Darcy family for decades, and Mr. Darcy specifically, meant he knew his client's wishes and was ready with a dozen propositions to discuss, contracts written, bank drafts awaiting signatures, and so on.

Mr. Daniels quietly pursued his search for information on the Marquis of Orman while Colonel Fitzwilliam's "spies" were unreachable and doing heaven-knew-what in their intelligence hunt. There was nothing for Darcy to do other than maintain his extreme diligence. Lizzy was cautioned daily, a reminder she comprehended and obeyed to the best of her ability. Yet, as the days turned into a week since leaving Hertfordshire, even Darcy began to relax and pushed the worries aside.

Maundy Thursday dawned bright and sunny. The Holy Day set aside to commemorate the Last Supper of Christ with his apostles began the Easter events Darcy most enjoyed, his delight compounded now that Alexander was old enough to attend. Church bells resounded from a multitude of steeples as they rode to St. Marylebone Parish Church for the service. Alexander sat mesmerized throughout the foot-washing ceremony and adaptive Passover Seder, finally falling asleep in his father's lap during the choral worship. He missed the ritualized stripping of the altar sacraments in symbolic preparation for the Good Friday mourning services, but Darcy was content to observe the solemn proceedings with his family close.

The weather for Good Friday reverted to cold and blustery with rain threatening. Lizzy opted to stay indoors with Michael rather than subjecting the infant to illness, but the ominous skies did not deter Darcy from taking a thickly coated Alexander to watch St. Sepulchre Church's reenactment of the medieval Easter Sepulchre liturgy.

Carved sepulchres of stone and wood created for Easter commemorations were once a common fixture in ancient churches. Some were simple works of art depicting the burial place of Christ with sleeping soldiers or visiting women carved as a niche in the wall of the church. Other sepulchres, such as this one, were large, elaborate sculptures with the entire story of Christ's burial and resurrection conveyed in detailed etchings surrounding and on the tombs. Steeped in history and a fair amount of mystery due to lost documents and the ritual being banned during the Reformation, this ceremony was a highlight whenever Darcy managed to be in London for Easter.

Darcy, Alexander, Georgiana, and George joined a large gathering observing the formal rite. Sacred hymns recounting the Passion were sung by the choir as four dark-robed, barefooted monks walked soberly down the aisle carrying a red velvet-draped cushion upon which rested a plain wooden cross with an exquisite effigy of Christ in gold. Reverently, the cross was placed beside the candle-encircled sepulchre, the monks falling to their knees and bowing before the image with foreheads touching the floor. Lifting mere inches to bestow a kiss to the sculpted feet, they then crept backwards as the waiting monks lowered to their knees and in the same humble pose approached the cross to kiss.

The assembled clergy completed that part of the ceremony, forming a ring of kneeling worshippers around the cross. It was then that the priest rose from his seat, and slowly descended the steps of the chancel and front of the nave until standing with his brothers directly before the cross. With calm deliberation he removed his traditional vestures to reveal an unadorned black cassock, his eyes never leaving the graven face of suffering as he handed the garments to a waiting monk, removed his shoes, and bent to his knees. Crawling forward, he too respectfully kissed the nailed feet of his Savior before rising and lifting the laden cross high above his head for all in the audience to see.

The heavy lid of the wooden tomb was opened and the crucifix placed inside with due pomp. Responsories were sung by the choir, sweet incense burned both inside and around the tomb, the lid closed and sealed with wax, and lastly covered with gold trimmed damask. The priest chose the first two sextons to be given the honor of guarding the sepulchre, a responsibility taken seriously and shared with other clergy in shifts until Easter morning.

"Papa, will Jesus be lonely inside the box?" Alexander asked as they left the church. It was the first words he had uttered since entering St. Sepulchre nearly an hour earlier, the boy studiously attentive to the ceremony throughout. The innocent query, asked with grave concern and a deep frown, brought instant laughter. The lighthearted response of the adults only increased Alexander's worry and tears welled in his eyes.

"Not at all, sweetling. First off, this Jesus is pretend. It is a statue only, as the real Jesus is in Heaven, right?" Alexander nodded, although not totally convinced. Darcy hugged him tighter, kissing the crease between the toddler's knitted brows.

Darcy tried to explain the concept of ceremony and symbolism with limited success, but Alexander's fears were not fully allayed until George said, "Jesus is taking a nap in the box, Alexander. He is tired after being carried about. The nice men will keep him company and open the box in two days once He is rested."

Darcy opened his mouth to refute that nonsensical explanation, but the cheery expression on Alexander's face halted him. In the end, he realized there would be plenty of time in the future to give theological lectures!

Saturday saw Darcy House besieged, much to Mrs. Smyth's horror. For some reason she never comprehended, the pristine dining room was converted into the official egg dyeing and painting chamber. The table was carefully draped with old linens and the fine furnishings removed to avoid damage or staining, but naturally there were a few mishaps that required harsh cleaning. Yet it was not the mess that peeved her as much as the ruckus caused by so many festive persons.

The boiling of eggs had occupied a portion of the kitchen staff's time on Friday, those cooled eggs now added to the dozens brought by Jane Bingley, Lady Simone Fitzwilliam, Mary Daniels, Marilyn Hughes, Harriet Vernor, Julia Sitwell, Amelia Lathrop, Chloe Drury, and Alison Fitzherbert. The babies were taken to the nursery for age-appropriate play while the other children eagerly flocked the cluttered long table. Baskets of eggs sat among the bowls of paints, dye, and adhesive to decorate with the glass pieces, feathers, beads, seeds, ribbons, lace, and more. Adult supervision was essential, especially for the littler children. Artistry was encouraged, some eggs a masterpiece of precision adornment and painting while others were sadly lacking any finesse, but each an expression of individuality and definitely colorful. The fathers aided the procedure for a time, managing to decorate one or two eggs themselves, before retiring to Darcy's billiard room and leaving the chaos to the women.

By late afternoon the last colorful egg was placed carefully into a basket awaiting Easter Day festivities and the exhausted children were returned to their respective homes. A purse-lipped Mrs. Smyth oversaw the dining room restoration, her abrupt manner noticeable to the maids and footman as indicative of her irritation, but the Darcys were unaware as they settled in for a quiet night alone.

On Easter Sunday Lizzy stood in the small dressing room attached to their bedchamber, staring out the wide window facing the backyard garden. She clipped the pearl necklace—which once belonged to her husband's mother and was gifted to her on her first night at Pemberley as his wife—around her slender neck, followed with a pair of pearl and diamond earrings as she watched the glittering waves of water cascading over the marble rocks in the fountain. The sun was shining, bathing the grass and spring flowers with warmth and light. Fortunately the inclement weather on Good Friday had passed without a single drop of rain. Hopefully this meant the lawns and ground of Hyde Park would be relatively dry and free of fresh mud patches for naughty boys to discover.

She turned at the knock upon her door, pleased but not surprised when Darcy entered carrying an enormous bouquet of flowers.

"Happy Easter, my love," he said, smiling as he bent for a kiss and handed her the white flowers.

"Happy Easter to you as well, dearest. Thank you. These are exquisite!" She pressed her face into the petals, breathing deeply. "So sweet," she sighed, closing her eyes in delight. "I saw some of these at Covent Gardens earlier this week. They are quite unique."

"The florist said they are *Lilium longiflorum,* a newly discovered lily bulb from a cluster of islands off the coast of China." He shrugged. "That was all he knew and I have not had the time to delve into the topic further."

Lizzy reached to stroke over his cheek, a gesture difficult to accomplish, as the bouquet was large and heavy for one arm. "Poor Mr. Darcy, forced to smother his unquenchable curiosity! I am surprised you were able to sleep."

"Indeed it was a struggle, but I was able to relax with the vision of your face amid the blooms. As always my imagination failed miserably as you are engaging beyond what my dreams prefigured." Stepping back, he swept his gaze over her gowned body with appreciation evident. "White becomes you, Mrs. Darcy. Did you acquire this gown here or before we left home?"

"It is a creation of Madame du Loire. Frankly, I am doubtful of the wisdom in wearing white when chasing children through the dewy grass and boggy ground at Hyde Park is the order of the day! Marguerite will have her hands full removing stains."

"She is skilled. And if the dress is soiled beyond repair it shall be worth the loss to see you wearing it all day. These touches of green are for me, yes?" He ran his fingertips along the satin ribbons and accents, all in shades of darker green, smiling at her affirmative nod. "Purest white and garden green. You are a walking lily. An Easter flower lovelier than these lilies, or the callas, narcissus, pussy willows, tulips, or hydrangeas arrayed in vases throughout the house."

"I trust you left some flowers behind for other households?" she asked with a laugh. "And hopefully one vase roomy enough for these."

"I am certain Mr. Travers will produce the perfect container." He offered his arm, turning toward the door when she slipped her free hand under the bend of his elbow.

"Or"—she drew closer to his side and halted his steps—"I can leave them here nicely wrapped in their moist tissues until we retire tonight whereupon we can spread them over the bed and make love amid your favorite colors."

Her face was lifted toward his, eyes bright with promise. Darcy kissed her nose, voice husky as he teased, "Sounds delicious, my wife, but I shall repress my desires ere I see how vigorous you are after chasing children around Hyde Park all day."

"I am certain I shall prove hardy enough to fulfill your desires," she responded smugly, propelling him forward as she continued, "even with a day of constant activity. After saying farewell to the last of our dinner guests we shall see who is most vigorous. Yes," she said at the grimace crossing his face, "I confess I bullied you into hosting Easter dinner here, but only because I know how important Easter is to you. I was only thinking of your happiness, my darling."

"Ha! If that were the case you would not have invited Lord and Lady Blaisdale."

"Well, indeed that was a misstep I hold faint misgivings of. Yet, what should I have said when Caroline heard Jane and I talking about the planned picnic at Hyde Park? She was profuse in her enthusiasm over the egg hunt and rolling. Even you would have been moved at her countenance of delight envisioning young John partaking of the festivities."

"I agree that Caroline's happiness at motherhood has given me pause in rethinking her marriage and general attitude, but nothing will ease my dislike of Lord Blaisdale."

"I do not much care for him either, William. However, he is Caroline's husband…"

"And she is Bingley's sister. Yes, I know the arguments. For the record, Bingley barely tolerates the man, not that Lord Blaisdale condescends to socialize with them on a frequent basis. In truth, I am surprised he agreed to this invitation."

"Perhaps he loves his wife and child more than you give him credit for. Whatever the case, there will be plenty of gentlemen for you to converse with. Leave his lordship to your uncle who relishes needling just for fun."

Darcy flashed an evil grin, Lizzy's laughter echoing down the corridor into the parlor where the family waited. Alexander dashed into the foyer, greeting his parents with an armful of colorful chrysanthemums.

"Mama! Papa! See my flowers for Jesus? Papa say we give flowers to God."

Darcy scooped the toddler into his arms, flowers and all. "It is true, Son. We will pin the flowers onto the tall wooden cross we saw outside the church on Friday. Once everyone decorates the cross with fresh flowers, it will be beautiful, busting with color as a symbol of God's life-giving nature."

"And then they will open the box so Jesus go free?"

"The box will already be empty, Alexander," George said, his voice dropping into a whisper. "It is like magic! The lid will be raised and, poof! Jesus will be gone!"

"Where?" Alexander asked, his eyes round with awe as George commenced a discourse on the Resurrection melding fact with fascinating hyperbole, keeping the youngster entertained during the carriage ride to church.

The fine weather held, to the delight of London's populace. Churches were crowded, the faithful weekly worshippers vying for space amid those who only attended on Holy days. Traffic was amplified, carriages crawling at a snail's pace as drivers struggled to find a clearer route or one not barricaded for a parade. Traditional Easter entertainments were scattered throughout the city, one not required to travel far to find a parade or dance or egg hunt or religious ceremony to honor Christ's resurrection.

For the sake of ease and proximity to Darcy House, the Bingleys and Darcys chose the Oxford Street parade. After the interminable trek to the church and back locked inside stuffy carriages, they were overjoyed to walk the short jaunt north to the home of Captain William Henry Percy on Portman Square. There they joined Lord and Lady Matlock, longtime friends of Captain Percy and his father, Lord Beverly, and others invited to observe the parade from the comfort and prime location of Captain Percy's parlor or walkway and steps.

Alexander was unimpressed with the waving strangers wearing elaborately decorated garments and bonnets, although the ladies kept mental notes of designs. His eyes were riveted to the horses. Some were military with full regalia worn by cavalryman and beast, while others were prized ribbon- and flower-garlanded racchorses with proud jockeys atop. In the latter case Darcy, member of the Jockey Club and a horse racing fanatic, enlightened a rapt Alexander as to name, owner, racing statistics, and so on, all of which the child absorbed while Lizzy laughed.

Both boys squealed with glee at the antics of the Morris Dancers. The dancers were dressed in costumes Elizabethan in general style but garish and accented with varying sized bells, loose scarves in a multitude of colors, and large bracelets and rings. Aided by rollicking tunes on pipe, tabor drum, fiddle, and a bagpipe, the dancers leapt and skipped from one side of the street to the next in a constant flow of movement. The bells and jewelry served a purpose other than ornamentation as each flick of the wrist or twist of a leg created a ringing note, the dancers' seemingly random antics in fact a precision choreography with music rising in the air. In addition to that, many of the dancers held swords that they whacked together as they twirled or struck against street poles or tapped onto the cobblestones, the metallic clangs blending with the rest.

Michael clapped his hands as they passed, bouncing nonstop on Lizzy's knees until she was sure she would have bruises! "I do believe our youngest son has an ear for music," she yelled over the din.

"Let us pray it is not only for lively tunes most often found in pubs and disreputable dance halls," Darcy yelled back. "A taste for sophisticated music would be preferred."

Lizzy shook her head, glancing to where George stood clapping his hands and dancing a jig. "The influence for unsophisticated music may be too intense!"

For the four-block walk to the Grosvenor Gate to Hyde Park, Alexander was carried on George's shoulders while Darcy held a squirming Michael, the infant refusing to sit calmly in his pram. Crowds of families were already gathered throughout the enormous park, blankets and shading canopies or pavilions haphazardly dotting the areas not designated for games.

The recognizable blue canvases belonging to the Vernors stretched between tall poles, shading the rugs spread over the damp ground on a level field preselected at the base of a knoll near the lake. Some of their friends had already arrived, the adults busily setting out food and eating utensils while the children played and formed instant friendships with every other child in the near vicinity.

Richard greeted them midway down the grass-covered slope, taking the basket of food and eggs from Georgiana's hands as he teased, "We thought you had forgotten the way! Or been attacked by a horde of hungry egg bandits. It is a mania, I declare. Why, Oliver has eaten a dozen already!"

"I have eaten two, Father, whereas you have eaten three and would have done another if Mother had not slapped your hand." The son of Lady Simone's first husband, now Lord Fotherby although not appearing particularly lordly with his sallow complexion and stumped posture, smiled fondly at his stepfather before turning to greet the new arrivals and take Lizzy's basket.

"Oliver can eat all the eggs he desires, or anything else for that matter." Simone's voice was light as she gazed at her stepson, only the barest hint of anxiety noticeable. Oliver despised references to his illness or public expressions of pity, bravely and stubbornly refusing to succumb to weakness. "You, however, must wait until the food is properly served," she finished, poking her husband in the upper arm.

"Brutality, I say," Richard said, rubbing his arm as if wounded. "The definition of a picnic is to pick at the food when one feels the urge. Back me up on this, Darcy."

"I am not about to argue with the mandates of your wife, Cousin. You are on your own."

"Traitor."

"I doubt you shall starve, Richard. Harry"—Lizzy turned to Simone's nine-year-old when they reached the picnic area—"would you please take Alexander and Ethan to join the Sitwell and Fitzherbert boys? Thank you, dear."

"And please take Fiona as well," Amelia Lathrop added, plopping her two-year-old into Harry's arms. Fiona screamed and kicked her legs, poor Harry recoiling from flailing limbs while trying to hold on. "Oh bother! Let the wee tiger down, Harry boy. She can run with the laddies for a spell until Mrs. Daniels arrives with her lasses, not that my Fiona will sit and play with dolls for more than five minutes, heaven bless her."

"Perhaps she will mellow with maturity, Amelia, especially if your baby is a girl."

"I am guessing she will corrupt the new bairn ere she learns to crawl. Or more likely it will be a male child as filled with the devil as she is!" Amelia caressed over her belly, shaking her head as she smiled.

"We need to add a few more girls to this generation. Deborah, Claudia, Fiona, and my Abigail are vastly outnumbered." Marilyn Hughes glanced at the pram where her baby slept. "They are doomed to be ruffians just to survive with all these boys. You two do your best to save our sweet girls from that tragedy!"

She nodded toward the expectant mothers Amelia Lathrop and Harriet Vernor, the latter touching her distended abdomen. "Third time lucky, let us pray. A baby girl would be most welcome to soften up my own ruffians. Stuart and Spencer would benefit from a female touch."

"I daresay the future will include plenty of opportunities for female babies."

"Are you slyly imparting momentous news, Julia?"

Julia Sitwell laughed, shaking her head vigorously. "Merciful heavens, no! Austin is not yet weaned, please God grant me a reprieve! Besides, after four boys I have accepted the fact that we can only produce male offspring, so would look for no assistance from me. I was merely pointed out that collectively we appear far from finished in creating English citizens."

"I can promise to do all in my power to ensure the future of our great land," Richard offered, smiling at his wife, who blushed and ducked her head. "Mr. and Mrs. Darcy are diligently attending to the task and those who are not *yet* married will eventually do their duty to God and country." He nodded toward Georgiana, who through the entire exchange had been scanning the shifting sea of bodies beyond their group. "Searching for anyone in particular, Georgie?"

Georgiana started at Richard's question, reddening at his knowing smirk, but answered calmly, "I was looking to see if the Daniels were amongst the people approaching. Not yet, but I do see Lord and Lady Blaisdale. He does stand out in the crowd to be sure."

"Caroline is fairly easy to spot as well," Charles said with a laugh. "The curse of being red-haired, not that you can see her hair with that ridiculous hat. Heavens! She has an entire garden on her head!"

The former Caroline Bingley, now the Countess of Blaisdale since marriage to Lord Blaisdale after a surprising and brief engagement two years ago, wore a gown of daffodil yellow—not the most flattering color for her—that was nevertheless of the latest fashion and richest fabrics with an elaborate, and enormous, Easter hat adorned with real flowers. The tranquility of spirit and softened attitude seen in smaller, private milieus since her satisfactory marriage and the birth of her son disappeared when in the public arena. Caroline's air of superiority had only increased with her elevated rank, as had her other annoying habits. Her current costume proved the point, as did the first words out of her mouth.

"Charles, I do hope our blankets are on a flat patch of ground and the canvas generous enough to adequately cover. I cannot allow the sun to color *my* son's face." She pointedly glanced to the rosy-cheeked and tanned Ethan and Alexander, who were playing tag with the other equally brown and sweaty children, Dr. Darcy dashing among. "Nor can my fair skin tolerate these fierce rays. Jane, dear, adjust your bonnet brim before you burn. Sun-darkened skin is vulgar."

"I have always preferred a healthy flush upon a woman's cheeks," Darcy interjected urbanely, "but have no fear, Caroline. We have these two large tented areas in a perfect location to observe the children during their games, and that smaller pavilion is for the babies. Will you be assisting young John hunt eggs? Several will be placed in plain view for the younger children to easily pick up."

"Lady Blaisdale," the Earl responded with emphasis, "will stay covered.

Our nurse will lead John, although why a one-year-old needs to grab eggs off the grass is beyond my comprehension."

"You will be pleasantly surprised then, my lord, to see how delighted even the youngest are at finding hidden eggs and watching them roll down the slope. It is a joy, I assure you."

He smiled faintly, green eyes doubtful. "I shall take your word for it, Mrs. Darcy, and hope I am delighted by the spectacle."

"Speaking of spectacles," Richard murmured, nudging Darcy and grinning.

George joined them, long limbs effortlessly crossing the field in a handful of strides. "If I could bottle the mysterious elixir that bestows unlimited energy to children I would be a rich man."

"You are a rich man."

"True, Colonel, true. But then I would live far longer and have more stamina to enjoy those riches! Lord and Lady Blaisdale"—he bowed—"welcome to our intimate Easter gathering. We attempted to rent the entire park for ourselves but alas the crown would not comply. I see Master Clay-Powell is anxious to exhibit his dose of childish vigor."

Caroline turned toward the trailing nurse, her face softening at the wiggling impatience of her son, who was frantically trying to escape the woman's firm hold. Even the icy Lord Blaisdale chuckled under his breath.

"Poor dear!" Lizzy laughed, linking her arm with Caroline's and gesturing toward the tent. "We have the babies together, Caroline. Come, let's sit in the shade and drink our cool tea while the young ones exhaust themselves. Tell me, how long has John been walking?"

The antics of the children occupied the bulk of the afternoon. All jesting aside, the number of offspring just from the couples in some way related to Darcy and Elizabeth numbered over twenty! Oliver Pomeroy, the Earl of Fotherby, was the eldest at seventeen, and probably would not have been considered in the list of children if not for his frail, immature appearance and delight in playing the games with them. The remainder ranged from ten years to infancy, all but the tiniest joining other children in the park to partake of the varied entertainments.

Every parent, relative, and nanny lent a hand in supervising the fun and controlling the army of younglings hunting, rolling, and cracking eggs in an assortment of games. Eventually the bunnies brought as a traditional part of Easter celebrations circulated to their section, the children freshly squealing in glee at the sight of rabbits jumping and frolicking in the grass. A few found new homes, including a fluffy gray one that Alexander fell in love with and who evoked a string of babbled *ba-ba-bas* from Michael. Darcy was not so sure about Lizzy's insistence that he was trying to say "bunny," but the animal was cute and the boys so enamored that he saw no reason to deny them another pet to add to the menagerie already at Pemberley.

As the sun crept toward the horizon, tired tempers flared and irritable cries grew more prevalent. Then Deborah Daniels stopped mid-step, crumpling into a heap onto the grass soundly asleep with thumb in mouth, leaving no doubt it was time to retire to Darcy House!

The Easter week festivities of 1820 ended minutes before midnight when Darcy bid farewell to Gerald Vernor and Albert Hughes after winning the last billiards game. He joined his sleeping wife in bed, the beautiful and fragrant white lilies not put to use that night, and his sleep was not darkened by unpleasant dreams. Attentiveness to any possible threat was instinctual, so he was not lax during the week. Yet the best diligence in the world may not successfully halt a threat that comes from within.

※

Geoffrey, Come tonight at ten o'clock while they are distracted by guests. I shall leave the gate unlocked. Prudence

With an evil grin marring his handsome face, the reader of the hastily scribbled note reached for the candle, applied the flame to the scrap of paper, and watched as it caught fire and burned down to ash.

It is almost too easy, and exceedingly pleasurable, he thought.

He sat back in the hard, wooden chair, eyes staring sightlessly at the roughly hewn wooden rafters of his rented rooms. Clamor from the streets bustling with Easter revelers drifted to his ears, but he paid no heed. His thoughts were consumed with weightier musings.

For too long he had been thwarted in improving his prospects and gaining the respectability he was due. His charm and education gave him an advantage for periods of time, but inevitably something went amiss. Numerous times he came close to winning fortunes while gambling or in a business proposition. His military career had crumbled and prestigious employment eluded him.

The source of all his woes traced directly to Fitzwilliam Darcy.

George Wickham grabbed the bottle of wine, lifting it into the air as if toasting. "To Darcy, my former playmate once as close as a brother. Soon you will be repaid for your envy of me and the spiteful treatment in the wake of your father's death."

He drank deeply while thinking of the past and the future.

While Darcy inherited Pemberley and everything that came with the estate, Wickham was purposefully thwarted and left to rot in mean conditions. Darcy seemed protected by angels, increasing in affluence and felicity, whereas Wickham grew despondent. His hatred grew exponentially with the disappointments.

After his discharge from the army, he wandered aimlessly and accepted any available job that provided for their needs. Oddly his only contentment was Lydia. She was a receptive wife, easily controllable and willing to do his bidding as long as he reaffirmed his undying love thirty times a day. Her housekeeping skills were nonexistent, but her personality did entertain and lighten his mood. Mostly she was as sexually insatiable as he, so the need to seek pleasure elsewhere did not drain their fragile finances.

Finally, he manipulated his way into a middling position of power at the inn in Devon. It was a comfortable situation and he almost forgot to be angry with Darcy.

Until he crossed paths with the Marquis of Orman.

Naturally he had heard of the duel and Orman's humiliation. Gossip of such magnitude reaches even the dregs of society, but military personnel especially hold duels in high esteem no matter how loudly the Church cries out. Yet aside from shaking his head in disgust at Darcy escaping injury or justice once again, he dwelt upon it no further. He had no idea that Lord Orman had settled in Devon.

A purchasing trip to Newton Abbot for the annual cheese fair and a necessary visit to a local brothel led to a chance remark. His paid bed partner, a delicious young trollop not a day over sixteen, commented on the "relief in entertaining a nice gentleman whose parts work like they should, and body isn't a mass of scars and twisted bones." He had found the comment amusing, then intriguing as the girl continued to chatter, and finally breathlessly exciting as a wealth of possibilities flew through his devious mind.

Overnight Wickham's resentment regenerated and he was alive with seething ire ready for an outlet. The mystery of why Devon, a part of the country he had no previous connection with, suddenly made sense. It was meant to be. Finally, he believed the fates were aligning in his favor. The threads of serenity gained in the previous months frayed beyond repair and his despair transmuted into euphoria.

Gaining an audience and earning the trust of the Marquis took months. Wickham learned patience as plot upon plot formed in his mind. Eventually, through constant persistence born of faith, he weaseled his way into Orman's presence and a mutual partnership of hatred and revenge was forged.

That Orman was on the fringes of insanity was obvious from the outset. But this was to Wickham's advantage. He immediately comprehended the possibility of a future beyond dealing with Darcy, and an unstable, crippled, and debilitated man of riches was a gift from God to his way of thinking. Wickham's duplicitous nature and scheming intellect quickly laid the foundation for indispensability, embezzlement, and, if necessary, blackmail. Yes, indeed, his future was secure.

Once he dealt with Darcy, of course.

Orman simply wanted Darcy dead and did not care how it was done. Storming Pemberley with shotgun blazing was his initial idea, one that took Wickham weeks to rebut. He argued for restraint and the need to learn the man's habits and schedule. Wickham envisioned greater possibilities and had to constantly remind the maniacal Lord of this fact. The Marquis's salivation over Darcy being in Hertfordshire—and Wickham having free access to him—was difficult to counter, but Wickham had worked too hard for too many months to act hastily.

He watched and connived for the best solution to hurt Darcy the most and reap the best lasting benefit for him. Knowing that Pemberley was nearly as unassailable as a medieval castle, he turned his attention to London. He spent hours in surveillance of Darcy House, learning the routines of the staff and searching for any weaknesses in the regulated Darcy chain of security. He cataloged each person he saw to ensure that none of them were familiar and, in that respect, he was also fortunate since his past visits to Darcy House were rare and long ago. Mr. Travers was the only one who may remember him, but the butler was easy to avoid since he rarely left the house.

Fully aware of his power over weak-minded, foolish women, Wickham had intended to charm a maid as a possible way into the mansion. Several ideas were formulated, but Mrs. Smyth was a surprising boon. Following her to the market at Covent Gardens on that fateful day was a sheer whim, one undertaken merely to learn more of the staff's actions. His impulsive introduction was brilliant and he was exceedingly proud of how it was working to his advantage. Once that relationship was established, his pathway to success was obvious. Finally, he had convinced Lord Orman of the plot's victory, needing only to wait until the Season in Town.

His smile turned to one of sheer lust, groin automatically responding to his imaginings of the pleasure to come that night. Never would he have suspected that his manipulation of the housekeeper would lead to where it had. She proved to be a valuable asset in a host of ways, the bedroom a bonus he received as further indication his plan was bound to succeed. Geoffrey Wiseman's courtship was considered respectable, so the staff members were comfortable with his occasional presence.

Jumping to his feet with a youthful vigor, he decided to splurge and dine at the Queen's Diadem. He would dress in his best suit and order the most expensive item on the menu. With a satisfied stomach and a long night of Prudence Smyth's enthusiasm satiating his other appetite, his strength would be at optimal levels for the momentous days ahead. Perhaps he should bring her a gift, he mused, a trinket to soften her further, although she was quite pliant after they made love and more than willing to rant against her employers. He chuckled, imagining that after a week she would be especially vociferous, providing him with the final details required to carry out his revenge. Better yet, he thought, groin tightening almost painfully, she will be wild in her rage, finding an outlet with a partner more than willing to transfer angry passion into wanton abandon.

Yes, it would be the best Easter of his life.

CHAPTER SIXTEEN
Disturbing Disclosures

THE MONDAY FOLLOWING EASTER dawned as most did these days. That is Lizzy was woken just before the sun made its appearance by the gentle ringing of the dampened bell installed near her side of the bed, alerting of a hungry infant. Some mornings the faint chime roused Darcy as well, the drowsy father asking his wife to bring Michael to the bedchamber for light play before they all returned to sleep for another hour or two. However, most mornings were like today in that he remained asleep, oblivious to his wife's leaving and returning.

Lizzy fed Michael, a task that took about thirty minutes before he was surfeited and once again asleep at her breast. It was difficult to leave him in these moments of tranquility, his angelic face peaceful as she rocked him. There were times when she simply could not bear to return him to his cradle, opting to stay awake and croon as they swayed together with his warm body pressed to her chest.

This morning, however, Lizzy discovered that her thoughts drifted to the vision of her handsome husband as she had glimpsed him when she cautiously arose to answer Mrs. Hanford's summons. Therefore, she did not hesitate in laying Michael back into his cradle, sparing only a few minutes to caress and bestow another kiss to his silky forehead. She returned to bed, the glow of golden sunlight illuminating the edges of the heavy curtains and brightening the gloomy chamber. Darcy was precisely as Lizzy had left him: soundly asleep with respirations deep and regular, sprawled on his back with the lightweight coverlet pushed down to below his naval so that his muscular, hair-covered chest was exposed. One hand rested above the coverlet on his abdomen; the right extended and laying in the depression where her body had been as if his subconscious knew she was gone from his side. As always, his full lips were parted, lashes heavy on stubbled cheeks, and hair mussed. To his wife he was the embodiment of sexiness and desire.

She stretched by his naked body, one hand commencing the familiar journey across the hard planes of his chest. She pressed her breasts against the heat of his flesh and placed moist kisses over his neck and jaw. His breath's cadence altered until it matched her accelerated pace, and his muscles instinctively responded to the tactile stimulation even if his mind was primarily unwitting.

"Fitzwilliam," she breathed against his ear. "Wake up. I want you."

"Lizzy."

She smiled at his sleepy response. He *never* called her "Lizzy" unless utterly overcome with passion or drowsily reacting to unconscious incitements, such as now. Darcy slept deeply and was slow to gain full awareness, especially when the rousing techniques were pleasurable and smoothly integrated with his dreamy musings.

His half-sleep state did not inhibit him responding in a number of physical ways, however. He turned slightly toward her, seeking the soft, curvy body with hands reaching to cup her breasts for titillating manipulation and a leg lifting to lock around her hips and pull closer. With eyes yet closed, he nonetheless aimed true, locking his lips onto hers for a prolonged, heated kiss.

"Hmmm… Are you awake now?" ·

"No."

"No matter. Stay asleep, my darling, and fly through your dreams as I love and adore you." And with that declaration she firmly pushed him backwards until he again lay flat and commenced a thorough, provocative investigation of all available places.

Darcy smiled with satisfaction. He was awake, of course, his mind no longer fuzzy from sleep, but rather happily dazed with rising sensations as his unparalleled lover worked her magic upon his body.

He *loved* when she woke him this way and took control! She knew every inch of his flesh better than he, knew precisely how to touch him and play over his body until his ardor rendered him weak with desire. At these times, her passionate nature was unleashed, her abandon a special thrill that lifted his fervor tremendously.

She was so beautiful! Her figure was lithe and sensuous in the pale light with her unbound hair cascading crazily over her slender shoulders with random tresses brushing over her lush breasts. He rested one hand lightly on her hip and spread the other over her belly while observing her glory and sensing every frenzied motion.

He knew—moments before she grasped his wrist and thigh with clenches strong enough to cause bruises if he was not sturdy enough to withstand the pressure—that she was ready to succumb to the spiraling vibrations. She arched over his knees and released a cry of extreme delight with his name interwoven. Every ounce of his considerable restraint was called forth not to ride the tide with her, but his wish was to first savor her happiness. Only when she collapsed onto his chest, shivers and gasps wracking her body, did he take control.

He rolled her over and resumed a gentle rhythm of loving, whispering sweet endearments and erotic phrases. His passion reverberated through his body and transmitted into hers as she progressively reacted with rekindled desire.

It was a morning greeting of the highest order. All concerns flew away, the only care being of that moment and pleasuring each other. Senses ruled and the only sounds were of the elation they acquired in this unique interlude of joining.

The sun was well over the horizon, rays of illumination and warmth reaching above the surrounding London rooftops to touch the garden behind their bedchamber and flood through the curtain gaps. Shadows remained, but a newly dawned day was firmly established before Darcy lifted from his comfortable location nestled into his wife's neck.

"Good morning," he whispered, blue eyes shining with love as he brushed his knuckles over her cheekbones.

"Good morning," she returned, her brown eyes radiating identical contentment.

"Best wake up I have had in, oh, a week or so?"

"I cannot be faulted for you typically rising before the sun, or your youngest son's appetite."

"I am assigning no fault, my love. How could I when nearly every night your love aids my cleansing slumber such that I am well rested and eager to rise for another day of marriage to you?" He kissed her pert nose. "Indeed, I rather prefer these surprise awakenings being a special treat. Now I shall have a smug grin on my face all day, likely receiving a wealth of taunts from Richard."

Lizzy laughed, squeezing and pulling his lean body firmly against hers. "At least you can now tease him in return. I forgot that you were meeting with him today. What else is on your agenda?"

"Dull business all morning, I am afraid. Mr. Daniels will be coming at ten. Until then I plan to attack the mound of documents accumulated on my desk. I fear I shall see little of you or the children after breakfast."

"You recall that we have an engagement tonight at Lord and Lady Hassert's? Of course you do." She chuckled at the vaguely piqued expression that crossed his brows. "Forgive me, dear. I know you would not forget. Well, then I shall probably not see you until we meet in our complementary attire and enter our carriage."

"Is your schedule as full?"

"Not as much as yours. I have nothing planned this morning other than to play with the children. I need to recuperate from the past weeks' excitement. Jane and Simone will be joining Georgiana and I for tea and playtime for the children. Mrs. Smyth looked to cry when I told her the news. I believe the Easter entertainments have frazzled her nerves. She so clearly adores children," she added with a sarcastic laugh.

Darcy smiled and nodded.

"Are you dining at Estad's?"

"Of course. It is the best in London, and fortuitously close to Angelo's. By the way, I know I spoke of taking Alexander to the studio to observe the fencing, but I fear I cannot take him with me as I desired. I have appointments with Duke Grafton and Mr. Clemens at White's immediately following. Thankfully, I had not revealed my plan to him so he shan't be disappointed. I will take him on another day and fence myself instead."

"Actually, that is fortunate. We can work together in the garden this afternoon when the sun is beyond the walls and not so scorching. I have those seedlings that Mr. Clark prepared for me yet to plant and have not had the time to do so. I want to plant them in the far garden, in the clearing between the cypress and willow trees. That is the most spacious area for the children to have plots of their own that will grow with them. Mr. Clark gave me some great pointers so I do pray the seedlings have not withered with the delay."

"I know Alexander is anxious to plant the sunflowers we brought from Pemberley. He is fascinated by sunflowers and I fear his displeasure when they do not fully complete their life cycle before we depart. I cannot make him understand the passage of natural time as yet."

"He will learn eventually, love. And we have his sunflowers at home to harvest and ease his disappointment."

Darcy laughed. "I warn you, he will likely spend more time building dirt structures and searching for insects. That is what I did as a boy. An appreciation for horticulture came much later."

"Well, a man of the earth like his papa should start with the earth, I believe. So he can dig all he wants. A little dirt never hurt anyone. Mrs. Smyth balked at the idea of dirt playing and nearly fainted at the idea of insects in the house when I asked for a glass jar to store any intriguing specimens he discovers."

"Mrs. Smyth will need to adjust. Examining God's smallest creatures is an educational pursuit and scrubbing through the ground makes a boy stronger."

"So, while I entertain the women, you and the other husbands shall be dining at Estad's. At least promise me you will take the time to kiss me good-day before you depart into the wilds of London?"

He smiled, stroking over her soft cheek. "I promise. And if it is kisses you want, we have a few more minutes before the urgency for coffee and food overwhelms. Come here, Mrs. Darcy."

⋘∙⋙

"Come," Darcy boomed into the air, the study door opening briskly to reveal the retired Colonel Richard Fitzwilliam. "Richard!" Darcy said with surprise, rising to greet his cousin with a handclasp. "Was noontime not soon enough to share my company?"

He extended a hand to the leather Chippendale across from his parchment-scattered desk, Richard dropping into it with a sigh.

"I thought you might be missing my smiling face, Cousin." He grinned, reaching to pour a cup of coffee from the silver pot sitting on the edge of the massive desk. "Seriously, please pardon the interruption, William. I know you are busy." He paused to sweep a hand over the mass of papers piled on the smooth, polished surface. "I thought you paid people to manage for you. What is the point of being obscenely rich if you have to work so hard?"

"You are lazy and an autocrat." Darcy accused with a shake of his head,

Richard shrugging and not denying the tease. "You know I prefer to attend to my business personally. However, I am striving to sell a few of my interests and consolidate. I would rather focus on the mills, Pemberley estate, and my horses, reinvesting some of my money into improving those areas. I am being pulled in too many directions, and I want to devote more time to my family and travel. It will take some time and I need to be wise in my choices, but a major thrust this year has been to begin liquidating and reinvesting into the estate and some stocks that do not require my involvement. Interested in part ownership of a German steel mill?"

Richard grunted. "As you said, I am lazy. And newly married, retired, and preparing to do my part in increasing England's population."

"Are you trying to tell me Lady Simone is burdened with a little Fitzwilliam?"

"Wipe that smirk off your face, and do not breathe a word to Elizabeth or I will dust off my rapier and run you through. We are not certain as yet and if my wife knew I was saying anything before she has the chance to proclaim the news to her lady friends, and especially my mother, she would skewer me herself."

"Your secret is safe, Cousin. I do pray you are blessed with a positive confirmation soon. Elizabeth will be beside herself with joy and Aunt Madeline will be uncontainable."

"After she recovers from her seizure. I swear she still thinks my marriage is all a happy dream that she will wake from imminently."

Darcy laughed. "As do we all, my friend. Now, why are you really here if it is not to make an announcement?"

Richard sat forward, suddenly a colonel even if wearing a finely tailored suit similar to Darcy's. "My associates returned from Devon."

Darcy's face lost all traces of jocularity, eyes intent and mouth set. "Proceed."

"Some of what they reported you already know, but I paid them to be thorough."

"I owe you for that, by the way."

Richard waved a hand dismissively. "Forget it. It is my pleasure and you can pay me in father-related advice." He reached into an inner pocket of his jacket, removing a sheath of folded papers as he continued. "I gave my associates little information other than names. I wanted them to be thorough without any prior biases or assumptions. Therefore most of the information written on these pages is redundant, as we already know the rumors. But they were assiduous in their search and record keeping. I spent most of last night after returning home sifting through this, much to my beautiful wife's vexation, so you owe me a drink or two for that sacrifice on my part."

He smiled, but Darcy only nodded, eyes on the pages in Richard's hands.

Richard cleared his throat and resumed. "As you know, after recovering from the wounds you inflicted, Orman retreated to his estate in Devon and sold the one in Derbyshire. All the stories say that he hid himself behind the thick stonewalls and steadfastly began drinking himself into an early grave. That is difficult to verify, but the estate fell into disrepair within months with more than half the employees let go, so he clearly was not managing effectively. And there is some evidence that the local distributors of spirits have profited from his full-time residency, so there is probably some truth in that rumor. All of this, in addition to his selling of the London townhouse he owned, led to talk of financial woes.

"You also know how the rumors of his injuries escalated. I specifically charged my associates to discover the truth. It was difficult, but they finally learned that he is not completely crippled. He is able to walk, but haltingly with a severe limp, extreme pain, and the use of a crutch. He is not too pretty between the scars you gave him and the beauty that Lizzy delivered to his cheek. And apparently the gash to his thigh area, with subsequent festering, rendered him impotent."

Darcy was genuinely taken aback at that, instinctively clenching his own thighs together at the horror of such a fate, before remembering that in Lord Orman's case this was likely a blessing.

Richard shook his head, reading Darcy's expressions. "It is not the positive you may imagine. Sure, he can no longer rape a woman, but he has transferred his anger, bitterness, and lechery to assaulting in other ways. Tragically that fact is the only way my friends were able to get any personal information. Orman never leaves his estate and no one visits him, except for select prostitutes from a local bordello."

"But… What in the world would be the point if he cannot…" Darcy waved his hand vaguely.

"Apparently his appetite is not diminished even if he is unable to perform. Do you really want me to give further details of Orman's perverted proclivities, William? No, I did not think so. The brothel is high class and the girls are well paid for their indulgence—and their silence, but fortunately for us, these types of individuals are also prone to gossip and are mercenary."

He paused, gazing at his grim, pursed-lipped cousin. Darcy looked near to retching, the topic of conversation one that highly insulted his moral sensibilities. "I will just leave it that my associates are not so delicate and had no trouble stooping to distasteful methods in order to glean information. They had a fine time in the pursuit, I assure you, and no young ladies were injured, but that is where some of my money went and why I would therefore not ask you to reimburse me."

Darcy nodded, too disturbed to reply.

"The important part," Richard continued, "is that the information tells me that Orman is not a man fully in the grips of sanity. Additionally, the men were able to waylay the town surgeon who treats Orman. The man is a sot with loose morals and poor medical skills. Why he was chosen and is allowed in Orman's presence may seem to be illogical, but his lacking ethics are the key. He gleefully spilled an ocean of information for two bottles of cheap port. His tales of Orman's requirements, such as opium and ether for dulling his pain and recreational purposes, grew wilder as he reached the end of the second bottle. But, if half of what he said is true, Orman is seriously deranged."

"And thus a man not to be trusted."

"Yes. But also a man who probably could not reason beyond the desire for personal pleasures and revenge."

Darcy sat back in his chair with a sigh, fingers methodically tapping on the cushioned armrest. "So, Elizabeth could not have seen him in Hertfordshire if he never leaves his house in Devon."

"Do not be too hasty, Cousin. I have not told you all."

Darcy lifted his piercing gaze, again alert and intense. "Wickham?"

Richard shook his head. "My men found nothing about Wickham. They asked all along the Devon roads especially at the inns, carefully mind you, but his name is unknown. But here is what is interesting. Some eighteen months ago, roughly, things began to gradually change around Orman's estate. Crops were being planted again, a few new tenant farmers were contracted, and the grounds were improved. Rumors are rife, mind you, and no one speaks with any credibility, but there is one constant. A new employee that no one knows well, or can give a good description of, now works for the Marquis. He is mysterious, but most agree his name is Geoffrey Wiseman."

Darcy hissed through grit teeth. "Geoffrey Wiseman. George Wickham. That is too much of a coincidence!"

Richard shrugged. "Perhaps. But…"

"Perhaps? You must see how this all fits?"

"I see that it is one way to interpret the vague information, but not conclusive. Even you must admit, Darcy, that there are probably thousands of men in England with the initials G.W.?" Darcy nodded, but his eyes conveyed no doubt in his assumption. Richard, despite his claim, matched Darcy's expression. "However, I concur that there are too many aspects to this tale that raise my hackles."

Darcy was scrutinizing his cousin carefully. Richard, Colonel Fitzwilliam as he would always be, was a man whose instincts were to be respected. Darcy waited, Richard finally collecting his thoughts and continuing.

"My associates returned without digging anything else up. They knew I wanted information as rapidly as possible. What I have told you is the extent of what they discovered, the remainder of the notes in these pages"—he tapped the folded parchment lying on the desk's edge—"giving specifics that you probably do not want to read. I, however, have done my own inquiring during this past week." He grinned, a flash of cold humor sparkling in his blue eyes. "After all, I have skills of my own and matrimony has not softened me totally, as you shall discover this afternoon at Angelo's."

Darcy grunted, and Richard's grin widened briefly before fading as he resumed his narrative. "Did you know that the Marquis of Orman owns a hunting lodge near London?"

Darcy did not respond verbally, instead unerringly pulling a folded document from the apparent chaos scattered over the glossy surface of his mahogany desk. He tossed the paper to Richard wordlessly, Richard opening and scanning the written words rapidly.

"Well, excellent."

"Mr. Daniels is highly ethical and aboveboard, but thorough and skilled in his own way. He learned of Orman's Surrey property, a modest plot of land with a tiny cottage owned by the family for a century. It has rarely been used, apparently, as Orman was never much of a hunter, and has reportedly been vacant for the past three years."

"That is not entirely accurate." Darcy's brow rose at Richard's words. "When I stumbled across this intelligence yesterday, and after reading through this report"—he again tapped the sheath of parchment—"I asked Artois to ride out there."

"What did he discover?"

"Not enough to form any clear conclusions, but the house is not unoccupied. There was a faint light shining from a top floor window, he said, but no other signs of habitation. He did not dare investigate too thoroughly in broad daylight and he was not prepared for clandestine spying. It could easily be a squatter, but I plan to take my friends and go back tonight for a closer look, with your permission."

"If Orman is around, this is probably where he would be. And with Wickham, if he is this Wiseman."

Richard nodded. "My thoughts exactly."

A knock at the door interrupted, Darcy giving the command to enter. It was Mr. Travers with the day's post. Richard used the intermission to pour another cup of coffee, sipping quietly while Darcy cut the strings securing a small package. He watched him withdraw a tissue wrapped miniature frame, oval and fancily gilded. The intense loathing marring his cousin's handsome face was marked and his naturally deep voice was grating and thick when he spoke.

"I asked Mrs. Reynolds to send me this miniature portrait of Wickham. It was painted the year before my father died. He wanted a remembrance of his steward's son, his godson. He was so proud of Wickham's accomplishments at Cambridge. I could not bear to tell him the truth, and it is almost a blessing he died before discovering it himself." Sadness and bitterness inundated his voice, eyes staring at the dimpled smiling face for another minute before roughly returning the painting to the confines of the box. He cleared his throat, the familiar serene regulation washing over his features before he lifted his controlled gaze to his cousin. "I plan to show it to the staff to see if anyone has seen him lurking about."

Richard's brows rose and he nodded with respect. "Very smart, Cousin. I should have thought of that myself! I am so impressed I may just let you score a point or two off me during our match."

Darcy laughed, brightening slightly. "As if you could possibly beat me. Save your pity points as I shall trounce you fair and square."

"We shall see."

They both grinned, knowing that it would be a vigorously fought battle with the outcome a pleasant mystery with fencing skills that were evenly matched. That fact, of course, was why they so enjoyed competing against each other.

Richard stood. "Until later then. I will leave you to your dreary business pursuits and see you at Estad's. I think I shall return home and see how my wife is faring. More babies." He shook his head, momentarily assuming the mournful pose from his bachelor days. "What is happening to us, Darcy? All this domesticity is like a virus."

"Really? I shall remember that, Cousin, and hold it over you."

But Richard just laughed, slapping Darcy on the back as they walked to the door. "Alas, my wife knows me well and teases me relentlessly about the invisible shackles on my ankles. Luckily, she also knows I would have it no other way."

For the Master of Pemberley and Darcy House, the morning hours after the departure of Richard Fitzwilliam elapsed in the company of Mr. Daniels and a pile of documents. A great deal was accomplished ere the solicitor left before noon. Appointments for further discussions were made, plans were set in motion, letters were dictated, and Darcy's hand was cramped from writing. Mr. Travers assisted as secretary, his aged hands steady and possessing a legible penmanship superior even to Darcy's firm script.

Final instructions for posting of missives and calendar bookings were being given to the butler when the second surprise interruption of Darcy's day occurred.

Darcy positively answered the tentative knock on his study door, both he and Mr. Travers rising when the interrupter was revealed as Lizzy.

"Mrs. Darcy," Mr. Travers greeted.

She nodded his direction. "Mr. Travers. Mr. Darcy."

"Mrs. Darcy," her husband responded, brows furrowing at the hint of a blush that highlighted her prominent cheekbones. "Is something amiss?"

"No, no. Not at all." Her flush deepened and eyes flittered away momentarily, Darcy frowning further. "I am so sorry to disturb, but, if it is not too inconvenient or ill timed, I was hoping to speak with you for a moment?"

Mr. Travers was already gathering the stack of papers on the desk corner before him, murmuring his intent to post the letters immediately, and not noticing the puzzled and amused expressions crossing his Master's features. He passed Lizzy, bowing again, and closed the door firmly behind.

Darcy stood before his chair, observing his wife as she bit her lower lip and fidgeted with her wedding rings. He was content that he could read her moods well enough to ascertain that nothing alarming was causing her strange actions but was unsure of the root source. She was a bit breathless and a becoming flush spread to the tops of her bosoms, which, he noted with a jolt, were rising delightfully with her respirations and perceptible under the clinging muslin of her lightweight spring gown.

"Elizabeth, are you well?" His voice cracked feebly, his blood suddenly racing by her apparent condition.

She glanced up, eyes flashing from sultry to sheepish as she approached. "Michael is asleep and Alexander playing. I was... thinking of you and... missing you." She nervously swept a loose strand of hair away. "I know you are busy, but wanted to see you and felt that I could not wait."

She bit her lip again, an unconscious mannerism that never failed to make his knees weak, glancing upward into his penetrating eyes as she now stood in front of him a mere two feet away. He could feel the heat emanating from her body, the flush a ruddy glow now, and he lifted a hand to entwine with the one she extended toward his chest.

However, before their fingers met she exhaled sharply and sidestepped, moving around the chair. Before his surprise allowed him to turn toward her she had placed both hands onto his shoulders, tugging decisively until he sank into the cushioned leather of his enormous chair.

"Elizabeth, what...?"

"I was playing with our son, bouncing the ball between us, while my thoughts became diverted!" Her hands were running over his nape, jawline, and through his hair, fingertips massaging his skin in that mixed therapeutic and seductive way she possessed. Her voice was huskily vibrant but with undertones of peevishness. "How inappropriate is it to be in the company of a two-year-old and begin to feel... That is, what kind of a mother am I to abandon my children so I can seek my husband in the middle of the day? In his study no less! It is not like we haven't... been together for days or weeks. Why, just this morning, not some six hours ago we... Aargh!"

Darcy was trying hard not to laugh. His smile was faintly lecherous, as her reminder to their morning interlude, instigated most forcefully by her, was a pleasant memory indeed.

"Dearest..."

"All I could think of as I tossed that infernal ball to our innocent baby was your body! Your hands and mouth and neck." She was leaning into him, breasts brushing over his shoulder blades and breath tickling the exposed skin of his ear as she nibbled on a lobe. "Fitzwilliam..." she whispered, and he turned his face toward her, meeting her glazed eyes for a brief second before she pulled away.

Instantly scarlet to the tips of her ears, she withdrew, back of her hand over her full lips. "I should not have infringed upon you with my... ridiculousness."

She backed away, retreating around his chair until leaning against his desk, locked by his blue eyes glittering with gaiety. "This is pathetic, is it not? Chasing you down while you work to bother you with my humiliating impulses. I know you are to leave soon, and…"

"Are you trying to politely say that your concupiscence is high and that you have sought me out for relief?" His left brow arched playfully. He would not have thought it possible for her blush to deepen, but it did. He chuckled, speaking with humor amid the resonance. "Have I ever given you the idea that I would not welcome your attentions? Or that your passionate nature and zeal for me is not an incredible stimulant to my own ardor? Is there any doubt that I am the type of husband, and man, who gleefully encourages his wife to express her wanton urges and willingly acquiesces?"

She shook her head, smiling and not attempting to hide her desire as he rose and stepped near. He spanned her slender waist, strong hands smoothly lifting and sitting her onto the flat top of his desk. Starting at her ankles, he rubbed upward along the quivering silkiness of her legs, sliding under her skirts. Her legs parted naturally as he bent forward, his large frame dwarfing her dainty body and overwhelming her senses. Brushing his lips over her ear he whispered, "If you desire me, you need only ask. I can assure you I will never deny your fervor if at all feasible to comply."

Lizzy released a throaty moan, her stasis broken as she seized his cravat and jerked his mouth to hers, deftly untying the knotted silk in seconds. That accomplished, she attacked his clothing and body with a direct assault that stunned him despite his invitation.

Oddly enough, considering the mania they possessed for each other and the wild liberalness of their lovemaking, especially during the first year of their marriage, they had never made love on his desks. His Pemberley desk was simply too cluttered, the risk of serious wounding or impalement too great, so the numerous trysts occurring in that chamber were fulfilled in safer if equally atypical locations. This room was not inviolate, it being a good thing that walls cannot talk, but the desk had mysteriously remained undefiled.

Until now, and they would henceforth wonder why they waited so long! Of course, the fact that Darcy would forever have to tear his thoughts away from decadent memories to attend seriously to work may be one logical justification for avoiding the site. Another was the crumbled parchment pieces and spilled ink. But neither was enough to outweigh the indescribable ecstasy attained. Plus, the vision of his half-clothed wife lusciously splayed over his work surface, her face glistening with the radiance of sensual satiation and lush lips ruddy and swollen from his kisses was a picture he would never be regretful of holding.

"Lizzy, my beautiful Lizzy," he whispered, lips grazing over the heated skin encasing her fluttering heart. "I do not know what impetus drove you here, into my arms, but I am grateful you did not resist the urge. I love you so!"

"I am not sure what impetus drove me either, William. All morning, even moments after rising from our bed and your arms, I wanted you again."

His laugh was guttural and replete with satisfaction, teeth delightfully nipping along her collarbone. "Please do not expect me to express the slightest unhappiness in that information!"

"No, I would not anticipate your overwhelming remorse or displeasure. Nor am I in any way displeased. It is just… Ooh! Something is poking my side and my leg is getting a cramp."

More laughter ensued, the aftermath of rising from the awkward position and adjusting clothing humorous. The poking quill was free of ink, Lizzy's dress spared that stain although the wrinkles were another matter. They ended up sitting on Darcy's chair with Lizzy nestled in his lap while he kneaded her thigh muscle free of residual spasms.

"There. Feeling better?"

"Much. The experience was worth any discomfort." She nuzzled into his neck, hand snaking under his loosened shirt to the hot flesh underneath. "You are amazing, my husband. In every way knowing how to ease my pains. Such a superb deliverer of delights and gratification." She kissed along his jaw to his ear with tongue feathering while her caressing hand grew bolder.

"My love? If you are attempting to re-seduce me I may be forced to disappoint. Even I have a limit to how rapidly I can recover, your obvious charms notwithstanding." She did not reply, nor did she halt her pointed fondling. He chuckled, squirming and clasping her hand as he turned and captured her mouth in a firm kiss. "Goodness! I have not seen you so amorous since you were pregnant with Michael! Not that you are not generally more than capable of matching my ardor, but it has been a while since you accosted me in my study. And no, I am not complaining in the slightest." He paused, noting the odd expression on her face. "Elizabeth?"

"What did you say about being amorous?"

"That I approve most highly. And if you insist I am positive we can repeat the performance later tonight."

He kissed her cheek, but she pulled him away to look into his face. Her mien was one of blended surprise and elation. Darcy frowned.

"You may be right, William," she whispered, and then shakily laughed. "I cannot believe it has not occurred to me!" She rose from his lap, pacing away a few feet while he watched her in perplexity. "Probably because I have not restarted my cycles so I had no gauge. But I have been sleepier than usual, my breasts have been aching"—she absently cupped her heavy breasts—"and for the past couple of weeks I have been mildly queasy, although I attributed that to traveling and not eating my usual diet. And I have been desiring you more than usual, not that I do not welcome the feeling, but still!"

"Stop!" He was on his feet, hands fisted at his sides. His face was as white as a sheet and his lips pressed so tightly together that small pressure wrinkles appeared. "Are you saying you think you may be... pregnant?" His voice was a bare whisper, cracking on the final word.

"I am not certain, of course, but it fits, and certainly is plausible considering us." And she waved her hand between their two bodies. Her face was glowing with joy, eyes radiant and unfocused, and thus not noting his pained expression or tone of voice.

Darcy stared for another few moments and then released a coarse whine, pivoting and lurching to the window. His mumbling, angry words reached her ears, "Irresponsible idiot! You should have done something to prevent this happening so soon."

"What are you saying, William? Prevent another child?" Her face was aghast, her eyes wide with astonishment. "Even if that were possible, why would you wish such a thing?"

"Is it not obvious, Elizabeth? After Michael, your illness, I..." He sighed in exasperation. "You have barely returned to a normal state, emotionally. It has only been a month since you quit drinking uncle's teas! How could this happen so quickly?"

"Surely you do not need me to answer *that* question?" She snapped, her eyes afire with irritation.

"No, of course not. I did not mean..."

"Conception occurs when it occurs, Mr. Darcy. Look at Mary. Two babies in short succession. I doubt if Mr. Daniels expressed unhappiness!"

"It is hardly the same. You were so ill, Elizabeth. And we… our relation-ship suffered so dramatically. I could not bear to have that transpire again!"

His voice broke, the stricken cast to his mien penetrating Lizzy's awareness. Her heart melted, although she remained somewhat annoyed. She crossed to where he stood ramrod tense by the window. She looked into his agonized eyes, reaching her hands to gently straighten his disarrayed clothing, injecting placating modulations as she spoke.

"Uncle George has assured us both, several times, that the likelihood of another such incident is slim now that we know what to watch for. He will be with me to assure I am well, and I shall not make the mistake of avoiding assist-ance. We have all learned to be cautious and diligent, my love. Furthermore, and most importantly, I have no intention of looking upon carrying our babies, as often as the Almighty chooses to gift us, as anything but the most miraculous of blessings. I do not believe that you feel any different."

He stilled her hands, clasping them between his own and lifting to kiss her fingers. "I love you, Elizabeth, beyond words. And I love our children. And, yes, I do want more. In time. But I cannot pretend that the idea of you being pregnant, now, so soon, does not terrify me. I simply cannot embrace the joy of the idea at this juncture. Please forgive me, dearest, but I…" He swallowed, closing his eyes for a moment, and resumed in a husky whisper. "I cannot…"

A knock at the door arrested his words and any further discussion. Darcy reluctantly pulled away, tucking his shirt and fastening the buttons on his jacket. He cleared his throat, face assuming a neutral expression with only faint lines of stress marring the calm semblance.

"Yes?"

"Sir"—it was Mr. Travers, opening the door mere inches—"your horse is waiting."

"Thank you. I shall be there momentarily."

The door closed, leaving the lovers alone. Lizzy was staring at her husband, emotions in turmoil but understanding his angst. He pleaded silently, eyes melancholy, even as she forced a smile.

He opened his mouth to speak, but Lizzy interrupted. "Have a wonderful afternoon, dearest. We shall talk of this later." She lifted on tiptoes to kiss his cheek and caress fingertips over his jaw. "All will be well, you shall see. I love you."

Then she turned and left the room without a backward glance.

Chapter Seventeen
Unleashed Revenge

H E LEFT THE HOUSE moments after she exited the parlor. Lizzy worried over his frame of mind disturbing his focus during the planned activities for his afternoon, but otherwise refused to dwell on the unknowns any further. If she was with child they would know soon enough, and she had no doubt that Darcy, once assured of her health, would be overjoyed. His all-consuming love and devotion to his family frequently stated desire for a bevy of children, and general good sense allayed any fears she had over his present trepidations.

Tea was taken on the Darcy House rear garden. The air was crisp with a slight chill but pleasant enough for an outside dining experience. The four women conversed and ate at the round table under the shaded patio while the four boys nibbled picnic-style on the open grass beside the fountain.

It was a quiet affair, despite Mrs. Smyth's predictions. Ethan Bingley and Hugh Pomeroy were not as placid as Alexander, but they were well-behaved children able to pass a few hours in backyard play. Nine-year-old Harry spent part of the time chasing the younger boys around the grass and playing with the new bunny, and the other portion with his nose pressed into a book.

The ladies were content to gossip and laugh. Georgiana accidentally mentioned Mr. Butler at one point, Jane then being let in on the secret. After the expected congratulations and teasing, mostly from Lizzy, a goodly amount of time was spent on marital advice, leading to more laughter and blushes from the shy Georgiana.

While Alexander napped, Lizzy retreated to Darcy's office to write a few letters. Georgiana was busy with her music, amid frequent glances out the window just in case a courier arrived—or better yet, a handsome man with curly blond hair. Servants moved about performing their duties with some noise attached, and Michael's cries for nourishment did pierce the calm twice that day. But otherwise, it was a tranquil Monday boding nothing sinister.

Therefore, it was with a spring in her step and smile that she laid Michael down after his late afternoon meal, gathered Alexander and their gardening equipment, and headed to the northeast corner of the yard. As Lizzy had surmised, the sun was located so that the harshest of its rays were blocked by the surrounding walls and tall trees. There was no breeze to cool the air, but this corner of the yard was partially in shadow at this time of the day. She would not need to fret over their son's fair skin or wear a bothersome hat to shield her face.

In one arm Alexander clutched the glass jar given with a disgusted cringe by Mrs. Smyth, and in the other he held tightly to the basket of sunflower seedlings transported all the way from Pemberley. Lizzy hummed throughout the transplanting, babbling to her son as he attended to packing the rich earth carefully around the root-ball of each tiny plant, his focus lost only when the gray rabbit hopped over to investigate from time to time.

She wore gloves to protect her hands, and a thick apron over the light-weight muslin gown of dark green specifically created for such gritty tasks. Alexander wore a child's dress of dark blue, a color that accented the tiny flecks of ultramarine lining the edges of his otherwise azure eyes. His hands and feet were bare, the dirt grains settling into the creases and between tiny toes. Side-by-side they worked, kneeling in the springy clover bordering the flowerbed, Lizzy's instructions of a practical nature and in sharp contrast to Darcy's scientific expositions.

"Feel how rich the soil is here, love. Filled with wonderful nutrients to help the plants grow. This spot receives sun almost all day long, and that is why the sunflowers will grow so well here."

"Papa say sunflowers look at the sun."

"Yes, they do tend to turn whichever way the sun moves. Very interesting to watch." She glanced to her son's round face, marveling at the intent wrinkles between his thick brown brows as he set each sprout into the holes she created.

It was always, "Papa say..." about everything. She did not think he stated, "Mama say..." nearly as frequently or with the same assured authority, but she did not mind in the slightest. His father was where he turned for education, steadfastness, and rough play; but to her he sought succor when hurt, babyish cosseting, and the fulfillment of daily essentials. It was a balance between his parents: Darcy the all-knowing, masculine, stalwart protector; and Lizzy the ever-present, mothering, empathetic attendant.

The planting and dirt play continued, both oblivious to the pair of eyes that observed their every move.

The stalker hugged the deep shadows cast by the four tall Mediterranean cypress trees lining the open glade near the rear wall of the mews. This corner of the moderate-sized enclosure that contained the Darcy House gardens, lawn, and patio was away from any open windows and hidden from easy view by sculpted hedges, bushes, and thick-trunked trees. The fountain that sat in the precise middle of the yard was not large, but the water bubbled, splashed, and trickled loudly. It was designed to mask the noises from without the walled sanctuary, but the interloper depended on its dampening properties to aid his scheme.

A final cap was the rarely used, small, recessed door that gave access to the endmost stall within the stables. As if by divine intercession, a plain wooden cart was kept parked there for the occasional hauling of rough materials. That his prey would choose this place to be alone and unguarded, trusting in the safety of their abode, was unquestionably providence.

It was almost *too* perfect, but Wickham was convinced his time for vindication and success was destined. The pieces of the puzzle had fallen from heaven into his lap, snapping together into a beautiful picture that was foolproof. He had duped the mighty Darcy, beguiled his way into the arrogant man's house, and would now prove his superiority by absconding with those his nemesis held most dear. Right from under his haughty nose.

Wickham allowed a thrill of victory to rush through his body before squelching the emotion. He must maintain cold control. All day he had lain in wait for them to garden as Prudence sneeringly revealed at one point last night. Now, all he needed was for the two to separate so he could deal with them individually before the other noticed, but patience was a virtue he had mastered.

It happened a few minutes later.

Alexander rose, walking with a sure gait for one so young, to the decoratively piled rocks amid the flowers. His father had taught him that the dark, moist areas under the rocks were the best places to find wiggling worms and pill bugs. He placed his jar onto the ground, making sure it was upright and near at hand, added a handful of dirt and some leaves, only then kneeling to upend the rocks and begin his quest. Lizzy, after assuring his occupation, turned to the wheelbarrow encumbered with the potted plants gifted by Mr. Clark to be added to the Darcy House gardens. She set to her task, humming and blissfully unaware of the horror that was about to be unleashed.

Wickham checked the thick, woolen scarf that covered his nose, leather-gloved fingers pulling the fabric tighter. With a practiced tug he loosened the cork plugging the narrow neck of an amber bottle and saturated the folded cloth held in the palm of his hands, careful to avoid inhaling the fumes wafting. With eyes shifting between Lizzy and the boy, he crouched low and crept away from the wall. It was easy to remain in the shadows or hide behind the thick copse. The trick was to avoid stepping on dry leaves or twigs, and not to scrape against the brush.

He skulked warily, crossing the four feet to where Alexander huddled in rapt attention. He paused, gauging the scene and preparing. A quick glance assured that Lizzy was occupied on the other side of the roughly five foot grassy plot, her back to him as she dug holes. Alexander was close, his tiny face the mirror of Darcy's and filled with childish delight as he observed the pill bugs crawling over his small palm. He was ignorant to the lurking menace and therefore had no warning, or later memory, of the hand that suddenly emerged between a gap in the branches and clamped over his nose and mouth. A startled indrawn breath of the sickening sweet fluid and he was on his way to unconsciousness without uttering a sound.

Even Wickham, who had seen the effects of inhaled ether used by Lord Orman to dull his pain and induce oblivion, was stunned at how rapidly it worked on the toddler. In the midst of his planning he had wondered if the liberal amount needed to sedate a fully-grown woman may be too much for the tiny body of the boy, but he had no choice in the matter and could only hope the youngster did not succumb before Darcy could watch.

Wickham's lack of precise knowledge meant that when Alexander so quickly reacted to the drug, his abrupt slump took Wickham off guard. The hand that held the cloth to the boy's face slipped, and Alexander landed facedown onto the arranged stack of rocks. The stones slid, falling in a clattering shower that was not noisy, but enough to cause Lizzy to turn her head to investigate.

Despite his momentary surprise, Wickham responded instantly. He lurched forward, bounded through the thicket, and dashed across the lawn in seconds. Lizzy released a sharp cry that was cruelly cut off when Wickham crushed her head between the wet rag cupped in one hand that pressed harshly over her face, and the other hand that painfully twisted into the hair pinned into a lovely arrangement on the back of her head. He hauled her upward, relishing the pain he knew he was causing, until she was facing him.

Her eyes were wild with fright as she met Wickham's triumphant gaze. There was immediate recognition, but also, to his amazement, a blaze of indescribable fury. With a jolt of astonishment he realized that she was holding her breath! Additionally, although he had expected some feeble struggling, she nearly overwhelmed his considerable strength by her strenuous counter-assault. She violently wrenched her head to the left while lashing out with her limbs. Her legs, stout and supple from years of walking, pounded into his shins with well-aimed kicks. Her hands contorted into dangerous claws, gripping and slashing with frenetic attacks to his face and neck.

Several hopping steps were required to avoid tumbling over, but he managed to collect himself and widen the stance of his stiffened legs, planting his feet into the soft turf. In desperation he tightened his grip to her hair, waiting for the muffled squeal of pain that she refused to release, and pulled her into his chest for additional support.

"Breathe damn it!" He growled, the fingertips holding the cloth digging into the tender flesh of her cheeks.

But Lizzy did not breathe. Instead she fought, frantically. Her body writhed and strained, every muscle contorting and contracting with incredible power. She grabbed on to his wrists, twisting the leather covering his flesh abrasively. She fisted her hands, raining clouts over his shoulders and upper arms. Her feet, encased in sturdy half-boots, beat into his shins and feet. The maniacal struggle led to an odd sort of dance, Lizzy's zealous maneuvers forcing him to sway and bend in order to maintain control.

He arched his head backward, both to avoid inhaling the ether or presenting an easy target for her fingernails, and held her in a crushing embrace. He knew she would have to breathe eventually, so he ignored the bruising blows peppering his legs and upper torso.

It seemed to last forever, although in truth less than two minutes passed before the need for air overwhelmed her. He felt her inspiration, marveling anew that even in her panic it was shallow. It was followed by fresh thrashing, but he sensed her weakening as another wheezing breath was taken and her flails lessened. He kept the pressure steady as her muscles began to relax.

Nonetheless, he was again taken by surprise at her resilience when she acted in a final, ferocious protest. She released an animal scream into the wad of sweet vitriol soaked cloth, raked the fingers of her right hand deeply across his left cheek while pulling the protective scarf away from his nose, and aggressively pushed with her legs and shoved her lower body into his. The combination again disrupted his balance, only this time he was unable to correct his equilibrium, and they toppled onto the spongy clover.

His clasp was lost, the ether-doused cloth falling forgotten to the ground, and Lizzy rolled away from his side. Wickham had enough presence of mind in his blinding rage and pain to follow after her, prepared to reestablish his domination. He sprawled bodily onto her, straddling her legs and pressing them together with his knees while his hands reached to encircle her slender throat. But it was not necessary. Her last outburst and gasping shriek had overwhelmed her, the drug finally penetrating to subdue her brain.

The only sound was his harsh respirations. He was so angry that his vision was hazy and mind clouded. It did not occur to him to consider that their struggle may have drawn attention, nor was he coherently able to halt his rage.

He lashed out, delivering a stunning slap to her slack face. "Witch!" he bellowed, following with another blow to the opposite cheek and additional foul expletives. He sat back on his heels, breathing raggedly, and then heaved to his feet. Sanity and calm were slow to be restored, but he had not planned this revenge only to allow one unsuspecting difficulty to ruin all.

His fingertips wiped the oozing blood away from the four stinging wounds rived into his left cheek. "You will pay for this, Elizabeth Darcy. Now it is not just about Darcy. Another score *will* be settled this day."

❦

"Point to Colonel Fitzwilliam."

The declaration rang out, but Richard did not experience the elation he normally felt when scoring one on his cousin. He frowned behind his protective mask, raising his left hand to signal a suspension. Pulling the mask away from his sweating brow, he approached his opponent.

Darcy removed his own mask and raised his arms in question, sword firmly gripped and by all outward appearances ready to continue the match. He was not breathing heavily and only a light sheen moistened his forehead, but that was all the more reason Richard knew something was not quite right.

"Do you want to tell me why I am beating you so easily?" Richard inquired, his voice low and a faint smile lighting his face. Still, he peered into Darcy's eyes with clear concern. "You are hardly trying, and have been distracted all afternoon. Are you yet disturbed over the information I gave you this morning? I did not plan to win on default." His tease was met with a blank stare.

"Put your mask back on, Colonel. The match is far from over." Darcy clapped the hood in place, gesturing with his sword arm, and resumed a precision fencer's stance.

The battle recommenced and although Colonel Fitzwilliam did ultimately defeat the younger man, it was not the resounding victory he suspected based on how it began.

Darcy managed to rally his focus and skill, but remained preoccupied and was not in top form. He could not bury his vacillating emotions over what had transpired with Lizzy that morning and all afternoon the iciness of fear raced uncontrollably through his veins. The four months since he and Lizzy rekindled their relationship and her mysterious illness faded was too short a time to expunge the trauma from his memory. The terror of revisiting such a place of agony was as real as if it had happened yesterday.

He hated that their interview was so abruptly cut short. He had not been able to articulate his feelings and to discuss with her as they always did until understanding was reached. The idea that she may be confused as to his concerns, reaching the conclusion that he wanted no further children, or fearing his displeasure regarding another baby, greatly weighed on his mind.

Indeed, he had not anticipated her conceiving so rapidly, so part of his shock was due to that. He was not an imbecile and knew precisely the mechanics of where babies came from. However, probably due to the fact that it had been well over a year between Alexander's birth and Michael's creation, he had somehow not given the possibility any thought.

Nevertheless, it was the worry over his wife's health that overwhelmed him and sent shivers of foreboding through his body. It had taken her so long to regain her physical stamina. Weeks after her mental and emotional status returned to normalcy—his uncle's stated diagnosis that it was primarily the breach with her husband that prohibited her spiritual recovery proving true—she had remained tired, weak, and delicate. For only the past month or so had her constitution and physique rejuvenated to her prior vigor and lushness. In fact, Darcy recognized with daily surging happiness, she was robust beyond what she had previously been. Thus, the hint of anything disrupting her hard-fought wholeness and vitality was enough to numb his bones.

Yet, oddly, amid the rivers of cold he began to detect a warm center of happiness. It began deep in his belly, almost touchable, and gradually spread to dispel some of the frostiness. It was bizarre and unexpected, but his mind was continually invaded with the image of a tiny face. A feminine, delicate, and beautiful face.

Numerous times he shook his head, forcing the vision to evaporate, but it kept returning.

Unlike his wife, Darcy had experienced no prescient dreams or inclinations with either pregnancy. Lizzy had known, each time, that the baby she carried was male. With Michael it was merely a "feeling," partially based, she admitted, on the fact that her body carried the infant precisely the same as Alexander. She did not have a crystalline dream as with her first pregnancy, but there was no doubt in her mind that she would be presenting her husband with his second son.

He did not believe the image that plagued his mind today was a premonition, but rather a divine message. As the afternoon progressed, he renounced the worst of his anxiety and cautiously allowed the possibility of further happiness to creep in. It was difficult to focus on business or manly pursuits while sensing a strange need to rush back to Darcy House and make amends with his wife now, not later.

He shook his head to dispel the disquiet and dipped the damp cloth into the cool water filling the porcelain bowl. He wrung the excess away, wiping over his neck, shoulders, back, and underarms. He did not have time to return to Darcy House for a complete wash prior to his appointment at White's, but like most gentlemen who frequented Angelo's Fencing Academy, he toted a clean shirt and cravat, as well as a bottle of his preferred cologne, to freshen up after a vigorous workout.

He splashed a palm-full of the musky concoction that Samuel provided onto his chest, forcing his thoughts away from holding Elizabeth in his arms while assuring her of his love and supreme joy in accepting the God-given gift of as many children as He chose to entrust to them. His concentration turned to the upcoming session with his business partners, rigid intellectual calculations snapping firmly into place, and he began pulling the crisply ironed linen shirt over his shoulders when the door burst open.

"Darcy," Richard flatly pronounced. "You are needed at Darcy House immediately!"

It was a nightmare. It had to be. There was no other explanation. It even felt like a nightmare with the racing heartbeat and fogged mind sensations typical of a horrific dream. Only usually she was able to wake herself when the terror grew too extreme. Upon waking, the negative effects would stop with the comforting familiarity of her bed restoring her wits. And then the dream itself would fade, the images once so disturbing quickly losing clarity.

This nightmare was not following that pattern.

Georgiana exited the nursery, the heaviness of her heart weighting her body down as surely as an oxen's yoke, and her vision dimming to the point where she was forced to lean against the wall and grasp onto a narrow table or fall to the floor.

She inhaled deeply, willing the tears away. After all, it had to be a nightmare, an especially vivid one but a nightmare nevertheless. It could not be real and any second now she would wake and the scenes would shatter into dust.

She pressed her fingertips against her burning eyes, realizing with increased dismay that closing her eyes only brought the dream into greater focus…

At slightly before three-thirty the doorbell had rung unexpectedly, Georgiana's heart lurching with the thought that it might be Sebastian as she jumped up from the pianoforte and dashed into the foyer. Her disappointment at discovering Lady Simone being greeted by Mr. Travers rather than Mr. Butler was smothered, and she embraced her cousin with true delight.

"Forgive me for disturbing your quiet afternoon, Georgiana dear, but I wanted to bring these books to Elizabeth before I forgot. Also, my painting of the stone pines in the Villa Doria Pamphili that she loved has been framed and I wished to give it to her right away."

"Never apologize, Simone. You are always welcome and Lizzy will be thrilled. She has an abiding love for wooded places, we have discovered. Come, she and Alexander are in the garden up to their ankles in dirt I imagine. I am sure they would both benefit from some cooled juice, if you could provide some, Mr. Travers?"

He bowed, heading toward the kitchen while Simone and Georgiana walked across the tiled entryway to the wide glass-paned doors that opened onto the garden courtyard. It was strange how, in retrospect, traversing the airy hall seemed a walk of doom lasting an eternity. Yet she and Simone barely noticed their steps as they chatted and laughed all the way to the far corner where Lizzy and Alexander were supposed to be planting sunflowers. And then the painfully long seconds as they puzzled over a scene that made no sense.

Gardening tools and unplanted seedlings sat unattended but undisturbed, the dirt holes and misplaced rocks a normal expectation when gardening. It was the utter silence that struck them first. Then the absence of the two who should have been digging and who did not appear, no matter how often they both scanned the bush encircled glade expecting them to jump out and yell, "Surprise!" Still, they would likely have assumed that Lizzy and Alexander were in the house if not for the random clumps of grass gouged from the ground, the crumpled cloth discarded beside a human-shaped depression, the gray rabbit lying in a heap next to the cloth, and the folded parchment nearby.

Georgiana shivered and opened her eyes. The hallway was empty and silent. Michael was finally asleep, rocked in his aunt's arms after the efforts of Mrs. Hanford to placate him with warm porridge and cow's milk proved successful. The infant's vocalized unhappiness at not having his mother's breast and gentle touch was an emotion they empathized with, but neither spoke openly about the calamity that had befallen Darcy House. Miss Lisa had stood by the dresser silently crying as she folded and refolded a pile of Alexander's freshly washed clothes.

Pushing herself away from the wall, Georgiana shuffled down the corridor wishing she could give in to her grief as Miss Lisa did. But then one should not cry over a nightmare, should they?

The period following the shocking garden revelation was identical to a dream. Someone screamed and Georgiana was still unsure whether it was she or Simone. She remembers bending to touch the poor rabbit, the warm fur and flutter of a heartbeat bizarrely relieving as if his life assured the survival of Lizzy and Alexander, wherever they were. Then there were shouts, running feet, and a blurred onset of commands and activity.

Simone scribbled a note, sending a groomsman to Angelo's where she knew her husband and Darcy were. Another message was dispatched to the hospital for Dr. Darcy. Mr. Travers took charge, although there was nothing to do but wait.

Georgiana clutched on to the note, afraid to read it after the look on the butler's face when he had, delivering it into her brother's hands when he stormed in less than twenty minutes later. She had no time to marvel at how quickly he and Richard managed to travel from Angelo's Academy in Soho to Grosvenor Square, her hand's shaking and heart breaking as he silently read. Then she shrank away from the fury suffusing his face as he turned to Richard, who was reading the letter over his shoulder.

"Wickham has taken my wife and son."

"Wickham?" Georgiana blurted, beyond stunned.

But Darcy ignored her, his eyes locked with Richard's. "It is not his handwriting," Richard began, holding his palm up to stay the scathing retort Darcy was about to deliver, "but I would agree it the logical conclusion. With no reason to deduce otherwise, we have the upper hand, as we know where to find him."

"We waited too long," Darcy interrupted, his voice shaking with rage and fear. "We should have… I should have…"

"It does not matter," Richard snapped, his voice commanding and in control. "All that matters is getting them back. Wait here and…"

"I am not waiting for a second!" Darcy yelled, the words echoing from wall to ceiling. "They have my wife and son!"

Simone and Georgiana flinched, instinctively stepping back a pace and reaching for the other's hand. But Colonel Fitzwilliam stood fast, his face grim but unperturbed.

"We need assistance, Cousin. There is no way to know what we are walking into. The best chance of success is with numbers. We need men who know how to handle weapons and are combat trained."

Darcy did not reply, instead pivoting abruptly and moving toward his study. Richard sighed, turning toward Simone. "Did anyone think to send for Dr. Darcy? Well done," he said when Simone nodded, his lips lifting in a minuscule smile that did not touch his eyes. "Darcy will require physical restraining, I fear." And after a quick squeeze to his wife's upper arm and the same semi-smile directed to Georgiana, he followed Darcy, mumbling, "Bloody idiot is probably loading his pistols."

What transpired in the study between Darcy and Richard was never revealed to the females, but within five minutes Richard exited. He briefly conferred with his wife, kissing her brusquely before leaving the house.

Through it all Georgiana stood glued to the same spot, her mind unable to veer from Darcy's firm proclamation of Wickham being the abductor. *It was impossible, all of it was impossible*, her mind screamed. Lizzy and Alexander spirited away by an unknown assailant to God knew where with unfathomable tortures being inflicted upon them was horrid enough to contemplate, not that she was allowing herself to contemplate it, but to think that Wickham…

Georgiana shuddered, her heart pounding to the point that she heard the blood rushing past her eardrums and felt the beats under the palms pressed against her breast. Wickham. The man she nearly eloped with so long ago. The man she knew to be unscrupulous and plagued by envy for her brother, but had never considered truly evil. Yet this act crossed into a place beyond evil into…

She shivered and gasped, and felt the room swimming before her glazed eyes.

"Georgiana, dearest. Come, let us sit down while the men deal with the situation." Simone's tender voice pierced through the haze, her hands warm and stabilizing where they grasped Georgiana's elbows. "Mrs. Smyth," she called to the lurking housekeeper, her eyes engaging Georgiana's steadily, "we require tea, very hot and very strong, as quickly as possible."

"Wickham," Georgiana squeaked. "How?"

"Let us sit before you fall down and I will tell you what I know of the situation."

A bitterly strong cup of scorching tea later, Georgiana persisted in believing it had to be a nightmare. But she was calmer and somewhat informed based on what Richard had told his wife of the matter since suspicions were raised in Hertfordshire.

"I cannot believe that Mr. Wickham could do this." Georgiana paused, not certain how much Lady Simone knew of her entanglements with Wickham and not prepared to delve into that portion of her past, especially not now. "That explains William's extra caution this past week, not that it has apparently been effective."

"Do not be harsh on your brother. I am sure he is berating himself enough as it is. I wish he were not alone…"

Noises from the hall caused them to glance toward the door, the stomp of feet and hasty greetings of Mr. Travers followed by the appearance of

Dr. Darcy, tall and serious faced with his dark, stained hospital coat covering the flowing suit of blue worn underneath.

"Ladies, can someone enlighten me as to what the bloody hell is going on?"

"I declare, Dr. Darcy, you must have flown from Whitechapel to arrive so speedily!"

"A fast horse can do wonders, my lady. Anyone I bowled over was instructed to convey my apologies to my associates and place the bill onto my account. Your note was understandably vague. Do we know what has happened? Does William know what has happened?"

"He is in his study awaiting the return of my husband with reinforcements. I am sure he needs you."

George nodded, robes swirling as his wide stride carried him out the door, narrowly missing Mrs. Smyth, who flinched away from his body and the disgusting diseases she was sure he carried upon his person. He did not notice, intent only upon talking to his nephew, and seconds later was in the study where he would remain for a long while.

Mrs. Smyth, once recovered from the trauma of almost touching the doctor's garments, delivered the message from Mrs. Hanford that Michael was awake and needing his mother.

Georgiana responded to the summons, as much to assist as to turn her mind away from the horrors that only grew worse. She informed the stricken nannies of Lizzy's absence as succinctly as possible, her emotions buried while attending to her nephew. Assisting Mrs. Hanford with the chore of inducing a thoroughly angry baby to ingest warmed, sweetened cow's milk and wheat porridge, and then rocking him to sleep while singing favorite lullabies had been an oddly comforting procedure that wrested her thoughts away from the drama beyond the nursery walls. At least to a degree as she was torn between envying Miss Lisa's tears and shamefully wanting to throttle her!

Now she stood at the end of the hallway desperately searching for the strength to continue walking. She flipped open the dainty pocket watch fastened at her waist, shocked to note the time now a quarter to five. Barely an hour and a half since she blithely walked into the garden with Simone. Her thoughts were so scattered and clouded that the passage of time had no meaning. It could have been fifteen minutes ago or half a day and she would feel as shocked and numb.

Mrs. Smyth passed with a tray of coffee and pastries, heading toward

Darcy's study, drawing Georgiana into the present. "Mrs. Smyth. Would you please tell Mr. Darcy that Master Michael is fed and asleep? I am sure it will offer some comfort."

The housekeeper nodded. "As you wish, Miss Darcy."

Georgiana watched her walk away, momentarily distracted by the woman's pained expression and clipped intonation. *She is definitely an odd woman,* Georgiana thought, *but I would not have considered her caring for Lizzy enough to be so distressed.* She shrugged, squaring her shoulders and entering the parlor.

"Needlepoint?" she exclaimed, so surprised that she released a humorless laugh. "You can focus on needlepoint?"

Simone did not glance up from her hoop. "I learned years ago that painful vigils passed quicker if my hands were occupied with something other than wringing my skirts. Precise stitchery requires concentration and calculation, thus keeping my thoughts away from dwelling upon the trouble of the moment and spinning wild with speculation. This is a new situation for me, to be sure, but I am well acquainted with periods of strain and waiting."

"Yes, of course you are. Forgive me."

"Nothing to forgive. But do not be deceived, my dear. I am frantic on the inside, doubly so as many people I love are in jeopardy and not just my son." The needle flashed, each stitch perfectly sewn. "Of course I now have trunks filled with completed samplers, garments, pillows, and so on. Quite beneficial for Christmas and birthdays."

She smiled at Georgiana, who again laughed, albeit briefly. "Richard has not returned?"

"No. I am sure he is acting as expeditiously as possible, but amassing an armed forced must take some time. I am fairly confident that whoever he enlists will be highly competent for the task."

"Armed forces. Loaded pistols." Georgiana sank heavily onto a chair across from Simone. "Lizzy and Alexander kidnapped from my house. While I was here just yards away! While servants moved about and…" She drew in a deep breath, clenching her fists to control the shaking. "Please tell me this is a nightmare from which I shall awake momentarily?"

"I wish I could, Georgiana, I truly do."

"Should we watch for them?" She glanced to the wide windows overlooking the Square, restless anxiety wrecking havoc on her attempts to calm. "Perhaps time will be saved if I alert William as soon as they enter the Square."

"They will come in through the mews," Simone answered with a shake of her head, continuing at the questioning expression on Georgiana's face, "Richard will be considerate of discretion. Best not to cause a scene. I am sure the neighbors are already spinning conjectures over what brought Mr. Darcy and Colonel Fitzwilliam galloping crazily into the Square."

"Oh! I did not think of gossiping neighbors! This is horrible enough without wild tales spreading through Town!"

"Breathe, my dear, before you faint."

"I cannot bear it, Simone. Please, tell me how you have learned to remain tranquil in crisis situations. How do you maintain your sanity and stay strong and act bravely? And do not say needlepoint!"

Simone shrugged, the needle continuing to steadily pierce the stretched linen in even strokes. "Tranquility and strength are illusions. And bravery in my case is more bravado. Trust me, crying and raging occurs. Frequently. All I have learned to do is choose the time for my emotional collapse when I am alone and not inconveniencing anyone. Well, generally so, I should say. I did try to kill my own father when my feigned acceptance and patience failed me."

She spoke in a lighthearted tone, almost as if jesting, but Georgiana knew the pain buried underneath her carefree words. Suddenly, Lady Simone dropped the hoop into her lap, reached across the narrow space, and clasped Georgiana's hand. "There is no shame in crying. You do not need to be brave or strong if tears are necessary. Releasing the emotion usually aids the rebuilding of one's fortitude and restores clarity."

Georgiana shook her head, opening her mouth to assert her intention to remain brave for her family when the door chime rang, jolting through the depressive pall heavy in the air as if a clanging cymbal. Nerves strung tighter than a coil, Georgiana jumped up, taking an involuntary step toward the doorway.

"Fret not. Mr. Travers will handle whoever it is."

Georgiana nodded but moved closer to the foyer to overhear. Mr. Travers's polite greeting transmitted across the expanse, but the response from behind the stout door was muted. Yet something in the hushed, mumbled tenor piqued her curiosity.

She opened the door further, peeking curiously through as a hand appeared with a folded envelope extended to the butler. "I shall see that Miss Darcy receives this as soon as she returns, sir."

The hand disappeared, the butler beginning to close the door, when the response reached her ears. "I would appreciate that, thank you."

Instant recognition swept through her body, the musical timbre of the male voice causing her heart to lurch with joy while also pulverizing the tenuous tethers holding her emotions in check. Her legs carried her across the tiled floor before she found her voice, then shouted, "Sebastian!" startling Mr. Travers into dropping the note.

Mr. Butler was equally startled, but responded with a broad grin of happiness which lasted about two seconds before the impact of his beloved's body knocked the air out of his lungs and nearly sent him sprawling onto the outside step. Thankfully, Mr. Travers grabbed one arm, the other instinctively clutching the wooden threshold for stability so he did not tumble with the clinging, sobbing Georgiana onto the stones, but his emotions at such a bizarre greeting were chaotic to say the least!

Years of experience paid off as the butler rallied rapidly, hauling on Mr. Butler's arm to bring him into the foyer and slamming the door shut. Then he retrieved the fallen note and walked away as if Miss Darcy weeping in a strange man's arms was a daily occurrence.

Although not adverse to having Georgiana locked within his embrace and not impervious to the fragrance of her hair and warm curves pressed against his chest, Sebastian was utterly flummoxed, his confusion not aided by Georgiana, whose words were indecipherable amid the crying. He held her tight, comforted slightly upon noting Lady Simone standing in the parlor doorway. But her expression was grave, sending additional alarms through his mind, and then the appearance of an armed Colonel Fitzwilliam from the dimly lit back hallway sealed the awareness that something was seriously wrong.

"Ah, perfect timing, Mr. Butler," Richard said, not a trace of humor or warmth on his face. "The ladies will need your added support. However, I would suggest that all of you retire to the parlor and shut the door as I do not think it wise for Mr. Darcy to see his sister in your arms right now, all considered."

And then he pivoted, sheathed sword knocking against a holstered pistol, walking purposefully down the left hallway.

CHAPTER EIGHTEEN

The Night of Reckoning

I have your wife and son. No harm shall befall them if you heed my demands, quietly and alone. 70,000 pounds will pay for their safe release. Make arrangements immediately. You will be contacted for further instruc- tions. Any hesitation or deviation from my dictates and they will die.

DARCY READ THE WORDS for the hundredth time. He had no need to read them, as they were indelibly etched into his brain and would likely never be forgotten. No salutation. No signature. The handwriting was not Wickham's, of that Darcy was certain, so he assumed it was Orman's penmanship. Of course, there was no way to know for sure, but he had little doubt.

He sighed, closing his eyes and dropping the clutched note to his side. The wait was killing him. It had only been an hour since the messenger had arrived at Angelo's and they had torn through the crowded streets of London to reach Darcy House. An hour that was an eternity.

At least he was calmer now, Richard succeeding in penetrating his irrational raving before departing to collect the necessary manpower required to deal with the situation. Of course it had required taking him bodily and slamming Darcy into the library wall to accomplish the feat, utilizing a strength that amazed his younger cousin who was physically larger. Richard had revealed a side to his character that Darcy was not familiar with: the commanding colonel who knew how to quell an entire company of men with a single look or growled demand. It was painful, and a bit humiliating, but the action had done the trick. Darcy's emotions were no less tumultuous, but at least he had them well buried and under a semblance of control. The arrival of his uncle was beneficial, the older man so accustomed to trauma that he was a stabilizing force.

Darcy glanced to the wadded fabric lying on the table by the window. George, who paced several feet away, had instantly recognized the odor emanating from the moist cloth as oil of sweet vitriol, or ether. The brief exposition that the doctor provided of the chemical compound had only added to Darcy's distress over his wife and son.

The questions of how this violation could have happened within the confines of his home were too numerous to deal with at the present time. His unquenchable fury over what he saw as a failure on the part of his staff was so monumental that he simply could not allow himself to dwell on it. Richard was correct. He needed to remain levelheaded and composed for the sake of Elizabeth and Alexander.

But it was horribly difficult. The chaotic clash of indescribable terror and unprecedented wrath warred within his body and mind unrelentingly. It was only by the grace and strength of God that he did not collapse. Or begin breaking things.

Although they had no conclusive, legal proof, everything pointed to Wickham and Orman being behind the kidnapping of his family. They planned to proceed as if this were the case, but on the slim chance that it was all a horrific coincidence and some other criminal was the abductor, he had written to Mr. Daniels for the funds to be delivered as soon as was possible. Darcy could care less about the money, and would pay far more to ensure the safe return of his wife and son. Nevertheless, he abhorred the idea of anyone escaping justice, especially if the lawbreaker was Wickham or Orman. But of greater importance was finding his family before they were harmed any further.

A soft knock at the door caused both men to jerk and whip about. "Enter!" Darcy barked, involuntarily taking a step toward the door.

It was Mrs. Smyth carrying a tray of hot coffee and pastries. Her face was pinched and gray, haughty eyes shadowed with deep emotion, but Darcy wasted no time wondering at her odd expression. She curtseyed and kept her gaze downcast as she cautiously approached the desk and sat the tray down. Under different circumstances Darcy may have felt shamed at having inspired such trepidation in his staff, but not today.

"Very good," George said, stepping up and pouring two cups of coffee while biting into a scone.

"How can you eat?"

"I can always eat, you should know that by now. It settles my nerves. I would encourage you to eat, but figure I will be ignored. I am going to insist you drink some strong coffee with several spoons of sugar, as you will need both. Doctor's orders."

"Forgive me, sir," Mrs. Smyth hesitantly interrupted, flinching when the stormy cast to her master's face turned her direction. She diverted her eyes, not wanting him to note the anger she felt over this violation to the house, it just one more proof, in her mind, at the downfall and imminent disgrace since marriage to *that woman*. "Miss Darcy wished for me to inform you that Master Michael is now asleep. He finally ate from the milk feeder offered, as well as some of the barley porridge Cook prepared, and Miss Darcy was then able to rock him to sleep. She thought this news would ease your mind."

Darcy nodded. "Thank you, Mrs. Smyth. Indeed that is excellent news. Please thank Mrs. Hanford for me. Assure her that her expertise and devotion are greatly comforting at this time."

He turned away, preparing to resume his blank contemplation of the flowering lilacs outside the study window, when a startled gasp from Mrs. Smyth caught his attention. He swung about just as the housekeeper lifted the miniature from the packing box sitting on the edge of his desk. She noted his movement, instantly attempting to drop the portrait into the box, but his rapid lunge prevented her concealing.

He latched onto her wrist, eyes engaging hers. "You recognize this man." It was not a question, her face clearly stating the answer.

"I..." She licked her suddenly parched lips, the seething anger in his glacial voice terrifying her and rendering her speechless.

"Answer me," Darcy whispered, a note of ruthless command ringing through the regulation.

"He... is a friend."

"George Wickham is your friend?"

"No," she stammered in confusion. "That is... I do not know... This is Geoffrey Wiseman."

Darcy did not respond. His gaze pierced through Mrs. Smyth, her body shuddering from what felt like visible beams of fire searing into her eyes. The grip on her wrist was painful, but the expression on his face was far more terrifying. He took a step closer, Mrs. Smyth withdrawing a pace reflexively.

"Geoffrey Wiseman, you say? And you know him? And have allowed this stranger into my house?"

"Fitzwilliam," George spoke softly, but Darcy curtly gestured for silence and never removed his savage gaze from her face.

"Sir, please."

"How long? How far has this man penetrated these walls? What have you allowed him to do?" She shook her head, visibly undone by the black, thunderous cast to her master's normally kind face. "Answer me!"

His shout reverberated around the room, Mrs. Smyth gasping in fright. She felt near to swooning by the assault of emotions and thoughts roiling within. *What was Mr. Darcy doing with a painting of her Geoffrey?* A surge of doubt stabbed her heart. The numerous questions she had sensed over the past months, questions that she submerged due to her entanglement with her lover, slammed into her forehead until the pain darkened her vision and stuttered her speech.

"I trusted him. I… loved him. He…"

"Was he your lover? In *my* house?"

"Yes! Oh, please, sir… I am so sorry… I…"

"Do you have any idea what you have done?"

Mrs. Smyth released a whimper, truly petrified. She remained puzzled over the identity of her lover and the man in the miniature portrait, but it was also abundantly obvious that Mr. Darcy was connecting the two and intimating he was the culprit in the Darcys' abduction. And worse yet, she was beginning to wonder the same. It was also obvious that Mr. Darcy was murderous in his rage, and she honestly feared for her life.

"Fitzwilliam," George stated in a firmer voice, his hand gently touching Darcy's rigid forearm. "Think. We now have the proof we needed. Calm yourself, and remember Elizabeth and Alexander. We can deal with Mrs. Smyth at a later date." He tugged on each finger gripping the housekeeper's wrist, prying his nephew loose.

It was a tense moment to be sure. Darcy yearned for a physical outlet for his considerable stress and Mrs. Smyth seemed like the perfect recipient.

How it may have ended will never be known as just then Richard rushed through the door.

"Forgive me for taking so long! I have ten men..." He stopped, his eyes taking in the scene and turning a questioning look to George, as Darcy refused to relinquish his focus from the shaking, weeping Mrs. Smyth.

"It appears," George offered, "that Mrs. Smyth has been befriended by George Wickham, alias Geoffrey Wiseman. He has been in the house, according to Mrs. Smyth. Recently?" She feebly nodded at the doctor's inquiry. "Indeed," he said, removing the last of Darcy's white-knuckled fingers from her wrist, the housekeeper collapsing onto the sofa.

"Excellent!" Richard boomed with a satisfied nod. "This is the information we needed. The connection to Orman. Surely Elizabeth and Alexander are in Surrey. We must make haste."

Darcy inhaled, gathering the frayed edges of his emotions and reining them in. He nodded, stepping away from the cowering woman. "Uncle, I expect you to take care of this." He waved a hand in Mrs. Smyth's direction, a steely-eyed George inclining his head in agreement.

"Trust me. You listen to Colonel Fitzwilliam, do you hear me, Son? He knows what to do."

Darcy glanced to Richard's grim, commanding face. "Very well. You are in charge, Colonel. I will obey your orders. But once my wife and son are safe, do not think about constraining me."

Richard grinned evilly. "At that point, Cousin, I will be assisting you."

⚘

Lizzy's memory of the hours and days following her abduction would remain hazy for the whole of her life. There would be some impressions so vivid, yet obviously so fantastical, that she knew they were generated by the drug. And then there were other momentous events described to her later that seemed unfathomable for her to be unaware of when she was front and center to the action. Even years later, when she allowed herself to muse on the experience, she would not be able to say for certain what was real or what was of her drug-induced imagination.

Her first memory, after Wickham overwhelmed her in the garden, was of a dimly lit staircase, seen upside down and moving. Her body felt weightless and disconnected from her eyes as if floating. She noted the individual tattered threads on the carpet runner covering the steps, but could not differentiate between one hand and the other. Both were dangling before her eyes, tied together with a knotted cord wrapped around her wrists, but they looked like a flesh-colored lump with no definition. She knew this was odd, that she should be alarmed or at least curious, but she was apathetic. She closed her eyes and returned to sleep.

Much later—*or was it only minutes?* she did not know or care—she heard voices. She tried to open her eyes but couldn't. No matter. She just listened to the voices. They were pleasant. Hollow, almost echoing, with drawn-out syllables. The words were mixed up, no order or sense. She found it humorous and wanted to laugh. Maybe she did laugh, but she never remembered for sure. She drifted off again with the funny voices soothing her.

Again, she was lifted. Her hands hurt, but she could not move them. She heard a name being called close to her ear, yet from miles away. *Elizabeth.* She was fairly sure that was her name but was uncertain. She opened her eyes to a face near her own. It was a cat! A cat with horrible breath and a massive scar cutting through the fur on its left cheek. How strange. The cat was talking to her. Hissing, really. *Silly cat, attempting to speak.* She smiled and began to giggle. The cat meowed and growled. A cat growling? How strange and amusing. She continued to giggle until sleep and dreams of talking cats consumed her.

On it went. Bizarre delusions melded with reality an uncountable number of times. Finally she woke to a clearer observance. Her vision was fuzzy and there was a loud ringing in her ears, but she felt the cushions of the sofa she was lying on. Her head was resting on a soft, threadbare pillow. Her hands were still tied, as were her feet, she sluggishly recognized. They were tight and in an awkward position that was uncomfortable but not painful. Her face was sore and both of her cheeks tingled. In fact, she gradually became aware of dozens of gnawing aches and sharp pangs all over her body. Her breasts burned with the need to feed her baby, and the thought, as nebulous as it was, caused milk to leak and wetly soak into the bodice of her dirt-stained gown.

Abruptly she remembered the garden and Wickham, and the panic rose to form a cold knot deep in her abdomen. But surprisingly, she was not as distressed as one would expect. A cold, detached voice within told her this was the drug's effects acting upon her mind, and she found this interesting, but could not decide if her lassitude was beneficial under the circumstances or a detriment.

She scanned the room, clouded eyes adjusting to the half-light. It was evening, dusk settling in the world without. Several lamps were lit and there was a glow emitting from somewhere behind her head that was probably from a fireplace. The chamber, clearly a parlor, was rustic with furniture of hewn wood and beamed ceilings of knotty oak. It was a large room, well-appointed and fine, but layers of dust and scattered cobwebs were observable even to her limited vision. She saw two windows from where she slumped on the sofa, both covered with thick drapes that allowed minimal light to escape or enter.

"She is awake."

It was George Wickham. She recognized the voice though it was slowed and monotone. He materialized in front of her, kneeling and obscuring her limited range with his smirking face. She blinked several times, but the filmy glaze did not disappear.

"Mrs. Darcy. How delighted I am to see you. Did you sleep well?"

"Alexander?" Her voice, even to her own ears, was grating. The effort to say that one word burned a pathway through her vocal cords and she winced in pain.

"He is nearby, asleep and well. He will stay that way, as long as you cooperate."

"Cooperate?" she murmured roughly between giggles. "I do believe you have me at a disadvantage, Mr. Wickham. I cannot see how I have much choice."

She was laughing uncontrollably, the ache in her throat increasing, but she could not stop. *Does he not see how utterly ridiculous this is? Does he not see the true danger?*

Wickham frowned, his face turning red. But this just made Lizzy laugh harder.

"Oh, Mr. Wickham! I would not worry about me. It is my husband who will be killing you."

The laughter was by then in gales, and the pain to her throat severe. A voice shouted from the background to shut her up, but it was not necessary for anyone to take action as the edges of blackness crept over her eyes. A dark tunnel that grew narrower and narrower until there was no light at all and she remembered no more for a time.

Minutes, hours, days?

Lizzy had no sense of time when she next rallied. Nor did she care. The only concern—in fact what brought her out of her drugged, unconscious state— was the violent pain and upheaval from her stomach. Her previous bouts with nausea and vomiting, even when pregnant, were minor annoyances compared to this affliction. She heaved until her midsection ached, long after the contents were evacuated. Her throat was on fire, but that was paltry compared to the hurt she felt in every muscle and the ague that enveloped her. She had absolutely no control over her body; the chills and shuddering ruled.

A man swore, and Lizzy felt the end of the sofa she was laying on give as he jumped up. It was Wickham, her clearing mind noting that he must have been sitting with her legs on his lap. The image was greatly disturbing, but fresh waves of tremors took over her thoughts. Breathing became increasingly difficult and painful, so she assigned all concentration to the mere act of inhaling and exhaling. However, she did hear another man laughing.

"Fortunate that I insisted on the tub sitting there, eh, Wickham?" Orman laughed, the sight of Elizabeth Darcy suffering highly amusing, as was the disgust on Wickham's face as he looked at the mess. "How badly do you want her now? Hmmm? Ready to take her this instant?"

Wickham ignored the gibe, crossing instead to a door located on the far wall. "You there!" he bellowed. "Leave the boy and come clean this mess. He will not be going anywhere."

The girl who entered at Wickham's bidding was dressed in a ragged gown, her emaciated frame unable to keep the neckline from gaping and showing her bony chest. She cowered, dropping an ungainly curtsey in Orman's direction before setting to the task Wickham ordered.

He stood away, covering his nose with a scented handkerchief until the job was done. "How is the boy?"

"Asleep, milord. Woke and got sick once. Fell ta sleep agin."

"You keep him breathing, understand girl?" Orman growled from his chair near the fireplace. "Thanks to *his* incapability in handling an infant, the whelp in there has been dosed with enough sweet vitriol for a grown man."

"You did not have a miniature ruffian pounding your shoulders and stomach, all while screaming directly into your ears. The monster actually bit me on the neck! It was nearly my life, as the imp thrashed so as I almost fell down the stairs, breaking both our necks. Be thankful I had the ether at hand. Should have known Darcy's progeny would be the devil's spawn."

Orman grunted. "Be that as it may, you are lucky you did not kill him. Keep him tied down and gagged, girl. I do not want the brat waking up and screaming for his mother. But keep him breathing or it will be your hide, understand?"

She performed her clumsy bob again, departing into the room where a trussed and muzzled Alexander lay on a narrow bed. Wickham closed the door firmly on the sight, turning to see Orman staring at him with derision.

"Do not make me retch," the Marquis said scornfully. "Does seeing the brat in such a state injure your tender heart?"

"Hardly. I am more concerned over him dying too soon, that is all."

Orman cackled. "He will recover enough to be conscious and crying out to his papa when we slit his throat. Ah, the look on Darcy's face while he watches his precious son and wife die! The joy, Wickham, the incredible joy!"

"Well," Wickham interrupted what he knew could easily bloom into a full-fledged manic tirade, "I shall allow you that task. I will take care of Mrs. Darcy in the way that best satisfies me. We shall both have our revenge before he dies."

"You are a fool," Lizzy rasped through clattering teeth, "if you truly believe you will get away with any of this. Fitzwilliam will not fall for your pathetic ruse or be taken so easily. He is stronger than you, Wickham, and always has been. This you know and you are afraid."

Wickham smiled confidently, only a glimmer of nervousness showing in the depths of his eyes. "How touching," he drawled. "The faith you have. All the more reason why taking you while your hero watches powerless to intervene will be so extremely pleasurable, for me anyway." He leered, one hand rubbing vulgarly over his crotch while lecherously scanning over her body.

He sat again onto the sofa, pulling Lizzy's lower legs and feet onto his lap and commencing a lazy caress over her bare shins.

Lizzy jerked her legs from his offensive touch, kicked powerfully with every ounce of her strength into his jaw, and watched his head snap backward as blood spurt from between split lips in a gushing stream along with teeth.

At least that was what she imagined doing. That was what her mind desired to happen. But her muscles and nerves betrayed her, refusing to obey the brain's command. Instead she cringed and quailed, her stomach threatening to again disgorge, and her weeps of anguish caught in her chest.

Wickham and Orman talked on, with glee, about the plans they had laid. How Darcy would be, even at that moment, collecting the funds to retrieve his wife and child, funds that they would enjoy, but were only a diversion. How he was probably agonizing over the loss to his fortune while also agonizing over the fate of his loved ones. How he would suffer all through the long night and all the next day before he received his instructions. How they would drop vague hints of Lizzy and Alexander's torment designed to torture him. How they would lure him with promises of a safe return, only to capture him when he played to their directives like a marionette. How they would follow through with the final monstrous assaults to Lizzy and an innocent child, ending their heinous campaign with Orman killing Darcy.

The declarations and fits of laughter blended in her weary, stupefied mind. Lizzy sensed the tendrils of oblivion creeping over her and she reached for them eagerly. She hurt, physically and emotionally, and yearned for the relative peace that sleep would bring her. Her last memory was of a loud bang and muted scream from somewhere far away, but she could not muster the curiosity needed to maintain a grip on her reason. Blackness again consumed her.

The ride from Grosvenor Square to the remote hunting lodge in Surrey, near the village of Oxshott, was uneventful. The twelve men on horseback drove their mounts hard, not bothering to talk, and crossed the distance in record time. Nonetheless, to Darcy it felt like an eternity. Only a few hours had passed since the suspected time of the kidnapping, fewer still since he had been interrupted with the news at Angelo's, but it was more than enough time for any number of gruesome punishments to have befallen his wife and child. No matter how hard he tried to squelch the visions, they occurred with alarming frequency. It was only the driving will to rescue them that preserved his sanity.

The calm, military proficiency of Colonel Fitzwilliam was a soothing balm at this time. Even in the midst of his turmoil, Darcy was consciously appreciative that he had such a man on his side. It would not be until much later, however, that he would be able to think back on his cousin's sapient leadership with the full amount of pride and awe it deserved. For the present, he could only focus on holding his wife and son in his arms, and putting this nightmare behind them. Luckily, he did have enough clarity and good sense to hearken to Richard's decrees.

They did not slow their galloping pace until they neared the narrow weald bordering the unkempt expanse surrounding the house. The colonel signaled a halt amongst the concealing woods. Each of the ten men he had circumspectly chosen for this mission dismounted in complete silence. They tied their horses to the trees, gathering around their commander in hunkering positions without crunching a single dried leaf. With a combination of gestures and pointed words spoken in hushed tones that were nevertheless crisp and comprehendible, their plan of attack was laid out.

Richard signaled Darcy, the only nonmilitary man in their company, to stay close to his side. Darcy nodded, knowing that this was as much to be sure the emotionally charged man did not do something stupid as it was to be sure he was front-and-center to the final rescue.

The other men fanned out in a rough semicircle between the trunks of oak, wild cherry, and birch. They crept silently, low to the ground, eyes scanning through the faint illumination of dusk, edging ever closer to the boundary of the concealing forest. Once the house was within easy sight, they halted again. More faint whispers and gestured commands were given. Darcy only understood about half of the communication, but then, his eyes were riveted to the lodge beyond the weedy, dilapidated yard.

It was not large, strictly being a temporary resting place for menfolk to lay their heads in relative comfort while hunting the plentiful game that inhabited the surrounding woodland. Fashioned from roughly carved logs and timber, it almost reminded Darcy of drawings he had seen of cabins in the American frontier. Although the current pressing point was to spy the land and collect necessary intelligence, Darcy did spare a moment's curious inventory of the architecture, grudgingly admitting that the rustic design was appealing. Moreover, on a practical level, it made this venture easy to delineate.

The land in between where they hid among the underbrush and the house was level, only some thirty yards wide, and conveniently dotted with wildly overgrown hazel, green hound's-tongue, herb Paris, and a number of other bushes and small trees. The house was dark with glimmers of light showing from one first floor window on the far corner and a group of windows on the second story. They waited, watching, unbelievably coming to suspect that there were no guards or servants in the vicinity, when an armed man walked around the corner.

Richard snorted in disgust, nudging Darcy with his elbow, and leaning for a murmured commentary. "Look at how he is holding his shotgun. Pathetic. Not looking around or alert. Oh, this is almost no fun at all." He signaled to one of his associates, Colonel Roland Artois, older brother to Kitty's husband Randall Artois, who nodded curtly, rose, and almost instantly seemed to disappear!

Darcy blinked in astonishment, as he would several times in the next few minutes, finally espying the enormous soldier with bulging muscles that looked to burst through the strained fabric of his lightweight jacket. He was melting into the darkness cast by the foliage, his hulking body appearing to magically fade as he furtively grew closer and closer to the unsuspecting sentry. The man stood nonchalantly by the wall, puffing on a glowing pipe, the shotgun negligently slung over his shoulder.

It was a thing of beauty. One moment he was there, in full view, and the next he was dropped to the ground. It happened so fast that if their angle did not allow the scene to play before his eyes, Darcy may have thought the man evaporated! In one smooth motion, the brawny warrior emerged behind the watchman, his arms and hands circling with a knifing twist and jerking clasp. The unfortunate man instantly went limp, Colonel Artois lowering them both gracefully to the ground amid the concealing bushes and shadows.

Darcy gasped. Richard grinned, delivering a wink to his cousin. "Do not fear. All the men have been instructed not to kill unless absolutely necessary." He shrugged. "Generally it is *not* necessary. There are ways to subdue and leave for future questioning. Can help when you need information, keeps down the mess and boring questions later, and gives the courts and lawyers something to prove their worth in this world."

Richard delivered another wink before growing serious and motioning to more of his assistants. Four more slunk away, two in each direction. "They will approach the house from the back and side, take care of any other *guards*," he emphasized with derision, "and stand watch around the perimeter. Ah, there is the signal."

The bulky figure of Roland Artois came into view from amid the brush, nodding at the colonel.

"Come. It's time to retrieve your family!"

The next span of minutes, again seemingly agonizing in their slowness, was rather exhilarating. If the stakes were not so high and Darcy's insides were not in a twisted knot of tension, he may have welcomed the thrill of the hunt. He was eager to confront Wickham and Orman, more than hoping there would be some resistance merely for the delight in dispensing some well-deserved physical pain! The awareness of his zealous barbarism elicited a sad smile, knowing that Elizabeth would scold him for the train of his thoughts while secretly swelling with pride.

Be strong, my love, his thoughts pleaded, I am coming for you and our son, and all will be well.

It was late in the evening, and although the setting sun still cast rays through the surrounding trees, inside the two-story lodge it was dim. No lamps were lit in the lower level chambers except for a glow from far down the hall in what they discovered was the empty kitchen. The only obvious illumination in the upper story came from the chamber at the top of the stairs and another further down the corridor. It was eerie, but certainly made stealthy reconnoitering easy.

Entering the house, investigating the empty rooms, and gathering before the dark stairway leading to the upper floor was accomplished expeditiously. The four soldiers assuredly secured the exterior and then, per the colonel's instructions, remained posted outside the house. There was no doubt in anyone's mind that they would provide safeguarding in a far superior manner than Orman's dismal protectors, all three of whom had been efficiently incapacitated.

The murmur of voices and movement could be detected from above as they cautiously ascended the long staircase leading to the upper floor, hugging the shadows against the wall. Richard was in the front of the line with Darcy on the next lower step and six soldiers bringing up the rear. Halfway up the steps the voices grew clearer, with words distinguishable and distinct.

"How badly do you want her now? Hmmm? Ready to take her this instant?"

At Orman's repellent words, uttered with a sickly humorous tone, Darcy stiffened and took an involuntary step forward. It was only Richard's steely grip on his right upper arm, fingertips digging in so harshly that he would note bruises on the morrow, along with a chary but determined push into the wall, which kept the enraged man from leaping forward into the room.

"Wait," Richard hissed. "We must be certain where they are. Trust me."

Darcy nodded, grimly setting his jaw and regaining mastery over his emotions. Fresh rage consumed him, but Richard's stern warning enabled him to seek the placid restraint he needed for his family's benefit.

The lurid exchange that followed was horrible for both Richard and Darcy to hear, but it furnished the required information. Locations could be determined and a vague grasp of layout ascertained. The surge of unfathomable joy Darcy experienced upon hearing Elizabeth's voice was immeasurable. The relief when he realized that, although ill, both she and Alexander were alive and not violated drove out the fear. All that remained was pure, cold, rational anger and the hunger to exact justice.

Tiptoeing with incredible caution, they ascended until on the landing. With the briefest of nods and hand motions, three of the soldiers passed by and headed left to the door down the hall behind which they now knew Alexander was hidden. The remaining three soldiers spread out behind Richard and

Darcy as they approached the parlor, careful to stay out of the light bathing the carpeted hall from the half-opened door.

The eight men carried a virtual arsenal of weapons. The military veterans held razor-sharp shortswords or daggers in their left hands, with two pistols holstered on their hips. The occasional gleam reflecting off steel and sundry materials fashioned into hard hafts proved the existence of additional weapons stashed upon their bodies. In fact, the man closest to Darcy, a wiry, short gentleman who nonetheless struck an imposing stance of coiled energy and cunning, had a dagger grip of what appeared to be bone carved with images of skulls, protruding from the top of his scuffed Hessian boots.

Darcy only had two weapons, not counting his hands. He held the comforting cold metal of a flintlock pistol in his right hand and a powder flask and balls in an accessible pocket if time allowed a swift reload. At his left hip he had strapped his sword, a colichemarde once belonging to his father. It was a favorite choice when he fenced, Darcy preferring something heavier that was efficient for thrusting, parrying, and cutting, and thus he was proficient with the blade.

The men stationed in the shadowy spaces near the bedroom door were tense, weapons at the ready, and eyes on the colonel, waiting for the final signal to spring into action. It was difficult for Darcy to entrust Alexander's rescue and safety to strangers, but he was confident of their expertise. And, frankly, he did not have much choice. Seconds before Richard delivered the "Now!" sign, Colonel Artois met Darcy's eyes. He solemnly saluted and inclined his head toward the closed door. It was subtle, but Darcy understood the silent communication. He nodded in return, feeling tremendous relief by the man's acknowledgement.

Richard made a sharp, slashing motion with the shortsword he held in his right hand. Instantly, the leader of the rescue team for Alexander, that being Roland Artois, opened the door with a massive shove, barreling through the gap and slamming the heavy wooden door into the wall with a resounding crack. The other two men were on his heels, rushing through with a ferocious shout.

The violent entry and ruckus was intentional, of course, and it worked as the colonel planned. A shrill scream erupted from the panicked young woman, who Darcy would later learn was the only person attending to his son, adding to the clamor invading the quiet.

After a split-second of startled silence from within the parlor, precipitous movement and cursing issued forth. The response was as Richard anticipated and their slight delay in action was purposeful. No signal was necessary as the waiting deliverers noiselessly sprinted into the room.

Darcy's eyes swung immediately to where he assumed his wife and Wickham were, the rapid scan of the room revealing it to be much as he had imagined.

A blazing fireplace was precisely in the middle of the outer wall with two large, partially draped windows flanking. A large, plush wingback of deep brown leather sat to the left of the hearth. Upon it rested the scarred and maimed Marquis of Orman. His sturdy, broad-pointed walking cane, an elaborate instrument of glossy cherry wood with a silver and brass handle shaped like a hissing snake, leaned against the chair's arm by his knee. Orman, as hoped, was leaning forward and turned to his right toward the chamber beyond, his face a study in confusion.

There were two sofas in the room, as well as two additional chairs. The one with Lizzy and Wickham was nearest to the door, the end where Wickham sat pointing toward Darcy.

Richard headed directly toward Orman, crossing the short distance before the stunned man had any clue that people had entered his supposed impenetrable sanctuary. Wickham instinctively bolted upward, his impetuous ascent not considering that Elizabeth was partly lying on his lap. As Darcy assessed the scene, his fury escalated as he helplessly watched his precious wife go tumbling to the floor in a heap.

He yelled a snarling challenge as he lunged forward.

Wickham swung about. The shocked expression on his face instantaneously disappeared when he saw Darcy. It was replaced with a look of such vicious hatred that, if Darcy had not been filled with his own overwhelming loathing and wrath, it might have given him pause. Yet, despite his steely resolve and preparedness, he was astonished by how speedily Wickham retaliated.

"No!" Wickham screamed, charging aggressively to collide into Darcy with a resounding clash. The impact was intense, Wickham barreling into the bigger man with incredible force. Darcy was knocked backward a step, but otherwise countered the attack with tightening legs and a shove with his torso. Wickham was unfazed, one hand latching fiercely onto Darcy's throat with squeezing fingers, while the other grasped and twisted the wrist that was aiming the firearm toward his chest.

Darcy wrenched his arm out of Wickham's clutches, whipping the pistol about and delivering a strong clout to Wickham's collarbone. He felt a surge of delight at the audible crack of contact on bone.

Wickham howled in pain and fury, but his assault did not lessen. The two men grappled together, squeezing, wrenching, and pummeling blows with increasing gusto. Energy and stamina were fed by their mutual hatred and ire, years of pent hostility seeking an outlet of a physical nature. Wickham did not have a weapon to use, but it was unlikely he would have used it any more than Darcy, both men perversely enjoying each landed punch.

They swayed and staggered across the floor, Wickham finally succeeding in slamming Darcy into the thick oak door.

The air was knocked from Darcy's lungs, the back of his head also striking the surface hard enough for him to momentarily see stars and loosen his hold. Wickham shouted a victory, administering a hard wallop into Darcy's midsection, and raising his leg in preparation for a crippling knee into the groin. Darcy, in spite of his pain and blurred wits, sensed what was coming and pivoted his hips away. Wickham's knee came into crunching contact with the oak, his body sagging in Darcy's arms.

Burying his hurt into a deep recess of his mind, Darcy rounded with a second clout of the flintlock, this one connecting with Wickham's left temple. The injured man yelped and reeled backward, Darcy following with a balled fist landing under Wickham's chin.

His head snapped back, hands desperately reaching for anything to correct his imbalance. He grabbed on to Darcy's jacket lapels, the men again wrestling together as they tottered crazily into the hallway. The strange dance lasted for only a few seconds, Wickham then securing one arm around Darcy's neck and clawing at the nape. Darcy knifed his left forearm downward with tremendous force, Wickham's long arm bone cracking, while simultaneously bringing the pistol to bear and discharging the round into the wailing man's abdomen.

Wickham released an inhuman squeal of agony, outrage, frustration, and disbelief. The bullet's impact buckled his body, blood soaking through his clothing in a flood. His rapidly weakening legs bowed and his body rocked unsteadily on the top step of the staircase.

He glanced upward, the fraction of a second stretching as he met Darcy's eyes with blazing defiance and mania apparent in his wounded gaze.

He opened his mouth to speak, but whatever he meant to say would never be uttered. With the final iota of strength remaining, he threw his uninjured arm over his lifelong enemy's shoulder, pulling with all his residual might, both of them falling over the edge of the staircase.

Wickham landed flat on his spine with a reverberating thud, Darcy's muscular body smashing onto him forcefully. The pistol went flying into the air, Darcy releasing it in desperation and flailing his arms wildly for some sort of purchase. It came dually in the form of a handy baluster and the clutching grip of Colonel Fitzwilliam. Richard firmly hauled on Darcy's left shoulder and side, staying his inevitable descent down the stairs.

Wickham was not so fortunate. The combined momentum of his fall and Darcy's impact sent his body tumbling and sliding crazily all the way to the bottom. His cries echoed through the air until fatally cut off when his neck snapped on the last step.

Richard and the wiry soldier pulled Darcy to a semi-sitting position on the floor.

"About time! Where have you been?" Darcy gasped.

"You appeared to have it under control. Besides, I thought you would appreciate your wife lying comfortably on the sofa. Come. I will help you up. You look horrible, by the way, and later I shall chastise you for not shooting him in the first place, but right now I think your wife needs you."

Darcy nodded, wincing with the pain felt from numerous parts of his body. With necessary assistance from each man, he was gingerly lifted to his feet. Richard held on to Darcy's arm to ensure stability and handed him his handkerchief.

"Your head is bleeding. Are you sure you are all right?"

"I will be fine." He blotted the back of his head but was already unsteadily moving toward the parlor. "Alexander?" he asked, glancing at the trailing Richard.

"He is with Artois in the bedchamber. He is still drugged but apparently undamaged."

Darcy felt torn, but the need to touch Elizabeth was calling him. He crossed the threshold, his eyes only for his wife. But, his peripheral vision did note that the Marquis sported a number of fresh cuts and bruises, and was trammeled and gagged in a far corner with two burly guards watching him. He was thrashing maniacally, his muffled voice raving and face bleeding and red as a beet with eyes bulging scarily. He appeared near to an apoplectic seizure, foam and spittle soaking through the muzzling rag. The unfazed warriors stood nonchalantly a foot away, passing a cigar back and forth for several puffs before roughly dragging the insane man out of the room.

Darcy spared scant thought to Orman's condition. He assigned immediate and total attention to his wife. Richard had positioned her body comfortably on the sofa, head resting on the pillow, and a blanket obtained from somewhere covering her lower body modestly. He had removed the rope bonds from around her wrists and ankles. She looked peaceful and beautiful, except for the snarls in her disheveled hair and the angry red marks on her cheeks that filled Darcy with fresh anger. Upon closer inspection he noted four circular pressure bruises the size of a man's fingertip on one cheek, and raw burns on her dainty nostrils. He dropped to his knees, clasping her hands and brushing kisses over her face, not aware that tears were falling from his eyes.

"Elizabeth, sweet, precious Elizabeth. Wake up! Look at me, dearest. You are safe. Alexander is safe. I am here and no further harm will come to you. Please! Elizabeth, open your eyes!" His alarm grew when she showed no sign of responding. Not a moan or sigh. He touched his fingertips to her forehead, recognizing what his frantic lips had not sensed. "Richard! She is feverish! Why?" He turned questioning, anxious eyes to his hovering cousin. "Does vitriol do this?"

Richard shook his head slowly. His face was naked with concern as he too touched gentle fingertips to Lizzy's forehead. "I do not know, Darcy. I have no experience with the drug."

Darcy withdrew, blinking the moisture from his eyes to commence a detailed examination of his wife. First off he noted the rope burns to her wrists, fingering them lovingly, and sending a silent thankful prayer heavenward that her delicate skin was only mildly abraded and not bleeding. He kissed each wrist before moving his tender touch to the ivory, unmarked flesh of her neck. If he had seen evidence of Wickham applying filthy hands to his wife's throat, he may have returned to the body lying twisted at the bottom of the stairs for a few well-deserved kicks!

He rested his palm over her heart, relieved to feel the steady beat. But, it was then that he became aware of the areas of patchy wetness and dried milk staining over the front of her apron covered gown. Additionally, and far more alarming, was the hard lumpiness of her breasts. He gasped, reaching to discreetly peel the fabric away from her chest. Richard, he noted in his periphery, turned away, leaving Darcy in relative privacy to examine his wife. He did not completely expose her, would not have in any case, but it was not necessary. The erythema spread in a fist-sized blemish over the top of her left breast. Carefully palpating, with tears stinging his eyes and fury freshly rising, Darcy felt the warmth and swelling of the starkly demarcated patch, the engorged milk pockets like little rocks.

"Richard, Elizabeth needs a physician."

"Very well. I shall send Helt to Oxshott..."

"No. Search for a carriage. Surely there must be one since Orman could not possibly sit a horse. We must return to London immediately."

"But..."

"No argument. No one will touch my wife but my uncle." He looked up at the anxious face of his cousin. "Hurry, please. The nicest carriage, if we have a choice, with the fastest horses. Cushions and blankets. She cannot be jostled more than necessary. Quickly!"

Richard moved to administer orders that were carried out hastily. Darcy turned back to Elizabeth, covering her completely before leaning to kiss her feverish lips.

"Do not fear, my love. All will be well. I love you and will not leave you."

"Mr. Darcy?"

"Papa!"

Darcy jerked at the overlapping voices, his eyes alighting on Alexander, who practically catapulted out of Artois's arms into the open embrace of his father. Alexander buried his tiny face into his father's neck, tears falling in waves, and arms and hands gripping adamantly as his little body shook. Darcy savored the sensations, his own body shaking with contained sobs as he clutched the vibrant life to his chest.

Cascades of murmured endearments and promises of safety fell from his lips as he planted dozens of kisses. He stroked over the soft back of his son. His firm hands and sturdy body were ready reminders to Alexander of his father's strength and devotion. Gradually the weeping and tremors lessened, Alexander finally withdrawing to gaze into his father's beloved face.

"I knew you come! I miss you and Mama, but I brave boy. I bite bad man, Papa! He got mad, but I not care. Kick him too. Bad, bad man! Bad man Mama not like. I told him you come and get me and he be sorry. Made me smell sweet water that made me sleepy and sick. Sorry, Papa, I try to be brave but I got sick. Nice girl washed my face. I sleepy a lot and my stomach hurt and nose hurt and..."

He spoke in a rush, gasping residual sobs interrupting the rambling dialogue. Darcy smiled through the commentary and brushed his hands and fingers over his son's body. But the toddler seemed fair enough, all things considered. He kept babbling, the innocence of youth to an extent already beginning to see the whole incident as a great adventure, especially now that his father was holding him safe and secure. He finally glanced away from Darcy's face and noticed Lizzy lying on the couch.

"Mama! Mama come with you, Papa? She asleep?"

"Yes, Son. She is asleep. We must be quiet and let her sleep for now, understand?"

The boy nodded, his eyes serious as he lifted one finger to his lips and made a shushing sound.

"Indeed," Darcy lifted his finger as well, whispering. "Very quiet. We will be leaving soon to return to Darcy House where Uncle George and Aunt Georgiana are waiting for you."

"Nanny and Michael too?"

"Yes, of course. They miss you very much. Nanny will want to hear all about your exciting adventure and how brave you were."

Alexander brightened, smiling and nodding. "Can I give Mama kiss?"

"Certainly! We can both kiss her, how about that? But gently."

Darcy leaned, Alexander firm in his grip, both placing soft kisses over Lizzy's cheeks. She stirred and released a faint sigh.

"Fitzwilliam?"

"Yes! Yes, my dearest! It is I, and Alex…"

"Fitzwilliam will kill you, Mr. Wickham. You know he will. Hunt you down like the animal you are. It is only a matter of time. Only time, time, time." She shuddered, arching her neck as her eyelids fluttered and opened. But the deep brown that Darcy so adored was glossy, the pupils largely dilated and not focusing. "So thirsty. Please, Mr. Wickham, water please. I need…"

She sighed, her voice dropping lower and her eyelids beginning to slide shut, before suddenly opening widely and looking directly at Darcy. "William. Where is Alexander?"

"Here, Mama!"

"We are here, Elizabeth. Both of us, see?" He was clutching her hand so tightly he knew it must be causing her pain, but she seemed impervious. Then, to his momentary joy, she did fix her gaze on Alexander and smiled faintly.

"I knew you would come. Your father always takes care of us, does he not, sweetie? Always, always." Her eyes slid to Darcy, the smile waning as the glassiness overtook her eyes once again. "I love you, Fitzwilliam." She groaned, her eyes closing in obvious pain as she grimaced. Her body shivered and shifted in discomfort, one hand feebly rising to lie on her affected breast. "I hurt, Mr. Wickham! Please, I need my baby! Please, it hurts so. Please, please."

Tears were falling uncontrollably from Darcy's eyes. Alexander was sucking his thumb, eyes large with confusion and fear as he looked from one parent to another. Lizzy's voice trailed off into silence, once again succumbing to the fever and trauma of the past hours.

"Papa," Alexander spoke in a shaky voice, "Mama be all right?"

Darcy swallowed, closing his eyes for a silent prayer as he pulled his son closer to his body for a tight squeeze. "Of course, my lamb. Your mother will be just fine. As soon as we get home, Uncle George will make her better and she can rest." He kissed the soft forehead, maintaining a firm embrace, as his voice fell for a whispered supplication. "Please, God, let her be all right. Please."

CHAPTER NINETEEN

Consequences and Conclusions

DARCY HELD HIS FEBRILE and delirious wife during the frightening drive through the dark, poorly maintained country roads leading to London, home, and the supreme medical expertise of Dr. George Darcy. Alexander refused to unclasp his arms from his father's neck, not that Darcy desired separating from his son for a second, until they were well beyond the "scary house with the bad man." Even then he loosened his grip only enough to nestle onto Darcy's lap with his mother's head comfortingly touching his small thigh.

Colonel Fitzwilliam and the bulk of his men remained behind to deal with the mess. One rider voluntarily risked life and limb to carry an express message to Darcy House, the occupants informed of the rescue and Lizzy's condition. Colonel Artois insisted on acting as armed guard to the Darcys, riding ahead of the carriage confiscated from Orman's lodge.

They encountered no obstacles, but the late hour with limited natural illumination and potential road hazards meant great speed was not a possibility. Therefore the ride took twice as long as it would have during the day. Heart pounding painfully and anxiety barely kept at bay, Darcy sat in the dark interior unable to see his wife's face except for brief seconds when the crescent moon's pale glow pierced through the trees. He was comforted by the press of Lizzy and Alexander's bodies, but the stretches of absolute silence from Lizzy when only the steady pulse palpated in her neck assured him of her life followed by interludes of nonsensical mutterings and thrashing escalated his anguish. The lights of London and finally Grosvenor Square had never been so appreciated.

The carriage was greeted with expectancy but subdued fuss. Mrs. Hanford plucked Alexander from Darcy's arms, managing to control her emotions until inside the foyer whereupon she squeezed his body and wept so uncontrollably that it was Alexander who ended up soothing the distraught nanny with gentle pats and murmured assurances. Before they reached the nursery he was recounting the adventure and his bravery in matter-of-fact tones that allayed the worst of her fears. After a warm bath and hot soup, the toddler was tucked into bed with Dog nestled tight and Miss Lisa curled beside for added security. He swiftly fell asleep and the atmosphere within the chamber was no different than on any other night.

Not so within the master's chambers. Darcy carried Lizzy into the house blazing with lit candles and lamps, ignoring everyone in his haste to safely deposit her onto their bed, where within seconds the examination by Dr. Darcy was underway. George was in full physician-in-command mode with the staff bustling about to implement his barked instructions.

"It is as I suspected from your scrawled descriptions, William," he said after a rapid evaluation. "She has developed a case of puerperal mastitis. The lingering effects of the ether may be contributing to her fever and delirium, but I believe it is the inflammation. We must reduce the redness and swelling, pray there is no infection, and control her fever. Marguerite"—he turned to Lizzy's waiting maid—"please assist Mr. Darcy in cleaning your mistress and providing comfort. I will see to those poultices I ordered."

He rose from the edge of the bed by Lizzy's inert side, reaching to clasp Darcy's hands. "Do not fear, my boy. She is healthy and astoundingly stubborn. A simple breast inflammation will not overwhelm her. However, I do pray there is not an infection brewing. I do not think it has gone to that degree but cannot be sure. I know of several herbs, most of which I have in my supplies. What I do not have I can obtain from the apothecary on the morrow. For now our greatest priority is to lower the fever and relieve her pain. For the first I have ice being chipped from the ice-cellar, and for the latter we need Michael."

"Michael?" Darcy glanced away from his wife's face to look at his uncle, brow raised in question.

"Indeed. A hungry infant will be best able to alleviate the engorgement, that causing the mastitis in the first place. Now, help Marguerite while I obtain a few supplies. But first, I am assuming Colonel Fitzwilliam is fine or you would have stated otherwise, but I am sure his wife would appreciate an update."

"Lady Simone is still here?"

"She rightly figured this was the best place to wait for her husband, but also would not abandon Georgiana, who has been distressed." He did not mention Mr. Butler, who had also refused to leave and was in the parlor still, saving that information for a more opportune moment.

"Of course." Darcy pinched the bridge of his nose wearily, nodding in agreement. "That is to be expected. Assure Lady Simone that Richard is fine. He is handling the aftermath. It may take a while so she may as well return home. Where is Georgie?"

"Georgiana is assisting with the poultices and will be along momentarily. Let me talk to Lady Simone and I will return." He patted Darcy's shoulder, squeezing once, and turned to leave.

Darcy sighed, closing his eyes and taking a minute to silently say a prayer, and then stepped to join Marguerite.

Lizzy's devoted maid was wringing cool water from a cloth, moving to apply the soothing and cleansing lave to her mistress, but Darcy gently took the swab from her hand. "I shall do this, Marguerite. Will you please remove her soiled clothing?"

Lizzy moaned frequently and murmured incoherently. Her eyelids fluttered, opening to slits several times, but she did not waken. Her fiery, flushed skin responded to the tepid bath with gooseflesh and shivering. Darcy examined her bosom, encouraged to note that the inflamed patch was not worsened and there were no additional erythematic areas. The hard, turgid milk-sacs were obviously painful when touched, but her nipples were of normal appearance. Darcy was hopeful that the latter was a positive sign.

Midway through the cleansing Georgiana marched into the room carrying a wailing Michael. Behind her came two maids, their arms burdened with towels, laden trays, and a bucket of ice.

"He was not too fond of being woken up in the middle of his night and only a few hours after feeding, but Uncle insisted." She spoke over the din to her brother, who approached with a frown etched between his brows. "Fortunately, your son has a tremendous appetite. Cannot imagine where he attains that character trait."

She attempted a warm smile but her eyes were red-rimmed and cheeks blotchy. Georgiana tiptoed to bestow a tender kiss to his cheek, speaking in a feigned casual tone. "It seems odd to me as well, letting him nurse when Lizzy is unaware. But it does make sense, Brother, when you consider the logic. Besides, Uncle knows what he is about." She glanced to Lizzy, whose reddened left breast was exposed as Marguerite applied one of the poultices Dr. Darcy had concocted. "It looks so painful. Here, take him to his mother. You know what to do better than I."

"Thank you, Georgie. Are you…?"

"I am fine now so do not fret over me. Just take care of Lizzy."

"Very well. Come, sweetheart, let us get you fed. Your mama needs you."

Normally, Michael latched onto the nipple instantly, quiet falling, never to be distracted until forced to relinquish one nipple for the other or when utterly sated. This time, however, his native volatility was compounded by being woken precipitously and then expected to nurse from an engorged breast with stale milk. Darcy patiently persisted through Michael's fit of temper until the infant settled in for serious sucking.

Darcy sat on the bed's edge, softly stroking his back with one hand while holding Lizzy's slack right hand to his lips. Georgiana knelt on the wide bed behind Lizzy placing the compress of crushed mint, ginger, and pepper paste to her forehead and rotated the tied bundles of chipped ice over her neck and shoulders. George entered the room minutes later, handing the poultice of fenugreek seed and dandelion to Marguerite.

"Give this to Mr. Darcy to smear on Mrs. Darcy's inflamed breast," he directed Lizzy's maid. "The smell is not too foul, William, so it should not disturb Michael, but for now apply it conservatively." He sat down in a corner chair, discreetly positioning himself so he could instruct without witnessing Lizzy's nakedness. "Once he is finished we will slather more on and wrap with a cloth. Keep moving the packs along her back, Georgie. We do not want her to become chilled. The fever should subside gradually. If there is an infection process fomenting, an elevated temperature is partially beneficial. William, rub the congested milk sacs, gingerly mind you, as Michael nurses. It will aid the release and press the herbal salve into the skin. Once Michael is finished, we will rouse her and force her to drink those teas."

He seemingly rambled without purpose, but his orotund tones with words falling in a lilting cadence were soothing. Darcy watched his wife's face, noting the occasional flashes of pain that crossed her brow as he massaged her softening breast. But he also noted the regular rhythm of her breathing, the lessening blotched pallor and ruddiness of her skin, and the increasing coolness of the hand pressed against his mouth. Together the signs were encouraging.

Michael finished his meal, his chubby body limp as Darcy nestled him against his left chest for burping. He kissed the infant's forehead, turning to look at his uncle.

"I doubt if I can wake him to eat more. This is his time of extended sleep with hunger well abated."

"No matter. He will make up for lost time tomorrow. For tonight I can instruct you how to alleviate some of the pressure in the other breast manually. First we must get Elizabeth to drink some fluids. Georgie, will you return Michael to Mrs. Hanford? Thank you, dear. Sit Elizabeth up, William."

Darcy was required to lend his entire body as support, Lizzy's flaccid form melding to the contours of his torso. He sat behind her, arms securing and broad chest a firm resting place for her back, and the bend of his neck and shoulder a solid prop for her head.

"Elizabeth," he voice lovingly commanded into her ear. "We need you to wake up and drink. I need to hear your voice. Please, Elizabeth, look at me. Squeeze my hand, anything to let me know you hear me."

She moaned, weakly arching her back and turning away from his pleading. But he continued on at Dr. Darcy's urging. He told her that she was home now, that Alexander was safe and asleep, that the threat to them was eliminated, that he loved and needed her, and so on.

George held one wrist between his fingers, counting the decreasing beats of her pulse. His other hand skillfully brushed over her neck and upper chest, palpating the changes in skin temperature. Softly, he directed Marguerite to administer the oral drops of belladonna, and then to change the herbal compress on her head to one of cool sandalwood paste. The teapot of steeped black elder, willow bark, chamomile, and lime flowers sat waiting on the bedside table.

Darcy kept up his train of verbal declarations of love and need, compelling her to respond. Eventually she did, with groans growing louder as she broke through the febrile haze and finally opened her glassy eyes.

"George," she slurred in surprise, not expecting his to be the first face she saw.

"Yes, Niece, it is me. Delighted to see you, but, if you do not greet the big fellow behind you soon, he may burst into tears."

Darcy was indeed teary eyed. His strong palm was already cupping his wife's cheek and nudging so that he could meet her gaze. "Tell me you know who I am," he whispered.

She frowned. "Of course I know who you are. My Fitzwilliam."

"Yes! Yes." He brushed a kiss over her lips. "All is well now, my heart. Uncle has some tea for you. I am sure it is foul…"

"I beg your pardon?" George interjected indignantly.

"…but you must drink all of it. It will help with the pain and fever. Do you understand?"

"As you wish. I am very thirsty." Her voice was listless with a note of confusion, her brow quizzical. Even so, she offered no objection, drinking the pungent tea wordlessly. Darcy murmured encouragingly throughout, caressing her arms as George plied her with three cups of the medicinal brew.

Finally she finished her required dose, the satisfied physician assessing her flushed skin and mild warmth with a smile and happy nod. "Excellent. Much improved, Elizabeth."

"She still feels hot to me, Uncle. Are you sure she is mending?"

"The fever is less and she is awake, if drowsy and befuddled. All to be expected." He smiled cheerily, patting Lizzy's knee. "Now she needs to sleep. Questions can be asked and answered tomorrow. Does that sound like a capitol idea, Mrs. Darcy?"

Lizzy inclined her head while fumbling to absorb his words without much success. The fringes of her memory niggled at her, some vague awareness buried behind thick clouds attempting to capture her attention and whisper facts that she should be concerned about. Yet all she felt was extreme weariness. The odd torpor weighting down her limbs was offset by the comforting sturdiness of her husband's body. She felt his breath on her cheek, smelt the wonderful aroma of his manliness and cologne, heard the potency in every word he uttered, and felt the loving touch of his fingertips. It all combined to imbue her soul with an overwhelming peace and assurance so that none of the troubling glimmers could penetrate her blanketing sense of security.

She muttered a few words, none of the room's occupants understanding what she was trying to say, and returned to her slumber.

George palpated the strong pulse in her neck and lifted one eyelid to gaze at her pupil, nodding with clinical satisfaction. "She is asleep, nothing else. This is good." He looked at his clearly distraught nephew, smiling and patting his knee. "Relax, William. She will be fine, I promise."

"Uncle, do you know if vitriol has any effect on unborn babies?"

George's brows rose, his eyes instantly returning to Lizzy and scanning over her body. "Are you sure? I have seen no signs of Elizabeth being with child."

"It is merely a conjecture based on... possible symptoms." He smiled wanly and laughed shortly. "Strange. This morning I was distressed at the idea of Elizabeth being pregnant so soon after her recovery, with the fear of a repeat occurrence all I could dwell upon. Now I find myself paralyzed by the prospect of our baby being lost or damaged in some way."

"Ether is used liberally in some places to dull pain. I have utilized it often myself for certain procedures, although I do not care for the aftereffects. I have never documented any direct sequelae from ether during gestation, William, but of course we will not know for some time. Do not fret about it at this juncture. I seriously doubt if this one exposure will cause any harm."

"But why..."

"I know you have questions, William, but I think most of them can wait. You look horrible and need rest of your own. Let me examine that scalp wound and apply an antiseptic unguent, then I order you to sleep."

Darcy held Lizzy for several more minutes before laying her comfortably onto the bed. He followed his uncle into the small parlor, falling into the chair with a loud groan. George cleaned the wound, pleased to announce that stitches were unnecessary, his fingers gentle in their ministration. Still, Darcy winced from the pain, especially the stinging salve, and gratefully drank the pungent elixir offered to dull the pain felt in his head and from numerous bruises.

Conversation was minimal. Darcy had so many questions that he hardly knew where to begin and the fatigue washing through his muscles prevented his tongue from properly functioning. He tried, however, but George was taciturn, finally halting the mumbled queries by placing both hands firmly onto Darcy's shoulders and stating, "No more questions or discussion, Son. I am convinced there is no infection since the fever is subsiding. The residual effects of the ether will be gone by tomorrow and the fever will likely break by morning. The mastitis will heal once Michael is allowed to nurse unrestrained. In a few days you will be scolding your impetuous wife for leaving the bed and wanting to walk to Hyde Park. Now, go get some sleep. You know where to find me, but I intend to do the same as all this excitement is stressful on my old bones."

He grinned, clapping his nephew on the shoulder, and left the chamber with a spring in his step far jauntier than the considerably younger Darcy could muster at that moment.

❦

Georgiana returned to the parlor after tucking Michael into his crib and taking a few minutes to kiss the sleeping Alexander. Simone stood as she entered the room, crossing to meet her for a firm hug.

"My dearest girl, all is now well, yes?"

Georgiana nodded, her smile genuine if fatigued. "Lizzy is feverish but responding to treatment." She included Mr. Butler in her reply, his face drawn with concern for everyone involved if slightly more so for his fiancée. "Dr. Darcy says she will be fine in no time at all, praise God."

"What of the… abductors?" Mr. Butler asked.

"I did not ask."

"Surely they have been subdued and apprehended," Simone offered. "I deduce that is what my husband is dealing with. And speaking of my husband"—she reached for her cloak and gloves—"I shall leave you now, if you do not mind, so I can have a hot meal ready when Richard returns. If he comes here first, tell him to go home immediately so his wife's anxiety will be allayed."

Georgiana recognized her honest emotion, assuring that she would bodily toss him out the door if need be. The laughter elicited at that image lifted everyone's heart, Simone bidding good night at that point.

Once alone, Sebastian enfolded Georgiana in a healing embrace, neither saying a word for several minutes.

He had sat beside her for hours, holding her hand and desperately wishing he could do more than merely listen in horror and wait while the clock loudly ticked into the silence. The ache to comfort her and express his love had escalated to a piercing pain. Georgiana's emotions, once released, had burst forth as a ruptured dam with tears and shivers bordering on hysteria even after retreating to the parlor as Richard recommended. Once that passed, she had grown nervous, clearly embarrassed by her upheaval. Lady Simone had left the room, silently indicating Sebastian ignore propriety and console the distraught young woman in any way possible. That, however, had proven difficult as

Georgiana remained flustered, busying herself with serving him tea all while profusely apologizing for the situation and her behavior, and then deflecting the conversation away to inquiries about his Easter, family visit, and so on. In the end he decided it was probably best to distract her with tales of his exploits, highly exaggerated to amuse, and deal with her ridiculous humiliation later.

Although he knew he could not stay much longer and risk further embarrassing her by being discovered alone or seen skulking away after midnight, the need to express his sentiments overrode all caution.

"Georgiana," he whispered, cupping her face with his palms and engaging her eyes, "I…" And then he could resist no longer, bending for a consuming kiss that spoke louder than any words.

For a long while the ticking clock was the only sound, unless one counted heavy breathing and moist lips in action. Mental clarity and restraint were slowly restored, Sebastian withdrawing but keeping the space between their bodies minuscule.

"I am glad that I arrived when I did. Being with you during this difficult time, aiding even in a small way, eases my heart. I cannot fathom how awful to hear later that you went through this trauma without me. We may not yet be wed, Miss Darcy, but I already feel responsible for you. Do not doubt that or my love for you."

She laughed shakily, attempting to nod with her head clasped firmly between his hands. "I have missed you, Sebastian, so much. And I am glad you were here too."

He kissed her again, tenderly, and then stepped back. "Now I should be going, despite my reluctance. You need to sleep and I am sure Mr. and Mrs. Darcy will need you tomorrow."

"When will you return?" Her voice caught, emotions still surging close to the surface.

"I am staying at my grandmother's townhouse. I shall wait upon your pleasure. See to your family first and when you deem it appropriate, write to Lady Warrow." He pulled on his overcoat, smiling at her worried expression. "I promise to respond with alacrity. After all, I have an official question to ask of your brother and have no intention of delaying any longer than absolutely necessary."

"Yes, indeed you do," she agreed with a hint of humor, "and, as difficult as it was to manage in my despondency and loneliness, I have several sheets of music I need your expert opinion on."

"I sincerely doubt I will have anything worthwhile to add to your brilliance, Miss Darcy, but I will delight in hearing you play the notes."

"You flatterer! The piece is meant to be played together and I am sure you will add some flair I did not envision, after your skill in rapid memorization is tested, that is."

"I adore a challenge," he countered, leaning to meet her lips for a final kiss, "and I adore you. In fact, I am crazy in love with you."

"I love you," she breathed, closing her eyes and rubbing her soft cheek against his stubbled one. "Shall I have a horse saddled?"

"No, thank you. I think a walk in the brisk air will do me good. It is not far. Attend to the present circumstances, Georgiana, but call for me soon. I need you," he ended simply, leaving seconds later, after another kiss.

Lizzy's fever broke three hours before the dawn, Marguerite changing the damp nightgown without the sleeping Darcy even aware. He did rouse at the angry voice of his son demanding sustenance, assisting the procedure since Lizzy remained languorous and addled. The baby did not seem to mind, nursing well from each breast, but Lizzy's condition worried Darcy.

"It is to be expected," George stated. "The fever, although lessened, is slightly elevated and the effects of the inflammation cause sluggishness. Add that to the residual ether sedation and I anticipate in may take a day or two for her to rally completely."

His assessment was correct. Lizzy slept most of the day and all that following night. She recognized Darcy and spoke dazedly of what had happened, but her haziness prevented curiosity as to how she was rescued or the condition of her abductors. Gradually, over the ensuing week her memory would return, but there would forever be gaps in her recollect mingled with bizarre images that made no sense. She was haunted by disturbing dreams, some powerful enough to jerk her awake, crying out in fear and reaching franticly for Darcy.

An oddly sweet odor to her breath and mild cough lasted for another twenty-four hours, also the aftereffects of vitriol, George said, as were her poor appetite and vomiting even with the bland soups and plain breads offered. The inflamed blotch marring her beautiful breast was gone in two days, thanks to Michael and the various medical treatments, internal and external, that their resident physician prescribed.

Alexander experienced lingering lethargy during that first day, his stomach was easily upset, and he too coughed. A honeyed tonic brewed by Uncle Goj remedied the unpleasant symptoms and after another night of restorative sleep he was physically one hundred percent cured. However, nightmares that he never remembered upon waking plagued him for weeks with Darcy called upon to pacify his terrified son until returned to sleep.

Observing their distress with no way to remedy it other than embracing caused him immeasurable pain, in some respects worse than their suffering. His sleep was disturbed by their nightmares and his own plagued dreams. The daytime hours were busy, allowing little time to rest until later in the evenings when the four of them gathered together in the large bed for play and stories, inevitably falling asleep in a tangle of limbs.

The laceration to his scalp was not large and healed without festering. The only negative effect was an annoying tingling as it healed and an occasional headache. His greatest physical pain arose from the wallop against the heavy oak door, the bruises scattered over his body, and muscles stressed during the altercation. Luckily, he was a quick healer and daily hot baths, soothing compresses given by his uncle for the biggest bruises, and deep massages from Samuel speeded his recovery.

The combination of bath, medicines, and massage definitely helped that first morning, Darcy exiting his dressing room prepared to deal with the consequences of the prior night's events.

Richard had not returned to Darcy House during the night, assuming his cousin would be otherwise occupied and trusting that Dr. Darcy would handle the medical needs with his typical brilliance. Besides, after taking care of matters as completely as possible considering the late hour and extending thanks to the men from his former regiment, all of whom had enjoyed themselves and shrugged off his thanks, he was exhausted and hungry for his wife's comforting arms.

However, knowing his cousin as well as he did, Richard rose early and rode straight to Darcy House after breakfasting with his new family. Once the hot pot of coffee was delivered to the combination study and library where Darcy sat waiting and steaming cups were held in their hands, Richard launched into his update.

"The men guarding the house were scum Wickham had hired. None of them had any idea they were working for the Marquis of Orman, content to take the money and ask no questions. The fear instilled by my associates and I, obviously military despite not wearing uniforms, was enough to subdue, especially after a spell in Newgate just for good measure."

He sipped gingerly, continuing, "My comrades enjoyed trussing them up and finding the ricketiest cart obtainable for the long ride back to town. A handful of coins to the gaoler and vague information on their crime will be enough to keep them in misery for a good while."

"Will they be executed?"

Richard shrugged. "It is easy to arrange that and they deserve it since they knew a woman and child had been kidnapped. Men of that ilk should not be roaming free for the next criminal to take advantage of. I will see what I can arrange and still leave your name out of it."

"Thanks. What about Orman?"

"Still raving and frothing at the mouth last I saw. Campbell and Willet took him to Bethlem. No news from them today, but I plan to visit the barracks when I leave here. I am not a doctor, Cousin, but the man seems insane to me. It might get tricky since he is a peer of the realm. However, if your name has to come into it, we can merely say he threatened you in some way and not mention Elizabeth or Alexander."

Darcy visibly relaxed, sighing and nodding in relief. "I will go to great extremes to prevent them being dragged into this and harmed in any way possible."

"Even lie?"

"I know, I know. It goes against every principle I embrace, but in this situation I will employ every ounce of my poker skills to bluff if need be."

Richard could not resist laughing. "Well, let us work on a plausible story since your skills at poker are dismal!" Darcy grunted but did smile, and Richard continued. "It will not be difficult to spin a tale. Everyone knows your past with Orman, and his insanity and living conditions are real enough. I say keep it simple and close to the truth. Call me a cynic, but I would be shocked if the authorities waste time on investigating too thoroughly. They will take one look at him, toss him into a cell, and happily confiscate what property and money he has in the name of the Crown. He will not be an enigma in that madhouse they call a hospital, I assure you. He can share a room with Lord Attenborough or Baron Warburton."

They spent a few more minutes hammering out the finer details and then broached the most distressing topic of all.

"What about Wickham? I am not crying at his demise, but he was, well…"

"Family," Darcy spat bitterly, "yes, I know." He paused for a large swallow of coffee. "What did you do with his body?"

"We took it to the yard, placed in the morgue for now. No questions will be asked, yet, but I cannot keep him there forever. May I make a suggestion?"

"By all means do."

Richard leaned forward. "From what I have deduced, the only person on this planet who will miss the wretch is Mrs. Wickham. I do sympathize with her loss since she appeared to love him. Therefore, I see no point in multiplying her grief by learning the truth about the man she was married to or how he died. Certainly knowing you were involved will add unnecessary strain that benefits no one."

"No argument there. I am not looking forward to telling Elizabeth he died at my hand, let alone sharing that with Mrs. Wickham and the Bennets."

Richard barked a laugh. "I would not worry about Elizabeth's reaction. Somehow I think she will show her gratitude and pride enthusiastically. As for the rest, here is what I propose: We know he left Mrs. Wickham over a week ago, sending her home or wherever while he came on to London. It does not matter what story he concocted for her benefit. All you have to say is that he was discovered dead on the side of the road, neck broken as a result of falling from his horse as far as can be ascertained, and you were contacted because of this."

Richard pulled a folded paper from his coat pocket, placing it into Darcy's hand. The parchment piece was yellowed with age and torn along the edges, the creases grimy after years of being stuffed into pockets, and the charcoal drawn faces smudged in places, but there was no doubt who the two smiling young men were even if their names had not been written underneath.

"I remember sitting for this," Darcy whispered mouth agape in shock. "We were days away from leaving for Cambridge. Mr. Wickham was proud that his son was to attend with me, intelligent enough to pass the entrance exams even though younger. He held such high hopes of his son's success." Darcy coughed around the tightness in his throat, not every memory involving Wickham an unhappy one, especially where Pemberley's previous steward was concerned. "Mr. Wickham requested his wife draw us. She was talented with charcoal, although not as much with paints. I have to admit that during this time, especially noting how happy his family and my father were, I completely forgot my misgivings where Wickham was concerned. For a while he was George again, my boyhood friend."

"It was among his papers, the only personal item. He did not even have a drawing or reference to his wife."

"Mr. Wickham had this framed. I remember it sitting on his desk. After he died, Wickham came for the funeral. I fulfilled Mr. Wickham's wishes in giving everything to his son, other than a few trinkets specified for others. I gave the picture no thought. Why do you think he carried it?"

"I do not know, Darcy. Perhaps in a twisted way he held a modicum of affection for the past. Or then again, maybe it was so he could look at your face and heap curses, Gypsy style. We will never know and I beg you not to let it distress you. For the sake of the present, it provides a reason for why you learned of his death and were left to handle it. And we can point to this and his past connection with your family, positive as far as most know, as a way to deflect any rumors that may arise."

"I find it difficult to believe he held any affection, so more likely the curse theory is the correct one." He folded the paper, handing it back to Richard. "Nothing ties him to Orman?"

"Nothing that I can see. Even my spies drew blanks on that count."

"What about Geoffrey Wiseman?"

"I will look into anything here in London, but he will disappear with no one the wiser, I suppose, except for your housekeeper, but I leave that in your capable hands."

"Next on my morning's agenda," Darcy said dryly. "The matter of Wickham can wait a day or two, can it not? I would like to talk to Elizabeth before contacting her family. Her insight will be invaluable, especially where Lydia is concerned."

"It is sensible to wait on this matter anyway. Two odd events, one a death and the other a crazed lunatic out for blood, involving you in the same week might raise an eyebrow or two. Best to space out the fodder for gossip."

Darcy frowned, scandal, even hinted, being something he abhorred.

"Do not worry too much, Cousin. Orman's madness will be the topic of choice, with vivid descriptions I am sure, not the death of a man no one knew. Wickham will not generate more than a sentence or two. As for Mrs. Wickham, with all due respect to Elizabeth and no wish to offend, I somehow doubt the widow will be grief stricken or lonely for long."

Darcy shook his head, unable to hold in a smile. "No, I doubt she will. Her mother will welcome her home with tears of joy, Mr. Bennet will probably be relieved, and I will make sure that her husband left a settlement to provide until husband number two is ensnared."

"That is generous of you, under the circumstances."

"Trust me, generosity has nothing to do with it, nor do I really care about Lydia, if you must know. I do, however, care deeply for my wife. And speaking of my wife, I need to check on her. Keep me informed."

"I always do. That is my lot in life, cleaning up your messes as usual, Mr. Darcy."

Darcy waved his cousin's gibe and grin away. "I think we are tied for rescuing each other, but you better watch your step or I will give erroneous parenting advice on purpose."

Darcy had refused to think of the housekeeper and her role in the abduction during the night. He did not ask George of her whereabouts until that morning after bathing and dressing, knowing that the incensed rage would interfere with the calm he needed for his family. Thus, it was mid-morning after talking with Richard and then spending time with his peacefully sleeping wife before he felt in control enough to broach the subject with his uncle and then confront the woman. The time allotted gave his mind the opportunity to rationalize the subject, deciding on the best course of action.

George had gleaned little of interest. Mrs. Smyth had been so shaken by her master's threatening anger that she was a puddle of tears and incoherency. In disgust he had given up on any questioning, banishing her to her quarters and assigning a footman to ensure she stayed put until Mr. Darcy said otherwise.

In truth, Darcy could care less how Wickham had finagled his way into Mrs. Smyth's good graces and thus into his house. Knowing the skill Wickham wielded at deception and charming women, he was not surprised and wondered why the possibility had not occurred to him. He might have been able to feel some pity for the obviously lonely, mislead woman, but the fact is that she had willingly allowed a stranger into his house and fornicated under his roof, rules that were broken in blatant disregard of his authority. Couple that with her ongoing, albeit suppressed hostility toward his wife and children, and his extensive patience was at an end.

What he was not prepared for, especially after George's description of how distraught she was the day before, was the blaze of defiance he was greeted with.

She marched into his study, Mr. Travers trailing, her face set into a haughty pose with spine stiff and hands boldly clasping the chatelaine of keys indicative of her office. Darcy sat in his imposing leather chair, composed and coldly authoritative. His momentary startlement at her demeanor did not show outwardly, nor did it cause his disciplined core to waver. Rather, it steeled his resolve.

"Mrs. Smyth, I am no longer interested in the details of your involvement with Mr. Wickham. Your misjudgment which led to your crimes is for you to bear. The proofs of your transgressions against the rules of this household, my rules, are more than sufficient to warrant your immediate dismissal. I order you to pack your belongings and vacate my house by this afternoon. My only concession, my last act of kindness if you will, for years of service will be to offer the availability of a carriage and driver to take you to a destination of your choosing. Under the circumstances I judge that more than fair."

"And what of my future livelihood? Am I to be given no recommendation for employment?"

Darcy's brow rose reflexively. "You cannot be serious? Do you honestly anticipate that I would write a letter of recommendation after what has transpired here?"

"Indeed, I would think you might consider the wisdom in securing me another post. But I will accept a letter as just payment."

Darcy was flabbergasted. But he was also irritated and perversely curious. "Please, do enlighten me as to why I should deem such absurdity 'wisdom' on my part."

She took a step nearer the desk, the whiteness of her knuckles as they gripped the metal and the ridges of her compressed lips the only obvious indications that she was not as assured as her words intended.

"Mr. Darcy, I know you are a gentleman whose reputation for propriety is of the highest importance. Positive regard amongst Society is valued by you. I would never wish to see your excellent name sullied even further than it already has been."

Darcy's face was impassive, his hands resting on the polished surface of the desk with body erect in his chair. He stared at her calmly and in silence, finally replying dispassionately, "I shall ignore the inference that my 'name' has in some manner been sullied, at least in your opinion. Let us proceed to the insinuation that I can in some way be further besmirched. I am truly curious as to what you refer."

She twitched, his relaxed query unnerving her. "People love to talk, Mr. Darcy, even if the facts are erroneous. Gossip can lead to scandal."

His eyes, those piercing eyes of glacial blue, bore unwaveringly into her face. "Indeed, this can be true. However, I still do not see how this pertains to me or any member of my household."

"Why… it is simple! Mrs. Darcy taken in the night, gone for hours with a man of the criminal element. One can easily imagine what probably transpired during that time!"

"And you have some sort of proof of this allegation?"

"I… I beg your pardon? Proof? But surely there will be inquiries?"

"Let me save your time and mine, Mrs. Smyth. Whatever you think happened yesterday may as well be a figment of your imagination. None shall utter a word of it to anyone. And if *you* do, no one will hearken to a disgruntled employee who has been discharged under disgrace for consorting immorally with one Geoffrey Wiseman, a known swindler who has disappeared."

"But, you said he was this Wickham."

"George Wickham is dead, madam."

She gasped, staggering backward at that shocking revelation.

Darcy continued in his calm but flatly commanding tone. "Mr. Wickham died several days ago from a fall off his horse while returning to his wife in Devon. Geoffrey Wiseman, however, is a thief who was improperly admitted to the townhouse of a valued, well-regarded gentleman of London Society by his housekeeper. If need be, those will be the facts circulated. Tell me, Mrs. Smyth, who do you think will be believed?"

"Sir, please."

"I will take the chatelaine now, Mrs. Smyth. You have two hours to gather your possessions. The carriage will be awaiting you in the mews for a destination of your choosing, outside of London. You are dismissed. Mr. Travers, see Mrs. Smyth to her quarters."

Chapter Twenty

And Life Continues On

Richard Fitzwilliam and George Darcy were practically clairvoyant in their assessments regarding Lizzy.

Two days passed before she was clear-headed enough to hear the entire tale of brave deeds and daring rescue. The death of Wickham and status of Lord Orman brought only relief and a suppressed glee that she knew was unattractive but could not hide from her husband. Darcy glossed over the more gruesome details, Lizzy not murderous enough to require a precise picture of Wickham's broken, bloody body or Orman's breakdown, but his theatrical tendencies emerged in recounting the exploits and suspense. Largely this was unconsciously done, but he did hope that inserting a fantastical element to the adventure would dilute the reality of how dangerous and terrifying it truly had been.

She was immeasurably proud of her spouse, extolling his courage with a wealth of glowing adjectives until he blushed and begged her to stop. He attempted to downplay his injuries, but naturally she saw through his dissembling and was not satisfied until personally examining the healing bruises and scalp wound.

"Now, if you are appeased with my health and vigor, I wanted your advice on how to proceed with the announcement of Wickham's death."

"You have notified no one?"

He shook his head, apprising her of Richard's counsel on the subject. "I would have proceeded but was not sure how you felt about telling your father. Goodness knows your mother must not know the truth, but perhaps Mr. Bennet should. Yet I am unsure the wisdom of troubling him over your health when it no longer matters."

"No, please do not tell him. There is no point, as you say. I am fine and do not wish to burden him unnecessarily."

"Agreed. Then I shall write immediately, as if I have just been informed. I trust he will know how to contact Mrs. Wickham?"

"I have her address written in my directory, not that I have bothered corresponding in ages."

"Oh, I did not know. Excellent. I shall dispatch a courier with the news and funds to transport her and whatever belongings she has to Longbourn."

"That is more than you should do, William."

"Let us pray she will mature through her grief and make wiser choices in the future."

Lizzy shook her head sadly. "I fear your optimism destined to be disappointed. Most likely she will lament for as long as it takes to ensnare another man when he takes pity upon the poor widow, Lord forgive my uncharitable attitude."

Darcy smiled, kissing her forehead before replying, "I forgive you if that counts, but then I am as uncharitable since I said much the same to Richard."

"What is the current status of Lord Orman? He has said nothing of the abduction?" Her eyes were large and haunted, the shadows underneath darkening against the pallor his name increased.

"The Marquis is under evaluation at Bethlem and not saying anything worthwhile," Darcy assured in a firm tone. "George has seen the patient daily and is keeping abreast of the situation. The diagnosis is not definitive, the doctors hoping to cure in time, as all doctors do, but that does not look to be imminent or probable. He raved bestially for over a day without ceasing, so I am informed. A straitjacket was required to prevent self-injury, as he was devil-possessed in his mania. His words were recorded, most indecipherable or nonsensical, and my name was mentioned. Or at least 'Darcy' was mentioned, but nothing beyond that. Then, yesterday afternoon he abruptly passed into a stuporous petrifaction. George calls it catalepsy or cataleptoid insanity. I have no idea what it means, but the prognosis is poor, he says, and the condition prevents any verbalization."

Lizzy shuddered, Darcy drawing her closer against his side with a sturdy squeeze. They lounged on their bed, Lizzy yet weak and needing to recuperate further before moving outside their chambers. "I pray he never recovers," she said with heated conviction. "It terrifies me to imagine him loose again, no matter how assured the doctors are of his revived mental state."

Darcy agreed and prayed for the same without a shred of remorse. He did not vocalize his vengeful thoughts to his wife, settling for tender caresses to the raw rope burns on her wrists and gentle kisses to the fading bruises on her cheeks as a means to convey his protectiveness. His heart was stone where it concerned Lord Orman and his conviction firm that the madman would never take one step beyond the asylum's walls. Whatever was required to ensure Orman's incarceration and safe distance from his family would be done—legal or illegal.

Dr. Darcy, although not trained as a physician for mental ailments, had some experience with madmen of varied types. "Lord Orman's condition is as horrible as I have ever seen, William," he said the previous evening after returning from Bethlem and a conference with the physicians there. "Some patients reanimate, but not typically. Caring for their basic survival needs takes top priority over mental treatment, and maintaining physical health when they refuse to eat, drink, or move is extremely difficult. I suppose you can deduce what the common outcome is without my illuminating."

Indeed Darcy could, mustering not an iota of sadness in the idea.

"Well," he said to his wife, "if he ever does return to reality and coherency it will be far in the future. No need to fret about it at this point. And since there is no evidence of an abduction ever occurring, it does not matter what claims he asserts. You have been stricken with a nasty cold but are rapidly mending. That is all anyone need know, unless you chose to reveal otherwise."

"Thank you, my darling." She sighed deeply, closing her eyes as she wiggled into the warm mattress, her arms tight around his waist and head on his chest. "I trust you to manage as fitting." And moments later she was asleep, Darcy holding her for nearly thirty minutes before pulling away to attend to the final disposition of Mr. Wickham's body to Hertfordshire.

In the days that followed Darcy strived to create a façade of normalcy by conducting business as planned and keeping most of his appointments. It was difficult, as residual anxiety affected his concentration and produced an aversion to leaving the house. George calmed his fears, wisely pointing out that his appearance in public would quash any rumors that might be swirling about and that physical activity was the best balm for a wounded spirit. "Much like climbing back on the horse after a nasty fall," he said with a wink.

Darcy did frown and equivocate some, but he knew the recommendation was sound. He was reassured by Georgiana's steadying presence, trusting that she would inform him instantly if his family needed him. Therefore, he met with Mr. Daniels and other business associates, scheduled interviews with potential housekeepers, engaged in a rigorous bout at Angelo's, and enjoyed one rousing race around the military horse track with Richard and several others. The constant activity did help restore his mental equilibrium and expend the residual anger coiled within his body. Nevertheless, his thoughts were never far from Darcy House and he returned home as quickly as possible. Evening engagements were canceled so he could spend the hours alone with wife and sons, the three needing his strength and comfort during the long hours of darkness where nightmares stalked.

The excuse of Lizzy suffering a spring cold was accepted since it was a common ailment. Of course her lady friends were worried, sending well wishes and colorful blooms to cheer her, but they understood her need to rest and preference for solitude. Jane and Mary came by with fresh soup, a special family recipe served when any of them were sick. After a heavy application of powder and rouge to hide the fading bruises and donning a long-sleeved gown to cover her healing wrists, Lizzy welcomed them with honest enthusiasm. She was delighted at the interruption to her bland convalescence. Yet, within seconds of asking about her illness, before speaking the rehearsed pretext, she burst into tears.

Needless to say the sisters were baffled and distressed. Georgiana, who possessed no skills in the art of deception, was instantly in tears as well and helpless in salvaging the situation. Lizzy blurted the entire truth in one long sentence, words stumbling over each other and largely incoherent. But finally the story was told in its entirety and the relief Lizzy felt in talking about her memories and experience was strangely cathartic. Georgiana and Darcy had thus far been her only confidants, but Lizzy tended to hold back and gloss over the dreams that plagued her sleep to spare their distress.

After talking with her sisters she was amazed at how much freer her soul felt. A weight was lifted in sharing every tiny detail with them, many that grew clearer or were newly recalled in that hour. That night her sleep was undisturbed except for vague visions shrouded in mist that lacked the power they once wielded. It was then that she realized it was best for her state of mind to be honest. She decided she would rather her closest friends know the truth, trusting in their secrecy and empathy, than perpetuate a lie. Darcy agreed but insisted on channeling the information through the husbands rather than her reiterating and reliving the trauma, and during a long, relaxing afternoon at White's, he sketchily outlined the incident.

"I trust that you each know your wives' temperaments best," he said, "and can edit the tale as befitting. Please stress that Elizabeth is recuperating rapidly and free of any residual sequelae. In fact, her temper is chafing at the convalescence Dr. Darcy and I are insisting upon." He smiled genuinely, his wife's rising waspishness a sure sign of her restoration to the woman he loved. "All I ask is that questions are kept to a minimum unless initiated by her."

To the latter they all agreed.

George Darcy was clairvoyant in his assessment that few days would pass before Darcy was scolding his wife for complaining, vociferously, that she was perfectly fine and ready to enjoy the marvelous spring weather. Darcy stubbornly insisted she walk no further than their terrace and garden. Grudgingly and with some grumbling, Lizzy complied with his overprotective demands since her stomach remained delicate and fatigue struck at odd moments even after all other symptoms resolved. Considering what had transpired it was logical to assign her complaints to that, but neither had forgotten the possibility of a pregnancy even if the topic had not been broached.

On the morning of the fifth day when she lurched up in the bed, inhaling forcefully, with one hand clamped over her mouth and the other searching frantically for the blanket edge, Darcy knew it was time to discuss his feelings on the concept of another baby.

She returned to bed, shaky and pale, sheer force of will preventing disgorgement this time at least.

"Do not smile at me, Mr. Darcy," she snapped, which only caused his smile to widen. She crawled under the quilt, pointedly lying so that her back was to him, and mumbled grumpily, "I am not in the mood for smiles. Smiles will surely increase my nausea and I may chose to turn your way rather than dash to the chamber pot. Purposefully."

He caressed one hand down her arm, bending to plant a soft kiss to her shoulder. "I apologize, love. Dare I inquire as to what is irritating you most, being cooped up inside or your nausea? If it is the former I believe I have a solution that may elicit a smile, despite your displeasure for the gesture."

"What solution?"

"Oh, nothing too extravagant. Merely a gathering in Hyde Park on the morrow with all of our friends."

She turned her face toward him then, the corners of her mouth lifting although her eyes narrowed. "You are not teasing me, are you?"

"Would I do that?"

"Ha! Yes, you would!"

He shook his head. "Not about something as vitally important to the workings of the universe as a picnic I wouldn't. Dining outside is serious business."

Now she was smiling and turned toward him. "A picnic? Truly? That is a marvelous idea! Who have you invited?"

"Our closest friends. The Bingleys, Vernors, Daniels, Drurys, Lathrops, Fitzherberts, Fitzwilliams, and so on. And I plan to extend the invitation to Mr. Butler after we speak today, since I am fairly certain he will be betrothed to my sister as a result of our converse."

"You figured that out all on your own?"

"Happy to see your sense of humor has returned, Mrs. Darcy. Indeed the puzzle was rather easy to solve since every day he finds himself in the general area of Grosvenor Square, spontaneously pausing to extend his respects. The casual offers to accompany Georgiana on walks or shopping excursions that no man in his proper state of mind would desire to suffer through was a large clue. But if that had not penetrated my thick skull, even I am not so dim-witted or unobservant to miss the loving glances and surreptitious caresses."

"She has been waiting until the time was right, not wishing to add to your distress. I told her she was being ridiculous and that you would be thrilled. You are, are you not?"

"I can think of no impediments to the match. He is a good man and clearly in love with my sister. I recognize the pose when it is sincere. Furthermore, I like him."

"I regret that I have been unable to interact with him more. Of course I am hearing of his perfection via Georgiana, but that assessment may be slightly skewed."

Darcy chuckled and nodded. "Indeed the term 'perfection' may be over-reaching, but he is a quality gentleman. I may not comprehend the musical discussions that frequently arise, generally choosing to vacate the premises when that topic is attended to, but he is equally versed in estate matters, horsemanship, and politics. He is also proficient at the billiard table."

"Well that seals it then! As long as he is not better than you," she teased.

"Surely I am allowed to retain one area of preeminence in my sister's eyes since all others have been transferred to Mr. Butler?"

He smoothed the hair away from her bright face, bending to kiss each humorously glittering eye and then her lilting lips.

"So were you smiling due to your sister's betrothal or the picnic?"

"Both fill me with delight, I confess. However, the impetuous for this particular smile, as saddened as I am by your peaked stomach, is the fervent hope that your lingering symptoms indicate we are blessed with a new life on the way."

He spoke barely above a whisper, running one hand down her satin-gowned torso to rest upon her flat abdomen.

Lizzy touched his cheek. "Is this honestly how you feel, Fitzwilliam?"

"I will not lie or pretend that my initial reaction was not one of terror. I confess this and apologize for how I responded, Elizabeth."

"It was your heart and natural given the situation."

"Perhaps. Nevertheless it was wrong of me. I want you to know, beloved, that all afternoon, before any of the tragedy to follow, I realized how mistaken my sentiments." He told her then of his visions of a daughter and his tremendous remorse at departing the house with unsettling tensions between them. "I chastised myself a fool, mostly for not conveying my feelings adequately or prioritizing us and our relationship over an afternoon's entertainments. To be frank, my thoughts regarding a baby so soon were tumultuous still, until faced with the horror of losing you, Alexander, and our unborn child. That I would include her, or him, in that appalling possibility added to my distress as you cannot fathom, Elizabeth, but it clarified how I truly felt about the idea."

His hand continued to rub gentle circles over her belly while the other pressed her palm tight against his cheek. "Every child will be welcomed and loved immensely, my dearest, whenever God chooses to bless us. Please forgive my lack of enthusiasm and any heartache my poorly chosen words caused. Trust me when I say that every shred of doubt or dismay has been erased with only joy remaining."

Lizzy responded by weaving her fingers into the thick hair on the back of his head and drawing him back to her mouth with firm insistence.

The other arm clenched around his back, aided by a leg thrown over his hips, both working to drag him onto her body. It was a demand and affirmation Darcy complied with, his hands greedily skimming over her satin-gowned flesh and pressing her against his chest.

For several minutes they kissed as if starved, rousing desire fueled by the need to erase the turmoil of the past week. Breathing erratic, Darcy parted from her lips to whisper, "Is this a thank-you for arranging the picnic or for granting my sister's happiness or both?"

"Neither," she retorted with a chuckle. "Or perhaps those points add to my hunger for you, but primarily it is simply that we have not made love since a week ago on your desk…"

He interrupted with a husky growl, trailing suckles along her neck, "What a titillating vision to conjure now!"

"Indeed. And as nice as a reenactment may be, I do not wish to delay even to walk there."

"Elizabeth, are you sure we should do this now when…"

She clamped her palm over his mouth, eyes blazing with passion and irritation. "I am not constructed of glass, Fitzwilliam! Why is it that every time I develop the merest sniffle or cough you insist on believing me barely strong enough to raise a teacup and far too weak to engage in activity remotely strenuous when I insist I shall recuperate swifter if allowed to move about and maybe even make love to my husband, no matter how annoying I consider him at the moment, and when will you get it through that stubborn brain of yours that I *am* tough and if strong enough to birth babies I can…."

The verbal lashing that showed every sign of continuing on indefinitely was halted when he finally managed to peel her gripping fingertips from his face and clamped his mouth firmly over hers. The kiss startled her into silence, but did not last long since Darcy lost his battle in repressing laughter.

"My spunky wife is back in full form, praises to God!" he gasped amid the laughs. "And, I pray, your vacillating temper is further indication of pregnancy." He traced a fingertip over her knitted brows, still chuckling as he continued, "I plead guilty of zealous guarding when you are incapacitated in any way and shall make no promises to ever change, as it is my character and duty. But believing you made of glass? Not at all! More tempered steel and pyracantha thorns are you, Mrs. Darcy! If I doubted your strength, and I never have, the doubt would have been erased after examining the gouged earth as evidence of how you fought Wickham. And do not think I did not notice the scratches on his cheeks. Gave me a thrill, I must tell you. I could not be prouder."

"Then why the persistent mollycoddling?"

"I *mollycoddle* because I enjoy taking care of you, Elizabeth. If my attentiveness disturbs you I will try in future to reign in my need to excessively hover."

"Well, no," she mumbled, lowering her eyes in contrition. "I do appreciate your concern and know I am blessed to have a husband who cares so thoroughly." She glanced upward into his glittering eyes, voice again surly as she added, "Even if he is a nuisance about it."

"A nuisance am I? Hmmm, then perhaps I should leave and not stay home with you all day as I planned. I would not wish the label to advance from nuisance to burdensome pest!"

She lifted her chin, piercing him with a stern glare. "You may stay home, if you promise not to baby me or limit my activity. I want to move beyond this chamber even if it does tire me and I want to make love! Will you agree to my terms?"

"Did you totally miss my clever innuendos and unveiled glances when I announced I had canceled my appointment with Lathrop so I could remain at Darcy House today? Either I have lost my skills or your perceptions are still blunted from your illness, in which case perhaps we should wait a while longer," he teased.

Lizzy harrumphed but did flush faintly. "Not on your life! Now you have committed to the course, so do not try to back out of it again!" And she forcefully pulled his entire body back onto hers, not that he had moved too far away, with limbs insistent in their assault and mouth eager to reengage.

The bulk of their nightclothes were removed and both far along the road to full arousal before any words were spoken. Darcy pulled away, primarily to doff his shirt, but paused to ask, "Clarify one thing. When was it that I tried to back out of loving you?"

"When you asked if I was sure we should do this now. After waiting for nearly a week I was in no mood to listen to reasons why we should not be together." She pressed her fingertips to his lips, her eyes shiny with emotion. "Loving you, having you love me, is what is needed to restore us both, Fitzwilliam. We need to erase any vestiges of fear over what might have been. We need to immerse ourselves in the other, loving hard to declare our vitality and passion."

"I could not agree more, dearest." He resumed his roost atop her, their naked flesh melting together as he smoothly embedded himself deep within her, commencing a slow rhythm. He drew her bottom lip between his teeth, his tongue sweeping across before releasing to speak between kisses. "The only reason I have not ravished you days ago and proven my burning need for you is simply because time has been against us, Elizabeth. I have been as exhausted as you and torn in numerous directions. I did not want to rush our lovemaking, and that was what I was about to ask before you flared at me."

He rose on his elbows, maintaining the steady thrusts that were rapidly causing every coherent thought to flitter out of Lizzy's brain, and encircled each milk-heavy breast with a broad hand. "I only meant if we should wait until after Michael needed you." He bent and licked over one taut nipple, Lizzy's laugh lost in a throaty moan of pleasure. "But now it is too late. He must learn patience as I no longer care to be a concerned father." He moved to the other nipple, applying the same treatment. "Right now I am the impassioned lover intent upon his wife. I trust this pleases you and fulfills your terms?"

Lizzy nodded, limbs squeezing tightly and body rocking to match his exuberant tempo, and her breathy *yes* in answer to his question was repeated over and over as a fervent affirmation of her pleasure.

Darcy entered his study precisely at eleven o'clock smiling and whistling. In every way the morning had passed delightfully. The refreshing lovemaking with his incredible wife was followed by a visit from Michael, and then Alexander, the four of them breakfasting together. Once the boys returned to the nursery, Michael for a nap and Alexander for his lessons in the alphabet with Mrs. Hanford, he and Lizzy sat on the terrace overlooking the back garden. They talked about general topics, such as the mundane matters of household management and society gossip he had noted for her benefit, as well as weightier subjects involving their children.

"Has it occurred to you that this baby, if you are indeed with child, would probably be born around Christmas time?"

Lizzy's eyes widened in surprise and the teacup heading toward her mouth halted mid-air. "I… Well, no, I didn't… Are you sure?"

Darcy laughed, mostly because she was now tapping out the months with her fingertips on the arm of the sofa they sat on. "We cannot say for certain, of course. But it is a rough guess since we are well into April and you are just feeling symptoms." He swallowed a mouthful of tea and watched her face. "I rather like the idea of a baby as a Christmas present."

She turned to him with a smile that was so brilliant and countenance so animated with joy that his breath caught and his teacup also hung forgotten in space. They stared transfixed while their hearts quickened, finally leaning for a soft kiss. They never cared to analyze how it happened, but in short order they ended up back in their bed with no ready recollection as to how they got there other than vague images of clothes shed in haste—proven by the scattered garments trailing all the way to the terrace—a vast amount of kissing and touching, and someone slamming the door with a resounding crash.

Taken all together, Darcy was in an excellent mood when he greeted Mr. Sebastian Butler, who was early for their appointment and awaiting him in the sunny room.

"Mr. Darcy"—he bowed—"thank you for agreeing to meet with me today. I know your time is precious and concerns heavy at the moment. May I inquire as to Mrs. Darcy's health?"

"Thank you for your solicitude, Mr. Butler." He sat down in the leather wingback near the window, waving a hand toward the identical Chippendale on the other side of the small square table bearing a pitcher of lemonade and two glasses. "Lemonade?" He poured two tall glasses of the cool beverage, speaking as he did so, "Assuming I am correct in my deductions based on the week's interactions, I am guessing Miss Darcy is forthright with you and has revealed that Mrs. Darcy is not suffering from a cold."

Butler took the glass, meeting Darcy's gaze boldly but with a hint of worry. "Thank you. And you are correct in your assumption. I hope you are not dismayed by Miss Darcy's disclosure of a private matter or, worse yet, angry at her?"

Darcy smiled and shook his head. "I have never found it easy or natural to be angry at my sister for anything. Rather it is most comfortable for me to indulge and spoil liberally. I daresay you may encounter the same difficulties."

"I already have," the younger man confessed with a laugh.

"Glad to hear it. Truthfully, if the relationship between our branches of the family were the same as two years ago when we first met, Mr. Butler, I would not be forgiving in the least. I am a very private person and this particular situation is emphatically one I do not want discussed openly." He paused, piercing

Mr. Butler with an intense scrutiny. The moment stretched, Sebastian maintaining the contact, his face open and relaxed. Finally Darcy nodded, visibly loosening his posture and easing back into the cushioned chair. "Obviously the relationship between our families has altered and I am thankful you were here as a support for my sister. Your company and dependability were invaluable. I owe you a debt of gratitude, Mr. Butler."

"Thank you, sir, but you owe me nothing. It has been my pleasure, and relief, to be here for Miss Darcy and to comfort as possible."

"It is easy to identify the nature of your relationship with my sister so unless I am grossly mistaken in my conclusions, I presume you have a request of me?"

His smile was friendly, in truth his heart overjoyed at his sister's great fortune. Therefore, he was surprised when Mr. Butler sat his glass down and leaned forward with a serious cast to his face.

"Indeed you are correct, Mr. Darcy. My feelings for Miss Darcy are strong and sure. I am not at all being melodramatic when I say that I would be crushed beyond repair if your response to my desires regarding Miss Darcy were not granted in a positive way. I believe she would be crushed as well." He lost his composure briefly, clearing his throat before continuing. "My affections for Miss Darcy are genuine and intense, as is my respect for her and appreciation of her relationship with you. In the weeks we spent together as friends prior to our sentiments maturing to love, we talked frankly, on dozens of occasions, about our families. I am sure it is no surprise to you, sir, that Miss Darcy is devoted to her family, primarily you. I easily comprehend this, as my devotion to my sisters is as powerful. It is out of this comprehension and respect that I wish to be honest before formally asking for Miss Darcy's hand in marriage."

"Is there some impediment to your union I am unaware of?"

"No! Not in any way you might imagine. I promise that. My heart is set and constancy on my part, and I trust on Miss Darcy's part as well, is not in question. Please, bear with me as I explain."

He paused again, taking a large gulp of lemonade to wet his parched throat. "You know, of course, that as the eldest son I will someday inherit my father's title and lands. God willing this will not occur for many years or decades to come, but I want to assure you, Mr. Darcy, that my ancestry and estate are dear to me. Miss Darcy will be a wonderful Lady Essenton, I have no doubt, and I will be blessed to have her by my side in that capacity, when the time comes. However, you may not fully appreciate that music has forever been my first passion. I have single-mindedly pursued this course; it is a drive that has unfortunately created some tension between my father and I. Additionally, my focus on music nearly caused me to lose Miss Darcy, both of us misinterpreting our goals and desires profoundly."

He chuckled then, sitting back into the chair and shaking his head. "I am not sure if you can empathize, sir, but young people newly in love can be stupid about it!"

"You might be surprised how well I empathize, Mr. Butler," Darcy answered dryly.

"Well, it appears we both have intriguing stories to tell. The point I am struggling to make is that although my love for Miss Darcy supersedes everything else, I am not prepared to give up on my dreams and studies. Nor does Geor... Miss Darcy wish me to." He blushed at the slip, but Darcy just smiled, nodding for him to continue. "And this brings me to the crux of the matter. The truth is that among the numerous attributes I love about your sister and the commonalities we share, our musical passion and gifts bind us in a unique way."

He scooted forward in his chair, zeal etched upon his face and in every gesture. "Mr. Darcy, do you realize how phenomenally talented your sister is? She is incredibly gifted in both composing and playing, and this is not just a lover speaking. I recognized her talents well before my heart was lost. Furthermore, I have shared her work with professors and musicians at the Conservatoire in Paris, each one impressed by her skill. We both recognize that we do not possess the brilliance of the great masters, but our hearts are as one in our yearning to embrace this shared passion. In fact, we have discovered our inspiration and proficiency improved with collaboration."

"Mr. Butler," Darcy interrupted, "so far all you have said merely affirms my pleasure in granting you the hand of my sister, so I am confused as to where the conversation is leading. Georgiana is transparent in her feelings toward you and vice versa, and despite my distraction this past week, I have not been unaware of the piano music constantly drifting through the halls. I make no claim to possess a finely discerning ear for music, but I will attest that what I have been hearing is fantastic."

Sebastian's head lifted in pride, his gray eyes bright. "Thank you for the compliment. You are correct, however, in that I have been rambling a bit. Very well, I shall be blunt." He took a deep breath and kept his eyes steady upon Darcy's face. "Mr. Darcy, I humbly and with all my heart bare before you, ask for the honor of marrying Miss Georgiana Darcy. I promise to fulfill every vow placed upon me by God and the love I hold for her. I have tendered my heartfelt proposal to her and she has accepted. We will bow to your wishes in the matter, but our prayer is that you will agree and allow us to marry before the summer is over as we mutually desire relocating to Paris, where we are enrolled for study at the Conservatoire in the fall."

Darcy blinked in surprise. "Georgiana has been accepted into the Conservatoire?"

"With honors, sir."

Sebastian controlled the urge to squirm impatiently in his chair, waiting a full minute for a silent Darcy to respond. When he did, the surge of relieved energy was so intense Sebastian experienced a moment of extreme lightheadedness and almost missed the words uttered.

"I cannot believe she has kept silent." Darcy's voice was an awed murmur, followed by a shout of amazement. "This is extraordinary! I am no longer sure which brings me greater delight, her fortune in securing a quality man who loves her or this incredible accomplishment. By God, a Darcy studying in Paris! And music no less." He laughed again, grinning and blue eyes shining when he refocused on Mr. Butler's face. "I cannot recall the first time Georgiana sat on a piano stool. My mother attempted to teach me how to play, and I learned the basics, but lacked the aptitude or interest. I remember once when Georgie was seven I sat beside her on the bench of our old harpsichord, turning pages as she impressed Father and me with new material she had been practicing. She began a sonata by Scarlatti, one of the few pieces I knew how to play tolerably well, so I joined in. We played all three movements, Georgiana smiling and nodding encouragingly throughout. I knew my poor proficiency was unmatched to the skill she wielded even then, but she adjusted her tempo to my dismal performance, laughing and applauding as if it were brilliant and the highlight of the evening."

"Yes, I can imagine the scene. She is eternally gracious and encouraging."

"Indeed, I shall not argue that truism. However, she later forced me to sit at the harpsichord as she explained my errors, enumerating each one and demonstrating the proper way to play the notes. She was patient and kind, but also amazingly firm that I practice until I learned it correctly!"

They both laughed, Darcy shaking his head. "Tenacious and passionate, at seven! And now to study with the masters in Paris. I should have foreseen this future coming to pass, yet I never have imagined it. Thank you, Mr. Butler, for inspiring my sister to fulfill this dream."

"Then you are not disturbed by the idea? Of her attending the Conservatoire, I mean."

Darcy lifted a brow, tone conveying his astonishment. "Not at all. Did she believe I would be? Is that the reason for the secrecy?"

"She was unsure. I was unsure. From your perspective, all of this"—Sebastian waved his hand—"me, Paris, marriage, must appear abrupt and overwhelming. Compound the matter with the notion of a woman studying, a concept not as accepted in England as it is abroad, and we feared your opposition."

"A few years ago I would have balked at the prospect, I admit. And I am certain I would not allow her to dwell in Paris as an unmarried lady." He shrugged. "Then again, surrounding myself with highly accomplished and extremely independent women as I have these past years has broadened my thinking. At least to a degree, since I am relieved she will be accompanied by her husband."

"Her husband," Sebastian repeated dreamily, a ridiculous grin upon his face. "I do adore the vision that phrase conjures." At Darcy's low chuckle he collected himself with a start, flushing and clearing his throat. "Then, I… May I conclude we have your blessing, Mr. Darcy? Have I the honor of formally announcing Miss Darcy is my betrothed?"

"Indeed you do, Mr. Butler."

Sebastian exhaled in a gush, closing his eyes for a moment before jumping up with the unleashed enthusiasm of a man giddy in love. "Thank you, sir! You have no idea how happy I am! How happy *we* are at your approval."

"You are mistaken, Mr. Butler. I have perfect knowledge of how happy you are. Discovering one's partner in life is a divine gift." He rose and extended his hand to his future brother-in-law. "I have hoped and prayed for Georgiana to be as fortunate as I have been with Mrs. Darcy. You have brought happiness and relief into my life by treasuring my sister, and I thank you for that."

"I do treasure her, very much. I want you to know as well that I have planned our immediate future most carefully. Lady Warrow owns a *maison de ville* in Paris where we will reside with every comfort Miss Darcy deserves and is accustomed to. Money is plentiful so she will want for nothing. We both have friends there, so she will not be without society and companionship. My mother is already renovating a suite at Whistlenell Hall and organizing a grand reception before we leave to Europe, though I warned both actions were precipitous, and my father is gradually adjusting to the idea of Miss Darcy as my chosen bride…"

"I beg your pardon?" Darcy interrupted roughly. "Why would he need to adjust to the idea? Does Lord Essenton have an issue with Miss Darcy?"

Sebastian sucked in his breath. "Forgive me, Mr. Darcy. I should have explained the difficulties with my father more thoroughly. Be assured that Lord Essenton has never, not once, spoken against Miss Darcy in any way. How could he? She has impeccable manners, a lovely personality, culture and beauty, excellent credentials…"

"I know all this. No need to state the obvious. Yet he does not approve?"

"His… reluctance is not based on Miss Darcy in particular. Rather it is his displeasure with the path I have chosen in life. Or, to be blunt, his displeasure with me not walking the path he prefers I do. I respect my father greatly, sir, but he and I have not always seen eye to eye."

Sebastian straightened, jutting his chin and suddenly looking years older than twenty-three. Darcy's brow lifted at the abrupt maturity; Sebastian continuing in a firm timbre, "I alluded to some of this in regards to my musical pursuits. Lord Essenton has never comprehended my desires and I regret to confess the battles have been bitter at times. His displeasure pains me, but I am not a man to be bullied and have pursued my studies regardless."

"I see. Has he learned to accept your choice?"

"He tolerates it, primarily due to my grandmother's influence and support. Yet also because I have promised him innumerable times that music and my dreams of study and composing do not supplant my love for our estate. He does not concur, but I see no reason both cannot be a part of my life. I think that despite my verbalized conviction he persists in considering it a phase I will grow out of."

Darcy was nodding and rubbing his chin. "I know Lord Essenton more by reputation than personal familiarity, but do believe I can guess that he now sees marriage as a distraction and further upset—especially to a lady as passionate about music as you. Correct?"

"Partially this is the case. Mainly I think he is simply so accustomed to disagreeing with all I do that the argument comes naturally and without forethought." Sebastian shrugged, but his expression revealed his sorrow while remaining resolute. "However, the other area we have long disagreed upon is his insistence that I marry a cousin on my mother's side. To be frank, the lady in question disgusts me for numerous reasons, but even if that were not the case, I have steadfastly refused to marry anyone other than whom I chose: a woman I love and who meets the standards I require, not my father. I trust you can understand and not think less of me for being a disobedient son?"

"Oh indeed," Darcy said with a laugh, clapping the younger man on the shoulder and steering toward the door. "I can completely understand and now my opinion of you has risen dramatically! What is it about marrying cousins that so appeals to older relatives?"

Sebastian frowned at the question, but Darcy was not expecting an answer. "Now, we better end this conversation since I am sure Georgiana and my wife are at the extreme ends of their patience. Actually, I am surprised Mrs. Darcy has not stormed into the library demanding we speed matters along!"

Instantly upon exiting the library the sound of piano music was heard escaping from the nearby parlor. Sebastian's puzzled frown turned to a smile and he began to chuckle even before Darcy spoke. "At least my sister is managing to remain calm. But then music always soothes her."

"I do not think it is working very well," Sebastian countered, stopping in the hallway and waving a hand toward the distant doorway and the invisible notes floating on the air. "The cadence is too harsh through here, the notes are rushed, and I can hear her nails striking the keys." He paused to listen. "And... There, yes, I knew she would muddle that particular chord if she were vexed or agitated!"

"That is not a positive sign. If my sister is strained then Mrs. Darcy is probably bleeding from needle-pierced fingertips or pacing to resist throwing something. We best hurry..."

"What in blazes could be taking so long?" Lizzy's strident declaration followed by the heavy thud of a book onto a tabletop interrupted his words. The music abruptly died with the end sound composed of random keys chiming discordantly when Georgiana's hands slammed down.

"You do not think he could be saying no, do you?"

"Of course not! He has probably taken Mr. Butler off to the billiard room to celebrate with a game and brandy! I may have to strangle him!"

The men's appearance on the threshold went momentarily unnoticed as Lizzy continued to rant of how she intended to punish her spouse, her tirade stopping when Darcy cleared his throat.

Georgiana gasped, frozen for a span of seconds with hand to her breast, but the stasis broke at the sheepish but dazzling smile Sebastian directed her way. She flew off the piano bench and was across the room before her fiancé took a breath, barreling into his body and embracing tightly.

Darcy was gazing with lifted brow at his irritated wife, Lizzy not appreciating his humor at the words she knew he must have heard. Yet they both melted at the sight of Georgiana's effusive happiness. Then Darcy was taken aback when she left Mr. Butler's arms after mere moments to launch into his.

"Thank you, Brother! Thank you! You have made me the happiest woman alive! But did you have to take so long?" And she actually punched him in the arm.

"Hey! We had numerous matters to discuss, such as your admission to the Conservatoire, Miss Darcy."

"Are you pleased?" He nodded once, grinning. "So we can marry soon and be together in Paris studying?"

"Georgiana, I would never stand in the way of love being fulfilled, or your musical ambitions for that matter. I am incredibly proud." This time he enfolded her within his embrace, not letting go for a long while.

Sebastian was unable to steal his beloved away for private kisses and conversation for hours, but the afternoon and evening brought immeasurable joy nevertheless, as he grew closer to the people dearest to his future wife. Preliminary plans were set in motion for a late spring wedding, the men frequently lost in the ensuing discussions, and not a single person thought of the recent traumas.

Love remained the greatest healing force, so it seems.

CHAPTER TWENTY-ONE

On the Banks of the Serpentine

Y OU LOOK ABSOLUTELY BEAUTIFUL, Mrs. Darcy."

He crossed the room, fingers lifting to tie the bonnet strings under her chin.

"Thank you, dearest. I desperately need to stretch my legs, so I also thank you for allowing me to leave the house."

"Since when have my allowing or not had any bearing on your actions, especially walking?" He shook his head while laughing. "I can recall perhaps a handful of occasions when my dominating demands were harkened to when you disagreed with me. In this instance I surmised this venture wise for everyone involved, as it may improve your grouchiness."

"It *will* improve my grouchiness, I can assure you. Being cooped up irritates me…"

"Yes, I know," he agreed with a teasing lift to his left brow.

"I shall not deny it. And I will only partially blame you and the good doctor for keeping me chained to the house since I admit to not being hale enough to journey far. Of course, a large part of that is entirely your fault, Mr. Darcy."

"Ah, I see we are going to start that standard accusation again, even before we are certain." He grinned, extending his arm, which she readily took.

"Indeed we are. I am preparing you for the eventuality, whether I am with child now or at a later date." She tiptoed and planted a firm kiss to his dimpled chin. "How do I look? Well enough?"

He grasped her chin between his thumb and forefinger, turning her uplifted, smiling face side-to-side. "Hmmm… Rosy, if a bit pale from want of sunlight. Eyes clear, lively, and sparkling. Cheeks full and nose pert. Adorable in every way and full of youthful vigor. Quite perfect, my dearest wife. Perfect."

"Thank you."

"As stunning and hearty as you appear, are you sure you shall not be overcome with nausea midway along the promenade?"

"I make no promises. But my stomach is currently stable and I do not plan to embarrass you in front of all London society."

"I was only thinking of you possibly messing this gorgeous gown. I would be standing there foolishly grinning and declaring to any onlookers that my divine wife may soon be presenting me with a daughter."

"Ridiculous man. Now who is leaping ahead before we are certain? In all seriousness, thank you, William, for planning today and setting aside your business to be with us."

"Nothing pleases me more than the thought of spending an entire day with my family and our friends. Besides, I need this outing and respite from the chaos as much as you."

"Are you sure nothing will interfere? No pressing affairs that Mr. Daniels will insist must be attended to immediately or the fate of Pemberley will teeter on the edge of destruction?"

He winked, lowering his voice in mock secrecy, "I told him I was leaving the country for a while so he would not pester me." She laughed and shook her head, Darcy continuing in a normal tone, "I am all yours today. Did you doubt my assertion?"

She shook her head, eyes flaring with sudden mischief and promise. "No. Merely wanting to reaffirm. I intend to prove my healthiness to you, my husband, so you will no longer worry and annoy me with your overbearing attentiveness. I want to walk the garden paths, frolic with the children, laugh with our friends, and eat until bursting. Then"—she leaned into his body, mouth brushing against his ear—"later while the children are napping I will further prove my robustness by removing all your clothing and ravishing you all afternoon until you are begging for mercy." She seized the lobe between her lips, tugging decisively before running the tip of her tongue over the sensitized skin.

Darcy growled deep in his chest, pulling her body hard against his torso. Huskily, he responded, "Do not tease me if you are unsure of the outcome."

She placed her smiling lips lightly over his. "I am acutely aware of the outcome and prepared to ensure you are not disappointed."

"I am never disappointed with you, Elizabeth. However, I will admit the prospect as you outline it is abundantly appealing."

He brushed his lips over her collarbone, Lizzy squeezing tightly. "You have been so patient and devoted, Fitzwilliam. My love for you has grown to another level through this trauma. I cannot explain it, but I know it to be true. Your care for our sons and me has been remarkable. My gratefulness is not the root cause of my yearning to love you, but I will say that the emotion augments my desire. Truthfully, as much as my pride hates to admit it, I do feel vulnerable these days. It may be pathetic, but activity clears my mind and erases the residual fear. Vigorous loving declares my vitality in a special way that heals me, not to mention how enjoyable it is to love you."

She ended her statement with a teasing smile, but Darcy sensed the unease underneath. His embrace was tender but stalwart, gazing into her eyes for several heartbeats before whispering, "Elizabeth, I love you."

The consuming kiss that followed conveyed his boundless love and happiness, Lizzy returning the searing exchange wholeheartedly. Instinctively their hands kneaded and stroked as mouths battled gloriously. Lizzy's escalating ardor was felt deep in her belly, in those hidden places that only his touch could reach. Darcy's heightening passion was felt pressing hard into his wife's lower abdomen.

Both of their hearts were pounding, the mutual rush of blood and heavy breathing drowning out all extrinsic sounds and Darcy had taken a sideways step toward the bed when they were interrupted.

"Mama! Papa! I got bread cumbs for the duckies! Nanny has Michael dressed and sent me to get you. Hurry! Carriage outside!" Alexander had barreled into their legs, grabbing on to skirt and breeches, and was tugging insistently. Darcy and Lizzy staggered at the forceful impact, clutches steadying the other as they separated a pace. Lizzy burst into laughter, Darcy turning his red face and aroused body away from his son. Fortunately Alexander was innocently impervious, although as he grew, his awareness would follow a similar path as Darcy's with regards to his parents. Frequent embraces of an intimate nature would be a matter of course for the numerous

Darcy offspring to witness, their parents' love and passion multiplying as the years progressed.

But for now the toddler was only interested in picnics and play at the park. His parents followed him to the foyer, his piping voice nonstop in expressing his enthusiasm. George scooped him up, playfully planting his large hand over the child's mouth.

"Uncle Goj!" He exclaimed as soon as his mouth was freed. "You smashing my bread! How duckies eat them now?"

George rolled his eyes and then winked at Lizzy and Darcy, the group chatty as they filed onto the street and into the parked carriage.

The short drive south on Park Lane to the Hyde Park Corner entrance on Knightsbridge took longer than typical due to heavy traffic. It was a gorgeous day in April with crowds of merrymakers taking advantage of the placid temperatures in dozens of outdoor pursuits, carriages and horses and pedestrians vying for space on the walkways and avenues. The sun shone brightly, but a steady breeze off the Thames cooled the air. Scattered white puffy clouds offered breaks in the sun's direct intensity and created interesting shadows along the ground.

The intriguing combination of shadow and clouds fascinated Alexander and finally halted his tongue. From his perch on Uncle Goj's lap, he could study the patterns formed by the cottony clouds high in the azure sky and the silhouettes moving over the land. Darcy kept a close eye on Lizzy, but she appeared perfectly fine as she sat beside him chatting with Georgiana, who sat across holding a wiggling Michael and next to George with his sedate burden.

The ladies fluttered fans, but more out of habit and to keep the dust away from faces sheltered by wide bonnet brims. It was tolerably warm and the open calash permitted the gentle wind to waft over their bodies. George, of course, was attired in a flowing Indian garment of lightest silk, pale blue with edgings in navy that accented his sapphire eyes. His head was hatless in defiance of proper fashion, and a flashily embroidered and beaded pair of new juttis adorned his long feet. The cut left most of his upper feet bare, Darcy frowning upon seeing the scandalous footwear, but George just grinned and wore them anyway.

Lizzy and Georgiana were gowned in dresses of finely woven muslin as thin and loose as modesty would allow. Georgiana's was dandelion yellow with lacy sleeves capped upon her shoulders. Lizzy was similarly clothed, her gown a fallow-brown trimmed in copper with layered half-sleeves. Their wrist-height gloves were netted for ventilation, leaving the greater part of their arms bare and unprotected except for the matching shawls currently bunched at their elbows. Fashionably protecting their fair faces from the harshest rays of the sun were brimmed hats strategically placed to shield while also accenting elaborate coiffures and jewels.

Darcy, naturally, was resplendent and every inch the dashing English gentleman. From his tall, felted beaver hat to the tips of his polished, mid-calf Wellington boots, he oozed 1820 style. Although he did own a large collection of longer trousers and pantaloons, Darcy still preferred breeches, today wearing a calf-length pair of beige nankeen precisely tailored for his muscular lower body and tucked with barely a wrinkle into the tops of his black boots. His brown-and-gray-striped waistcoat and jacket of Prussian blue were sewn from lightweight kerseymere, the lacy white cravat tied elaborately but loose, all designed to withstand the soaring heat and humidity of a London summer.

As usual, it was his professional valet who selected the day's attire, Darcy rarely having an opinion on the subject. Samuel was well aware of the societal nuances in dress and accoutrements that were essential for the various meetings, activities, and places that filled Mr. Darcy's schedule, knowing it better than Darcy did. Today he had decided that, although still April and the average temperatures not rising to drastic levels, his Master would be worried over his family and thus would need to be comfortable. Of course, Darcy did not know this was Samuel's reasoning, simply donning the individual garments with barely a glance. His only disagreement was on wearing gloves or taking a walking stick. He did not care for the ridiculous affectation of a dandified cane when he was perfectly capable of walking unassisted and he also wished to keep his hands bare and unencumbered so he could delight in the touch of his wife and sons.

He reached across to rescue the increasingly rambunctious Michael from Georgiana's questionable grasp. She smiled her thanks, but otherwise maintained the steady prattling conversation with Elizabeth. Lizzy's cheeks were rosy and eyes alit with delight as they turned onto the spacious access through the massive gates at the corner entrance to Hyde Park.

The King's Road, built by William III in 1690 as a direct route between Kensington Palace and St. James's Palace, was one of several carriageways cutting through the enormous royal park, but it was by far the largest and most popular. It was broad enough to easily accommodate three carriages abreast, thickly paved with a sea of coarse gravel from the Thames, and lined with manicured lawns, hedges, and footpaths. With over three hundred lamps positioned to illuminate the thoroughfare at night, this avenue held the distinction of being the first in the country to be artificially lit, a fact Londoners were proud of. Officially named The King's Road, the corruption of the French "Route de Roi" led to the more common, humorous name of Rotten Row. Of course, there was nothing "rotten" about it, the avenue pristinely maintained and scenic with a stunning view of the Serpentine's glittering blue waters through the trees and bushes to the north.

The fine carriage emblazoned with the Darcy crest was admitted to Hyde Park, the guard nodding briefly to the driver. The true "fashionable hour" for promenading and flirting would not be until later in the afternoon, but at this earlier part of the day, Rotten Row was far from empty. Several equally fine carriages were making their way west along the avenue, mixing in with the dozens of pedestrians and equestrians roaming up and down the graveled track. The clamor of hooves, wheels, and raised voices was intense, even with the relative sparsity in noontime visitors. Lizzy and Georgiana began waving at people they knew, Darcy nodding sedately as well, but the driver did not halt. Under orders from Mr. Darcy to proceed west until signaled to stop, he urged the horses at a stately pace.

They traveled roughly a mile, slowing for occasional brief conversations with known acquaintances either mounted on magnificent steeds or reclining in opulent carriages. Finally, when nearing a grouping of tall cedars and a bubbling fountain near a diverging footpath, Darcy addressed the driver and instructed him to halt. It was here that the occupants disembarked for their exercise.

The Darcy House footman jumped down to open the calash doors and then turned to assist Mrs. Hanford from her perch next to the driver. The perambulator was untied from the rear footboard and a protesting Michael secured inside the cushioned bed with a wide, leather strap spanning the opening. Darcy had been forced to emergently fashion a restraint for the small baby carriage two days before they departed Pemberley, after Michael exploded in a fit of temper while strolling with his parents and brother through the private garden. He had dropped his favorite toy, a ring of metal keys that clanged so beautifully when shook, arching his back and kicking his legs so violently that it was only Darcy's swift reflexes that saved the contorting infant from tumbling to the pebbled pathway. It was an incident that had never remotely occurred with Alexander, taking both parents utterly by surprise. The agitated father had marched into the stable yard and enlisted the aid of the mechanical wizard Stan in the project. So far the shackle was working fairly well to keep Michael in place, but Darcy remained vigilant.

"Calm down, you rascal!" Darcy knelt by the pram, tucking the folded blankets and padding around his irate son, propping him safely so he could see over the edge without escaping. "Here are your keys and your rattles. Elizabeth, do we have one of those biscuits he loves? Excellent. Here you are, sweet. Yum. There, much better, yes? Now can we take our walk? So many pretty flowers and people to capture your attention. Let us pray, that is." He leaned to kiss the soft forehead, wiping the tears off the ruddy cheeks. Michael gnawed on the hard cookie and reached one hand toward the beloved face of his father. Darcy snatched the chubby fingers between his lips, nibbling until Michael erupted in bubbling giggles.

"And what, pray tell, will you do when he begins to walk? Put him on a leash?"

Darcy glanced upward into the grinning face of his cousin Richard, a smiling Lady Simone on his arm. "I certainly hope such a drastic step will not be necessary, but with this one I may have no option." He smiled at his son, bestowing another kiss before rising. "Glad you could join us, Cousin. Lady Simone." He bowed. "A delight to see you. You are well, I trust?"

"Quite well, Mr. Darcy. Thank you. Elizabeth, you look especially radiant. I was so worried for you."

"Thank you, Simone. I am fully restored, partially due to your husband's efforts. I have not had the opportunity to thank you properly, dearest Richard." Lizzy reached to take his hands, squeezing firmly.

"Please, Elizabeth, you shall embarrass me!" Darcy coughed at that ridiculous statement, the colonel ignoring him. "I was delighted to be of service. Besides, your husband needed me to watch his back. Pathetically inept without me to take care of him."

She shook her head, face serious. "I shall not allow you to jest or make light. I know what you did for us, and I can never adequately express my appreciation. If not for you, your associates, and your intervention, we may not be here. And William could have been…"

She choked on the words, lowering her head to compose her emotions. Darcy touched her lightly on the small of her back, a tender caress as he spoke into the unsettling moment. "Mr. and Mrs. Bingley approach, dearest. Alexander, run and greet your cousin Ethan."

Lizzy smiled, her emotions again in check as she scanned the group of people milling about the lawn. She looked up at her serene spouse. "I see you have indeed invited everyone we know to join our excursion to Hyde Park."

"I may have mentioned it to one or two people. How they chose to spend their time is outside my purview."

Lizzy laughed at his bland statement and squeezed his arm once before joining Simone to accost her sister. The women welcomed each other, voices musical as they ambled the trail leading toward the river's edge where the blankets were spread. Lizzy's joy in the out-of-doors was evident to her husband, who turned a carefree face toward Bingley as he neared.

"Elizabeth appears her usual lively self," Bingley noted, inclining his head to George and Richard in greeting, "and the weather today is perfection for a picnic. Grand idea, Darcy. We have the tents erected and enough food to feed half of London."

"That is unlikely once I eat my fill."

"We considered your attendance, Dr. Darcy, and have provided accordingly," Bingley countered with a wink to his friend.

The four gentlemen assumed a knot trailing leisurely behind the ladies with the children and nannies in between. They exchanged pleasantries for several minutes until Darcy touched Richard's sleeve, pausing in his steps.

"What is the verdict from Newgate?" he asked, eyes intent upon his skipping son.

"Guilty, all of them, on numerous charges. As pathetic as they were as guards, each one of them possessed histories of crimes that continued to grow with further investigation. In the end, my brilliantly fabricated story was irrelevant. Rather disappointing in a way, but I am glad to see it done. Frankly, I am weary of remembering the night, as exciting as it was in some respects."

Darcy frowned, but George chuckled. "Rethinking your decision to retire, Colonel?"

Richard shook his head. "Not in the least. Domesticity fits me, I have discovered to my surprise." George snorted humorously, Richard continuing with a laugh, "I have happily foregone tramping through blood and mud, as have you the jungles and deserts, all for the sake of a fine meal and warm bed. We are not so dissimilar, Dr. Darcy."

"True, true." George mourned.

"Surely there are no legal consequences, is there, Darcy?"

"No, Bingley. Mere formalities to appease the authorities. They only spoke with me once, and Colonel Fitzwilliam twice. Orman remains silent and his helpers are grossly ignorant and untrustworthy, so nothing damning there."

"What did you find when you went to Bethlam, Dr. Darcy?"

George shook his head, his expression unusually serious when he answered Bingley's question. "Horrid place. Diseases of the mind have never held much interest for me, I am afraid, so I cannot judge with confidence. But his caretakers and the doctors say he is beyond being cured."

"Based on what the newspapers have written, I was under the impression that the new building in Southwark is impressive and modern. Is this untrue?"

"Oh, it is a fine building, Mr. Bingley. Well constructed, spacious, on a lovely plot of land, and with a fresh water supply. It is the attempts at psychology and healing of mental illnesses that leave much to be desired. Not that I have any enlightened ideologies, but what takes place at the aptly named Bedlam is frequently inhumane, although they do try."

"I have difficulty mustering any remorse for what Orman may be suffering." Darcy's voice was strained, his eyes hard as he stared straight ahead toward his wife and son.

"I comprehend your sentiment, William. We all do, naturally. But I think even you would be softened by what takes place there."

Darcy did not respond to his uncle's assertion, feeling not a twinge of compassion for the insane Marquis.

George continued, "Be that as it may, Orman has earned a private cell and is receiving better than normal care. His wealth affords that, at least for now."

"His wealth is not as vast as one might expect. Mr. Daniels did further probing and, in addition to what the inspector told me today, I believe Lord Orman's fortune has been largely squandered. For years I have heard the rumors of his decadent lifestyle and mismanagement of his estates. I witnessed it myself. It is just one of a dozen reasons why I loathed him long before he attacked my wife." Darcy's normally warm baritone was cold, the contempt evident under the careful regulation of his speech. "He has massive debts accrued, no legitimate heirs, and his crimes are innumerable. My solicitor said that the Crown would likely assume his properties eventually, the subsequent liquidation of his inheritance being confiscated to pay his debts with little left in reserve for his use. Again, I cannot evoke the slightest sorrow or compassion."

He looked at his uncle with eyes glacial. George nodded and said nothing more. An uncomfortable silence fell. It was clear to all involved, especially those who had known Darcy for extended periods of time, that his mind would not be changed or fury soon relinquished.

They resumed their stroll to the end of the path. The joined waters of the damned River Westbourne and the onetime natural springs that randomly dotted the center acres of the recreational grounds in the heart of London had, since 1730, formed the curved pool spanning the interior of the vast park. Named the Serpentine by Queen Catherine, whose idea it was to revamp the royal hunting and leisure preserve nearly a century prior, the lake was now a prime locale for socializing and diversion among the upper echelons of the ton while away from their country adobes.

Alexander, Ethan, Hugh, and the other children were squealing with glee at the numerous hungry-looking ducks swimming on the surface of the crystalline waters. Harry Pomeroy, a mature youth of nine whole years, stood with the older boys watching the frolicking youngsters, they refusing to cavort as the babies did, but their eyes shone nonetheless.

A wide lawn stretched along the southern shore where they stood and the untamed tree- and shrub-dotted northern banks were visible across the river. The gardens retained a wildness about them that was pleasing to the eye, if not as relaxing as a more sculptured landscaping would be. A sizeable amount of the northern acreage was yet forested and reserved for royal hunting of the deer that freely roamed. Only Kensington Gardens to the west, those lands that surrounded the Palace and were segregated from the rest of the park by the harmonious sunken fence established as a boundary in Queen Catherine's day, were truly designed and manicured to any great degree. Here in Hyde Park proper, there were only a few areas that could be considered formalized or groomed, such as Rotten Row and the Ring north of the Serpentine.

"I read that his Majesty is considering a renovation of Hyde Park," Bingley said in an effort to break the silence.

"Indeed," George answered. "He has requested the presence of architects, engineers, and gardeners from all over England. One article said that John Rennie is designing a bridge to span the Serpentine and that Decimus Burton wants to erect a grand entrance of some sort at the corner."

"What? Nash has not been invited as yet?" Even Darcy chuckled at Richard's remark.

"Give it time, Colonel. I am sure the eminent John Nash shall be involved eventually, but I also heard a rumor that our new King wants to renovate Buckingham Palace and has enlisted Nash for that project."

"Excellent. I can imagine Parliament is thrilled at those drains on the treasury."

"No politics today, gentlemen," Darcy interrupted, speaking for the first time since halting. "Let us focus on our families. Speaking of which, Richard, your stepson approaches."

"Father Richard, Mr. Darcy, Mr. Bingley, Dr. Darcy." Harry Pomeroy bowed to each man before turning to his stepfather. "The boys wish to remove their shoes and stockings and walk in the water. Do they have your permission?"

The fathers nodded their approvals, Richard adding with a smile, "You may join them, Harry. I am sure the water is refreshing." The older boy lifted his chin and frowned, saying nothing as he turned to rejoin the children currently screeching with joy as they tossed bread by the handfuls and were enveloped by a cloud of quacking ducks. Richard laughed softly, shaking his head. "He thinks he is so grown-up. Reminds me of another boy I once knew." He glanced slyly at Darcy, who, as typical, ignored his cousin and kept his attention focused on the six men approaching.

"Darcy! Thank you for inviting us. It is a fine day for a leisurely hour in the park."

"You are most welcome, Sitwell. I knew Elizabeth would appreciate visiting with her friends. How are you, Gerald?"

"Excellent. Could not be better."

"I know why you are wearing that grin, Mr. Vernor," George said with a smile. "Mrs. Vernor will be soon presenting you a third child by the looks of things. Congratulations."

Gerald Vernor bowed, his face beaming. "Thank you, Doctor. It could be any day now, so we are anxious. We waited so long after Spencer that we were beginning to think that was the end of Vernor children. But God has blessed us, and we are humbled and deeply appreciative. The boys are even more excited to greet what they are convinced will be a little brother."

"Marilyn can barely contain her glee," Albert Hughes said with a chuckle. "The fact that your child will be mere months younger than ours was not lost on her, I can assure you. And Michael is close in age as well. Our gatherings will surely be lively affairs for the next dozen years or so."

Darcy smiled, remaining mum on the possibility of yet another Derbyshire baby to join the mix. The symptoms Lizzy experienced were ambiguous at best, neither of them yet credibly trusting the notion so keeping it a hopeful jest for now. Even the eagle-eyed, intuitive diagnostic skills of Dr. George Darcy were not adequate to confirm the inconspicuous signs.

Mr. Hughes continued. "Darcy, as soon as we return home for the summer I need to bring Christopher to Pemberley. He is anxious to transition from pony to stallion, and I will have him ride none but your thoroughbreds. Marilyn would prefer a colt, but I think I can sway her to accept a smaller stallion."

George laughed. "Sway her, you say. I am not married, mind you, but that does not seem like an enviable proposition. I wish you well in that endeavor, Mr. Hughes."

Mr. Sitwell spoke in his quiet voice. "Mrs. Darcy appears well, Darcy. Julia was extremely distressed at the horrible truth. She wanted to rush over to Darcy House yesterday afternoon immediately, but I urged her to wait until today."

Darcy nodded, his gaze on his wife, who was currently being embraced by a tearful Julia Sitwell. Lizzy, Jane, and Simone had joined Chloe, Julia, Marilyn, Harriet, Alison, and Amelia, who had arrived earlier to set up the blankets and picnic essentials. The gentlemen stood at the edge of the pathway, near enough to hear the murmur of excited voices if not individual words. Lizzy turned to catch Darcy's eye. She was smiling broadly, her face shining and filled with happiness. She mouthed *thank you*, Darcy inclining his head slightly in response.

"Lord Orman has always been a scoundrel, but I never thought him capable of something so heinous. Wickham either, for that matter," Mr. Vernor murmured with a visible grimace. He shared a look with Hughes, whose pale face and unnerved eyes revealed a similar inquietude at men they have known for decades behaving evilly.

Hughes cleared his throat, speaking hesitantly and not gazing directly at Darcy when he asked, "I know you are undoubtedly weary of discussing the matter, Darcy, but I am nonetheless intrigued if you have discovered how Orman and Wickham devised such a heinous act."

Darcy continued to stare at Elizabeth, the pain cloaked behind a neutral mien but notable nevertheless. "Orman was not completely in his right mind,

Vernor, not that that excuses his actions. And we saw what Wickham became, his sanity undoubtedly questionable as well," he responded coldly, proceeding then to give the bare outline of how the two wicked men consorted and plotted.

"My God," Vernor whispered, truly shaken. "I had no idea. Darcy, I am... stunned. And so sorry."

Darcy barely hid the grimace the memories evoked. "Thank you, Gerald. I must reiterate that this is to go no further, gentlemen. I trust you in this." Darcy met each of the men's eyes, holding firm with a stern stare.

"You know we are trustworthy, Darcy. As are our wives," Mr. Fitzherbert verified.

They all reaffirmed their silence, Darcy finally sighing and relaxing. "Elizabeth and I want to forget the whole episode. She is well and Alexander is safe. That is all that matters now. Any subsequent talk will only lead to ridiculous insinuations and upset my wife. I will not allow that."

Darcy never spoke of intimate details or publicly acted in an improper manner, but the intense relationship he shared with his wife was known to his closest friends. These men had known him for years, or, in the case of Gerald Vernor and Albert Hughes, for all of his life. Therefore, they could readily interpret the unconscious gestures and expressions that crossed Darcy's normally constrained body whenever Mrs. Darcy was present or mentioned. All of them had been witness to tender interactions that were, in most cases, so naturally done that neither was aware of it. Darcy's friends were no longer shocked or perplexed by the unexpected choice he had made, all truly caring for Elizabeth and happy for the subtle alterations to Darcy's severe personality. None of them experienced the same intensity in their marriages, so were honest in not comprehending how stricken Darcy probably was by the recent attack. Still, they did love their own wives and children, empathizing and agreeing with the need for secrecy and protection.

"You know we would not wish for gossip, and desire Mrs. Darcy forget it ever happened. Do not fear from us, but what of your staff or others involved?"

"And what of the legalities?" Stephen Lathrop added his concern to Vernor's.

"The magistrate was uninterested, for the most part, and there were few queries," Richard explained to the new arrivals, saving Darcy from answering. He gave the same summary related to Bingley, finishing with a warm smile and glance toward Lady Simone. "My wife took pity upon the pathetic, nearly starved, and dimwitted girl used by Orman and Wickham as a slave and God only knows what else. She has been sent to the Fotherby estate to be employed as a kitchen scullion. That will be a far better life for her."

"Those of my staff who are aware of anything beyond Mrs. Darcy being ill are trustworthy." A cloud crossed Darcy's face, his lips setting in a stern line. "All loose ends have been accounted for," Darcy concluded decisively, the image of Mrs. Smyth's rented hack wheeling away from Darcy House a perversely happy one.

Mr. Drury, as if divining Darcy's train of thought, asked, "Have you interviewed my housekeeper's sister as yet? I scanned her résumé before referring her to Mr. Daniels. It appears impeccable and I can attest to Miss Inglorian's competence in managing Locknell Hall. If her sister is half as capable, she will be a fine housekeeper for Darcy House."

"Elizabeth and I have an appointment with her tomorrow. Thank you for the recommendation, but I trust you will understand my caution. I intend to explore all candidates thoroughly and not be hasty in hiring. In fact, Mr. Daniels is supposed to deliver a report today on his findings for the three women we are considering, Mrs. Hass one of them."

"No, of course I understand your caution, Darcy," Drury assured him.

"And speaking of Mr. Daniels, your junior solicitor approaches now," George inserted.

"I apologize for being late, gentlemen. I cannot fathom the mystery of it, but apparently one small child refusing to wear shoes can delay an entire household! Then we stopped at Darcy House to deliver a sheath of papers from my father. I think you will be pleased with the applicants, sir. Are you sure Mrs. Darcy is constitutionally restored to manage three interviews tomorrow? It can be exhausting."

"My wife thrives on such challenges, Mr. Daniels. The activity will be good for her."

"Mrs. Daniels will be happy to hear that. She was concerned, naturally, although it does look as if Mrs. Darcy is recovered."

Silence fell among them, each man lost in personal thoughts of the staggering events while watching their wives and children. Darcy again studied his wife, but she was laughing gaily while nibbling on pieces of cold pheasant and pickled beets. He smiled at the odd dietary combination, praying that it portended of a blessed addition to their family. With her woman's monthly cycles not resumed after Michael's birth, there was no way to gauge when she may have conceived, or if she had, therefore they were forced to wait for a surer sign than strange cravings or vague nausea.

"Dare I ask what of Wickham? How have you dealt with that, Darcy?" Mr. Vernor broached in a low voice.

"Circumspectly, Gerald. We agreed that there is no reason for the family to know what happened. Aside from Mrs. Daniels and Mrs. Bingley, of course."

"Will he be buried in Hertfordshire then?"

Darcy met his lifelong friend's eyes, understanding the unasked question. "I pray Mr. and Mrs. Wickham are unable to observe events on earth for a host of reasons. If they can, then I must trust they understand why their son will not rest alongside them at Pemberley."

The men nodded, none disagreeing with his sentiments, and George laid a consoling hand onto his nephew's shoulder, his voice matching the proud cast to his face when he spoke. "William has paid the burial expenses and wrote a letter to the Bennets eloquently expressing his belief that the Wickhams would appreciate their son being buried where his wife will some day rest."

The surprise at that gesture was clear upon each face, Clifton Drury whistling and verbalizing what they all thought, "That is generous to say the least, Darcy. Under the circumstances, it is a remarkable action on your part."

"Generosity had nothing to do with it, I assure you," Darcy said bluntly. "I was only thinking of my wife and how to minimize her distress. Wickham's body has been sent to a Meryton mortician who will handle the process with Mr. Bennet's direction henceforth. I am done with it. They are awaiting Mrs. Wickham's arrival, who we just heard today from Mrs. Bennet diverted to Bath after Major General and Mrs. Artois's wedding. A dispatch has been sent. Beyond that, I do not care, to be brutally honest. My family will be leaving for Rosings soon, thus the mourners will not include us."

"I am happy to hear your plans for Kent have not changed, since new scenery is a wonderful remedy, although Mrs. Hughes insists the seaside best cures her troubles and boredom. Her prescription is several weeks for complete healing, of course."

"Oh have no fear, Mr. Hughes"—George laughed—"Mrs. Darcy highly enjoys her visits with Lady Catherine! I believe the stimulus of confounding witless Mr. Collins and sparring converse with Lady Catherine will invigorate more than gallons of seawater or gales of sea air."

Darcy grunted, wincing at their laughter and the vision drawn by Dr. Darcy's statement. Yet he could not resist a smile—hidden behind a rubbing thumb over his lips—at the undeniable truth of how Elizabeth behaved and the guilty entertainment he reaped whenever dwelling at Rosings. "Elizabeth's pleasure is derived from visiting with Mrs. Penaflor and Mrs. Collins, strolling the gardens and walkways of the Park, and upon this occasion seeing our new niece," he stated firmly with an attempted glare at his uncle.

George shook his head, not the slightest repentant. "We shall see which brings her greater relief. I know I am most delighted by annoying Lady Catherine, but then my faults are blatant and myriad compared to Mrs. Darcy."

"Be sure to take careful notes since I shall not be there to bask in the fun," Richard requested.

George sketched a check mark in the air, the two exchanging impish grins. Darcy broke into the laughter coming from his friends, voice serious, "You should come with us, Cousin, and not to harass our aunt but to visit Anne and Raul. I doubt they will make the trip to Town this season so soon after Margaret's birth. The boys would enjoy Rosings Park and the clean air would benefit young Oliver."

"We had considered it. However, now we think waiting until later in the summer might be best. Rigorous travel is inadvisable at the moment."

"Is Lord Fotherby's health again poor, Colonel? I thought his new treatment regime was an improvement."

"The medicines I and Dr. Angless are using are helping, Mr. Lathrop, but not a cure, sadly. Nevertheless, Lord Fotherby is fit enough to travel I would imagine. Somehow I do not think it is his constitution Colonel Fitzwilliam is concerned about."

Richard flushed but could not completely hide the light in his eyes even as he attempted to glare at a smirking George. "Just once I wish you were not so skilled as a diagnostician, Doctor."

Vernor and Hughes puzzled the pieces first, Gerald whistling while Albert extended a hand that Richard automatically shook. "Congratulations, my friend! Well done! Babies and more babies!"

"No public announcements as yet, gentlemen. I am leaving that honor up to Mrs. Fitzwilliam when she decides the time is appropriate. I dare you to cross my wife on that count, Dr. Darcy!"

George pressed a finger to his clamped lips, the other men subduing their congratulations to happy smiles and minute gestures.

"In lieu of my cousin gaining the spotlight with his public announcement, how about I offer one of my own." All eyes looked to Darcy, who was broadly smiling but gazing over their shoulders toward the picnic area. He indicated the young man approaching with an elderly, stately woman on his arm, Lord and Lady Matlock flanking, and said in a voice bubbling with pride, "Come. Let us join the ladies before they consume all the food. I am parched and famished, plus I wish to proclaim our recent great fortune to the entire assembly."

He stepped away from their cluster, Richard muttering in mock disgust, "Oh God help us, he is going to make a speech. So much for slaking our thirst and hunger."

"Fear not, Colonel. There is plenty for all, and while everyone is distracted over William's announcement, we can dive in unnoticed and steal the best morsels. Come! No slight intended, but feminine company is preferable to a group of prosy old men!" And with a swirl of silk around limber, bony legs, Dr. Darcy flounced across the lawn toward the reclining women.

"Prosy?" Gerald Vernor asked.

"Old?" Albert Hughes commented drolly. "Has he forgotten who the eldest of this group is?"

"This is my uncle we are talking about here," Darcy said with a chuckle. "Do chronological years really enter into the equation?"

There was no need to answer the redundant question, so they merely shook their heads and followed the doctor's mincing steps—in a suitable strolling gait—until reaching the canvas sunshade where the ladies and children reposed.

"Lady Warrow"—Darcy bowed deeply toward his great-aunt—"I am pleased you could join us."

"I adore dining in the out-of-doors, Mr. Darcy. It is a delightful pastime as long as not undertaken too early in the day, mind you. I rarely rise before nine o'clock and it does take this old body far longer to reach a state proper for public viewing than it once did." She patted the perfectly coiffed silver curls bouncing youthfully at the nape of her neck, the other palm smoothing the fashionable French Empire gown of white lawn that draped her slim body.

"My Lady, you surely jest! Your beauty shines as brightly as ever and you appear no older than I recall from my youth."

The marchioness fluttered her fan as daintily and coquettishly as a maiden, but her eyes sparkled with a sultry gleam present in few mature ladies. "Dr. Darcy," she drawled, "where you learned to charm and flirt is a story I long to hear, since I know you did not obtain the skill from my brother, God rest his soul."

George extended his arm, Lady Warrow leaving Mr. Butler's side to take the offered support from her nephew, winking as he murmured in a secretive tone, "Indeed it is a dazzling tale, Aunt, but unlikely fit for fragile ears."

"Thankfully my ears have not been remotely fragile since I was sixteen, so I shall look forward to the conversation. For now, however, we must content ourselves with tales of young, innocent love. I assume you wish to inform the group of our mutual happiness, Mr. Darcy, but you better hurry or I shall blurt it out myself."

Darcy bowed, grin still broad as he extended his hand to Georgiana. She had managed to remain sitting on the blanket next to Lizzy and not bolt upwards the second Sebastian entered her vision through the greatest of willpower. Now it was as if she was released from a restraining tether and she did jump up, practically hopping across the short distance to take her brother's hand. At this point there were few doubts in anyone's mind as to what the news was since Sebastian and Georgiana were staring at each other in utter adoration.

"My friends and family members, it is my great joy to announce that Mr. Sebastian Butler has won the heart of my sister, Miss Georgiana Darcy. That his heart has equally been wrest away by Miss Darcy has been affirmed via several sources, most emphatically by the wrester. Thus, it was fairly easy to grant Mr. Butler the honor and privilege of her hand in matrimony when he sought my permission."

He took their hands and linked them together within his own, continuing in the same resonant timbre, "Join Mrs. Darcy and I in congratulating the betrothed couple!"

From there on it became noisy, laughter and overlapping conversations ruling long into the afternoon. Richard congratulated Darcy on announcing in a concise manner, to which Darcy responded with words that shall not be repeated here. Georgiana and Mr. Butler somehow managed to stay within two feet of each other all afternoon, even when playing with the children. Lady Simone broke her self-imposed plan to delay voicing her hopes by first whispering her suspicions to select ladies, and then two or three others, and before long the whole group knew, thus making it unnecessary for the Fitzwilliams to remain mum. The gentlemen expressed unknowing surprise at the news, Simone too busy receiving congratulations to notice those whose acting skills were inadequate. Richard proved to be as long-winded and emotional at speeches as Darcy ever was, a fact Darcy jumped on with taunting glee!

Harry eventually broke down and removed his stockings, ending up getting wetter and muddier than anyone else. In fact, the only youth who maintained his poise was Oliver, the nearly eighteen-year-old resisting the urge to act other than an Earl should without too much difficulty. Michael's encounter with the water, while held by Lizzy, elicited squeals of delight but the flapping ducks brought lusty yells not easily quenched. Fiona Lathrop fearlessly joined in with the boys, earning instant respect to be remembered for years to come.

The ducks decided braving the screeching children was worth the treats delivered, but apparently the frogs and lizards disagreed, since not a one was discovered no matter how exhaustive the searching. Dozens of bulrushes were broken during the amphibian/reptile quest and many more were stripped for the pleasure of floating seeds, but luckily the groves were plentiful so the visible effect was negligible.

Kites were strung but the breeze never grew brisk enough to gain altitude. Lawn games were more successful thanks to the level turf. The slopes and valleys located nearby served well for tag and tumbling. Butterflies, moths, and assorted flying insects drifted about, much to the delight of Stuart Vernor and Andrew Fitzherbert, who were fascinated by bugs and captured several interesting specimens for their collections. Julia Sitwell set up her easel, as did her eldest son, Rory, the two capturing the rippling waters of the Serpentine in watercolors with impressive skill. Sebastian withdrew his Tromlitz flute and Georgiana her Celtic lap harp, the expert musicians dazzling everyone with a variety of tunes.

The adults were tireless in their enjoyment of the sunny weather, fine food, and companionship, but the younger children succumbed to extensive play and full bellies. Lugging inert bodies back to the waiting carriages proved harder than carting the loaded baskets down had. Those, at least, were now nearly empty and servants arrived to assist with the larger items. Nevertheless, it was late in the afternoon before they were fully unloaded at Darcy House and the Darcy boys were tucked into their respective beds for naps.

Darcy fell onto the settee before the unlit fireplace in his and Elizabeth's bedchamber with a loud sigh. He was waiting, rather impatiently, for his wife to emerge from her dressing room. The vague references to *freshening up* and *getting comfortable*, whispered in a sultry drawl, did not induce relaxation, but instead instigated certain bodily reactions of a heightening nature.

Elizabeth dearly enjoyed surprising her husband. Of course explicit visual or tactile inducements were unnecessary, but he knew she would not see it that way. Therefore, his mind was pleasantly wandering. Would she wear the over-sized shirt of his that still drove him insane? Would she appear deliciously naked? Perhaps wearing one of the devilish costumes that her modiste designed? Would her hair be yet pinned up so he could thrill in releasing each lustrous tress? Or down in a cloud of fluid waves shrouding her elfin face and delicate shoulders? Would she splash her alabaster skin with her signature essence of lavender or the special musky jasmine that she wore as a treat just for him?

The musings meandered as he removed his shoes and jacket. Again, it truly did not matter; anything she chose was guaranteed to provoke him into a raging inferno of wanton desire. Merely the thought of her was affecting him and his next sigh was more of a moan as blood rushed in a hot surge through his vessels.

He reached a hand to loosen the suddenly constricting cravat just as the door opened. His breathing hitched and hand halted halfway toward his throat, the brief paralysis broken with a cleansing release of air as his eyes swept over the woman who utterly owned his soul. A brilliant smile illuminated his face as he drank in the vision of Lizzy gliding across the short distance.

Her hair was down, tumbling chocolate curls framing her cheeks and falling to her waist in a lush veil. She had chosen to remain in the creamy tan gown with copper trim that she had worn that day, only without any undergarments thus allowing the sheer muslin to cling to her flesh and offer tantalizing hints of the perfection underneath. The fact that a portion of his brain had been disrobing her from this particular dress all day made her choice to keep it on all the more stimulating.

He extended one arm, palm upward, murmuring gutturally, "Ah, Lizzy. What are you trying to do to me?"

She smiled in return, taking the offered hand and lacing her fingers between his, but moved around the narrow settee until behind him. She leaned down, kissing each fingertip ensnared amid her fingers, only then answering his question with a hot whisper against his right ear. "I think you know precisely what I am trying to do. And that I am succeeding admirably."

He moaned, dropping his head onto the back of the sofa and gazing into her eyes. "You were succeeding before you entered the room, my lover. Now you are killing me!"

"You can handle the stress, my virile husband." She moved her hands to his shoulders, kneading through the fabric of his waistcoat.

"That does feel wonderful, but I have to say that my shoulders are not the prime area of my body screaming for your touch."

Smiling as she lowered her mouth to his, her kiss was every bit as penetrating upside down as it was straight on. Darcy cupped her face in his large, warm palms, preventing her straying away from his lips. Nimbly she unbuttoned the waistcoat and top part of his shirt, fingertips grazing over the hairs and skin revealed in the gap before attending to the knots of his neckcloth.

Lizzy had no proof, and could certainly never ask, but she had come to believe that Darcy's valet drew some sort of mischievous enjoyment in fabricating new, intricate knots for his master's cravat. Samuel was just as stoic and professional as on the day Lizzy met him as a new bride, marriage to Marguerite not visibly loosening the strict propriety that encased him, but upon occasion she had seen an odd gleam in his eye when Darcy exited his dressing room. He knew that Lizzy was as apt to undress her husband as he was. Darcy, of course, despite his adherence to proper fashion, was not a dandy and therefore paid scant attention to how his neckcloth was tied. But Lizzy saw the humor in it, delighting in the challenge and added thrill as she deciphered the puzzle, unveiling her spouse's manly neck to her seeking caress.

Today she only loosened the wrapped silk, leaving the looped fabric around his neck and pulling the shirt collar free. Only then, after sliding her palms down his chest to the edge of his breeches waistband and stroking back up to his flexing shoulders, did she withdraw from the delights of his mouth to pepper soft kisses over his face. Straightening, she looked into his half-lidded eyes and clasped the hands that cradled her face. She kissed each palm before releasing them and moving to stand in front of him at his bent knees. There she paused to run her gaze over every masculine inch of his figure, noting the indications of his fervid desire with rising zeal.

Darcy was breathing heavily, lips plump and ruddy from the pressure of her mouth. His skin was alive and tingling from her caress, his heart harshly pounding and arousal aching. He groaned, shifting restlessly on the couch and pressing anxious palm into his thighs as the need to touch her overwhelmed. His frayed restraint faltered dangerously when she unclasped the two buttons between her breasts and proceeded to inch the gown's sleeves off her shoulders until the décolletage slipped lower. When she then delivered her special seductive smile and bent nearer, offering an abundant display of her bosom in the process, he knew his control was a breath away from being lost. Fortunately, she grasped the dangling strands of his cravat and tugged upward before he literally took matters into his own hands!

Requiring no further inducement he leapt to his feet, broad hands instantly spanning her slim waist and drawing her tight against his body. "Elizabeth," he moaned, lips traveling hungrily over her neck. "You do delight in tormenting me."

A rapid undressing commenced while edging toward the bed. Darcy murmured endearments and erotic phrases as typical while grazing over her bared skin. Lizzy silently absorbed the spiraling sensations, allowing her hands and mouth to express her desire. Until, that is, Darcy reached to unwind the cravat from around his neck.

"No," she gasped, staying his hand. "Leave it on. I find it alluring."

He laughed softly. "As you wish, my love. Let me take you to our bed."

They stretched onto the down coverlet, bodies sinking into the fluffed surface as they eagerly reached for each other. Instantly their limbs entwined, hands stroking and fondling, and kisses vehement. Lizzy twisted one long end of the hanging neckcloth around her forearm, grasped the ruffled knots still intact at his throat, and pulled his body onto hers, welcoming his weight with a satisfied sigh as the established rhythm of loving was initiated.

She kept one hand entwined with the white silk, kissing and licking the exposed skin of his neck as they swayed together. Darcy growled, voice rough against her ear, "Is the effect of my cravat as you anticipated, love?"

"You tell me."

"Indeed I would answer affirmative. And here I thought it was the removal of my neckcloth that aroused you. How inventive of you to leave it on."

"I would never wish to be boring."

"That is absolutely impossible." He shifted to bestow a scorching kiss, accelerating the undulating pace. "Making love with you shall never be boring. That I can promise."

"No, I do not believe it shall," she agreed with a promising lilt and lifted brow. Then without any warning she forcefully pushed against his body, Darcy understanding the purpose and rolling smoothly onto his back with his lover in tow and crushed against his torso. Their steady rhythm recommenced after a brief hiccup, and Lizzy resumed her oral play at his neck.

Darcy closed his eyes and arched his neck, a sonant hum expressing his satisfaction at her antics. He caressed lazily over her silky skin, happy to relax and drift with the pleasurable sensations as she unhurriedly trailed kisses and unraveled the complex ties.

Finally she released the last binding and lifted onto her elbows to begin slowly unwinding the damp material from around his neck. Darcy watched her with interest, noting the arch expression in her feverish eyes that meant she had something else planned.

Exchanging a lusty grin with her more-than-willing spouse, Lizzy sat up astride his hips, palms smoothing the trailing silk over his chest all the way to where their bodies joined. Then she lifted the strips of cloth and tickled over the hard ridges of muscle and taut nipples as he writhed underneath her. The ends of her long hair brushed his skin, one leg slithered supplely over his with tiny toes tantalizing. Her whole body energized his sensitive nerves until he was both dazed from the intensity while also alert in anticipation for more.

With a leisurely motion she pulled the silk from his neck and held it to her nose, inhaling deeply. "It smells of you," she whispered. "Of your cologne and natural scent. The process of unraveling the ties as I draw closer to that hidden part of you that is only for me to touch is vivifying."

"Elizabeth," he growled with need, thrusting upward hard and deep. The previous cat-like purrs of contentment had turned to breathy moans and the gentle caresses to demanding strokes. He suddenly yearned to kiss her amazing lips—still wearing that teasing, sensuous smile that drove him crazy—and encircling her wrists with hot hands he tugged.

Instead of complying Lizzy chuckled and evaded his grasp. "Patience, love," she admonished, waving her finger and fluttering the cloth over his face. Then she tossed her hair, arching her back and exposing her long neck to twine the white silk around, pulling the fabric slowly through her fingers and down between her breasts.

"How do I look?" she asked huskily.

"Far better than I ever have while wearing it, I assure you," was his guttural response.

She smoothed the tails lying in the valley of her chest and over her belly, all the while watching the open-mouthed mesmerizing intensity of his stare. When she reached the dangling tips at her naval she bent slightly, feathering the edges along his abdomen and groin. The response was fierce, his body shuddering and muscles clenching as an animal growl burst from his throat.

"Inventive enough?"

But the words barely escaped her lips before he sat up, large hands encircling her waist with urgent purpose. Simultaneously his mouth clamped onto hers, the kiss as demanding as the savage pace he set. Meeting his every stroke, Lizzy wound the silk over his shoulders and tied a loose knot at the nape of his neck. The ends she clinched amid her fingers, holding fast while embedding into his thick hair.

Long minutes later he lessened the furious movements, withdrawing from her lips and resting his forehead upon hers. Voice a hoarse rumble, he said, "Your inventiveness drives me mad, Elizabeth. My desire for you is uncontrollable, especially when you toy with me. God, how I love and adore you!"

"I love you as deeply, Fitzwilliam, especially the uncontrollable you." She smiled into his glazed blue eyes, resuming the wild pace previously set. "I enjoy driving you mad... as you do me. No... need... to... stop..." the latter whispered breathlessly into his ear, punctuated by licks and suckling kisses.

Darcy swallowed and moaned, skimming his hands upward to cup her breasts, thumbs rubbing over her nipples. "Yes! Oh, yes, my Lizzy!"

Later, quite a while later, Darcy pulled his wife's body tight against his shivering side. With a contented sigh Lizzy nestled comfortably, head lying on the firm pillow of his upper left chest and hand stroking over the drenched hairs covering his muscular torso. She burrowed closer, squeezed his waist, and planted a kiss on his breast. "I love you."

"I love you, Elizabeth. So very much."

Silence fell. They listened and absorbed the natural noises of breathing, strong hearts beating, and stroking fingertips. They were wrapped in a warm cocoon of peace and words were not necessary to convey the depth of feeling.

"If you are not already with child," Darcy's subdued rumble broke the calm, "perhaps we conceived this afternoon. It was remarkable," he finished with understatement.

There was humor in his tone but also a hint of hopefulness. She squeezed his waist once again before recommencing a tactile investigation of his figure.

"You no longer have any fears at the possibility? No lingering dismay for the ill timing?"

"I never felt dismay at the idea of another baby, my heart. My fears were only for your health and for our relationship." He paused, voice dropping into a husky timbre. "Those fears were ludicrous. I should have trusted in what we have learned and in what we have built together. God in His mercy has given us many blessings and He will care for us."

She lifted onto her elbows, lying half over his body, and looked into his eyes. "I have a strong suspicion that this afternoon's assignation shall have no bearing on a conception that has already occurred, but it is nice to hear your positive thoughts on the subject. After all, there are dozens of rooms vacant at Pemberley to fill."

"A dozen may be difficult to accomplish"—he laughed—"even for us! I am content to fill a portion of the bedchambers and leave the remainder to be occupied by visiting children. Pemberley has her limits and with the rapid procreation happening around us, I daresay there may come a day when we reach maximum capacity!"

Life Is an Adventure

DEPARTURES WERE BECOMING AN ordeal these days. Two small children required an astounding amount of luggage and space, not to mention the addition of two servants and their bags into a second carriage. At least George had never hired a valet, his decades of traveling fast and light fostering self-sufficiency. Georgiana was to stay behind with her companion, Mrs. Annesley, in the care of Richard and Simone, so Samuel, Marguerite, Mrs. Hanford, and Miss Lisa were comfortably situated together without a third carriage necessary.

Adding to the sheer volume of persons and baggage to safely stow aboard with footmen working overtime, saying good-bye was now a grand spectacle. Alexander associated leaving his Aunt Giana behind to the long separation while she toured the Continent and no amount of explanation placated. Thus the tears and dramatics were on a massive scale, Darcy finally forced to pry the sobbing toddler out of his aunt's arms and plop him onto the seat next to George, all of them attempting to ignore the tears and downcast expression that was as humorous as it was piteous. Not wanting to augment the perceived tragedy of the parting, everyone else jumped into the vehicle, Darcy knocking on the roof as the signal to move the second the door closed, and barely said farewell to the waving Georgiana and Mr. Butler.

Thankfully, Michael slept through the leave-taking foolishness—his temper tantrum not to start until the stop at Swanley—and Alexander regained his cheeriness when unfamiliar terrain was seen. "Where are we now, Papa?"

"We are in Eltham, Son. London is officially behind us and we are on the edges of Kent."

"Be there soon?"

"Not as yet. Cousin Anne and Lady Catherine live far south and Kent is large." He smiled and ruffled Alexander's curls, the boy wearing a slightly confused expression.

"Do you remember your cousins Anne and Raul?"

Alexander's frown deepened at his father's question, his young mind trying in vain to place faces to the names that were vaguely familiar.

"It has been over eight months," Lizzy noted. "Do not worry on it, love. You will remember once we arrive, especially when you lay eyes on scary Lady Catherine."

"Elizabeth," Darcy chided, without extreme emphasis, returning his attention to Alexander and ignoring Lizzy's smirk. "Your *Aunt Catherine*," he stressed, "will be thrilled to see you." Lizzy snorted. "But I suspect you will have the greatest fun playing with the Collins twins. Do you remember Miss Rachel and Miss Leah?"

Alexander thought on it for a few moments, and then brightened. "We played with furry little dogs on lawn, yes, Papa?"

"Indeed you did, although I might suggest refraining from mentioning that fact to your Aunt Catherine. She prefers to think of her corgis as special dogs who do not play with children." He paused, Alexander's confused face at such a bizarre concept initiating a lengthy dialogue on show quality dogs versus dogs that protect and are to be played with. Clearly Alexander thought that was the strangest idea imaginable, a notion Darcy could not argue with.

Nevertheless, between reminders of the various Rosings and Hunsford inhabitants, canine discussion, and observations of the passing scenery, time passed swiftly. After a brief halt to rest the horses and quiet Michael, he definitely not adjusting to carriage travel despite the recent journeys, they resumed their course. Alexander hopped between his father and Uncle Goj, depending on which window offered the most exciting view.

It was as they passed the iron gates marking the northern boundaries of Rosings Park, the Gothic spires of the mansion visible in the distance beyond the trees, that Alexander's hazy memories from his visit here the prior year began to reemerge.

"That the dark house, yes, Papa?"

Lizzy laughed. "Yes, it is quite dark, especially compared to Pemberley. Narrow, twisted hallways with few lights and gloomy tapestries combine for an interesting dwelling place. Not sure about you, but I am always relieved to walk out the door into the sun."

"I wonder if Anne secretly looks toward the day when she is in control and can rip those horrid wall coverings down," George muttered, eyeing the approaching house with a sour cast. "I pray she discards the dreary carpets and more than half the furnishings. Only then will the place be moderately hospitable."

"Have no fear, Son. It really is not that bad," Darcy addressed to Alexander with a stern warning to his uncle. "You will not be alone and I insist on lamps in our quarters."

But Alexander appeared the opposite of fearful. Rather he was grinning and bouncing on the seat. "Big house with real armor knights! And swords and shields and, and, pemmants, and canon, and…"

The adults burst into laughter, Darcy squeezing the exuberant child tight. "You would remember the armory! Perfect place for a boy to play, although it is best we do it quietly when your Aunt Catherine is away, agreed?"

Alexander nodded, his grin as broad as Darcy's. "We have adventure, Papa? Exciting adventures?"

"We shall play adventures, how about that? I think we have had enough adventures lately, thank you." Darcy's voice was light and grin intact, but he could not control the shiver that ran through his muscles.

Lizzy leaned for a soft kiss to Alexander's cheek, her hand warm and reassuring on Darcy's thigh. "Life offers plenty of adventures, my sweet. Let us pray for only the normal ones of fun and play and siblings and travels from here on out, shall we?"

The nods of agreement were vehement, the silent prayers soaring heavenward. Michael chose that moment to release an ear-piercing screech of delight, apparently agreeing with the sentiment, and although they all winced, it was a humorous moment. Thus with laughter and lifted hearts the final short bend in the road was taken. The family universally welcomed the coming visit with loved ones and embraced the longer road of life that stretched out before them.

Historical Notes

ETHER WAS DISCOVERED IN 1275 by Spanish chemist Raymundus Lullus, but it was Valerius Cordus in 1540 who synthesized ether into "sweet oil of vitriol" and praised its medicinal properties, chief of which was the alleviation of pain. His contemporary, Paracelsus, noted that sleep was induced when chickens ingested the liquid. The name was changed to "ethereal spirits" or "ether" in 1730 by German scientist W.G. Frobenius. Friedrich Hoffmann (1660-1742) combined it with ethyl alcohol and marketed it as "Hoffman's Anodyne" as a treatment for cramps, earache, dysmenorrhea, and toothache. James Graham (1745-94), proprietor of the Temple of Hymen and the Celestial Bed, was a noted addict, habitually and publicly inhaling a couple of ounces several times a day. At this time ether became a recreational drug, along with nitrous oxide, with users celebrating parties called "ether frolics" to enjoy the hallucinogenic, euphoric effects before falling asleep. By 1790, inhaled ether was widely used by doctors in England to treat patients with consumption and other pulmonary ailments. It would not be until the experiments of Dr. Crawford Long in 1842 and Dr. William Morton in 1846 when cloths soaked in ether and inhaled by patients during minor surgery intrigued the serious medical community to develop techniques using ether as an anesthetic.

In 460 BC, Hippocrates described postpartum "fever," which produced "agitation, delirium, and attacks of mania." The 11th century writings of the gynecologist Trotula of Salerno note that, "if the womb is too moist, the brain is filled with water, and the moisture running over to the eyes, compels them to involuntarily shed tears." Famed French psychiatrist Esquirol (1772-1840) wrote of the "mental alienation of those recently confined and of nursing women." That some new mothers experienced unusual symptoms including melancholy all the way to psychosis was documented, but largely ignored by the medical community until 1858. Marcé's *Treatise on Insanity in Pregnant, Postpartum, and Lactating Women* specifically delineated accounts of puerperal psychosis and depression, paving the way for greater studies and acknowledgement.

The fields of physiological and clinical chemistry—the study of chemicals in bodily fluids and how they work in the body—began in Britain in earnest around 1750. Dozens of physiologists lectured and researched, writing theses on the subject. It was this exploding area of science that gave Mary Shelley the ideas for *Frankenstein*, published in 1816. They built upon the ideals first proposed by others, including Descartes, who believed that life could be fully explained by chemical and physical principles alone.

Mental illnesses have been recognized from the dawn of time, although not well understood in general. Despite the inhumanity of many asylums and the bizarre "treatments" applied, there were doctors who strived to understand mental illnesses and apply science. The medieval Islamic physicians were highly advanced. As early as the 7th century they built hospitals and provided psychotherapy, medications, and even music and occupational therapy! The 11th century Persian physician Avicenna coined the term "physiological psychology" and associated mental illness with emotions. He also pioneered neuropsychiatry, recognizing the neurologic pathology to dementia, epilepsy, melancholia, and stroke, to name a few. England's Bethlem Royal Hospital in London was founded in the 13th century and, despite the negative reputation, was the world's first center for research and healing of the mentally ill. The location and official name has changed, but for more than 750 years Bethlem has been a part of London and maintained its specialization. In 1948 it combined with Maudsley Hospital and continues to be a leader in mental health research and services.

All of these sciences, and many others, interrelated and built upon each other. Physiological psychology—the branch of psychology that studies the biological and physiological basis of behavior—would not be referred to as such until around 1880, but the foundations to this understanding were laid in the centuries prior.

Acknowledgments

GROWTH IS AN INEVITABLE BY-PRODUCT of being an author, but we do not get there alone. At least not as easily or with our sanity intact!

Trailblazing authors in the Jane Austen genre who boldly declared that writing characters created by another are a valid form of literature and worthy to be published are on the top of my list for thanks. They faced the ridicule first, forged ahead with the help of equally brave publishers, and made it possible. Now the number of published Austen fiction writers is expanding daily. So much so that a bunch of us formed a blog to share our love of Jane Austen and our pride in delving uniquely into her world—Austen Authors at www.austenauthors.com.

A special thank you to Carrie Flores, Regional Director of the Central Valley California JASNA. Carrie reached out to me and welcomed me with an open heart. Her kindness combined with the friendliness of others within our group has allowed me to be a part of the Austen community in a way I did not previously think was possible.

Huge thanks go to the Romance Writers of America, the Beau Monde Regency chapter, and the Yosemite Romance Writers for their amazing support, feedback, resources, education, and friendship. I am so proud to be a part of this fine organization.

Hugs to each one of my Casablanca sisters! I love these ladies and honestly cannot imagine where I would be right not without their insights and encouragement. CasaBabes rule! And if you don't believe me, come to www. casablancaauthors.blogspot.com and I'll prove it to you.

To my fans: I wish more than anything I could personally meet each of you, sign your books, and have lunch! I can't express the depth of my appreciation for the emails, positive comments, participation on the blogs, interactions on Facebook, and so on. You inspire me to continue and to try even harder.

Deb Werksman, my fabulous editor—warmest thanks imaginable flying your way! You push me each time, finding new ways for me to improve my skills as a writer, yet always with love, respect, trust, and latitude. The blend is phenomenal and I know how blessed I am to have you.

Above all, to my family who suffer through this craziness with me! Your love and encouragement bolsters me. Somehow you have survived the insanity, probably better than me, and keep me focused and strong. Steve, my love, Emily and Kyle, my sweet babies: I owe it all to you.

Finally, I give all credit to the Lord. None of the rest would matter without Him. "I can do all things through Christ who strengthens me." Amen.

About the Author

SHARON LATHAN IS A NATIVE Californian currently residing amid the orchards, corn, cotton, and cows in the sunny San Joaquin Valley. Happily married for twenty-four years to her own Mr. Darcy and mother to two wonderful children, she divides her time between housekeeping tasks, nurturing her family, church activities, and working as a registered nurse in a neonatal ICU. Throw in the cat, dog, and a ton of fish to complete the picture. When not at the hospital or attending to the dreary tasks of homemaking, she is generally found hard at work on her faithful laptop.

For more information about Sharon, the Regency Era, and her bestselling Darcy Saga series, visit her website/blog at: www.sharonlathan.net or www.darcysaga.net. She also invites everyone to join her and over twenty other published Austen literary novelists at her group blog Austen Authors: www.austenauthors.com.

In the Arms of Mr. Darcy
SHARON LATHAN

If only everyone could be as happy as they are…

Darcy and Elizabeth are as much in love as ever—even more so as their relationship matures. Their passion inspires everyone around them, and as winter turns to spring, romance blossoms around them.

Confirmed bachelor Richard Fitzwilliam sets his sights on a seemingly unattainable, beautiful widow; Georgiana Darcy learns to flirt outrageously; the very flighty Kitty Bennet develops her first crush, and Caroline Bingley meets her match.

But the path of true love never does run smooth, and Elizabeth and Darcy are kept busy navigating their friends and loved ones through the inevitable separations, misunderstandings, misgivings, and lovers' quarrels to reach their own happily ever afters…

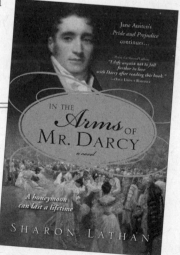

"If you love *Pride and Prejudice* sequels then this series should be on the top of your list!"
—*Royal Reviews*

"Sharon really knows how to make Regency come alive." —*Love Romance Passion*

978-1-4022-3699-0
$14.99 US/$17.99 CAN/£9.99 UK

My Dearest Mr. Darcy

Sharon Lathan

Darcy is more deeply in love with his wife than ever

As the golden summer draws to a close and the Darcys look ahead to the end of their first year of marriage, Mr. Darcy could never have imagined his love could grow even deeper with the passage of time. Elizabeth is unpredictable and lively, pulling Darcy out of his stern and serious demeanor with her teasing and temptation.

But surprising events force the Darcys to weather absence and illness, and to discover whether they can find a way to build a bond of everlasting love and desire…

Praise for *Loving Mr. Darcy*:

"An intimately romantic sequel to Jane Austen's *Pride and Prejudice*…wonderfully colorful and fun." —*Wendy's Book Corner*

"If you want to fall in love with Mr. Darcy all over again…order yourself a copy." —*Royal Reviews*

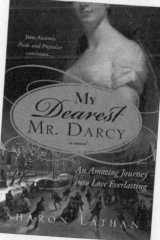

978-1-4022-1742-5
$14.99 US/$18.99 CAN/£7.99 UK

Loving Mr. Darcy: Journeys Beyond Pemberley
SHARON LATHAN

"A romance that transcends time." —*The Romance Studio*

Darcy and Elizabeth embark on the journey of a lifetime

Six months into his marriage to Elizabeth Bennet, Darcy is still head over heels in love, and each day offers more opportunities to surprise and delight his beloved bride. Elizabeth has adapted to being the Mistress of Pemberley, charming everyone she meets and handling her duties with grace and poise. Just when it seems life can't get any better, Elizabeth gets the most wonderful news. The lovers leave the serenity of Pemberley, traveling through the sumptuous landscape of Regency England, experiencing the lavish sights, sounds, and tastes around them. With each day come new discoveries as they become further entwined, body and soul.

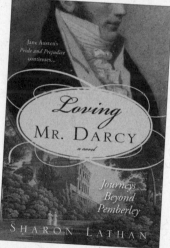

What readers are saying:

"Darcy's passion for love and life with Lizzy is brought to the forefront and captured beautifully."

"Sharon Lathan is a wonderful writer… I believe that Jane Austen herself would love this story as much as I did."

"The historical backdrop of the book is unbelievable—I actually felt like I could see all the places where the Darcys traveled."

"Truly captures the heart of Darcy & Elizabeth! Very well written and totally hot!"

978-1-4022-1741-8 • $14.99 US/ $18.99 CAN/ £7.99 UK

Mr. and Mrs. Fitzwilliam Darcy: Two Shall Become One
SHARON LATHAN

"Highly entertaining... I felt fully immersed in the time period. Well done!" —*Romance Reader at Heart*

A fascinating portrait of a timeless, consuming love

It's Darcy and Elizabeth's wedding day, and the journey is just beginning as Jane Austen's beloved *Pride and Prejudice* characters embark on the greatest adventure of all: marriage and a life together filled with surprising passion, tender self-discovery, and the simple joys of every day.

As their love story unfolds in this most romantic of Jane Austen sequels, Darcy and Elizabeth each reveal to the other how their relationship blossomed from misunderstanding to perfect understanding and harmony, and a marriage filled with romance, sensuality, and the beauty of a deep, abiding love.

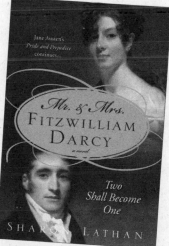

What readers are saying:

"This journey is truly amazing."

"What a wonderful beginning to this truly beautiful marriage."

"Could not stop reading."

"So beautifully written...making me feel as though I was in the room with Lizzy and Darcy...and sharing in all of the touching moments between."

978-1-4022-1523-0 • $14.99 US/ $15.99 CAN/ £7.99 UK

A Darcy Christmas

AMANDA GRANGE, SHARON LATHAN, & CAROLYN EBERHART

A HOLIDAY TRIBUTE TO JANE AUSTEN

Mr. and Mrs. Darcy wish you a very Merry Christmas and a Happy New Year!

Share in the magic of the season in these three warm and wonderful holiday novellas from bestselling authors.

Christmas Present
By AMANDA GRANGE

A Darcy Christmas
By SHARON LATHAN

Mr. Darcy's Christmas Carol
By CAROLYN EBERHART

978-1-4022-4339-4
$14.99 US/$17.99 CAN/£9.99 UK

PRAISE FOR AMANDA GRANGE:

"Amanda Grange is a writer who tells an engaging, thoroughly enjoyable story!"
—*Romance Reader at Heart*

"Amanda Grange seems to have really got under Darcy's skin and retells the story with great feeling and sensitivity."
—*Historical Novel Society*

PRAISE FOR SHARON LATHAN:

"I defy anyone not to fall further in love with Darcy after reading this book."
—*Once Upon a Romance*

"The everlasting love between Darcy and Lizzy will leave more than one reader swooning." —*A Bibliophile's Bookshelf*

WICKHAM'S DIARY

AMANDA GRANGE

Jane Austen's quintessential bad boy has his say…

Enter the clandestine world of the cold-hearted Wickham…

…in the pages of his private diary. Always aware of the inferiority of his social status compared to his friend Fitzwilliam Darcy, Wickham chases wealth and women in an attempt to attain the power he lusts for. But as Wickham gambles and cavorts his way through his funds, Darcy still comes out on top.

But now Wickham has found his chance to seduce the young Georgiana Darcy, which will finally secure the fortune—and the revenge—he's always dreamed of…

Praise for Amanda Grange:

"Amanda Grange has taken on the challenge of reworking a much loved romance and succeeds brilliantly." —*Historical Novels Review*

"Amanda Grange is a writer who tells an engaging, thoroughly enjoyable story!" —*Romance Reader at Heart*

Available April 2011
978-1-4022-5186-3
$12.99 US

Mr. Darcy Takes a Wife
LINDA BERDOLL
The #1 best-selling Pride and Prejudice *sequel*

"Wild, bawdy, and utterly enjoyable." —*Booklist*

Hold on to your bonnets!

Every woman wants to be Elizabeth Bennet Darcy—beautiful, gracious, universally admired, strong, daring and outspoken—a thoroughly modern woman in crinolines. And every woman will fall madly in love with Mr. Darcy—tall, dark and handsome, a nobleman and a heartthrob whose virility is matched only by his utter devotion to his wife. Their passion is consuming and idyllic—essentially, they can't keep their hands off each other—through a sweeping tale of adventure and misadventure, human folly and numerous mysteries of parentage. This sexy, epic, hilarious, poignant and romantic sequel to *Pride and Prejudice* goes far beyond Jane Austen.

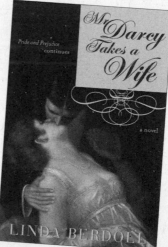

What readers are saying:

"I couldn't put it down."

"I didn't want it to end!"

"Berdoll does Jane Austen proud! ...A thoroughly delightful and engaging book."

"Delicious fun…I thoroughly enjoyed this book."

"My favorite *Pride and Prejudice* sequel so far."

978-1-4022-0273-5 • $16.95 US/ $19.99 CAN/ £9.99 UK

Mr. Darcy's Diary
AMANDA GRANGE

"A gift to a new generation of Darcy fans
and a treat for existing fans as well." —AUSTENBLOG

The only place Darcy could share his innermost feelings...

...was in the private pages of his diary. Torn between his sense of duty to his family name and his growing passion for Elizabeth Bennet, all he can do is struggle not to fall in love. A skillful and graceful imagining of the hero's point of view in one of the most beloved and enduring love stories of all time.

What readers are saying:

"A delicious treat for all Austen addicts."

"Amanda Grange knows her subject...I ended up reading the entire book in one sitting."

"Brilliant, you could almost hear Darcy's voice...I was so sad when it came to an end. I loved the visions she gave us of their married life."

"Amanda Grange has perfectly captured all of Jane Austen's clever wit and social observations to make *Mr. Darcy's Diary* a must read for any fan."

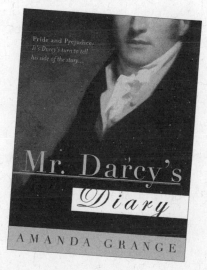

978-1-4022-0876-8 • $14.95 US/ $19.95 CAN/ £7.99 UK

Darcy and Anne

Pride and Prejudice continues…

JUDITH BROCKLEHURST

"A beautiful tale." —*A Bibliophile's Bookshelf*

Without his help, she'll never be free…

Anne de Bourgh has never had a chance to figure out what she wants for herself, until a fortuitous accident on the way to Pemberley separates Anne from her formidable mother. With her stalwart cousin Fitzwilliam Darcy and his lively wife Elizabeth on her side, she begins to feel she might be able to spread her wings. But Lady Catherine's pride and determination to find Anne a suitable husband threaten to overwhelm Anne's newfound freedom and budding sense of self. And without Darcy's help, Anne will never have a chance to find true love…

"Brocklehurst transports you to another place and time." —*A Journey of Books*

"A charming book… It is lovely to see Anne's character blossom and fall in love." —*Once Upon a Romance*

"The twists and turns, as Anne tries to weave a path of happiness for herself, are subtle and enjoyable, and the much-loved characters of Pemberley remain true to form." —*A Bibliophile's Bookshelf*

"A fun, truly fresh take on many of Austen's beloved characters." —*Write Meg*

978-1-4022-2438-6
$12.99 US/$15.99 CAN/£6.99 UK

WILLOUGHBY'S RETURN

JANE AUSTEN'S *SENSE AND SENSIBILITY* CONTINUES

JANE ODIWE

"A tale of almost irresistible temptation."

A lost love returns, rekindling forgotten passions…

When Marianne Dashwood marries Colonel Brandon, she puts her heartbreak over dashing scoundrel John Willoughby behind her. Three years later, Willoughby's return throws Marianne into a tizzy of painful memories and exquisite feelings of uncertainty. Willoughby is as charming, as roguish, and as much in love with her as ever. And the timing couldn't be worse—with Colonel Brandon away and Willoughby determined to win her back…

Praise for *Lydia Bennet's Story*:

"A breathtaking Regency romp!" —Diana Birchall, author of *Mrs. Darcy's Dilemma*

"An absolute delight." —*Historical Novels Review*

"Odiwe emulates Austen's famous wit, and manages to give Lydia a happily-ever-after ending worthy of any Regency romance heroine." —*Booklist*

"Odiwe pays nice homage to Austen's stylings and endears the reader to the formerly secondary character, spoiled and impulsive Lydia Bennet." —*Publishers Weekly*

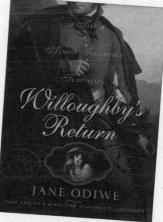

978-1-4022-2267-2
$14.99 US/$18.99 CAN/£7.99 UK

THE OTHER MR. DARCY
PRIDE AND PREJUDICE CONTINUES...
MONICA FAIRVIEW

"A lovely story... a joy to read."
—*Bookishly Attentive*

Unpredictable courtships appear to run in the Darcy family...

When Caroline Bingley collapses to the floor and sobs at Mr. Darcy's wedding, imagine her humiliation when she discovers that a stranger has witnessed her emotional display. Miss Bingley, understandably, resents this gentleman very much, even if he is Mr. Darcy's American cousin. Mr. Robert Darcy is as charming as Mr. Fitzwilliam Darcy is proud, and he is stunned to find a beautiful young woman weeping broken-heartedly at his cousin's wedding. Such depth of love, he thinks, is rare and precious. For him, it's love at first sight...

"An intriguing concept...
a delightful ride in the park."
—*Austenprose*

978-1-4022-2513-0
$14.99 US/$18.99 CAN/£7.99 UK

The Plight of the Darcy Brothers
A TALE OF SIBLINGS AND SURPRISES

MARSHA ALTMAN

"A charming tale of family and intrigue,
along with a deft bit of comedy." —Publishers Weekly

Once again, it falls to Mr. Darcy to prevent a dreadful scandal...

Darcy and Elizabeth set off posthaste for the Continent to clear one of the Bennet sisters' reputations (this time it's Mary). But their madcap journey leads them to discover that the Darcy family has even deeper, darker secrets to hide. Meanwhile, back at Pemberley, the hapless Bingleys try to manage two unruly toddlers, and the ever-dastardly George Wickham arrives, determined to seize the Darcy fortune once and for all. Full of surprises, this lively *Pride and Prejudice* sequel plunges the Darcys and the Bingleys into a most delightful adventure.

"Ms. Altman takes Austen's beloved characters and
makes them her own with lovely results."
—*Once Upon A Romance*

"Humorous, dramatic, romantic, and
touching—all things I love in a Jane Austen
sequel." —*Grace's Book Blog*

"Another rollicking fine adventure with the Darcys
and Bingleys...ridiculously fun reading." —*Bookfoolery & Babble*

978-1-4022-2429-4
$14.99 US/$18.99 CAN/£7.99 UK

Mr. Fitzwilliam Darcy:
THE LAST MAN IN THE WORLD
A *Pride and Prejudice* Variation
ABIGAIL REYNOLDS

What if Elizabeth had accepted Mr. Darcy the first time he asked?

In Jane Austen's *Pride and Prejudice*, Elizabeth Bennet tells the proud Mr. Fitzwilliam Darcy that she wouldn't marry him if he were the last man in the world. But what if circumstances conspired to make her accept Darcy the first time he proposes? In this installment of Abigail Reynolds' acclaimed *Pride and Prejudice* Variations, Elizabeth agrees to marry Darcy against her better judgment, setting off a chain of events that nearly brings disaster to them both. Ultimately, Darcy and Elizabeth will have to work together on their tumultuous and passionate journey to make a success of their ill-timed marriage.

What readers are saying:

"A highly original story, immensely satisfying."

"Anyone who loves the story of Darcy and Elizabeth will love this variation."

"I was hooked from page one."

"A refreshing new look at what might have happened if..."

"Another good book to curl up with... I never wanted to put it down..."

978-1-4022-2947-3
$14.99 US/$18.99 CAN/£7.99 UK